A RAGE
IN PARADISE

RALPH ARNOTE

A TOM DOHERTY ASSOCIATES BOOK / NEW YORK

FIC
ARNOTE
R

This is a work of fiction. All of the characters and events portrayed in this novel are either fictitious or are used fictitiously.

A RAGE IN PARADISE

Copyright © 1997 by Ralph Arnote

All rights reserved, including the right to reproduce this book, or portions thereof, in any form.

This book is printed on acid-free paper.

A Forge Book
Published by Tom Doherty Associates, Inc.
175 Fifth Avenue
New York, NY 10010

Forge® is a registered trademark of Tom Doherty Associates, Inc.

Library of Congress Cataloging-in-Publication Data

Arnote, Ralph.
    A rage in paradise / Ralph Arnote.—1st ed.
       p. cm.
    "A Tom Doherty Associates book."
    ISBN 0-312-86198-2
    I. Title.
    PS3551.R558R3   1997
    813'.54—DC21   96-52690
                                         CIP

First Edition: June 1997

Printed in the United States of America

0 9 8 7 6 5 4 3 2 1

Dedicated to Angelique

And, the unique people of the burbs: Barbara, Dolores, Detlef, Murry, Elmor and Edna, Maurine and Ken, Carol, Ted, the Bob with the big bike, and Cynthia who should have stayed in the city.

A RAGE
IN PARADISE

1

Cliff Blaylock felt good. He felt so good that he burst aloud with song as he walked quickly across the parking lot. "Way out west they have a name for water, wind, and fire!" Or was it earth, and wind, and fire? Damn it, he could never recall more than a line or two of the songs he really loved.

It was almost dark. The big suburban hotel was situated in a clearing within a densely wooded area in northern New Jersey. The regional coin and stamp show had drawn a big crowd. He had been forced to park at the far end of the parking lot abutting the woods.

Blaylock walked more swiftly as he approached his car. In his left hand he carried a tooled leather briefcase containing a collection of vintage gold coins. Also, deep in a pocket inside the case was his latest acquisition, a piece he had wanted all his years as a collector. He sighed heavily as he thought about handing over seventy-eight thousand dollars for a single U.S. cent, a 1793 Chain cent, known as the AMERI. The cent, in mint state, was one of a kind.

Sandy, a perfectly wonderful wife by almost any standard, never really understood his compulsion to collect rare coins. He regarded the purchase of the AMERI only secondarily as an investment. To him it was a piece of history, part of the first batch of coins ever to leave the first mint in Philadelphia. Fortunately his success in life allowed him such extravagance. There was a good chance that George Washington himself had touched that coin. Sandy would humor him. She would probably glance at the AMERI, shake her head, smile, and return quickly to her own task of the moment.

He reached his BMW, parked next to a big beige van, the only two vehicles now left in that dark area. Cliff Blaylock reached into his pocket to activate the remote door opener. Just as he heard the thump of the door lock, the door of the van opened and a tall, wide-shouldered man stepped out. Blaylock froze as the man steadied a handgun on the top of his BMW.

The man's voice came from behind a ski mask. "Now, slow and easy like, put that fancy briefcase on top of the car and slide it over here."

Blaylock hesitated. Another man jumped from the van and circled the BMW. He shoved Blaylock against his car, wrested the briefcase away and slid it over the roof of the car to his partner. That instant bought Blaylock enough time to reach into his own jacket and grip a small revolver. He twisted and fired point blank, twice into the chest of the man behind him, and then slumped to the ground with him as the wounded man fell. Blaylock scrambled along the ground trying to position himself for a shot at the fallen man's armed companion on the other side of the car.

He was too late. The van screeched into motion and accelerated across the parking lot. Blaylock stood up, then looked down at the man on the ground, now lying with one leg under the BMW. He bent over and ripped the ski mask from the prone figure. Blood was running from his mouth. Then he moaned and moved to sit up.

"Mr. Blaylock . . . what did you do that for?" The man tried to say more, but then slumped back down, motionless.

Blaylock stared at the man who knew his name, and then gasped. It was Willis McCord, the young man who lived next door to him. He had just shot his neighbor, a boy he had known all his life. He dragged Willis from under the BMW, glanced around, and saw no one in the fast growing darkness. He was almost a hundred yards from the hotel building. He knelt over the now motionless body. He tried unsuccessfully to feel a pulse. There was none. Blood had pooled in the area from where he had dragged him. Trembling, he stood up. "My God! I've killed Willis McCord," he whispered into the darkness.

Blaylock looked in the direction the van had turned. There was virtually no traffic on this Sunday night. He climbed into the BMW, took another quick look around, and then sped out of the lot. The road ahead was empty. Now, still shaking and sweating profusely, he roared down road after road in the rural area looking for the van. All he could remember was that it was probably beige, had a shiny luggage rack on top and a tire mounted on the back.

After awhile he reached Chestnut Ridge, which abutted an entrance to the Garden State Parkway. He toyed with the idea of getting on the Parkway, but then realized that it was hopeless. He decided to drive back to his house in Stag Creek. He could feel the hair standing on his neck. There was a good possibility that the man in the beige van knew who he was and what he had done.

Cliff Blaylock pulled a handkerchief from his pocket and mopped his brow. He was now driving slowly. He thought of going immediately to the police and telling them everything. He even turned down Stag Creek Road toward the police station, but passed it by when he got there. Nothing would bring back Willis McCord.

He drove home. The house was dark. Sandy was playing bridge this evening. She would be home late.

He went inside and into his den, where he sat in darkness for a long time. For the first time, he thought of the AMERI and his small collection of gold coins. The man in the van now had a tidy little fortune. He had it all to himself. There would be no need to split it with Willis McCord.

He found himself sobbing uncontrollably whenever his thoughts returned to Willis. The kid next door was everyone's favorite kid. He had often told Sandy that if ever they would have a son, it would be nice to have a kid like Willis. He couldn't shake the enormity of what had happened from his mind. He sat still now for a long time. Maybe he would go to the police in the morning and explain the whole thing when he was rested. Better yet, he would write it down, exactly how it all happened, and make sure it was all correct. He shook his head. But nothing would bring back Willis.

He sat in the darkness for about an hour before getting up and switching on a light in the den. He walked to the bathroom and looked in the mirror and then washed his face in cold water. What would he tell Sandy? Or, should he tell Sandy? Could life go on and have him never mention the subject to anyone? Obviously not.

He was distracted by the sound of car doors slamming outside. Returning to the living room, he could see the white and red flashing lights spinning in the McCords' driveway next door. A tightness returned to his throat as he looked through the window. Two police cars sat in the McCords' circular driveway. He could make out the figures of three officers walking toward the door. The McCords were in for the shock of their life.

He gulped and then walked back into the den to wait for Sandy. This wasn't a bad dream. It would never go away. He had shot and killed Willis McCord.

He slumped into a recliner in the den, watching the reflection of the flashing lights on the wall in front of him. The two police cars were soon joined by a third. God damn that guy with the gun! If it hadn't been for him, he would have never fired his own. Still, he didn't feel that he had panicked. He reasoned it was a shoot-or-get-shot situation. Yes, he thought, I'd better write it all down.

He sat staring at the wall ahead of him until he heard the key turn in the lock of his own front door. That would be Sandy, home from the bridge club.

"Sandy, I'm here in the den." He steeled himself to appear normal. Sandy could read him like a book, but he would rather face her with the tragic story later if he could, much later.

"Cliff, what's going on at the McCords' house? There are police cars all over the place."

"I . . . don't know. I just noticed them a few minutes ago. Maybe they heard a prowler or something." He walked over to the window and stood next to Sandy, looking at the police cars. "How was the old bridge game?" He noticed a slight waver in his voice.

"Dolores and I absolutely slaughtered them. In fact it turned into quite a cat fight. You, my dear, would have been greatly amused." Sandy put her arms around him and hugged him. "Cliff, we are so lucky. We had to listen to all of Marnie's problems. She and Sam are on the rocks. On top of all that, she kept making stupid bids until Alice completely lost her cool. I think I'll put the bridge club on hold for awhile." She kissed him, and then changed the subject.

"How was the coin show? Did you buy the AMERI?"

Cliff pulled away from her, trying to compose himself. Lying to Sandy was a difficult thing to do. "Oh, yes!" he replied, trying to feign enthusiasm. "I . . . I bought it at my price."

"Good! Now you will be fit to live with." Sandy was distracted by another flashing light outside. "Oh, look, another police car. What can be going on?"

Cliff stood watching with her at the window, grateful for the dim light. He could feel his eyes becoming moist again. "I . . . I don't know. I guess you'll find out all about it from Adrienne in the morning." Adrienne McCord had a much closer relationship with Sandy than he had with Alex. Alex traveled a lot, but Sandy and Adrienne had become close neighbors over the years. "Sandy, I'm beat, I think I'll turn in if you don't mind."

"Oh, really? I'd think you'd be all excited, wanting to celebrate the crazy old AMERI." She kissed him intensely, trying to provoke a response.

He nodded his head toward the McCords' driveway. "I guess I'm a little nervous. I wonder what in the hell is going on over there."

Sandy stared at the flashing lights and shook her head. "I've never seen anything like that before. I'll call Adrienne in the morning. I hope it's nothing about Willis. I don't see his red Corvette anywhere."

Cliff just shook his head slowly, fearful of speaking. He could feel himself start to shake at her mention of Willis.

In bed, Cliff feigned sleep as he lay turned away from Sandy, staring out the window. Their bedroom was on the opposite side of the house from the McCords, but as his eyes grew accustomed to the darkness, he could see the faintly pulsating reflection of the flashing lights on the tall trees. He thought of the missing AMERI for the first time since Sandy's casual mention of it. It seemed of such small importance now. He would have to file a theft report with the police. Did he dare? He would have to think very carefully about what he would tell them.

Again he started to sweat as he stared out the window, and fought the impulse to get out of bed, drive to the police station, and tell the whole story. Bob Tucker came to mind. He was the only lawyer he knew well. He made up his mind to call him in the morning and tell him about the whole thing. Yes! That was what he would do. He would call Bob Tucker after he wrote it all down.

2

Willy Hanson stood in the cockpit of the ketch *Tashtego*, stretching to lash the mainsail to the long boom. Ginny was at the helm guiding the ketch through the now gentle swells as they entered the channel to Great Salt Pond. It was Sunday night. Most of the weekenders had left. They would have a choice of moorings once they reached the marina in the idyllic Block Island haven. The trip from Wood's Hole had been a little more than he and Ginny had bargained for. The backlash of a squall came a little closer to land than early predictions, and they had to work hard to move the ketch *Tashtego* through thirty to forty knot gusts. Their planned lazy afternoon had turned into a demanding bit of seamanship.

Ginny beamed a broad smile toward Willy as they now slipped gently down the channel. "Willy, that was fun! What were you getting so excited about?" Her waist-length jet hair tossed in the breeze as she pulled on the wheel to guide the *Tashtego* around a welcoming buoy.

Willy grinned back at his soul mate of six years. "I have an aversion to big rocks in the water. Now tell the truth, did you really know where the hell you were?"

"Ha! You'll never know the answer to that, will you, lover?" The main now secure, Willy stood beside her at the wheel. She hugged him roughly and kissed his lips. "Just wanted to get your juices flowing. Any objection?"

"You always do that anyway. You don't have to flirt with boulders bigger than the *Tashtego*." He kissed her gently. Her violet blue eyes, set wide on her sun-bronzed face still reflected their color in the evening haze.

"There, Willy, grab that one with your hook." Ginny pointed to an approaching mooring bobbing in the water, and then expertly brought the *Tashtego* about. Willy hoisted the line aboard and secured it to the mooring. The two of them then busied themselves securing the *Tashtego* for a night in Great Salt Pond.

They had sailed together aboard the *Tashtego* for over five years, and worked swiftly and efficiently together at the task of keeping the showy ketch shipshape and seaworthy. The six-foot, muscular Hanson had retired early from a career in publishing to write, sail, and play amateur detective on occasion. The latter was never planned, but the adventurous and sometimes violent life of Willy Hanson just naturally led him to a life of an atoning avenger, and Ginny was always his willing partner.

Whenever he was asked where he had met the strikingly beautiful Ginny, he would usually say, quite casually, that he had picked her up on a jetty near Long Beach. Actually it was partially true. It was also true that the *Tashtego* belonged to Ginny. It didn't take long for the two of them to bond together and become loving partners in the adventure of life.

Having completed their tasks in silence, Willy now sprawled on a side cushion in the cockpit, his back propped against the cabin bulkhead. Ginny emerged from the cabin with a small chilled pitcher of Tanqueray, two glasses, and a jar of queen-size stuffed olives. "Mmm, you're getting quite predictable, dear. How did I know that you were going to do this?"

"Predictable! Willy, that's not nice at all. No woman wants to be called predictable." Ginny sat in front of him on the broad side cushion. She poured their Tanquerays and then leaned back onto Willy's chest. Receiving her in his arms he buried a kiss into the nape of her neck. "Now, Willy, tell me about the Blaylocks. I believe you called them Cliff and Sandy. Where do you know them from, and why are we spending a night at their house?"

"They are perfectly nice people, Ginny. I worked with Cliff in New York in my civilized days before I met you. He collects rare coins, like I do, but in a very major way. Cliff's collection is among the finest in the country I suppose. He is a good businessman, honest and a wee bit too conservative to ever take the big leap. We've always been good friends. I have put off staying at his place when I come east for years. His invitation is always very sincere. So just humor me for the one night. You'll like Sandy."

"And where do they live? I know you told me, but I've forgotten."

"Stag Creek. It's a sleepy little town in northern New Jersey. Not a bit ostentatious, just a pleasant place to raise a family and commute to New York City. Cliff and Sandy moved there about fifteen years ago, I guess. Cliff's done well. I suppose they could live anywhere, but they stay snug in Stag Creek."

"Any kids?"

"I don't think so. I know they had planned to once, but something didn't work out. I think one of them just can't have them, for some reason or another." Willy snuggled her close and kissed her again on the neck.

"Let's see," mused Ginny. "This is Sunday, so we will sail to Connecticut tomorrow, and then rent a car and drive down to meet them Tuesday evening. Sure you don't want to go alone?"

"Not a chance. What would I do for amusement?"

"Is that why you keep hanging around my boat? You find me amusing?" Ginny twisted her torso toward him, looked him in the eye, and started to brush soft kisses against his chest. Then she twisted further, and slumped against him as her kisses intensified.

"Ginny, it's not completely dark out here. Do you think this is wise?"

"Damn it, Willy, do you want wise or do you want unpredictable?"

He leaned over and buried another kiss into the hollow of her neck. "I'll take unpredictable."

3

Henri "Heavy" Laval drove the Cherokee van down the Palisades Parkway, taking great care to merge into the slow moving line of traffic and merely keep pace. Aggressive driving might get him home to Chelsea earlier, but it could also attract attention. The Palisades Parkway was jammed with the usual Sunday night traffic of weekenders returning from the Catskills and the lakes of upstate New York.

The tooled leather briefcase lay on the floor of the van in front of the seat next to him. It had a good heft to it. The weight gave him cause to believe that it was loaded with the heavy metal he sought. Willis McCord had assured him that the owner was a gold nut, a collector of "noted repute," he had called him. Laval grimaced and slapped at the steering wheel. The dense traffic had extended all the way from exit six in Rockland County to the approaching George Washington Bridge.

He eyed the toll collector warily as he approached the bottleneck at the toll booths. If anyone had gotten a number on his van, this would be a place that they would check traffic.

The sullen faced toll collector grabbed his money and stared at the next car. Laval sighed with relief. He would soon be hidden away in his familiar surroundings in Chelsea. Once across the bridge, he swung south along the Henry Hudson Parkway, content to crawl southward along with more heavy traffic.

Willis McCord had turned out to be a fool. Not only had he panicked, but he had been wrong about Blaylock. "The guy wouldn't know one end of a gun from the other," he had said.

Laval cursed. He wondered if the kid was aliv
wasn't.

Laval thought back over his relationship wi
as he drove. He was almost certain that the ki
by name. He did know him by his street name, Heavy.
the Hudson, Heavy was unknown. The only place Heavy would
raise an eyebrow would be in Chelsea where a few dealers de-
pended on him. Some of the narcs were onto him, but he knew
how to handle those guys.

Heavy Laval glanced at the tooled leather case again. If the
weight of the case was indeed caused by gold, the contents would
more than pay the tab owed him by McCord. The kid had a powerful habit for the best kind of stuff, and he was getting to be a
problem. He didn't seem to realize that Heavy Laval had a piper
to pay also.

Laval steered his van into the narrow garage in Chelsea, lowered the door, and went upstairs with the briefcase. "Peaches!" No
answer. He walked into the living room and sat on the sofa. He
loosened the belt that bound the tooled leather case.

Strange, he thought, that there were no fancy locks or latches
on the heavy briefcase. He spilled the contents out on the coffee
table. The clank and glitter of gold greeted his senses. He quickly
counted forty one-ounce gold coins. Most of them were bullion
coins, but several were vintage collectors coins with premium
value. There were several small gold coins of lesser value. He
quickly figured that strictly on the basis of bullion value at four
hundred dollars an ounce, there was more than twenty thousand
dollars on the table. Yeah, that would even McCord's tab and put
a little bonus in old Heavy's pocket. He looked around, wondering where Peaches was. She always liked big paydays.

He picked up the ornate briefcase, thinking that the best thing
he could do would be to stuff it in some garbage can along
Twenty-first Street. He peeked inside. There was a tiny zippered

ouch in one corner. He opened it and removed a small envelope, and shook its contents onto the coffee table.

A single coin, encased in a see-through plastic envelope fell out. Laval picked the thick piece of copper from its plastic holder. Inside a rather crude circular chain link frame were two words, ONE CENT. The other side of the copper cent bore the legend, The United States of AMERI.

"Shit!" he murmured aloud. "Now I have twenty thousand dollars and one cent." Gold was easy to move. The odd collector coin might be worth a few bucks, but he preferred gold. He dropped the strange coin into his shirt pocket, not thinking much more about it.

4

Oh my God!" Sandy screamed, staring, wanting not to believe what she was seeing on the small TV screen in her kitchen. "Cliff! Cliff! Come look at this!"

The morning news switched to another story and she raced up the stairs to wake Cliff. "Oh Cliff, it's terrible. I can't believe it! Willis McCord was killed last night in the parking lot of the Wellington Inn."

Cliff Blaylock gaped at his wife, wild eyed from a night without sleep. "How do you know this?"

"It was on the morning news. Oh Cliff, Adrienne must be out of her mind. No wonder there was such a big commotion in front of their house last night. One of the police cars is still there."

Blaylock rubbed his eyes trying to put his thoughts together. "This is terrible," he mumbled. "Sandy, give me a minute and I'll be right downstairs. Maybe you ought to call Adrienne. Oh God, I don't know what to do. How did it happen?"

"They don't seem to know many details. They said he was shot last night at least twice by an unknown assailant in a remote section of the parking lot next to the woods."

"Shot! I thought you meant he had a car accident." Cliff was amazed with the ease that the lie came out of him. He continued. "Incredible! I went to the coin show at the Wellington Inn. Of course it was still daylight when I left." He was again startled by the matter-of-fact tone of his own voice, and made a quick decision to keep Sandy in the dark for the time being.

In a few minutes he had slipped on a robe and walked downstairs to join Sandy at the kitchen window overlooking the McCord property. He watched with her as a policeman walked toward his cruiser accompanied by Alex McCord. They talked for a few moments before another police car appeared. Alex McCord got in and was driven away. The other officer returned to the house.

"Cliff, I am going to walk over and see if I can see Adrienne. She must be all alone there. Maybe there is something I can do."

"Why don't you call first?"

"I've tried several times. Maybe the phone is off the hook."

"Go ahead. Let me know if I can do anything." Cliff watched her all the way to the McCords' front door. She spoke briefly to the policeman who apparently left momentarily to carry a message to Adrienne. He returned and opened the door for Sandy.

Cliff began to think of his own problems. He pictured the shooting in the parking lot. By now, he had probably tested his memory a hundred times for details. Could it be possible that no one had witnessed the shooting? He must have been in the lot for a full minute before he drove out to look for the van. He had seen no one. Not a single other car moved in the parking area. There had been a brisk, cold breeze. No one would have lingered outside longer than necessary.

He went out the side door to where he had parked the BMW next to their garage. Inside the garage, he found a heavy terry cloth beach towel that had lain on the workbench since an outing last summer. He selected a carpenter's hammer from the pegboard behind the workbench and wrapped the towel around it several times. Then he returned to the car and took careful note of where he stood. The McCord's house was hidden by his own. His garage was abutted by dense woods that hid a large water reservoir beyond. His nearest neighbor's house was obscured by the same woods.

He had to act quickly before Sandy returned. He stood quietly in thought for a moment next to the BMW, glanced all around again to make sure he was all alone, and then slammed the hammer into the rear seat window on the driver's side. The muffled noise startled him. He hadn't expected it to be that loud. Reaching inside, he activated the door latch. Then he shook the towel vigorously, reentered the garage, and put it back on the bench. He hung the hammer in its place on the pegboard. Warily he strolled back into the house, glancing around him as he walked, trying to make certain that he hadn't been observed.

Cliff Blaylock sat quietly at the kitchen table sipping a cup of coffee, staring at the McCords' house. He rubbed at the stubble on his face. At the age of thirty-nine, he had made a horrible mistake. Success as a literary agent had created an idyllic life for himself and Sandy. The athletic pair had fell in love during college days where he had starred as quarterback on a perfectly miserable team. Now he thought about Sandy sharing the misery of a record-breaking losing streak with him. When they finally won their last game of his senior year, they had celebrated by eloping. It was the rashest, most unpredictable thing in his life, until now.

A half hour passed before the two women became visible at

the door. They hugged each other and continued in conversation for several minutes, when Sandy pulled away and started walking toward their house.

Tears ran down both cheeks as she entered the kitchen. "Oh Cliff, that poor woman. I just didn't know what to say. How can you say anything that matters at a time like that?"

"I'm sure you did your best, dear. Adrienne thinks of you as a good friend. I'm sure she needs your attention now." Cliff put his arms around Sandy. "Where did Alex go?"

"He went to identify Willis. He was in pretty rough shape. I guess it's necessary, though."

"Do they have any idea who did it?" Cliff felt the little waver come back in his voice as he asked what seemed to be a perfectly logical question.

"No. Supposedly they have some leads they are checking out. My God, Cliff, things like this are not supposed to happen out here. That's really why we live here."

"Things like this are unpredictable. They seem to happen anywhere these days." His voice quavered sharply as he spoke.

"Cliff, are you okay?" Sandy brushed her hand through his hair.

"Yes. I do have a problem. I hesitate to tell you about it at a time like this. Fortunately, it is nothing to compare with the hell the McCords are going through. I feel almost lucky." He turned away from her and walked toward the door leading to the driveway.

"What is it, Cliff?"

"We were robbed last night. Someone broke into my car and stole a folio of coins I had brought from the coin show. I just discovered it this morning when I went out to get them."

"Oh Cliff! That's horrible. Did they get your rare cent?"

"Yes, damn it. I've been sitting here deciding when to call the police. Compared to the troubles next door, it is pretty insignif-

icant. But I guess I'll have to file a report. There are insurance reports and all that have to be made."

"Might as well get it done, darling. It'll get your mind off all
this for awhile. I'm going back over to stay with Adrienne until
her sister gets there. She's flying in from Cleveland." Sandy
paused, looking thoughtful. "Someone must have followed you
from the coin show. Why didn't you bring your briefcase inside?"

"Oh, hell, I don't know. We've lived here for years. Half the
time we don't even lock the door to the house. You know that. The
BMW was locked up tight. They actually smashed a window.
Nothing like that ever happens around here."

"We can't say that anymore, honey." Sandy stared soberly at
the house next door. "Strange about Willis."

"What's strange?"

"Adrienne says he's been spending a lot of time in the city.
He told Alex last week that as soon as he started his new job
he wanted to get an apartment in Chelsea or Soho. Alex blew his
top. I guess he and Willis have been arguing something terrible here lately. Now, of course, Alex is feeling very bad about
that."

"Willis was twenty-two, I think. It doesn't surprise me that he
wanted to live in the city if he worked there. I wonder why Alex
kicked up such a fuss. I always thought the kid was an all-
American boy." His voice wavered again as he felt the pounding
in his chest.

"You okay, Cliff? You're white as a sheet." Sandy brushed her
hand gently across his brow.

"Yeah, I'm okay. You better get back to Adrienne."

"Willy and Ginny will be here tomorrow, Cliff." Sandy
paused. "I'm glad. Maybe that will help us get our minds off all
this."

Cliff watched her as she crossed the lawn toward the Mc-
Cords. I doubt it, he thought to himself. I've killed poor Willis
McCord and things will never be the same.

5

eavy Laval paused in front of the window of a tiny coin shop on Ninth Avenue. "Maybe you ought to do it." Peaches was primping at her wild mop of permed blonde hair in her mirrored image in the window. "Just ask him what it is worth. Tell him you found it in a box of stuff your grandfather left you."

"Why me? Why don't you take it in yourself? What if he makes me an offer?"

"Take it and then get the hell out of there. Don't get into a long conversation about it. That's why I like gold. You get the value every day, printed in the paper." Heavy Laval steered Peaches to the door of the small shop and then walked alone down Ninth Avenue. They had spent most of the day selling the gold bullion coins, a few at a time all over the city, feeling it was too risky to dump them all in one place. The old copper cent held no interest for him. He was willing to take whatever Peaches could con out of the small shop's owner.

He watched her push a buzzer on the door of the coin shop. Almost all the coin shops they had visited this day had some sort of security entrance. Most of them were laughable, thought Laval. Everyone had let him in. He made a mental note of several dealers that looked like an easy mark for a quick heist someday. The day was not totally wasted.

Heavy Laval walked back down the block. What in the hell could Peaches be doing? She had been in there about ten minutes. He peeked in the window pretending to study the dusty items scattered in display. She was standing in front of a display case with her mini-skirted fanny cocked to one side, like she always did when she was turning on the charm. The man behind the counter looked like an old geezer. Leave it to Peaches, she would con the old guy out of a few extra bucks.

He paced the block once more. When he passed the shop again, the old man was standing next to her in front of the counter. They were both bending low over a large open book. He noticed that the old man was touching her shoulder. The bastard better not get any crazy ideas like taking her in the back room. That was what made him crazy. Peaches would flirt with anyone. "But I only sleep with you," she always told him. So far as he knew, she had never lied. But he always wondered where she learned all that crazy stuff she did in the sack.

He walked on down to the corner again, and spun around impatiently, and there she was, walking toward him. She caught up to him, shrugged her shoulders, and handed him the small envelope containing the copper cent. "I think the old guy has the hots for me. He wants to do a little research."

"Research?"

"Yeah, he says old pennies are not his specialty. He wants to talk to an expert about the penny. He says it's probably phony, or it's worth a lot of money, maybe even thousands if it's real."

"You're kidding!" Heavy Laval walked Peaches around a corner. She had a smug sort of a smile on her face. She was holding something back. He squeezed her arm until it was uncomfortable. "Okay, what'd he offer you?"

"Heavy! Damn it, you'll leave a bruise." She pulled away from him and rubbed at her arm. "He said he would give me five hundred bucks, just on spec, if I wanted to make a quick deal. Says it might be phony."

"Five hundred bucks! And you didn't take it. You're stupid, Peaches. Go back and say you changed your mind."

"No, Heavy, you're stupid. Do you think that dumpy little shop would pay me five hundred just on a gamble? It's worth more, Heavy, a lot more."

"Thousands?"

"Yep, he's going to check around and make me an offer this evening. He promised he would be fair. He likes me, you know. He gave me his card with his phone number at home." Peaches fished the coin dealer's card out of her small handbag and handed it to Heavy Laval.

It read, JONATHAN FINEHOUSE, ANTIQUES AND RARE COINS. Heavy fingered the card thoughtfully. "Baby, you should have taken the five hundred, quick cash." He snapped his fingers in his face. "Now he's gonna start nosing around. Other people will know about it, and start asking questions if it's worth all that money."

"Heavy, don't make such a big deal out of it. He just wanted three or four hours to check things out. I'll call him tonight. We'll take it or leave it and then never see him again. Okay?" She planted a kiss on his lips, lingering, her tongue prying its way into his mouth.

After several moments he mumbled, "Okay, Peaches. It'd be nice to wind up with a few grand out of the deal, I suppose." He patted her affectionately. "I guess a few hours don't matter. If all you can get is the five hundred that's okay too."

Now they were walking down Twenty-first Street in Chelsea toward their flat. Peaches had turned him on. He quickened their pace, visualizing their afternoon together. He had told her nothing about the circumstances involving the acquisition of the coins, and didn't intend to.

His thoughts raced back to the dark parking lot of the Wellington Inn across the Hudson in New Jersey. Willis Whatzisname had been shot by the owner of the coin folio. That was that bastard's problem. Why should he worry so damn much? It would be perfect if Willis were dead, he thought. He was free and clear, with his pockets stuffed full of money. Why not let Peaches see if she could swing a big deal?

When they reached their apartment, Heavy Laval followed Peaches up the stairs leading to the door of their flat. He found himself getting aroused as he gaped at her saucily swiveling hips in front of him. His groping hand probed under her miniskirt. Predictably she paused on the stairwell and permitted his fingers to find their quest.

"Heavy, is that all you ever think about?"

"Yeah. I notice you ain't complaining." The key rattled in the lock, and they entered their flat. Laval flopped on the bed, grabbed the TV remote and began to channel surf, hoping he could find one of those sleazy panel shows featuring the usual assortment of creeps and their hot babes. A newscast promptly halted his surfing. The announcer unmistakably mentioned the name of Willis McCord. He became totally oblivious to Peaches' slow strip at the foot of the bed.

There it was, in vivid color, the Wellington Inn nestled in the green woods of New Jersey. The camera zoomed in on the parking lot and focussed on the area framed by yellow tape tied to trees and sawhorses.

The announcer was explaining that this was the scene of the crime last evening when, "Willis McCord, a local honors student at Rutgers University, was slain in the parking lot by two gunshot wounds to his chest. Police reported that the incident had occurred at approximately seven o'clock the previous evening. A bellman at the hotel discovered the victim after hearing the shots, and then the sound of a vehicle screeching in acceleration across the parking lot toward the hotel exit. Police had no comment when questioned about a possible suspect."

Laval found himself elated by the news report. Willis was dead, and the bellman's report didn't seem to offer much detail. The valet station at the front entrance of the Wellington Inn must have been at least a hundred yards from his van.

"What'ya watchin' baby?" Peaches was now in the buff, busy propping herself up by a pillow next to him. She stared at the tail end of the news report. "Hey, Heavy, it's me, remember. It ain't fair to get a gal all steamed up and then change the menu. Ain't ya hungry anymore?"

Heavy Laval turned his attention abruptly from the television set to Peaches, now squirming impatiently beside him. "Education, baby, that's what they call it. Some jerk got iced in a parking lot in New Jersey and the police are running around like chickens with their heads cut off. When you're in my business, and somebody makes a monkey out of the cops, you better sit up and go to school."

"Your business! I thought it was our business."

Heavy Laval rolled his weight toward her and pawed her lewdly. "Yeah, baby, and this is my business too. Just don't forget who the boss is." Laval was feeling good. Why shouldn't he? He didn't kill anyone and he had gotten away with the loot.

A scowl crossed his face. Of course, there was the matter of the guy in the BMW. The news report hadn't mentioned anything about him. Laval paused in his attention to Peaches and lifted his head, staring off in deep thought. What if the guy in the BMW had flown the coop too? He was out there somewhere. Laval doubted that he had got his plate numbers in all that scrambling for cover. He decided that he would read the papers later in the day. He would like to know who the guy was, just in case there were some loose ends to take care of.

"Heavy, for Pete's sake, what are you mooning about? Just tell me if you've got something better to do. It ain't fair to get me all hot and bothered and then suddenly go into a dumb funk. What's bothering you, Heavy? Do you have something to tell me?"

Heavy's attention snapped back to the undulating figure in front of him. "Hey, old Heavy's got some things on his mind. There are more important things than this you know." He lewdly probed at her again and then grinned. "But this will do for right now."

6

It was now nine A.M. Cliff Blaylock nervously paced his office in their home. Today was a day he was to have commuted to New York. Luncheon had been scheduled with one of his authors who was delivering a much awaited manuscript. He called and broke the date, pleading a case of the bug that was going around these days.

From his office he could see a portion of the McCords' home that included the front driveway and the police cruiser that still sat there. He couldn't keep his eyes off of it. Sandy was still over there keeping company with Adrienne.

He had printed Bob Tucker's phone number on the scratch pad in front of him. The more he thought about calling his lawyer, the more he became confused as to what he would tell him. He had watched the story over and over again as it was repeated on the morning news. There was no real hint that the police had an inkling of the real circumstances of the murder of Willis McCord.

Instead of calling Tucker, he finally reached a decision to call the police, not in the McCord matter, but to report the burglary of the coins from his car parked in the driveway. Yes, that must come first, he thought. It would make little sense for him to delay reporting a theft of that magnitude. He dialed 911.

Within minutes a Stag Creek police car pulled into his driveway. Blaylock tensed as he watched the officer exit the cruiser and walk toward his house. He wondered if he could make his story sound logical as he met him at his front door.

"Hello, I'm Patrolman Hinkle of the Stag Creek police. You called about a robbery, sir?"

"Yes, officer. My car was broken into last night by someone who smashed a window to get inside." Cliff Blaylock joined the patrolman and walked around the house to the BMW.

The patrolman circled the BMW and stopped in front of the smashed window. "Say, that's a shame. A beautiful car like this smashed like that. Have you been inside the vehicle since the robbery sir?"

"Not actually. I opened the door, looked inside for my briefcase, and then I checked the trunk, to see if I might have put it in there." Blaylock heard his voice come out nice and steady. He felt very confident now.

"What was in the briefcase, sir?"

"Well, there was about twenty thousand dollars in gold bullion coins, and various other collector specimens worth a total of about one hundred thousand dollars."

The policeman snapped his head to face Blaylock, eyes agape. He was obviously startled at the size of the loss. "If you don't mind my saying so, sir, that's a lot of money to be left in the driveway." The policeman backed several feet away from the car, crouching down when he spotted several shards of glass on the surface of the smooth blacktop.

"I know that. I feel like a fool. I returned late from a coin show at the Wellington Inn. I left the briefcase under the seat, and locked the car. I intended to drive to the bank in the morning and put everything back into a safe deposit box. In all the years we have lived in Stag Creek, there hasn't been a whisper of trouble. I guess I never even considered the possibility of theft."

"A hundred thousand dollars!" The policeman emitted a low whistle. "If you don't mind sir, I'm going to get an investigative unit out here to give the place a going over. There may be some prints around. Does anyone but yourself use the car, sir?"

For the first time, Blaylock felt himself choking up. The thought of an investigation would mean a lot of questions. "No . . . no, hardly ever. Sandy, my wife . . . she uses it once in awhile."

The policeman crouched again near the small shards of glass, and then glanced up at the smashed window. Blaylock thought he seemed to be puzzled by something. Now he could feel his heart pounding. He wanted the investigator to leave.

"Must have made a loud noise, Mr. Blaylock. It would take quite a whack to break that small window. Did you or your wife hear any unusual noise?" Patrolman Hinkle rose from his crouching position and slowly paced off several steps, measuring the distance from the shards of glass to the BMW. They appeared to be at least ten feet from the vehicle.

Blaylock shook his head. "We didn't hear anything. I have no idea when it happened. My wife, Sandy, might have been next door. She's a good friend of the McCords. She's been over there trying to help. Quite a tragedy over there, wasn't it?" Blaylock was hoping the officer could be diverted from his investigation.

Hinkle nodded his head slowly in the affirmative. "Yes it was." Commenting no further about the problem next door, the officer was now making some notations on a paper held to a clipboard. "Mr. Blaylock, I would appreciate it if you would not move the vehicle until our investigators go over the area. You have sustained quite a large loss. Our boys may be able to turn up something that will help. Maybe there's some prints around."

"Sure thing. I can use my wife's car in emergency." Blaylock followed the officer back to the front of the house and watched him as he called in a report to the station.

When he finished his radio call, patrolman Hinkle again began writing notes on his pad. The young officer was the picture of decorum as he went about his work. An insane urge crossed Blaylock's mind. He tried to imagine the look that would come to the officer's face if he were to blurt out, "Hey, by the way, I shot and killed my neighbor's kid last night." A perverse desire to laugh followed this mental picture.

Finally, having finished his report, the patrolman left. Blaylock again circled the house, walked back to the BMW and stared at it. Hinkle had placed a small coin on the garage apron next to the two small shards of glass, which he had left in place. His stomach fluttered nervously. Why would he do that, he asked himself. Then he remembered shaking the shards of glass out of the towel. There were probably other smaller ones around. So what? Any perpetrator of the crime could have done the same thing. Still, he felt uneasy. He wished Sandy would return from next door.

Inside again he poured another cup of coffee and sat quietly to wait. Then he remembered this was the day Willy Hansen and Ginny were coming to visit. He groaned. The crimes would no doubt become a topic of conversation.

Bob Tucker again came to mind. The longer he waited to tell someone about the crime the more intricate his lies would become. Yet he couldn't make himself pick up the phone. Then, he snapped to attention, sweating. The gun! He had to get rid of the gun. Blaylock climbed the stairs, went into his den, and ran his hand under a blanket on the closet shelf. He found the zippered leather case that held the revolver.

Downstairs, he found Sandy's car keys on the kitchen counter where she always left them. He picked them up, shoved the heavy leather case under his jacket, and then walked out to Sandy's car.

Blaylock drove to a convenience store, went in and bought a couple of newspapers. That was not unusual for him. It was the same thing he did on many a morning. Soon he found himself driving south on Stag Creek Road, the winding narrow street that led the length of their town. After a mile or so, he made a sharp left and crossed the small creek that wound its way through town.

Parking near the bridge, partially hidden by surrounding woods, he got out and walked a few steps back to the bridge and stared down at the swirling water. He glanced around him, mak-

ing certain he was unobserved and then reached inside his jacket
and pulled out the leather case. Glancing around one last time,
he dropped it into the murky water, and then hustled back to the
car.

Driving back to his house, he still felt ill at ease. He thought
about the small creek, now running bankful as a result of recent
rains. Then he remembered that at times during dry spells, it had
so little water in it that one could jump across it in many places.
Someday the gun, registered to him, might be found.

But that would be someday, probably when the demise of
Willis McCord would be forgotten. Or would it?

7

A lex McCord, tall, darkly handsome, stood inside his living
room looking out the window at the policeman who had finally left them. He sat in the police car in their driveway, using
his radio and sipping at coffee. Strangely, he had not yet shed a
tear over the news about Willis. The boy had been in trouble for
over a year. It had been a wonder that he had not gotten into trouble with the police before. He now wished that he had. Perhaps
the boy would still be alive.

"Alex, if there is anything at all we can do, please let us help."
Sandy Blaylock spoke as she made her way to the front door. "Adrienne needs some rest, but I suppose it won't happen for awhile."

Alex walked Sandy to the door. "Thanks, Sandy. Adrienne
needs your support so much. You've been wonderful." As he
opened the door he noticed that the police car that had been in
front of the Blaylock house was gone now. "I saw you had a visi-

tor from the local police this morning too. I guess they'll be nosing all around."

"Oh Alex, I had forgotten all about it. But we had a little trouble last night. Someone broke into Cliff's car and stole some coins he had taken to the show at the Wellington Inn." She bit her tongue, sorry that she had brought up the Wellington. "I suppose Cliff called them to investigate."

"Really! That's too bad. I know that Cliff takes his collection very seriously. It's strange, we've never had any such trouble in this neighborhood." He shrugged as his mind went back to his own problems. "Thanks again, Sandy. Be sure and drop in on Adrienne a little later. She needs you."

Alex McCord watched Sandy as she walked back to her house. A scowl replaced the affable demeanor he had displayed toward her when she had been present. Soon, he returned to Adrienne now resting on a couch in a family room. She lowered her eyes, avoiding direct contact with his.

Adrienne McCord, now approaching forty years of age, was still a dark, mesmerizing beauty. Her svelte figure would still do justice to any fashion runway. It was at such a showing where Alex had first spotted her when she was barely seventeen. Today her long jet hair, usually meticulously groomed fell around her face, making her dark eyes look even darker.

"If you would have just gone into the city with him now and then, Alex, maybe this all wouldn't have happened." Tears filled her eyes again, now circled from the lack of sleep. "Oh my God! It could have been so different." Adrienne lifted her arms and let them fall helplessly into her lap. "I guess you are going to smoke that filthy thing in here."

Alex McCord was tamping tobacco into the bowl of a meerschaum. He promptly stopped and glared at Adrienne, stuffed the pipe into his jacket pocket and returned to the front window across the room. Life was hell before, he thought to himself. Now it will be hell forever.

"Oh, Alex, smoke if you must. What difference does it make now? Will anything make a difference anymore? How long will it take us to care about anything?" Adrienne mopped at her eyes with a tissue, staring at the back of his head. "Alex, I will be leaving you. . . . Did you hear me?"

"Yes, dear. I hear you. Frankly, Adrienne, I want to warn you about ranting frivolous chit-chat. I hear it all loud and clear now, just as I have for the last five years. I don't give a damn about it anymore. In fact, I never did." Alex walked out of the room without looking at her. He turned in the doorway and pointed his forefinger at her emphatically. "My advice is for you to call Dr. Birch as soon as you can. I don't think he is much of a shrink, but he evidently gives you something I cannot."

"Alex! We've just lost our son! How can you talk to me like that? Where are your feelings? You're a monster, Alex. If you would have given the boy a little more of your time, this wouldn't have happened. I hate you, Alex!" Adrienne McCord burst into tears.

Alex McCord reddened, glared at her for a few seconds, then again turned his back on her and walked out the front door. He retrieved the meerschaum from his jacket pocket and lit the tobacco. He began to pace the driveway and soon found himself in the area of the swimming pool.

Adrienne was a wreck, he thought to himself. She would never get over the loss of Willis. Nor would he, for that matter. He sighed heavily, trying to rid himself of the unceasing feeling of hopelessness. If he had only cracked down harder in the beginning, he thought, the first time they had found cocaine in his room, maybe things would have been different. He could still hear Adrienne's words spoken back then. "Alex, please don't be so hard on the boy. He's not the only one in the world experimenting with drugs. He's not a bad son, Alex."

Of course, dicipline was difficult. After all, Willis had once found cocaine right there in their home. Adrienne had slipped up.

What a waste! An honor student, no less, a boy who had everything, everything but common sense. That was a commodity hard to find in his mother.

Alex McCord walked slowly around the pool, puffing on the meerschaum. The home in Stag Creek had never been impressive enough for Adrienne. She was always pushing him to build in Saddle River, or Smoke Rise.

Stag Creek was a perfectly decent suburb, with enough rural character to make it a delightful contrast to the city. But Adrienne always wanted something more elegant and showy. Not that money was any problem. They could afford to live anywhere. His gem importing business was thriving. But to pull up stakes and start over again with Adrienne was an abominable thought to him. Now, with Willis gone, things would continue to get worse with her. He felt sure of that.

McCord's attention was drawn to another police car entering his driveway. It was the same officer that had been there the previous evening. He had spotted him in the pool area, and walked toward him after getting out of the police car.

"Mr. McCord, I hate to bother you again, but we thought we should pass along some information." The officer hesitated as McCord circled the pool.

"No bother at all. You've got your job to do. Do you have a suspect?"

"Oh no, Mr. McCord, nothing like that. I wish we did." The policeman glanced at some notes on his clipboard. "We located your son's Corvette. It was parked in the far end of the lot at the Wellington."

"Well, that would figure wouldn't it." McCord nodded his head at the policeman. "I suppose we might as well have it towed over here."

"Well, that will be impossible right now, sir." The officer was eyeing him closely. "I'm afraid we are going to have to impound the car, sir."

"Really?" He looked questioningly at the officer. "Well, what-ever you say, I guess. Why must you do that?"

"There is a problem, sir. There was a substantial amount of cocaine found in the vehicle. We are going to have to check it over carefully."

McCord stared glumly at the young policeman. "There must be some mistake. Are you sure it's Willis's car?"

"No doubt about it, sir. I'd know the vehicle anywhere. I've seen it right here in your driveway many times. Sorry sir."

McCord sighed. "Well you just do what you have to do. I'm going inside if you don't mind."

He turned and walked rapidly toward the house. Cocaine, in-deed! And now there was no Willis to yell at. His memory flashed back to the day he first saw the red Corvette in his driveway. Adri-enne had gone with Willis to drive it home from the dealer, all totally without his consultation and approval. He realized it was sadistic, but he couldn't wait to get inside and tell Adrienne the news. As far as he was concerned, they could haul the Corvette to the dump and leave it there.

8

Heavy Laval fingered the card thoughtfully. "Jonathan Fine-house, what kind of a name is that? Was he an old man?" He never did get a real good look at him when Peaches was showing him the coin.

Peaches shrugged. "Yeah, he was an old guy, but not too old, if you know what I mean. He kept trying to get a better look at my boobs. I'd rather not go back to his shop after hours, if it's all the same to you, Heavy." Peaches ran her fingers through Laval's heavy black hair. "Besides, I don't want to get dressed again. You've got me all tuckered out. Mind if I take a little nap?" She pulled away from Laval and rolled over, squirming to the edge of the bed, putting as much distance between her and Laval as she could.

"Sure, babe, you just do that. I've got to go out and take care of some business. Mr. Finehouse can wait until we need a few bucks someday." Laval sat on the edge of the bed and pulled on his shoes. Still sitting, he slipped on his shirt and read the address on the business card again. He drew up his denims and fastened the big silver and turquoise buckle.

As he put on his leather jacket, he patted the inside pocket to feel the heft of the snub-nosed .38. Glancing over his shoulder one more time, he could see that Peaches was sound asleep.

Heavy Laval walked the length of the block and shut himself inside one of the phone booths located on the corner, then dialed the number of Jonathan Finehouse.

"Antique Shop," the old man answered on the first ring.

"Hello, Mr. Finehouse?"

"Yes it is, but I'm about to close for the day."

"Mr. Finehouse, my wife was in to see you today. It was concerning a rare penny we found in her grandfather's stuff. He passed away recently."

"Oh yes, the 1793. I offered her five hundred dollars for it."

"She thinks it's worth a lot more, Mr. Finehouse. She said you were going to check into it for us."

"As a matter of fact I did just that." The old man hesitated. "You tell her to bring it in and I will give her nine hundred fifty for it."

"It's getting dark, Mr. Finehouse, and she's all tuckered out. Do you mind if I bring it over right now?"

"How will I know you? I don't open the door for anyone after dark. You know how it is here on Ninth Avenue."

"I'm a tall guy. I have the business card you gave my wife. I'll hold it against the glass. I can be there in ten minutes."

"Good, I will wait for you." The old man hung up.

Laval smiled as he thought to himself. I bet you will, you old bastard. That big fat penny has to be worth a lot more than nine fifty. We'll just see. Laval walked slowly toward the tiny coin shop only a couple of blocks away. The darker it was, the better it would be. This one would be duck soup, he thought.

Finehouse stared at him for several seconds as Laval held the card against the window. He was probably frightened by his size. Laval produced the coin from his shirt pocket and held it against the glass.

"Oh no! Don't scratch it!" The old man fairly shouted at him, as he reached to open the latch.

Laval grinned at him and dropped the coin back in his shirt pocket as he entered the shop. Finehouse flipped the latch behind them.

"I always clear out of here by this time. One can't be too careful these days." The old man eyed Laval's broad shoulders warily and then quickly walked back behind the small counter at the rear of the shop. "So, let me see the specimen again."

"The specimen?" Laval shrugged.

"The 1793, I just want to make sure about it if you don't mind."

Laval handed him the coin and watched as he examined it with a jeweller's eyepiece. "Very nice. Very nice. You are lucky I have the cash, young man. I seldom keep much on hand. Baseball cards and a few Indian head cents are about all I sell here, mostly to kids." He set the coin gently on the counter and stepped behind a curtain, and quickly returned with an old cigar box.

Finehouse quickly counted out nine hundred fifty dollars and pushed it across the counter. From his angle, Laval could see that there was more money in the box. "I'll just take it all if you don't mind."

Finehouse stared at the snub-nosed .38. "Oh my. Please, please, just take the whole box. Take your cent, too . . . Please, just go." The coin dealer quivered nervously as he continued to plead for Laval to leave.

Laval motioned at the curtain to his back. "Get behind there, quick!" He stuffed the cent into his pocket and followed the old man behind the curtain, and dropped him with a savage blow of the steel revolver against his head.

He scooped up the contents of the cigar box, and left the rear of the store, pausing to douse the lights as he passed a switch in the narrow shop. He waited at the front door until there were no pedestrians in sight. He set the latch to lock as he closed the front door, then proceeded to saunter casually down Ninth Avenue.

Within minutes, he returned to the apartment. Peaches was sitting on the edge of the bed. "I found a way to have my cake and eat it too," he told her, grinning broadly. "Hey, that must be the proverbial lucky penny." He tossed the fat wad of bills onto the bed. "Add it up, babe."

He watched as she slowly counted the money. "Hey! There's over three thousand dollars here."

Laval tapped his forefinger to his brow. "Just stick with me, baby. Let's celebrate and order in some pizza."

9

Willy Hanson and Ginny had secured the *Tashtego* in a slip at the Cedar Island Marina in Clinton, Connecticut. The sail into Long Island Sound from Block Island had taken longer than expected, and they were hustling down Route 95 in the old Porche, trying to make Stag Creek and the Blaylocks before dark.

"It's been a long time since I have been there. I hope I can find it in the dark," mumbled Willy, as he tried to find a new station on the radio. "Cliff Blaylock used to work with me before I retired and became a useless rogue. Nice guy. He got me mildly interested in rare coins and the gold bullion market at one time. He made some money at it. With me it was just a hobby. Now I've ditched all my hobbies and have become Ginny DuBois's slave."

Ginny turned her azure eyes toward him, registering a lazy smile. "Some slave you are. I spend all my time following you all over the world chasing bad guys. It's lucky my slave hasn't gotten us both killed." Ginny stretched across the console and planted a wet kiss on his cheek. "What's next, Willy? Now that you've become a world-famous detective, it seems you're out of work."

Ginny kidded him a lot about his investigative exploits. Actually, the life-style had been thrust upon them by circumstances in his personal life. Yet, in a short time he had acquired the reputation of a top private investigator, successful enough that he had written books about it. And the books had done modestly well.

"That's all behind us baby. Now we're going to sail around the world and make love in a thousand ports."

"Is that all we're going to do?"

"Of course not. In time, I will grow old, get fat, ugly, and bald. You will retain your beauty long after I deteriorate, and then ditch me for royalty, probably a young prince who still has the vigor to hoist a main or haul an anchor."

"Oh good! I've often wondered how I will wind up. I'll try to live up to your expectations."

"Wouldn't do you any good, Ginny. I'd have to challenge the young prince to a duel. I would cheat and kill him, and then kill myself. You would be left all alone in eternal misery." He glanced at Ginny. She had dropped off to sleep. She didn't wake up until he swerved into the Blaylock's driveway in woodsy Stag Creek.

Cliff Blaylock walked outside to greet the Porche. "Willy, you old war horse. You haven't changed a bit." Blaylock pumped his arm vigorously when he got out of the car. "And you must be Ginny," he added after she had circled the Porche to join them. "Come on in, you arrived just in time. Sandy was fixing us a batch of martinis."

"Sounds good to me," said Willy. "Cliff is a Tanqueray man, Ginny. That's where I got the habit."

Ginny smiled warmly as the two of them followed their host toward the house. Suddenly, Cliff Blaylock stopped short. The warm smile of his greeting left his face as he stared intently at two police cars pulling into the McCords' driveway next door. He continued to stare as one policeman got out of his car and joined the other who was accompanied by a man in civilian clothes.

Willy and Ginny stood quietly. Blaylock didn't move until the three men went inside of the house next door. He seemed totally preoccupied for what Willy thought was an inordinate amount of time. It was almost as if he had forgotten his newly arrived guests.

"What do you suppose is going on, Cliff?" Willy asked, feeling uncomfortable about going ahead to the house without Cliff.

"Oh . . . they've had a tragedy next door. They lost a son last night in a shooting."

"Really! Right here in Stag Creek?"

"Oh no. It was at a hotel near here. There have been policemen coming and going all day long. It's been a big shock. He was a nice kid . . . I . . . I don't know who would do a thing like that." Cliff Blaylock's voice faltered as he spoke. He was obviously shaken by the incident.

"Gee, Cliff, you must feel terrible," Willy said softly. "That's pretty close to home. You must know the people well."

"Yes we do . . . well, I don't really. But Sandy is pretty close to the boy's mother." Blaylock again stopped to look at the front door of the McCords' house. One of the policemen was now standing in the partially open door.

Willy looked at his friend's face. He was obviously shaken up. "Cliff, you once told me that this town had won a prize or something for being the most crime-free town in the country. Just thank God you don't have much of this kind of thing."

Blaylock looked blankly at Willy, not quite following him. "Oh yes . . . you're right. Nothing much ever happens in Stag Creek. Well . . . let's go inside."

Sandy Blaylock greeted Willy with a hug. "Willy! You still look the same. And you must be Ginny! You know, I've read so much about you and Willy in the papers that I feel like I know you."

Ginny shook the hand of their enthusiastic host. Sandy was short, blond, and very athletic looking. Her reference to the papers no doubt referred to a high profile murder case that she and Willy had recently been drawn into. "Yes, life with Willy gets pretty exciting sometimes. Cliff was telling us that you've had some excitement right here in Stag Creek."

"Yes! Can you believe that we were robbed? It's unbelievable. Over a hundred thousand dollars worth of Cliff's coins were taken."

"That's terrible. But I was referring to the trouble next door that Cliff was talking to Willy about. When were you robbed?"

"Only yesterday. Right in our driveway!"

Willy noticed that Cliff was standing quietly, listening to their conversation. "Cliff, it looks like all hell has broken loose in your little town lately."

"Yes, as a matter of fact it did. I hope that the police can get to the bottom of these things. It all has made Sandy and me quite nervous."

Willy eyed the couple closely. Sandy seemed to be handling the situation quite well. Cliff seemed much on edge. "Well I would say that the law of averages has caught up with you here in Stag Creek. There probably won't be another crime for years," Willy said, trying to offer a word of optimism.

"I must say, I've heard enough about the mess for now. Let's get the martinis rolling, Sandy." Cliff lifted the icy pitcher and began to fill the frosted glasses. "It would be nice if I could retrieve the coins, but they're probably gone forever. Most of them were bullion. They can be turned in almost anywhere. Of course, the AMERI was something special. I had always dreamed of owning one."

"Oh yes, now let me see," mused Willy. "The AMERI was the first American cent, 1793, I believe. I remember some sort of a story to the effect that someone goofed at the mint when making the die for the coin. When he started to spell out the word, America, he ran out of space. He wound up with AMERI, right Cliff?"

"Yes, Willy, that's basically true. But this one was in mint condition. It cost me a small fortune." Cliff Blaylock hesitated. After all, to him, the slaying of Willis McCord and the loss of the AMERI was all one event. He found he had to be very careful when he talked about one crime, not to mention the other. "In the driveway . . . they took the AMERI from the car in the driveway. . . . Oh, well. That's what insurance companies are for I guess." Blaylock downed about half the martini in one belt.

As they finished their drinks, the two men filled each other in on the publishing events in New York lately. Cliff Blaylock was still pretty up-to-date about happenings at Willy's old company by virtue of his contacts as an author's agent.

"So what's really selling these days, Cliff? What should my next book be about?" Blaylock seemed oddly quiet, reticent to prolong any conversation. Willy kept trying to draw him out with questions that were answered in a word or two, without real interest or enthusiasm.

"Celebrity and crime. Basically that's what's selling. If you can combine the two, you might have a winner." Cliff spoke matter-of-factly and then returned to his quiet preoccupation with other thoughts.

Sandy picked up the slack in the conversation. "I think that losing the AMERI has Cliff in another world. Anyway, I have an announcement to make. We didn't know exactly what time you folks would get here, so I've just made a reservation at a restaurant nearby. You all must be famished. So why don't we go there now, relax, and maybe we'll all feel better."

"Good idea, Sandy." Cliff seemed anxious to leave.

They drove to the Prospect Inn, a restaurant located only a short drive from the Blaylocks' home. Cliff led the way to the dimly lit quadrangle bar adjoining the restaurant. "Another Tanqueray, Willy? I'm having a double. Sandy's always a good designated driver. She doesn't drink enough to fill a thimble."

Willy smiled at Sandy. "Good! I'll drink to that. Sobriety is a grand virtue, Sandy."

"Well it's the only one I've got, other than trying to humor Cliff when he gets in one of his funky moods. Is Willy always so bright and cheerful, Ginny?"

"Hardly ever. It's just an affectation. Actually with all the troubles around your house today, I think Cliff has a perfect right to be as lowdown as he wants to."

"Thanks, Ginny." Cliff smiled weakly as the bartender approached.

"Good evening, Mr. Blaylock. Lots of excitement up your way I hear." Teddy, the bartender was just making conversation. It was a good bet that not much happened in tiny Stag Creek that he did not hear of.

"Yes, Teddy. We're trying to forget it for the moment. Willis, you know, lived right next door."

"I feel sorry for the old man and his mother." Teddy leaned across the bar to where just the two men could hear him. "Between you and me, the kid's been a terror. But, of course, who could expect anything like this."

Cliff Blaylock tensed visibly. "Willis . . . Willis was a good boy, Teddy. Nobody knows that better than Sandy and I. Sometimes the things you hear in this town aren't exactly true."

The bartender eyed Blaylock carefully. His words in defense of the McCord boy were unexpected. Teddy shrugged. "Well, you ought to know him better than I do. Glad to hear it. I hope they find the bastard who did it."

Blaylock stood and abruptly turned away from the bar, not commenting on the bartender's words. Then he turned back quickly and changed the subject. "Teddy, this is Willy Hanson. All he drinks is Tanqueray, three fingers neat. Make sure you collect your money."

Willy grinned and shook the bartender's hand. "If that's the way my friends talk about me, wait until you hear my enemies."

Teddy nodded soberly at Cliff Blaylock. "He's good people. He's just got a lot on his mind tonight."

The hostess paged the foursome and they were led through the dining room to a dimly lit table by a window. The two women dominated the conversation, Sandy taking the lead with her guests as Cliff dropped into his silence again.

It wasn't until the after dinner drinks that Willy made one more attempt to draw Cliff out of his shell. "You know, Cliff, from what I know of coin collecting, it might be easier than you think to locate your missing 1793 AMERI."

Blaylock shook his head slowly. "I don't see how it can be easy. In fact I've already given up on the idea of finding it."

"How many 1793 AMERI cents are left in the world?" asked Willy.

Blaylock looked thoughtful for a few moments. "Oh, maybe a couple hundred in varying condition. But only one or two in anything resembling the mint state of the one I had. Most of them are found in much lower grades."

"What was yours worth?"

"Willy, I paid seventy-eight thousand for it, and it was a bargain. I'm just hoping my insurance coverage holds up." Blaylock went on in a halting voice to explain how the coins had been stolen from his BMW parked in his driveway.

Willy listened, rather amazed that he would leave the valuable coins in the car, locked or not. "Isn't it true, Cliff that nu-

mismatic rarities, like the AMERI, are well known among a core
of serious collectors? I've heard that many such coins actually
have pedigrees identifying a list of owners over many years."

"Yes . . . yes . . . that is certainly true of this one." Blaylock spoke
slowly, trying to see the implication of what Willy was saying.

"Cliff, I'm thinking that whoever took your briefcase might
not know what they have. Perhaps they were after the gold bullion. No matter what the reason for the theft, when they go to sell
the AMERI, wouldn't that raise a lot of eyebrows at most coin
dealers?"

"Yes it would. Most collectors or dealers have never seen one
close to the mint state of the one I bought."

"In that case, Cliff, the person who stole your AMERI is much
in the position of selling a rare painting or well-known antique.
In order to get top dollar for it, he would have to approach a
knowledgeable collector or dealer."

The hair began to bristle on the back of Blaylock's neck. He
saw what Willy was driving at. It was very possible that the
AMERI would turn up very soon. The burly, unkempt thief of
his coin who was Willis McCord's companion might not be a serious collector. He strongly suspected that they were after the gold
bullion. In that case, the man might easily decide to take it into
almost any coin dealer for an appraisal or for whatever cash he
could raise.

"Do you have a photograph of the coin, Cliff?"

"No, I don't. But the previous owner probably has one. Such
photographs sometimes accompany an appraisal."

"I'll tell you what I would like to do, Cliff. Ginny is going to
visit a few friends in the east over the next few days. I'm just going
to goof off and stay out of trouble. If you don't mind, I'll just poke
around a little, and talk to some major dealers so that they can be
on the lookout for your coin. In this day and age, many of them
are probably connected by computers. If I act carefully and

quickly, we might get someone to put the finger on your thief in a hurry."

Blaylock stared out the window, watching the taillights of cars disappear down Stag Creek Road. "Oh, Willy, don't bother. That's a lot of trouble for you. I can do the same thing over a period of time. Let the insurance company worry about it."

Willy looked questioningly at his friend. Cliff Blaylock wasn't talking like the aggressive fighter he knew him to be. "Nonsense! I want to do it out of my own curiosity. Wouldn't it be great to nail that bastard? Tell you what. I won't charge you a dime for my trouble."

Blaylock shrugged. It was really unlikely, he thought, that Willy would come up with anything within a few days. He decided he would do everything he could to hamper his investigation. If Willy did "nail that bastard," he would also nail the one guy in the world who could identify the killer of Willis McCord. "Willy, I have accepted the fact that the AMERI is lost. Don't bust your butt on this. The guy might carry a gun."

10

Boccacio Lamas didn't like what he read. The entire operation had gone smoothly for a long time. The supply and distribution system for the east coast had run without a glitch. Now all of a sudden there was the bundle of newspapers in the pouch from New York.

Lamas placed the stack of papers on the deck beside him, kicked his feet up on the deck lounge, and gave orders to be left alone until he had read them all. He didn't mind violence when he planned it. But he didn't like surprises. High profile homicide was lunacy. You never knew when some politician or do-gooder was going to crawl out of the woodwork and try to make a name for himself.

He glanced up from his reading to watch the steady stream of pleasure boats heading down the Intra-Coastal Waterway toward the channel into the Atlantic Ocean near Fort Lauderdale. The flat-water day was ideal for cruising far beyond the jetties, perfect for partying, and burning a few hundred gallons of fuel tearing up and down the Florida coast. Fat cats with their bikini-clad pets, with pert little noses, just waiting to be stuffed with high-grade snow to keep them cool in the tropics. No problems here at all. Why the big rigamarole up north? He picked up the first paper, the *New York Post*, and began his reading. Virtually the same story appeared in all the papers, with little variation. The *Daily News*, the *Bergen Record*, and the *Newark Star Ledger* all gave the story page one treatment.

It seemed this rich kid, athlete, honor student, had been shot in a rural hotel parking lot. His fancy red Corvette had two kilos of cocaine stashed in the side panels. Not that two kilos set any record, but it all happened out in some sleepy bedroom town, in one of those fancy suburban hot pillow hotels. Obviously the case had everybody fired up because such events hardly ever erupted in such places. In New York, Miami, or Detroit such a crime might not have even made the papers.

Lamas tossed the last of the papers on the deck. Two kilos may not be a lot, but it was just enough to make someone come up short of cash. He had already made some inquiries and expected some answers before the day was over. What worried him most were the elections coming up soon. Because of all the ingredients, there was little chance the story would vanish overnight.

Boccacio Lamas put his massive arms in the air and clasped his hands behind his head just when Veronica came on deck all spruced up in a bikini she had taken out of her tiny clutch bag the night before. Only last evening she had flown in from Atlantic City and was itching to add a Florida tan to her well-toned curves.

"Whatcha thinkin' Bocco?"

"I'm thinking you better put some clothes on before the Coast Guard decides to come aboard and have a safety inspection. One of those hot young officers might decide he'd like a close up look-see."

She walked over, slid her hands through his thick hair and then began to massage his shoulders. "You didn't complain last night."

"I didn't have to share you with the whole world last night." Veronica flipped a towel around her shoulders and continued to massage Bocco's neck as he returned to reading the papers.

"Vinnie! Bring me a phone!" Lamas barked out the order as he caught sight of the first mate of the Calypso Magic. Two kilos wasn't much, but someone must know how this kid in the parking lot got it. And that someone better have damn well covered his tracks. Right this minute was the time to nip any trouble in the bud. Also, if someone was trying to horn in on his territory, he had to find out quickly, so he could join Percy LeRoy. He closed his eyes for a second and tried to picture Percy, looking up at the Verrazano Narrows bridge with an anchor chained to his feet.

Within seconds Lamas was brought a telephone and dialed the number back in New Jersey. A familiar voice answered the phone with a loud grunt. "Hey Red, you dumb fuck, are you wide awake?"

"Jeez! That's no way to talk, boss. I'm up early, bustin' my chops, taking care of business."

"Did that include reading all the morning papers?"

"Papers? Hell I ain't got time for papers."

"What the hell's going on up in Bergen County? Who paid who for the two kilos in the red Corvette? And who lowered the boom on the nice little college kid?" There was a long silence at the New Jersey end of the line.

"Oh, that... don't worry boss, it ain't our guy. I've already put some feelers out. I'm tellin' you it ain't our product. The dumb kid must have brought it in from someplace else. You got no worries, boss. How's the fishing?" Red Irons tried to change the subject. He had no answers.

"Never mind the fishing. I want to know who's rocking the boat up there. Maybe you need some help from Miami."

"Boss, you worry too much. I don't..."

"Enough crap, Red. I want some answers!" Lamas clicked down the receiver, feeling a little better. Maybe it wasn't his problem. Or maybe Heavy Laval down in Chelsea was trying to cross the river again. If it was, he had to know. Red would probably talk to Heavy first. After all he had been caught operating in Jersey once before.

Back in Hoboken, Red Irons stared at his telephone, now emitting a dial tone. He felt uneasy. He didn't like Bocco to be upset. Things were going pretty good. Doing business to the New York bedroom trade up in the burbs didn't have a lot of headaches like the old days in the city. He had a neat setup, and nobody had rocked the boat for a long time.

He picked up his copy of the *New York Post* and reread the account of the shooting. Nowhere did it mention who the shooter might have been. The kilos had been found in the kid's Corvette. Willis McCord was his name. He shook his head to himself. He had never heard of a Willis McCord. The more he thought about it the better he felt. The kid had to have bought the stuff somewhere else.

His thoughts turned to Heavy Laval. He had made a contact in Hackensack a few months back, and had been warned by Bocco himself. Besides, the burbs weren't Heavy's style. Out in the bedroom towns, Heavy still looked like Hell's Kitchen. He was a fish out of water. Still, I better check him out, Bocco thought, as he dialed his number in Soho. Bocco would ask if he did.

Peaches answered the phone. "Heavy, it's for you."

"What ya want?" Heavy shook his head and rubbed his eyes trying to wake up. "This better be friggin important."

"Why did you ice the kid up in Bergen, Heavy?" Irons decided to act like he knew something.

"You're way out of line, papa Red. I heard about it on TV. A guy would have to be nuts to use his weapon up there like that. Anything else, papa Red?"

"Yeah, I'll see you this afternoon, about three o'clock at Murry's over on Ninth Avenue. We got a lot to talk about." He set the phone in its cradle before Heavy could say anything else, just like Bocco had done to him.

11

Cliff Blaylock stirred in his sleep. He opened his eyes and read the digital clock on his night table. It was four-fifteen in the morning. He stared at the clock without moving, not wanting Sandy to awaken and share his restless night. Their dinner the night before with Willy and Ginny had served only to accentuate his anxiety. Willy had asked a lot of questions about the AMERI. Predictably, he had acted like the friend he was, trying to help.

The damned AMERI was just a side issue. The real issue was the fact that he had shot Willis McCord, and time was passing by. He watched the digital clock register its new numeral for each passing minute. He cursed to himself for not having the guts to go to the police and make a clean breast of everything. Could he tell the story and make anyone believe him? As far as he knew, the McCord boy had carried no weapon. His story about the large man with a ski mask leveling his gun at him would sound like something trumped up. It would sound like a lie.

And what about the large man, with the guttural voice? Did he know who he was? Did he get the plate number off his BMW? Would the man even care about things like that? After all, he had gotten away with the loot.

Without thinking, he smashed his pillow into a roll and stuffed it under his head. Sandy stirred next to him.

"You awake, dear? I wish you would try to sleep. There is nothing you can do about the robbery, you know. Is that what's bothering you?"

"I guess so ... I'm sorry. I didn't mean to wake you. I think I've done all the sleeping I'm going to do tonight. I think I'll go downstairs. Maybe I'll go over and get the morning papers. I've got to get this whole thing off my mind."

"The whole thing?"

"The robbery, damn it, the robbery ... I guess the situation next door is bothering me too. It's hard to believe Willis is dead."

Sandy encircled him with her arm. "Please, honey, try to rest. Everything will be alright within a few days. I think Willy and Ginny think you're a real grouch."

"Really? Was I that obnoxious at dinner?"

"Yes you were. But I'm sure Willy understood. He is a fine friend to have, Cliff. I like him, both of them for that matter."

Turning toward her, Cliff kissed her cheek. "I love you, honey. I'm going downstairs for awhile."

With that he got out of bed and slipped on a pair of trousers and his shoes. He then tiptoed downstairs, passing the guest room housing Willy and Ginny, and went into the kitchen. His hand went to a bruised area on his ribs where Willis McCord had gripped savagely at him the instant before he died. My God! he thought. Would things ever be normal again?

He sat by the big picture window in the kitchen looking across at the McCords' house in the distance. It was dark except for a weak light in their bedroom upstairs. For the first time since the murder, he noticed that the police cars were no longer out front. Sandy would say that things were returning to normal. But he knew that things would never be the same again.

"Hey pal, did you eat too much!"

Startled, he turned to face Willy Hanson, who had left the guest room to enter the kitchen. "Good morning, Willy, I guess I've woke up the whole house."

"Not a chance. Ginny sleeps like a log. I get a few hours, and then my mind starts going. It's always been that way. You've had a lot of excitement, Cliff. Insurance might cover your loss, but still, robbery is an eerie feeling. You feel that you have been violated. And it's worse when it happens at home. It will take some time to get used to it, Cliff." Willy looked at his friend, hands clasped on the table in front of him, staring fixedly at the house across the way. "Now what if you had their problem, over in that house. You'll be able to get another AMERI someday. They won't be able to find another son just like the one they had."

Cliff turned to face him. Willy noticed that his eyes were moist. In fact the man was sweating, in obvious discomfort. "Hey pal, can I do anything? You look like hell. Maybe it was too much brandy. Your friend Teddy serves a healthy belt."

Blaylock forced a smile. "No, it isn't that, Willy. I guess it's just everything. I'm sure you're right. Time will take care of things." He stood and stretched. "Tell you what, Willy. I'm wide awake. The gals won't be up for hours. I'm going to go over to Park Ridge, buy some morning papers, and stop by the diner. Have some bacon and eggs. Want to join me?"

"Hell yes!" Willy was enthusiastic, happy to see that his friend seemed to be pulling out of his doldrums. "I take it they've got hash browns and Tabasco."

"No doubt about it." Blaylock forced a weak smile. "Let's get out of here before we wake the women up."

The short ride to the neighboring town took only several minutes. Willy noticed that Cliff Blaylock had clammed up again, as they made the trip in silence. He drove slowly, staring ahead thoughtfully. There was absolutely no other traffic at this hour. Willy wondered if Cliff really wanted to be alone, but after all, he had asked him to come along.

After parking at the all-night diner, Cliff paused to feed coins into several newspaper machines, selecting a *New York Post,* a *New York Times,* and the *Bergen Record.* "Might as well see what the world is saying about us. It's been a long time since Stag Creek made the news." He registered another weak smile.

"Hey, smell the coffee and the bacon. You know, Cliff, I've been all over this country and there's no place like an all-night diner in New Jersey for breakfast." Willy was bubbling with enthusiasm, not shared by Cliff Blaylock who was still in his quiet funk.

The waitress brought them coffee and waited while they quickly ordered breakfast. Cliff then began turning pages in the Post. HONOR STUDENT'S CORVETTE LOADED WITH DRUGS! The headline on page two screamed at him. He immediately became absorbed in the follow-up story on Willis McCord, which reported that several kilos of cocaine were found in the slain youth's red Corvette.

The article went on at length to speculate that the shooting might have occurred as a result of a dispute over drugs. McCord's car was reported discovered in a far corner of the rambling Wellington Inn parking lot, several hundred yards from the area where his body was discovered by a parking valet. If the police had any knowledge of the killer's identity, there was no mention of it in the newspaper account.

Cliff pushed the newspaper in front of Willy and began sipping his coffee. "The whole world's going crazy, Willy. I would have bet anything I had that the McCord kid wouldn't be involved with drugs."

Willy scanned the article. "Evidently the shooter got away. If they have any idea who it was, they are sure keeping it quiet. They may find some clues in the Corvette." Willy continued reading the account that ended with a brief biography of Willis McCord. "It's a damn shame, Cliff. Do you suppose his parents have any idea that he might have been involved with drugs? It's bad enough that the kid got murdered. Now they're faced with this news."

"It's a shocker. I'll bet they didn't know. I find it all hard to believe." He stared out the window of the diner, picturing again in his mind the burly frame of the man holding a gun pointed at him. If Willis hadn't circled the car and got involved, he himself might have been shot. In a strange way, whether intentional or not, the kid might have saved his life.

Willy saw Cliff's eyes moisten again as he continued to stare out the window. The tragedy was having a profound effect on the man. He tried to picture himself in the same circumstances, and imagined that he would also be much concerned about the loss of a neighbor. Willy picked up the *Bergen Record* and began leafing through it, deciding to leave Cliff to his own thoughts for awhile. A follow-up story in that paper contained virtually the same information.

A two-column headline on the next page caught his attention. DRIVEWAY ROBBERY IN STAG CREEK NJ YIELDS 100,000 IN RARE COINS. The brief account told of the break-in of the BMW. It gave Cliff Blaylock's name, but no address. "Hey pal, cheer up! You made the papers." He pushed the paper in front of his companion.

Blaylock's first thought after he finished reading it was again of the man who had leveled a gun at him. If he read today's *Bergen Record*, he would know his name and the town he lived in. That damned AMERI! It too was mentioned in the police report cited in the paper. It was like he had left a calling card for Willis's partner in crime.

He pushed his breakfast aside. His stomach was churning. He had an overpowering hunch that he would soon hear from the broad-shouldered man in the ski mask.

"Why in the hell would they put that in the paper?"

Willy shrugged, trying to follow Blaylock's thoughts. "Cliff, a hundred thousand is a big theft. It's news by any definition, especially from a car parked in a suburban driveway. I guess some reporter got wind of it somehow. What are you worried about? The thief certainly knows where you live. He might have followed you from the coin show."

"The bastard!" Cliff Blaylock nodded at Willy's faulty logic. "Yeah, you may be right about that."

"By the way, Cliff, how far away was the coin show? How far would the guy have to tail you?"

"Only a couple of miles." Cliff hesitated, then decided to identify the hotel. "It was the Wellington Inn."

"Really? The same place where your neighbor's kid was shot?"

"Yeah. It must have happened later." Cliff fell silent, hoping that Willy would get off the subject.

Willy looked closely at his friend. He was definitely acting strangely. But then he had been through a lot. "It must be a charming place, Cliff. Remind me never to stay there. Eat your breakfast, pal. Tell me about the Giants this year. They got a chance?"

Cliff sighed heavily, pleased to hear the change of subject. "I doubt it. I think they need a whole new team."

The rest of the breakfast conversation consisted of sports and small talk about the things that had happened in their lives since they last had met.

It wasn't until they were driving home that Cliff again brought up the subject of the robbery. "Willy, I've been thinking. If you do have a little time to spare, why don't you check with a few coin stores and see if there has been any talk about the AMERI."

"Sure! Be glad to, Cliff. I'll tell them I'm looking to buy one and see if I get any nibbles. If we handle it carefully, we might get a line on that son of a bitch."

"Don't get yourself in trouble, Willy. Hell, I'm almost willing to pay a modest ransom to get the AMERI back. For a collector like myself, it was the acquisition of a lifetime. Can you understand that?"

Willy shook his head in disbelief. "No, I really can't. After what you've been through, I'd be mad enough to kill."

12

Jeanie Finehouse Nicholson lived in White Plains, in Westchester, north of New York City. She and her husband had left New York City several years back, so they would be closer to his law practice in Westchester. Their comfortable house in affluent White Plains had been little attraction for her father, Jonathan Finehouse. He had been born and raised in Manhattan, a native New Yorker who had seen the best of his times in the city. Despite frequent invitations from Jeanie and Carl to pull up stakes and live either near or with them, the old man had demurred. Business in his small antique and coin shop had deteriorated over the years, and now her father was talking seriously about moving for the first time.

Jonathan had stayed in the city in a small apartment near his shop on Ninth Avenue, content to visit his family on infrequent holidays or meet with them occasionally when they came into the city. However, his Saturday morning phone call had become a ritual, and now it was about noon, and still no call. Jeanie pushed the redial button again and there was still no answer from his apartment.

She tried the coin shop, even though he had been closing it lately on weekends. There was no answer there either. Her father was highly disciplined in his ways. She could not remember him missing a call before.

She decided to drive into the city. Carl was busy working on a brief in his study. She decided to make the trip alone. It would give her an opportunity to do a little shopping.

After rapping at the door several times, she used her key to enter his apartment. He wasn't there. Her father was a stickler for neatness. The bed was made, but the newspaper folded neatly on the kitchen table was three days' old.

She walked the short distance to Ninth Avenue to the coin shop. The small shop was locked. Missing however, was the closed sign that he always put in the window when the shop was closed. Using a key he had once given her, she entered and walked through the narrow store. She pulled gently at the curtain in the rear, and then screamed.

Steeling herself, she bent over the figure slumped on the floor, and then ran sobbing from the shop. Seeing no police, she ran into the small bodega next door and asked the counterman to call the police. "Please, my father, next door. I think he is dead."

Within minutes the police were on the scene. One of the grim faced officers returned quickly to the front of the store where she waited, explaining her identity to another policeman.

"Mrs. Nicholson, your father is dead, of course, apparently for some time. I'm sorry."

"How? . . . why? Can you tell what happened? Oh my god!" She fell trembling into the officer's arms.

The policeman helped her to a stool behind the counter. "Can we call someone for you? We have to notify an investigation unit. You just sit right there. We'll be here with you for awhile."

"Investigation?"

"Yes, Mr. Finehouse sustained a blow to the head. It couldn't have been self-inflicted."

The tears came again. "I can't believe it. . . . He was coming to live with us soon. Perhaps he fell, or had some kind of an attack."

"I don't think so, Mrs. Nicholson." The officer tried to comfort her. "The detectives will be able to tell more about it. Do you know if there is a cash register on the premises?"

"No . . . he hasn't used one for a long time. What money he kept here was in a cigar box back there." She pointed to the curtain. "Oh my God! What monster would do a thing like this?"

"Mrs. Nicholson, does that look like the cigar box he used?" The policeman pointed to the box on the floor, open and obviously empty.

"Yes." She started to walk over and pick it up.

"No, no. Please don't touch anything, Mrs. Nicholson, until the detectives have done their work."

"May I call my husband?"

"Of course. Let us do that for you."

The telephone was on a counter behind her stool. A neat paper was thumbtacked to an area next to the phone. Her father had always put a clean sheet of paper there to start each week. There was just one entry on this sheet. In the neatly lettered hand of her father, was the name Peaches, and then a local Manhattan number. The policeman saw her reading the number.

"Do you know who that is, ma'am?"

She shook her head negatively, and then started to shake again, a spate of tears flooding her cheeks. She looked pathetically at the officer. "We told him it was time to leave the city. And now look . . ." She shrugged and turned her palms up in hopeless despair.

13

Heavy Laval walked down Ninth Avenue. He was still early for his appointment with Red Irons at Murry's, so he stopped into Buster's Hotsy Topless to check out the latest attractions. A six-foot, deadpan brunette, all skin and bones mechanically bumped her way through her routine, which was totally ignored by two aging men customers.

He frowned at the barmaid in disapproval. "Jeez! Where'd Buster dig her up. She'll chase away all the customers." He ogled the barmaid from head to toe, and decided she was far more of an attraction than the dancer. He ordered a draft beer. "Hey, you should be the one dancin'. I'll bet you could fill the joint up."

"No thank you, mister. I'll do a lot of things, but I don't flash it in public." She accommodated him by stretching languidly, showing off a provocative silhouette.

"Last time I was in, I told Buster I had a babe for him. I guess he didn't believe me." That's what I'll do, he thought to himself. I'll get Peaches working on all the old guys at the bar. "I'm getting sick of making all the bread while she chills out on the soaps all day."

"You know Buster?" She eyed him suspiciously.

"Sure. Name's Heavy. Just ask him."

"Heavy?" She smiled for the first time. "Bring your girlfriend in. Buster's in a tight spot now. He needs some fill-ins. He keeps pestering me to do it. No chance! If he keeps it up, I'll get a real job."

"Hey, I'll do that. I'll bring her around, maybe tonight."

"Any experience?"

Laval grinned lewdly. "She has lots of experience shaking her fanny. All she has to do is stand up and do it instead of lying down. She's hot as a pistol, too."

"Maybe she won't want to if she sees this dump."

"She does what I tell her to. That's the way it is, baby. What's your name, anyway?"

"Tracy. Look, Heavy, I'll tell Buster you're bringing in a girl tonight. He'll make her do a gig or two for tips, just to see if she's got the nerve."

"No problem." Heavy Laval downed his beer and looked at the time. It was fifteen minutes until his meeting down the street with Red Irons. He smiled as he pictured Peaches tossing it around up on the bar. It would be good for business he decided, his business. At lunchtime a lot of the suits came into Buster's. They'd walk over all the way from Park Avenue. What these punks needed was a little snow in their life.

Laval downed his beer, left, and walked quickly another half dozen blocks down Ninth Avenue, and entered Murry's Oyster Bar right on time. Murry eyed him nervously and then nodded his head toward the rear booth. He could see Red Iron's unruly mop of red hair from where he was. He hated the bastard. He would ask a lot of questions and try to trip him up. An in-person audience with Red Irons was a rare request. He seldom left Hoboken, much preferring to stay in Jersey. Irons was the boss as far as Heavy knew. Someday he would love to find out who controlled him. He'd like to talk privately to that guy.

"Hi, Red. I hope you didn't come over here just to see me. I love to go to Hoboken, you know. It's a swingin' place. Lotsa little chickies over there like to breed." He grinned lewdly at Irons. Laval sat up straight in the booth, making his burly frame tower over his compact boss.

"Laval," Irons growled his name ominously. "You know why

you're nothing but a street man?" He paused for just a second, putting his flat hand in Laval's face as he started to answer. "Because you've got no fuckin' brains."

"Red, baby, you've got no right to . . ."

"Shut up!" Irons interrupted, glaring at him. "When I finish talking, maybe I'll let you say something." Irons stretched back in the booth, letting his jacket part just enough to show the butt of the nine millimeter under his armpit. He looked past Laval toward the bar up front. They were alone except for Murry, now reading a newspaper behind the bar.

Laval could see in a mirror behind Red Irons that they were alone in the place. The thought flickered across his mind that if Irons wanted to nail him he could do it right then and probably get away with it. He wished he had brought his own piece with him, but he seldom carried it in the daytime.

"The kid killed up in Bergen County was carrying our stuff." Irons paused, letting that sink in. "Now ask me how I know."

Laval hated this. He was playing games with him. "How do you know?"

"Because a certain red Corvette has been parked in your block a half dozen times this last month. Right there where you and the bimbo roll around in the sack, thinking nobody knows you're there. Don't ask me how I know." Red Irons was staring at him, not breaking eye contact for even a second.

Laval froze. He considered for a second that Irons might be bluffing, having read about the Corvette in the paper. But damn it, the car had been parked in his block several times. Red Irons knew something, but how much? How could he possibly know the circumstances of the shooting?

"I didn't do it, Red. I didn't shoot him." He looked him right in the eye. "And that's the truth."

"Now tell me you weren't up in Stag Creek." Irons was coaxing.

Laval had an idea that he knew the answer to his own question. He decided not to lie. "I was near there. I went up there to make a collection. The kid got a little behind and I gave him one more day. I got the payoff and left."

Red Irons tapped his hand against the table, the heavy gold and ruby ring rapping loudly with each tap. He appeared to be deep in thought. "Who iced the kid?"

"Red, honest to God, I don't know. I made the drop, picked up the dough, and left the parking lot. Somebody had to nail him after I left. Obviously he could have run into someone who knew he carried a lot of stuff. He had customers all over up there."

"Then why didn't whoever shot him take the stuff? The police found it in the Corvette."

"I don't know, Red." He paused, hesitating to compound the lie he had now begun. "But there is no way anybody can put the finger on us. I made the drop, got the money, and left. Everything was hunky-dory when I left."

"That's it?" Irons had an evil smile, still coaxing, like he knew more.

"Yep, that's it."

"Okay, Heavy. I believe you. If I ever find that you held anything back, you are going to get cold water company, out there under the Narrows bridge. Fair enough?"

Laval shrugged. "I got nothin' to worry about."

Red Irons sighed heavily, and appeared to relax. "Now, Heavy, there are two things I want you to do."

"Anything, Red. You know that." Laval felt exhilarated. He felt now that Irons had bought his story.

"First of all, I want to know if you're going to think of something later and suddenly remember you didn't tell me everything. Because I don't want to hear any surprises later on."

"Red, you've got nothing to worry about. What's the other thing?"

"There is the matter of Peaches. How much does she know?"

"Nothin'. She's only good for one thing. And she's damn

good at it." Heavy smiled, but found himself confronting a blank stare.

"I know what she's good for, Heavy. I asked you how much she knows?"

"Nothin' incriminating, Red. We don't talk business. I been thinking about putting her in a topless joint, so she can drum up a few suits for customers."

Red Irons stood up, preparing to leave, and turned to give Laval one last piece of advice. "Do yourself a favor, Heavy. Get rid of her. Kiss her off. Find her a new boyfriend. Do it now, before it gets complicated and you have to really get rid of her. By the way, Laval, do you read the papers?"

"Papers?"

"Yeah! If I had a pusher that got shot, I'd sure want to know who did it, and why they did it."

"I read the *Post* and the *News*. The cops don't know who did it. Or if they do, they ain't telling. I ain't worried, cause I didn't do it!" Heavy Laval permitted his voice to rise in protest at being grilled again.

Irons grinned at him. "Just asking, Heavy." He pulled a section of a newspaper from his side jacket pocket. It was the *Bergen Record*. "Brought you a local paper from Jersey. The local paper does a better job. But they still don't seem to have a line on who did it." Irons shrugged, glanced at the article briefly, and tossed the paper in front of Laval and then turned and walked slowly toward the front door.

Laval watched him until he was out the door and out of sight. "The bastard," he muttered to himself. "He's got no business talking to me like that."

He picked up the paper and read the story in the *Record,* which was essentially like the others. When he turned the page to finish the balance of the story, his eyes were caught by a small headline. DRIVEWAY ROBBERY IN STAG CREEK NJ YIELDS 100,000 IN RARE COINS.

After finishing the story, his hand went automatically to his shirt pocket. He felt the bulk of the big copper cent through the material. The article described it as priceless! Laval read the account over and over. This Blaylock character from Stag Creek had evidently concocted a story about being robbed in his own driveway as a cover for the real story of the robbery and shooting in the parking lot of the Wellington Inn.

He fished the large cent out of his pocket. It fitted exactly the description of the AMERI in the paper. "Priceless," he murmured to himself. I wonder how much priceless is, he asked himself. It must be a lot more than the nine hundred fifty the old man had offered him.

He dropped the large cent back into his shirt pocket, jammed the newspaper into his jacket, rose from the table, and walked out onto Ninth Avenue. He hurried back to Peaches' apartment, thinking all the way about the strange coin. It figured, he thought. After all, the old man had practically doubled the price he had first offered Peaches. No telling what it was really worth.

Peaches was not home when he got there. Heavy Laval flopped down on the sofa and kicked his feet up. He read the article again. He had sold the bullion to all those dealers for around twenty thousand dollars. If the headline was accurate, the cent must be worth about eighty grand. Of course it could be a lot more or less. It was reasonable to assume that the reporter would merely pick up a ballpark figure.

He grew impatient. Where the hell was Peaches? He had concocted a plan that he had to discuss with her. He would find out exactly what the stupid cent was worth, and then he would sell it. This Clifford Blaylock over in Jersey, he would have no choice in the matter. He would have to meet his price. He grinned as he heard Peaches' footsteps on the stairwell. How could one man be so lucky. He'd get a nice piece of tail, and then tell her his plan.

14

Willy Hanson and Ginny were driving along the Merritt Parkway, on their way to the ketch *Tashtego*, the only home they knew. A chilly early October had brought the fall colors to a dazzling display. The heavily wooded Connecticut countryside mesmerized them. They talked of their plans to move the *Tashtego* down the coast during the next few weeks and hole up in Florida for a few days before sailing to the Virgin Islands. They had wintered in St. Thomas once before and had come to love the place.

"If the weather was always like this, I would never want to leave New England." Ginny sighed as they lapsed into silence.

"Ginny my love, the winters here can be brutal. Almost all the vessels the size of the *Tashtego* spend their winters in dry dock, with their owners huddled around a fireplace somewhere. I can't wait to get started down the coast before you get a real taste of winter. We'll move the *Tashtego* down to the Tappan Zee, just north of New York City. It shouldn't take more than a few days to poke around a few coin shops and see if we can help Cliff with his problem. Then we'll be Florida bound. By the way, Coley Doctor will be in New York in a few days working on one of his high profile divorce cases. We should see him before we head for Florida."

Ginny beamed at the mention of Coley Doctor. The lanky six-foot-seven private investigator was one of her favorite people, and had become Willy's closest friend. "Now that's great. It'll be good to see old Coley. I haven't seen him since we wrapped up the case in Hong Kong. How's he doing with his new flame?"

Willy shook his head. "I haven't heard. Coley's flames tend to burn out rather regularly, however." He smiled at Coley's checkered history of marriages and affairs. The tall black detective moved too far into the fast lane to be tolerated by most of his women.

Ginny chuckled. Coley and Willy had become unofficial partners in the world of private investigation. The three of them had been through some harrowing times together and developed a rare friendship. It was one of those things that lost none of its strength, even through months of separation.

"Willy, with all due respect to your friend in Stag Creek, I found him rather aloof, or perhaps preoccupied is a better word. Is he always that way? I think Sandy was embarrassed by the way he withdrew from conversation now and then."

Willy nodded in agreement. "So it was that noticeable to you? Cliff Blaylock was not his usual self at all. No question that the robbery had him upset. I can understand that, but his apparent insurance coverage should ease the pain. He was in another world most of the time. Frankly, I felt quite uncomfortable. If it wasn't for Sandy's graciousness, we would have left sooner."

"You're right there, she's a peach," Ginny agreed. "Willy, I think the tragedy next door affected Cliff a lot. He was always staring at their house. Once I actually saw him become teary eyed. He seemed on edge whenever Sandy talked about it."

"It was a hell of a thing. Put yourself in their place. They had no doubt seen that kid around most of their life. That's probably what was really bothering Cliff. Yet he didn't talk about it much." Willy shrugged. "You know when he acted the most strange? It was when he was showing me his BMW. He was very quiet, unless I pumped him for details. I was amazed that he hadn't heard the noise of someone breaking the window. The car was parked right next to the house."

"You know, I asked Sandy the same thing. She was amazed that she heard nothing. She says she is a light sleeper. It was a hell of a chance for someone to take to come right under their window in their driveway."

"You know, Ginny, if he wasn't my friend, and I hadn't known him for so long, I wouldn't believe him. You'd almost suspect an insurance scam. Put yourself in the position of the thief. Here's a sleepy little town where nothing happens for months on end. By the way, did you notice how quiet it was last night? Picture this thief going all the way, almost to the end of a cul-du-sac, smashing a car window, and then making his escape with a briefcase. Amazing!"

It was dusk by the time they reached the marina on the Sound near Clinton. As they pulled into the parking lot, the showy ketch *Tashtego* stood silhouetted against the setting sun, its wide spreaders and tall masts standing out from all the other boats tied up on the long guest dock.

Willy turned to Ginny, now dozing on his shoulder. "We're home, lover."

"Umm . . . got any plans for the evening?"

"Just a bottle of wine, a loaf of bread, maybe some cheese, and Ginny DuBois for dessert. It was much too quiet at Cliff's house last night. I could even hear the clock downstairs ticking."

"I know. I thought about attacking you once, but didn't want to embarrass your friends." Ginny snuggled closer to Willy in the small car. "Willy, I've been thinking about the first time we made love. In fact I have been thinking about it all the time you were driving. Do you remember?"

"It was in the cockpit of the *Tashtego*. Like a fool you had let the main sheet go into the wind. We were well into the Catalina Channel."

"You do remember!"

"Of course. It was very special. Everything we did that day was special."

"Willy, do it all over again just as you remember it, right here tonight, as soon as we get aboard. As Captain of the *Tashtego*, I will order the wine and cheese served later as dessert."

15

It had been almost a week since the robbery at the Wellington Inn. Heavy Laval tossed the stack of newspapers on the bed, then propped himself against the headboard. Peaches lay on her pillow next to him breathing noisily in a deep sleep.

Buster's Hotzy Topless was turning their life around. She would drag in about four in the morning, go to bed and sleep till afternoon. But she was bringing in the money, more each day. He slipped his hand stealthily into her pillowcase until his fingers closed around the small glass-beaded purse. He hesitated as she shifted on her pillow, then slowly retrieved the purse. He opened it and counted the contents. Six hundred dollars! Her best night yet. He stuffed three hundred back in the purse and returned it to the opening of her pillowcase.

He stared at her. They never really made love anymore. She was too tired for anything but an occasional quickie. He fingered the money he had kept. What the hell, he thought, if she kept bringing home this kind of bread, he could get all the loving he wanted somewhere else.

He started paging through the morning papers he had picked up at the bodega on the corner. Yesterday there had been a brief account of Willis McCord's funeral in the *Record,* and that was all. The New York papers had pretty much phased out the story.

There were lots of new murders, gorier and closer to home. Stag Creek, New Jersey, not even on the map he had bought, held little interest for most New Yorkers. Willis McCord would be quickly forgotten.

He paged impatiently through the *Post* and the *Daily News*. Nothing there, he tossed them onto the floor beside the bed and started leafing through the *Record*. There was a short follow-up story buried in the local news section. Police reported no suspects as yet in the case. A slug, possibly from a bullet fired by a .38 handgun, had been dug from a tree next to the parking lot. The article speculated that the slug had passed through McCord's body and lodged in the tree. The story repeated a previous report that an autopsy completed by the Coroner in Paramus, New Jersey, had revealed that McCord had traces of cocaine and other substances in his system.

Heavy grinned at himself in the mirror across the room. The police didn't have a single clue pointing toward him. Only he knew that the slug they had found would be a match for the gun fired by Clifford Blaylock. He would make Mr. Blaylock pay the price someday for killing such a nice young man. But first he would dangle him on a string for a while, until he got enough money for one of those fancy cabin cruisers he liked to watch racing up the Hudson River from Battery Park.

He slipped his hand under the covers encircling his fingers around her breast. "Hey Peaches! Wake up!"

"Heavy, what the hell are you doing? What time is it?"

"It's about time for me to leave. I got business uptown. But first I need one of your special quickies."

"You're a bastard, Heavy."

"And you love it!" He leered down at her as she turned toward him, eager to get it over with.

Fifteen minutes later Heavy Laval hailed a cab on Ninth Avenue. "Drop me off at Fifty-seventh," he ordered the driver. At

Fifty-seventh, he stuffed one of Peaches' tens into the hand of the driver. "Keep the change, pal."

He walked down the cross street, feeling good. Peaches never failed to make him feel good. And now, very soon he was going to be a lot richer than he had ever been.

He eyed the storefronts carefully until he spotted the sign, BLACKWELL'S NUMISMATICS, in fancy gold lettering. He peeked in the window. The shop gleamed compared with others he had visited while selling the bullion coins. A security door with a buzzer faced him. Inside, he could see at least two armed guards. The place was a small fortress. Heavy pushed the buzzer several times. A loud buzzing signal was activated that enabled him to open the door to be faced immediately by one of the armed attendants.

"Yes sir, may I help you?" The man eyed Laval closely. He wore rumpled but clean work clothes. Thick black hair was combed, but he needed a shave.

"My grandfather died here awhile back. We found a coin in his belongings. I would like to find out what it's worth."

"Why don't you step right over here, sir, and I'll get someone to help you." The attendant studied the powerfully built man, wondering if he had been wise to have let Laval in the door.

In a few moments, a tall distinguished looking man emerged from a back room and approached Laval on the other side of a counter.

"Yes sir, I'm David Blackwell. What can I do for you?"

"I've got this here coin. I'm wondering what I could sell it for?" Laval fished the large copper cent from his shirt pocket and tossed it on the glass counter.

"Oh my, please, let's don't scratch it. Copper is really quite soft."

"Soft?" Laval could feel himself getting nervous, as he watched Blackwell lean over the counter to eye the coin. He stared at it for several seconds.

"My word! It's an AMERI, and in magnificent condition it appears." Blackwell reached behind him and produced a felt-lined tray, then lifted the coin gingerly by its edges. He examined both sides for a few moments and then placed it down on the felt.

"It's a fine piece," Blackwell said, now examining the coin with a magnifying glass.

Laval started to perspire. The old man, Finehouse, had also called it a "piece."

"What will you gimme for it?" Laval mumbled, wishing that he had sent Peaches on this mission. There was something uppity and stuffy about this place that he didn't like.

Blackwell studied the man, glancing up now and then from the coin. He couldn't help but notice the grimy fingernails, and generally unkempt appearance of Laval. "It is an interesting specimen. I couldn't possibly give you an answer without showing it to one of my partners who is an expert on rare copper. I suspect it is something that could be put up at auction at quite a handsome figure."

"A handsome figure? What does that mean?"

"Well, if my colleague verifies it as authentic, I suspect it might bring many thousands of dollars at an auction. As I say, he is the expert on specimens like this." Blackwell looked at his watch. "The gentleman will be in at two o'clock this afternoon. If you want to bring it back, he'd be happy to talk about handling the coin for you. Perhaps he would even buy it himself."

Now Laval was getting confused. "Handle the coin for me?" Blackwell was now staring blankly at him. "Two o'clock. Okay, I'll bring it back." He reached to scoop the coin up off the felt.

Blackwell placed his hand over the felt. "Here, sir, let me fix this up for you." He reached under the counter and produced a soft paper envelope, picked the coin up deftly by its edges, and dropped it into the envelope and then into a larger one made of plastic. "Here, sir, I suggest you keep it in here. Every little scratch you get on it may cost you a thousand dollars." He winked, trying to be helpful, but found himself meeting a hostile stare from Laval.

"I didn't think it would be all this much trouble to find out what it is worth. I'll be back at two." Laval dropped the small envelope into his shirt pocket, and turned toward the door.

"Sir, if you'd rather not risk carrying that around, I would be happy to keep it in our safe until this afternoon. I'd give you my personal receipt for it, Mr. . . what is the name, sir?"

Laval waved his hand without answering and continued to the door. He had already figured out that the little piece of copper was worth a pile of loot. He'd make Blaylock pay dearly for it. With a patsy like Blaylock, maybe he wouldn't need Red Irons anymore.

16

Sandy Blaylock eyed her husband warily. It had now been a week since Willis McCord's funeral. At the last minute as they were preparing to leave the house to go to the funeral service, he had started perspiring and became nauseous. She attended the services alone. When she had returned a couple of hours later, he was still seated at the table in the kitchen fully dressed for the funeral, paging idly through one of her tennis magazines. He had absolutely no interest in tennis. He asked her nothing about the funeral.

This morning he sat in the same chair in front of the window that looked out across their lawn to the McCord's house behind a row of neatly clipped hedge. "Cliff, are you going into the office today?"

He lifted his attention from a newspaper. After a few moments he shook his head negatively. "What for?"

"What for?" Sandy spun on her heels and fairly shouted at him. "Cliff, I asked you a perfectly normal question that should have a perfectly simple answer. Are you going into the office today?"

"No," he replied reluctantly after a pause of several seconds.

"Thanks, Cliff. I am going into New York today, and I thought if you were going, I would go with you. That's why I wanted to know. I am not trying to pry into your business." If he heard her, he didn't comment. He continued the same intense stare at nothing in particular that had become so familiar over the past several days. "Cliff, maybe you should make an appointment with the doctor. I can't read your mind. For the last few days you have been a perfect ogre. In fact, when Willy and Ginny were here, he took me aside and asked me if you had a physical problem. You had acted like a jerk, Cliff, and you've been like that ever since."

"I'm sorry. I didn't know I was causing a problem. What would you like to talk about?" He spoke softly and started leafing through the newspaper in front of him. "I didn't realize that quiet civility was a crime."

"Quiet civility! That's not fair. Cliff, I think we need a vacation. I don't know what's bugging you, but something definitely is. Is there a crisis at the office?"

"Absolutely not." He tried to force a smile. "Everything is just fine at the office . . . and, Sandy, the way I feel has nothing to do with you. I love you, Sandy . . . you're really . . . well, you're everything to me."

She gaped at him. There was something almost pathetic about his demeanor. She walked behind him and bent down to kiss him. "Honey, I'm sorry, but I worry about you. I'll have Adrienne drop me off at the train station. Promise you'll tell me what's bugging you when you can, okay?"

"Adrienne? I'll run you to the train. You know that."

"Oh, Adrienne likes to keep busy these days. Maybe she would like to go into the city with me. I still think you should go to the doctor and get checked out."

"Don't worry. I feel better already. You're a jewel, Sandy." He returned her kiss with a peck on the cheek and then rose and walked from the kitchen.

Someday, I'll have to tell her all about it, he told himself as he walked away. He just couldn't hide it from Sandy forever.

Last night's phone call from the insurance claims investigator had set him off. He said he would drop by sometime this morning. There were a few routine questions he had to ask regarding the theft from his car. Routine questions? Why couldn't he just ask them over the phone?

Later that morning Sandy left the house and walked up the McCords' driveway. Adrienne opened the door to meet her. She looked like anything but a woman in mourning. A flashy red dress, slit high on her thigh moved subtly on her well-toned body as she strode toward her Mercedes in the driveway. He gaped at her as he usually did. Sandy was no slouch, but Adrienne McCord was a work of art. Even in his mental state, the woman still compelled him to stare.

The Mercedes passed near his house as it moved down the driveway. He saw Adrienne smiling, gesticulating with one hand while she drove, obviously engaged in animated conversation. How could she do that while he was sitting here stewing in misery. He drummed his fingers nervously on the table, wondering if he would ever be able to push the killing in the parking lot from his mind.

The door chimes snapped him from his trancelike state. He peeked out the window. A young man in a business suit stood waiting. He carried a satchel type briefcase stuffed with protruding papers. Blaylock opened the door.

"Good morning, sir. I'll Billy Baxter, Trans American Casualty."

Blaylock stared at the claims investigator, thinking that he didn't expect him so early. He had wanted to give the matter more thought before talking to him. "Come right in. I'm in a bit of a hurry this morning, so I'd appreciate it if we could get this out of the way quickly," Blaylock said hopefully.

The investigator followed him into his study, set the satchel on the end of a desk, and extracted a small clipboard. "Let's see now, Mr. Blaylock. Your claim amounts to just a few dollars over a hundred thousand, not counting some minor damage to your vehicle. Is that correct?"

Blaylock immediately took a disliking to the young man. He didn't like the way he plunged right into the matter without the usual chitchat about the weather, or some of the other civil little pleasantries that often precede a conversation between two strangers.

"Well, Mr. Baxter, I would say that it is a matter of your point of view. To me, the rare copper cent is virtually priceless. I can assure you that if the coin were properly put at auction it would bring far more than the amount listed in my claim."

The investigator looked at him thoughtfully for a few moments before speaking. "What would you say the replacement value of the item would be, Mr. Blaylock?"

"That is just my point. It is probable that there may not be a replacement at any price, anywhere in the world. The mint state AMERI is quite likely one of a kind." My assessment was based on a sale price between friends that was unrealistic. In fact, after some thought, I think the proper procedure would be to let an expert assess the probable value of the AMERI."

"And who might that be, Mr. Blaylock?"

"Well there are a few possibilities. There is an Early American Coppers organization that specializes in rarities such as the AMERI. If you contacted them, they might offer some advice." Blaylock read the skepticism on Baxter's face. The young man obviously had no familiarity with the world of numismatics. "Of course, there is Blackwell's in New York. They are one of the foremost coin dealers in the world. They would have someone there who could assess a value once given an accurate description and a photograph of the actual coin."

Baxter wrote down Blaylock's comments as he talked, asking that he slow down now and then so he could get it all correct. When he had finished he leafed through several pages he had brought with him. "Do you have the vehicle that was broken into on the premises?"

"Yes. You are lucky you came today. I'm taking it in to get the window replaced tomorrow. Come, I'll show it to you."

Blaylock led the way out the front door and then down the driveway to where the BMW was parked. Though he had used the car for local errands since the detectives had completed their investigation, it now was parked in a position very similar to the place where he had claimed it had been vandalized. He watched as the insurance investigator walked around the car, stopping to stare at the small shattered triangular window.

"Unusual," Baxter murmured.

"What's so unusual?" Blaylock asked, again feeling the tenseness in his voice.

"That small window is difficult to break. Most experienced thieves would smash the large window. Usually the smaller window gets broken when someone leaves the keys locked in the car. They think they are saving money by smashing the small window." Baxter walked around the car one more time, stopping briefly to glance at the small chalk circle where the policeman had first marked the spot where he had picked up the shards of glass. The penny was still lying within the circle. If Baxter was curious about the small chalk circle, he didn't say anything.

"Well then, I guess my thief wasn't experienced." Blaylock started walking back toward the front of the house, anxious to get the investigator on his way.

The investigator followed him slowly, continuing to make ad-

ditional notations on his pad. "The police report shows that shards
of window glass were found quite a distance from your car."

He turned to face Baxter who was still jotting a note on his
pad. "Yes, I believe so. Why?"

"Why? . . . We may never know. One would expect that if the
window were broken from the outside that the glass would fall
within the vehicle or right next to it."

Blaylock shrugged. "I'm afraid I can't help you there." He was
happy that Baxter was now shoving his clipboard into his briefcase. The mental picture of how he had shook the pieces of glass
from the beach towel flashed across his mind. He breathed easier, reasoning that a hypothetical thief could have done the same
thing.

Baxter offered his hand to Blaylock. "Thank you for showing
me around, Mr. Blaylock. We'll get moving on your claim right
away." He glanced back down the driveway and shook his head.
"Our thief surely took a hell of a chance, walking all the way back
there and smashing the window. It had to make quite a racket."

"I suppose so. But no one heard a thing. I sure hope they
catch the bastard."

The investigator climbed into his car, and again glanced down
the long driveway before backing into the street. Blaylock hoped
it would be the last time he saw him. His curiosity made him nervous.

Cliff Blaylock walked across his lawn to the edge of the road.
During his conversation with Baxter, he had seen the postman
stuff the daily mail delivery into his rural mailbox. Walking back
toward his house, he shuffled through the several envelopes.
There was one large manila envelope with his name and address
crudely lettered with a marking pen. It bore no return address.
The word, PERSONAL, was lettered in large print.

He tore the flap loose from the small metal clamp and reached
inside. Pasted to a sheet of typing paper was a newspaper photograph of Willis McCord. It was his graduation photo that had been

published in all the papers the day after he had been slain. Across the bottom of the sheet was a message lettered in the same dark marking pen as the address on the envelope. "Shame, shame on you!"

He stood frozen to the spot a few feet from his front door, nervously glancing around. He peeked inside the envelope and then studied the outside of it carefully. There was nothing else. There was also no stamp! The envelope had most likely been hand placed in his box by someone other than the postman. He could feel his pulse throbbing as he started to sweat.

Blaylock hurried inside his house, locked the door behind him, and examined the envelope and its contents again. He tried desperately to rationalize some explanation other than what seemed obvious to him. The man who had stolen his briefcase, the man in the ski mask who had driven away, the man who saw him kill Willis McCord, knew who he was and where he lived. In fact, he had been right there at the edge of his property and put the envelope in his mailbox. Now he was actually trembling.

Blaylock dashed up the stairs, into his bedroom, and ran his hand under the pile of blankets in the linen closet. "Idiot!" He cursed at himself, remembering that he had dropped the .38 revolver into the creek off Old Tappan Road. I must be going crazy, he thought to himself. How could I have forgotten that?

He turned around and slid his hand once again under the blankets, and then pushed the envelope as far back under them as he could. He saw his hand trembling. He would deal with the envelope later. Right now he needed time to think.

The phone rang, startling him. Hesitantly he picked it up from its place on his nightstand. "Hello," he answered weakly.

"Cliff, that you?"

He sighed with relief. It was Willy Hanson. "Yes, Willy. . . . Good to hear from you."

"Ginny and I just docked the *Tashtego* at the marina near Tarrytown. Had a beautiful sail down the Sound. It was a bear get-

ting through Hellgate against the tide, but God takes care of the
foolish sometimes." Willy hesitated, hearing no response from
Blaylock. "Anyway, Ginny and I would like to pop for dinner tomorrow night. Are you and Sandy free?"

"Sandy's not here right now, but I'm sure it'll be okay. We'll
meet you at the marina."

"Good. Any news about your AMERI?"

"No . . . I guess I've resigned myself to the loss. Don't waste
your time with much poking around, Willy."

"Nonsense. We'll talk about it tomorrow night. I've got an idea
or two." Again there was silence at the other end of the line.
"Cliff, you there?"

"Oh . . . yes. Sorry Willy. Someone's at the door," he lied. "See
you tomorrow around six." After little further conversation, Blaylock hung up the phone. He really hated the thought of having
dinner out tomorrow night.

He thought of the envelope tucked away on the closet shelf.
How could he ever feel safe anywhere again? He was sorry he had
tossed his .38 into the creek. Then he remembered that there was
another gun around the house. He had bought Sandy a small .22
automatic years ago. She had wanted no part of it and had hidden it away. He would find it and carry it himself.

He sat on their bed for a moment and then leaped to his feet.
He went to her vanity table and opened the lower side drawer as
far as he could. Feeling down under all its contents his fingers
closed on a leather clutch bag. He could feel the heft of the small
revolver inside. What luck! It was in the spot Sandy had put it
years ago.

He took it from the bag and jammed it into his pocket. Somewhere downstairs around his workbench he had only recently
spotted a box of shells. He would find them, right now while
Sandy was away, and load the bullets into the revolver. He vowed
to himself that he would carry the weapon all the time, feeling

certain that it would give him peace of mind through the days ahead.

Blaylock returned to the living room downstairs and sat in a club chair looking out over the front lawn. Every now and then he tapped the revolver that fitted comfortably in a side pocket of an old leather jacket. From where he sat, he could see his mailbox. The uneasiness and trembling began again. The fact that the thief who carried a gun when he confronted him at the Wellington Inn had possibly visited his mailbox was terrifying. He could be anybody. For that matter, he could live nearby, right there in Stag Creek.

17

Red Irons paced the arrival area at Newark Airport. It was a command performance. Boccacio Lamas was flying in from Miami. He was to meet his flight and then escort him to Nicky's marina near Barnegat on the Jersey shore.

He hated the thought of a meeting with Lamas. In fact he hated everything about Lamas. It was easy to dislike a man who had two luxury yachts, one on the Jersey shore and the *Calypso Magic* that spent most of its time in the Florida keys. Bocco didn't know what a social visit was. When he called for a meeting, he had something on his mind. And the son of a bitch was never straightforward about it. He dreaded the thought of actually boarding Bocco's *Jersey Trick*. There were bigger yachts around, but the *Jersey Trick* was all power and muscle. The sleek one hundred twenty footer handled the rough coastal water like no other vessel her size.

All those stories about Bocco came to his mind. This guy or that guy was always recalled as last being seen alive climbing aboard the *Jersey Trick*. Bocco had grinned at him once and told him he had made up those stories as a practical joke. A few days later Percy Leroy was invited aboard the *Jersey Trick*. Nobody had seen him since.

Red Irons looked at the postings on the televised arrival screen. The flight from Miami was reported on the ground several minutes ago. Since the beefed up security at all the airports, if you were meeting a flight, you had to wait at a special arrival area at the head of each concourse. From the vantage point he had selected it would be impossible for him to miss Bocco as he left the concourse.

He could see him now. Bocco was a couple of hundred feet down the concourse. He had wide shoulders and was wearing his perpetual frown. He had two expressions, the frown and the occasionally manufactured phony grin. Walking beside him, a couple of steps behind, was the babe. It had to be Veronica. The showy blonde's reputation had already come north via other recent visitors to the *Calypso Magic*.

Lamas paused for a second, as they passed. "Come on, Red. What'ya waiting for?" The three of them walked quickly to the baggage area.

"Red, this is Veronica." Bocco said as he glanced impatiently at his watch.

Veronica smiled weakly, but said nothing. She was attracting much attention in a form-fitting pink jumpsuit with the legs slit from her ankles to her thighs.

"Nice meeting you, miss. Did you have a nice flight?" Irons found it difficult to keep his eyes off her.

Bocco Lamas glowered at him. "Hell yes, we had a nice flight." He snapped his answer before Veronica could speak. Then he leaned over and whispered just loud enough so Veronica could also hear. "Just don't get any crazy ideas about crawling around in her pants!" This bit of advice was followed by one of his phony grins.

Veronica gave his remark a palms up shrug and smiled at him. "I think Bocco needs some rest. How far is the marina?"

Bocco again butted in. "An hour or an hour and a half depending on the traffic, providing Mr. Irons here doesn't get us lost."

"Not a chance, Bocco." Their luggage tumbled into the carousel quickly. Bocco shoved some bills into the hands of a skycap who followed them to the parking area below.

Irons couldn't help but gape at the torrid blonde as she piled into the back seat of the limo next to Lamas. Then he thought of the long drive ahead, reminding him that he would stay aboard the *Jersey Trick* that night. His hand slid subtly into his inside jacket pocket as he slid behind the wheel. The comforting feel of the cold steel made him feel better. What the hell. Bocco was acting perfectly normal. He would have known by now if he were in a bad mood.

Irons turned south on the New Jersey Turnpike. Within minutes he exited to the Garden State Parkway and headed south toward the marina near Barnegat. He could see that Bocco and Veronica were already locked in a clinch. Soon both heads disappeared. Good, he thought to himself. Now I can pay attention to the driving.

18

A nybody home!" Coley Doctor rapped the flat of his huge hand against the hull of the *Tashtego*, now tied up at Svenson's Dock near Tarrytown, New York.

Willy Hanson emerged from the cabin and grinned broadly at the six-foot-seven black detective. "I knew it had to be you. No one else would be that unkind at this hour of the morning." Willy glanced around the marina and noticed several others looking their way. "I hope you didn't wake up the whole marina."

"Willy, it's after nine o'clock. Everybody's moving around except you."

"Hi, Coley!" Ginny Dubois poked her head out of a forward hatch.

"Aha! Now I know why. With company like Ginny Dubois, who wants to wake up and see the cruel world?" Coley vaulted himself aboard, revealing incredible agility for a man his size. "Long time no see, pal." He extended his hand to Willy, still standing in the hatchway.

Willy greeted his friend warmly. It had been many months since they had worked together wrapping up a serial murder case in Hong Kong. The former basketball all-American looked fit as hell. It always puzzled Willy that Coley had eschewed the professional sports lure to become a lawyer, and now a quite famous and respected private detective. Willy and Coley had worked closely together on several cases that had attracted national attention. Their relationship produced several harrowing moments that welded a rare and lasting mutual respect and friendship.

Coley stood on the aft deck of the *Tashtego*, admiring the huge structure of the Tappan Zee Bridge spanning the Hudson River at its widest point. The bridge connected Westchester with Rockland County and the Catskill region to the north. Gazing through the main span on this clear morning, the skyline of Manhattan, twenty miles away, was clearly visible to the south.

"Magnificent! That's what it is, Willy. You guys know how to live. Everytime I've been on the *Tashtego*, it's been the most beautiful place around. No wonder you don't settle down and buy a house like normal people."

"Nothing fun about being normal, Coley. You know that better than anybody else," Ginny observed, joining Willy at the hatchway. "By the way, how is that beautiful Marissa these days?"

The hint of a frown crossed Coley's face. His rocky existence with the women in his life was legendary. "She is still on my list, Ginny. Believe it or not. But she is a hard one to train." Coley shrugged, then the frown turned to a grin.

"You working on anything big right now, Coley? What brings you to the east coast?" Willy rubbed at the stubble on his chin, hoping that Coley would be around for a few days.

"Nope. In fact I've got a couple days to take it easy. I'm waiting for some guy to get in from Paris with his wife. Got to follow them around for awhile and then get back to California."

"You're going to follow a man and his wife? Sounds pretty dull, Coley." Ginny smiled. Coley had a way for setting you up, and then letting the other shoe drop in a conversation.

"Yeah, except for the fact that he has another perfectly legitimate wife back in sunny Cal who wonders what the hell is going on."

Willy shook his head. "Same old Coley, going after the easy money."

"Hey man, I can't help it if these rich bastards can't handle their women." The smell of bacon and coffee drifted from the galley of the *Tashtego*. "Hey, I'm in time for breakfast."

Coley lowered his head to join them in the cabin "You know, I've been on a lot of boats, and none of them are built for a guy my size. What brings you two guys to these parts, Willy?"

"We're trying to move the *Tashtego* down to the Caribbean before we get stuck in the cold. We got sidetracked here for a few days. An old buddy over in Jersey has a little problem. I'm trying to help him Nothing really serious; he was a victim of larceny. He had a super-rare coin stolen."

"Doesn't sound very exciting. What's it worth?" Coley was still

looking at the idyllic splendor of New York framed by the Tappan Zee Bridge. "It's sure gorgeous here. I can't believe I'm just a
few miles from the Bronx."

"The coin might be worth a hundred G's, Coley."

"That's a little more exciting. Did he look in his sofa? That's
where I lose most of my change."

"It was in a briefcase he left overnight in the front seat of his
car parked in the driveway." Willy couldn't resist a smile as he said
it. It was a strange way to lose such a treasure.

"No kidding. That sounds kind of stupid. In fact, I'd say your
friend sort of asked for trouble. Has he got all his marbles, Willy?"

"He's a smart fellow. In fact, I'd say he's brilliant. You've got
to understand that he lives in Stag Creek. It's a quiet little town
where nothing goes on but eating, sleeping, taking the kids to
school, and running for commuter trains and buses. Sometimes a
year goes by without a reportable crime. You might say that Stag
Creek is the antithesis of the south Bronx."

"Sounds awfully dull. I still think your friend is stupid. A
hundred G's! That's enough to tempt a bunch of people. Human
nature comes in a lot of varieties, even in this Stag Creek place."

The three of them sat on the long cockpit benches of the
Tashtego, eating breakfast and conversing. Since Willy had started
the story of the missing AMERI, he continued to fill Coley in on
what he knew about it. "You know, Coley, I'm sort of a half-assed
collector myself. Cliff feels terrible about the loss, even though
he has insurance."

"Aha! Insurance! I'm surprised at you Willy. Where's your investigative instinct?" Coley winked at Ginny. "Your lover here
needs a longer vacation."

"Oh no, Coley. Don't even think it. You could trust Cliff Blaylock, even with Marissa. He's not like you and me. He doesn't have
a wicked thought in his head."

"Hmm . . . a dull man in a dull town. I still say it's probably in
his sofa."

"I've got a great idea." Ginny had remained quiet as Willy told the story of the robbery. "We're having dinner with the Blaylocks tonight. Remember? They are coming here, to the marina. Coley can join us and make his own judgment about Cliff."

"Good thinking, Ginny! Coley will loosen up the conversation. Cliff was in a real funky mood last time."

"Honey, he had a perfect right to be in a foul mood. Both he and Sandy were very upset about all the trouble next door. It happened the same day of the robbery."

"Trouble next door?" asked Coley.

"Oh yes! I guess I had forgotten about that. The young son of their closest neighbor was shot and killed in the parking lot of a local hotel near Stag Creek. Cliff and Sandy are pretty close to the family. You can imagine how upset they would be." Willy went on to describe what he had read in the papers about the shooting.

Coley listened carefully until Willy was finished. "Now let me get this straight. In the house next door to where a hundred grand robbery had taken place, on the same day, the neighbor's kid was murdered in a drug-related incident. All this happened in this quiet, sleepy little town, where nothing ever happens?"

"Yep." Willy thought back over their conversation with the Blaylocks. "There is another small coincidence, Coley. On the day of both crimes, Cliff attended a coin show at the Wellington Inn where the McCord boy was later shot. Of course, one crime had absolutely nothing to do with the other."

Coley shook his head and started to chuckle. "You know, the last time I got involved in the troubles of one of Willy's friends, we wound up chasing a serial killer halfway around the world. I'd love to have dinner with you folks if you promise me nothing like that is going to happen."

"Not a chance, Coley. Remember, Stag Creek has had its quota of crimes for a few years now." Willy reached into his jacket pocket and produced a folded piece of yellow paper that obviously belonged in the yellow pages of some phone book.

"So you're one of those guys." Coley watched Willy as he ran his finger down the yellow page. "It seems like everytime I look for something important in the yellow pages in a hotel room or wherever, somebody's torn out the page I need. That's a rotten habit, Willy."

Willy made several checkmarks on the page. "Coin dealers must be going out of business. There are only a half dozen listed here. Two of them are right over in White Plains, just down the road. Want to play detective for a couple of hours Coley?"

Ginny bowed out. "If you guys don't mind, I'll hang around the *Tashtego*. There is a ships stores shop in the marina. I'm going to bring the *Tashtego* up to snuff. We seem to be low on a lot of things." The *Tashtego* had been in Ginny's family a long time, and she took great pride in keeping her seaworthy.

"Aye-aye, Captain. We should be back shortly after noon. Any plans Coley?"

"Nope I plan to run into the big city tomorrow to check on an old friend." Coley beamed. "She was a pretty little thing about ten years ago. I got Marissa's permission."

"Coley, you lie! Marissa and I are friends. I warn you I will tell her everything."

"You can't do that, Ginny, because you don't know everything. Let's go play detective, Willy. Ginny's getting mean."

"Let's go. My idea is to prowl around all the large coin shops and see if anyone has been approached about the AMERI. They are a pretty clubby bunch, those coin dealers, and probably connected by computer. They talk to each other a lot. The coin was stolen only about ten miles from here." He pointed to several dealers in the listing that he had circled. "One of these dealers could have been contacted. If not, we will put them on alert. I'd like to see Cliff get the AMERI back. He was really down in the dumps."

As Willy looked at a roadmap, Coley drove south along the Tappan Zee. Within fifteen minutes they had found the first coin dealer on their list in White Plains. The man was basically a bullion dealer, not evincing much interest at all in old copper coins.

No one had approached him lately with such a rarity. In fact he hadn't seen an AMERI in years. He flipped through a catalogue and found a listing for the coin. "Gentlemen, I doubt if you'll ever find what you are looking for. A mint state AMERI may not even exist. It would cost you all a lot of money if it did. There is a club, Early American Coppers, national in scope. Their collectors are a pretty close-knit group. I suggest you talk to one of their members."

"Like who?" Coley asked.

"There's an old gent who runs a shop in downtown White Plains, Elmor Hanford. I don't know of anyone else near here who might help you. Here, let me get you his number." He turned around to look for a phone book.

Willy pulled the yellow page from his pocket. "Never mind, I have his address right here. Hanford Coins, on Fourth Street."

The man looked at Willy reading from the ripped yellow page, and nodded his head slightly. "Sir, I hope you didn't rip that page from the directory we keep in the building lobby here. That is a great disservice to advertisers." The man was scowling at him.

Coley scowled along with him. "I'm surprised at you, Willy. Young punks tear up those phone books. You ought to know better!"

"Sir, I didn't get this from your directory." Red-faced, Willy followed Coley out the door. "Coley, your sense of humor is going to get you in trouble some day. Now what do you think that man thinks about us?"

"He thinks you're a jerk, and I'm a pretty nice guy." Coley laughed gleefully. "It's fun playing detective with you again!"

Elmor Hanford turned out to be an elderly gentleman who listened quietly as Willy discussed his desire to locate a mint-state AMERI. Shaking his head, he looked at Willy and then Coley, eyeing them up and down before he spoke. "I've been in business here for over thirty-five years, and I've only handled one AMERI. It was far from mint state, very low grade in fact. It still sold for a very nice price. I doubt if what you want really exists."

Coley handed the man a card and produced his private investigator's credential. "Mr. Hanford, if you have any inquiries about such a coin, I'd appreciate a call. It just might have been stolen."

"Really!" Hanford scrutinized both men again and smiled faintly. "I should have known you were investigators of some sort. I wish I could help you."

Willy became engrossed in a glassed display case that held a number of old copper cents. The display included a number of coins starting with the 1820s, but nothing at all prior to that.

"You care to look at something more closely?" asked Hanford. "There is really nothing exciting there for the serious collector."

Willy shook his head, thanked him, and the two of them headed for the door.

"Wait a minute!" Hanford caught them just in time. "There was something . . . it's been over a week." He was in deep thought, as if trying to recall something.

"What was it, Mr. Hanford?"

"I did get a call from an old friend. I didn't think much of it at the time because I wasn't able to help him."

"A call about an AMERI?"

"Yes, exactly! This man runs a small shop down on Ninth Avenue in New York. A woman had brought in an AMERI in amazingly good condition. He didn't say it was in mint state, however. He said she wanted to sell it and asked me if I would be interested in it, or if I had a customer who might be."

"And?" Coley nudged Willy. This sounded like pay dirt.

"I told him I had no use for it. I suggested that the woman should be directed to Blackwell's down on Fifty-seventh. They would be more informed and up-to-date on the value of such a coin."

"A woman?"

"Yes, yes, a pretty woman Jonathan said." Hanford smiled. "Yes, Jonathan is my age but he still knows a pretty woman when he sees one. She said the coin was an inheritance."

"Jonathan who?" asked Coley.

"Jonathan Finehouse. He has a small shop down in Chelsea. Just a moment, I will call him for you." Hanford dialed a number and then waited as it started to ring. "It just keeps on ringing." Hanford looked at the clock on his wall. "He should be in. It's a very small shop. He might have left for a few minutes. He does that sometimes. He just puts a card in the window." Finally Hanford shrugged and hung up the phone.

"How about the woman, Mr. Hanford. He didn't happen to give you a name did he?"

"Well sort of . . ." Hanford smiled broadly. "But I think the old rascal made it up. He called her Peaches."

"Sounds like Mr. Finehouse is a live wire," observed Coley.

"Oh . . . don't go getting the wrong idea. He is a fine man. He has a daughter here in Westchester. She married a lawyer, I believe. Can't think of her name right now."

"Do you happen to have the address of his coin shop?" asked Coley.

"Certainly, I have it here someplace." The old man fished a small address book from an old roll-top desk. He methodically printed the address and phone number on one of his cards and handed it to Coley.

"Thanks, Mr. Hanford. Here is my card. There is an 800 number on it for my answering service. If you think of anything else or hear any more about an AMERI, give me a call."

Willy and Coley left the shop and walked rapidly back to Coley's rental Buick. Coley was elated. "Wow, how do you like that, pal. We struck a nerve right off the bat."

"Maybe, Coley, maybe. All we know is that someone had an AMERI down on Ninth Avenue. Hanford didn't think it was in mint state. It could mean nothing." Willy was much less elated about the apparent lead.

"Willy my boy, I am going to drop you off at the *Tashtego* and head downtown. Want to come along?"

"No, I think I'd better stay with Ginny. I don't want to interfere with you and your old flame. I take it you will check out Mr. Jonathan Finehouse while you're downtown."

"Yes, and I'll follow it up with a visit to Blackwell's if it's okay with you."

Willy could see that Coley was really pumped up about their lead. "Hell yes. Might as well touch as many bases as you can. Ginny's anxious to get to the Caribbean. I'd like to be off by next weekend."

Willy opened the door to exit the car at the marina. "Remember Coley, we expect the Blaylocks at the marina about six-thirty. I'm anxious for you to meet Cliff."

"I'll be there," Coley assured him. "Maybe we'll have some good news for him."

By the time Coley reached East Side Drive, traffic was light. He followed it down to Twenty-third Street and proceeded to go crosstown to Ninth Avenue where he parked in a lot within a couple of blocks of Jonathan Finehouse's coin shop.

"Is that a misprint?" Coley pointed at the sign as a parking attendant approached. It read FIRST HOUR $13.00.

"Look big guy, you wanna park or don't ya?"

"Yeah, little fella, I do."

"Don't gimme any shit pal. You get this chit, I get your car."

For a fleeting moment, Coley thought about parking somewhere else and then remembered he was on Ninth Avenue in New York City. The man was actually pretty civil.

Coley walked down Ninth Avenue. He hadn't spent much time in the east for years, but Ninth Avenue looked pretty much like he remembered it. There were some new shops in renovated buildings and a considerable ration of porn shops and sleazy bars interspersed.

There it was. The lettering on the window was minus a few letters, but it was clearly readable as Jonathan Finehouse, Antiques and Rare Coins. The interior was unlit. He pressed his face close to the window and then tried the door. It was locked.

A small card was taped to the inside of the glass. Coley crouched to read the print. OUT OF BUSINESS. *STORE* FOR RENT, and then a phone number. Coley jotted the phone number on a piece of paper.

He backed away from the store front. The shop looked like it had been vacant a long time, yet the dealer in White Plains had told them that he had talked to Finehouse only a few days ago.

Coley walked into the small bodega next to the empty coin shop and approached the young clerk behind the counter.

"I'm looking for Mr. Finehouse. Do you know where I can find him?"

The man looked puzzled and shook his head negatively.

"I'm trying to locate the man in the coin shop next door. It's important that I reach him."

The clerk again shook his head.

Coley flashed his investigator credentials. The man studied it for a moment and then spoke. "Mr. Finehouse is dead. He got beaten to death in there." The young clerk pointed to the coin shop. "The police know all about it. You should talk to them. I know nothing."

Stunned, Coley backed away from the counter. "When did it happen?"

"I know nothing, except I heard it was a robbery." The clerk turned away from him and fidgeted nervously with some items on display. He obviously was not comfortable discussing the subject.

Outside, Coley hailed a cab for Blackwell's on Fifty-seventh

Street. Hanford in White Plains had said it was one of the most prestigious coin merchants in the country. It would be a good starting point. He made notes as the cabbie headed uptown. After checking out Blackwell's, he decided he would check with the NYPD precinct down in Chelsea before picking up his car. Maybe they had a line on the Finehouse murderer. The homicide was an amazing development, and probably not connected at all with his case. Hell, heists in that neighborhood were probably daily events.

Coley buzzed his way through the security doors and entered Blackwell's. The guard led him to a nattily dressed man working on a display of gold coins near the rear of the shop. Coley introduced himself by showing his private investigator credentials, and briefly telling the attendant about the stolen AMERI.

"David," the man called to another man sitting at a small desk in the rear who quickly joined them.

"Sir, I'm David Blackwell. Can I help you?"

"I was telling your friend here about a stolen 1793 cent, I believe you folks call it an AMERI. It was stolen over in New Jersey. I'm just checking around in behalf of the owner."

David Blackwell eyed the tall, sharply dressed black man closely before he spoke. "I saw one a couple of days ago. It was a handsome coin, very close to mint state. A man brought it in for an appraisal, and then left before we could help him. He never came back." Blackwell went on to describe the tall, beefy unkempt man who had not given him a name.

Coley tensed with excitement. "I take it these things are pretty rare."

"Exceedingly. The one I saw would fetch a nice figure in an auction. The only one like it that I have ever seen, conditionwise, is in a museum. I always thought it was one of a kind."

Coley's blood raced. "Then it is quite likely that the one the man brought in here might have been the stolen coin."

"I'd say it's almost a certainty, sir. If I may say so, I don't believe that the man I saw in here knew quite what he had. He pulled it out of his shirt pocket, totally unprotected, like a subway token. Said it was an inheritance. He was an unkempt seedy looking fellow. Actually, I fear for the coin."

"Fear for the coin?"

"Yes, it is copper, really quite soft. It can be scratched or stained easily, which would be a terrible shame. I even offered to keep it in my safe for him, but he walked away. I did put it in a protective envelope for him." Blackwell shrugged. "It was all he would permit me to do. He didn't even leave a name."

"By the way, Mr. Blackwell, did you happen to know the owner of a small coin shop down on Ninth Avenue, Jonathan Finehouse?"

"Yes! Delightful old gentleman. He is one of the old timers in our business."

"Not anymore, Mr. Blackwell."

"Oh?"

"He died a few days ago. There was evidently a robbery in his shop, and a struggle."

"That's horrible news. I can't imagine that I haven't heard."

"I don't think they found him for quite some time. Mr. Blackwell, I would appreciate it that you call me if the man carrying the AMERI comes in again. Of course, the police should be called first; I'm going to bring them up-to-date as soon as I leave here."

"Absolutely . . . I knew Finehouse pretty well. Down in that neighborhood anything can happen. Of course, that's pretty much the story of New York these days."

"Sorry to bring you bad news. Sir, I want to tell you something else. Be very careful. I have information that Finehouse looked at that same AMERI about ten days ago. If you see this big heavy guy, call the police right away. Don't try to cope with him yourself."

"Don't worry, I'll also post my security staff to be on the lookout and do likewise."

Coley left Blackwell's and glanced at his watch. It was two

o'clock. There was still time to go to the Chelsea NYPD precinct before heading back to the marina to meet the Blaylocks. He couldn't wait to report to Willy. The case was beginning to facinate him.

19

Cliff Blaylock sat in his study attempting to concentrate on a manuscript. His normal work schedule had been devastated by his inability to find peace with himself. The last words of Willis McCord had replayed in his mind a thousand times. The envelope in his mailbox reduced him to a state of nervous anxiety that he could not live with. Now, there was this damn dinner with Willy and Ginny. In a few hours he would be meeting them at the marina in Tarrytown.

He flung the manuscript onto his desk and glanced at his watch. He had seen Sandy and Adrienne return from the city and enter the McCord home over an hour ago. What was she doing over there, he wondered. What were they talking about? Of course, he hadn't been civil to Sandy for several days. He had to get a grip on himself. Sooner or later she would blow up and demand an explanation. He dreaded the thought of going out to dinner with Ginny and Willy.

Then he had a delightful thought. Maybe Sandy had forgotten all about their date in Tarrytown. That would be wonderful. He could call the marina and beg off. He wouldn't have to sit around for hours and try to act civil and participate in all the inane dinner conversation. Then he again thought of the damned envelope.

The telephone rang, jarring him from his thoughts. He decided to let the answering machine do its job, but then realizing that it might likely be Sandy, picked it up.

"Is this Mr. Blaylock?"

The gruff male voice was unfamiliar. "Yes, what can I do for you?"

"Actually, Mr. Blaylock, you can do quite a lot for me. If you want me to keep our little secret, you can get a hundred thousand bucks together in tens and twenties and hundreds. I'll give you about forty-eight hours to do that, until Friday morning. By the way, Mr. Blaylock, did you get the nice picture of Willis McCord I sent you?"

"Willis? . . . I have no idea of what you are talking about."

"You're lying, Mr. Blaylock. We both know very well what happened. Now look here, Mr. Killer! You pay close attention or the whole world will know what happened to that poor boy come Friday afternoon. I'm told that a hundred thousand is a reasonable price for the old penny."

Blaylock pushed the caller identification button, but the the screen revealed nothing. It was evidently another area code or the caller knew how to get around the device. "How do I get the money to you?"

"Now that's bein' nice, very nice. No use making a big hassle out of this. Don't worry, just get the money together and I'll tell you how later on. Poor Willis McCord. You've caused me a lot of trouble. I expect to be paid for my troubles. Good-bye, Mr. Blaylock."

"Wait! Please!" Dead silence and then a dial tone came from the phone. The bastard! Cliff Blaylock pulled Sandy's small .22 automatic from his pocket and hefted it nervously in his hand. What the hell, he reasoned, he had killed once. Actually the caller was responsible for his action. Killing the caller would sort of wipe the slate clean.

"Darling, I'm home." It was Sandy, entering the side door.

Blaylock jammed the automatic back into his jacket pocket. "I'm in the den, dear. Been doing some work here on the Huffer manuscript."

She entered the den, leaned over and bestowed a warm kiss upon him. "Cliff, you look great! It is so good to see you working again. You have no idea how much I have worried about you."

"Well time takes care of everything, you know." He was surprised to find the words come out easily. "I guess we are still on with Willy and Ginny tonight?"

"Of course! We'll have fun, Cliff. I like your friends. Do me a favor and try to get Willis and the AMERI off your mind for the evening. Poor Adrienne, she went smashing through a four martini lunch in the city today. Alex is being a total bastard. He is constantly blaming Adrienne for being too permissive with Willis. Do you know that the boy used cocaine regularly through college?"

"Really, where did he get it?"

"According to Adrienne, that's not much of a problem. In fact, Cliff, she surprised me, said that she and Alex tried it a few times. Alex told her that it might perk up their old libido. Isn't that a kick! Adrienne always looks like she stepped right out of *ELLE*. Can't imagine Alex having a problem."

Cliff nodded, picturing his statuesque neighbor for a moment. "Is that what you girls talked about at lunch? I wonder what you told Adrienne about me."

"Don't be silly, Cliff. She had the four martinis, not me. Besides, I couldn't bear telling anyone in the world that life was that dull."

"Is it?" The momentary elation she had seen in Cliff faded from his face. Now he was staring out the den window again toward the McCord house.

"Okay, Cliff, snap out of it. Go get yourself ready. I'm kind of anxious to see this fancy yacht your friends cavort around the world in. Let's be on time. I told Adrienne about our evening. I think she could have been easily convinced to tag along. Alex is out of town."

Blaylock put his arms around her. "No thanks. I have all the woman I can handle right here."

"Attaway Cliff! You're beginning to sound promising. Let's be rude and surprise them by being early."

Blaylock hurried upstairs to dress for the evening. He couldn't help but wonder what kind of an experience it would have been to have Adrienne join them for a social evening less than two weeks after he had killed her only son. He doubted that he would ever be able to be in her presence again for any length of time.

It was just after five P.M. when Cliff and Sandy pulled out of their driveway in Stag Creek. A few short woodsy, winding blocks later they turned north on Stag Creek Road. There was virtually no traffic as they went north a few miles toward Orangeburg road where he made a right turn and soon entered New York State.

As they drove along the Tappan Reservoir, Cliff slowed down a bit out of deference to a police cruiser who occasionally hid around the bend ready to nail the occasional speeder. A vehicle closing the gap behind him did likewise.

"Where are we eating tonight, Cliff? I remember Ginny said that we were having cocktails aboard the *Tashtego*, we'll watch the sun go down, and then go out."

"I don't know. Willy said that he had scoped out someplace along the Hudson near Dobbs Ferry. I guess we'll go there."

Cliff glanced in his rearview mirror as they approached the Palisades Parkway, pulled into the right-hand lane and made the cloverleaf that took them north on the parkway. The van behind him made a similar move, coming very close to his rear bumper. As they pulled into traffic on the parkway, the vehicle dropped back several hundred feet behind him behind several other cars.

It wasn't until he rounded the off ramp to the New York

Thruway toward the Tappan Zee Bridge that he noticed the same vehicle about a hundred feet behind him. It had been there now since the side streets of Stag Creek. He tried slowing down a little, but the vehicle stayed its distance. When he was able to speed up, the driver in the rear seemed to keep pace.

At the east end of the Tappan Zee Bridge, he had to slow down to pay the toll. The vehicle behind lined up next, pulling close to his rear bumper. It was a beige Cherokee, with darkly tinted windows and a shiny oversize luggage rack on top. He had looked for a vehicle like that every time he had driven for the past two weeks. He had seen several, but usually they were going the other way. There were probably thousands of similar vehicles on the road, just like the one that had parked next to him in the Wellington Inn on that fateful day.

Immediately after paying the toll, he revved the engine and literally shot forward, roared into the right lane toward the first off ramp on the east side of Hudson River.

"Cliff! What the hell are you doing!" Sandy had been jolted awake from the temporary catnap she had taken in the toll line.

Cliff grinned at her. "Just thought I'd see if the new tune-up made any difference." The grin faded quickly. The beige Cherokee had sped up and was now on the off ramp a couple of cars behind him. As the other car made the cloverleaf, he could see the tire mounted on the rear. No doubt about it. The Cherokee was a carbon copy of the one at the Wellington Inn. Still common sense told him that there were no doubt many just like it.

He drove a short distance north through Tarrytown and then made a left down the winding road toward Svensons Marina, glancing frequently into his rearview mirror. He breathed a sigh of relief. The Cherokee was not visible. He made a vow to get a grip on himself. He couldn't go through life going crazy every time he saw a Cherokee.

Soon he pulled into the parking area abutting Svensons Marina. The *Tashtego*, tied up on an outer guest dock, was silhouetted beautifully against the red sky of the setting sun. "There's the *Tashtego*, Sandy. A real beauty, huh?"

"Cliff, it's gorgeous. You say they sailed it all the way to Hong Kong?"

"Yep, and a lot of other places. It's Ginny's boat. I'd say Willy has a good thing going for him."

"Cliff, that's terrible. You're saying that Willy loves her just because of the *Tashtego*."

"Just kidding. I'm just kidding. I'm not a bit jealous of either of them and their boat. Besides I get seasick. As idyllic as it seems, I'd make a real mess of it."

Sandy beamed. It was the first small talk she had heard from Cliff in a long time. Maybe he was getting back to normal. "You won't get seasick while we're sitting at the dock will you?"

"Of course not! We're pretty early. Maybe we'd better take our time."

They began to walk the long L-shaped dock that extended an arm far out, leaving a channel between the guest dock and a crushed rock jetty. They paused now and then to admire the reddening sky.

As they were nearing the *Tashtego*, they could see Ginny standing on the aft deck, waving her arms in welcome. "Ahoy there! Hurry, you're going to miss the sunset!"

Sandy walked rapidly ahead to meet Ginny at the foot of the short gangway.

Cliff turned to glance back at the long dock. His eyes moved through the marina and then to his car parked beyond. He grimaced and then scowled as he looked up the road that wound down from the top of the hill.

The beige Cherokee was parked alongside the road, perhaps a quarter mile away. He tried to block it out of his mind, reasoning again that there were a lot of them. His stomach felt queasy. I'm a damn fool, he told himself. The beige Cherokee had followed him all the way from Stag Creek in another state. He didn't lose him until he had turned down the dead-end road to the marina. The occupant of the Cherokee was probably up there looking at him. He knew where he came from and where he was now.

He now heard Willy and Ginny calling him from the cockpit of the *Tashtego*. He turned toward them, forced a smile and steeled himself for the evening ahead.

20

Coley waited patiently, watching the second hand swing around the clock on the wall of the NYPD precinct station in Chelsea. Detective Sean O'Reilly, an old buddy from law school had sat him in the tiny office, apologized for making him wait, and disappeared. It had been almost a half hour ago.

The bedlam in the police station was a mirror image of a popular TV show of the day. Screaming, cursing, and wailing drifted over the transom of the small office from a dozen others just like it along the hall. O'Reilly was writing up an arrest. He had said it would be only a few minutes. Coley groaned, trying to make his tall frame comfortable in the straightback wooden chair. He'd be late for dinner in Dobbs Ferry if he didn't get out of here soon.

"Jesus, Coley! Days like this make me wish I had finished law school." O'Reilly burst into the room and sat on the edge of the wooden table facing Coley. "It's a circus in here today. It's like every punk in town tried to beat up his wife or significant other. You get them in here, then they clam up, kiss up, and refuse to press charges." O'Reilly was sweating profusely. He removed his jacket and ran his fingers under the tight strap holding his shoulder holster.

"Well, you should come to LA. I'd give you a dime an hour to sniff around some mighty fancy quiff."

"I don't know how you do it, Coley. You call that police work, nailing some poor sap, so some broad can take him for the whole ranch."

"Just remember I asked. You'll get sick of this zoo some day." Coley grinned at O'Reilly and shook his head. He often wondered how guys like him could keep their cool in the bowels of Manhattan.

"Hey, Kathleen and I want to have you for dinner while you're in town."

"How many kids now, Sean?"

"Still two. We've stopped. We figure it's all we can have and do the best we can by. What brings you here, Coley?"

"There was a coin heist over in Jersey, worth over a hundred G's. So far the trail leads to an old coin dealer on Ninth Avenue who was beaten to death a few days ago."

"Jonathan Finehouse," murmured O'Reilly. "Not my case, but I'll take a peek at the paperwork. I heard the boys talking about it. I think they've come up with blanks so far. Let's take a look, just between you and me." O'Reilly left the room briefly and returned with the file and opened it.

Coley watched him skim through the detective's report. "He was struck by one powerful blow to the head, probably by a gun barrel. The trail was pretty cold because the body wasn't discovered for at least forty-eight hours. His daughter, a Jeannie Nicholson, came into the city from Westchester when she couldn't reach him on the phone and found him dead." Sean shook his head. "So far there are no real handles on the case. Usually a blow like that is not fatal, but whoever did it was strong, and lucky."

Coley handed him a card listing his 800 number. "Will you keep me posted? It's the only lead I really have. There was this coin dealer up in Westchester that said he got a call from Finehouse a couple of weeks ago. Finehouse was a good friend. Some-

one brought in a very rare coin. Said it was inherited from a
grandfather. Finehouse evidently called this guy in Westchester
for help in appraising it. He suggested he take it to Blackwell's up
on Fifty-seventh. Forgive me, but I killed a little time this afternoon and checked with Blackwell. Some guy, no name, big and
tough, did bring in a similar coin. He left and never returned."

"Anything else, Coley? You come to me for information, and
you've got more than I've got." O'Reilly was jotting down notes
as Coley talked.

"There's one more thing, probably not much. Hanford, up in
Westchester, said that Finehouse told him that a good-looking
woman had showed him the coin. He called her Peaches."

O'Reilly turned through the police report and suddenly sat
erect as he read the short list of collected evidence. "Bingo!" he
exclaimed, looking excitedly at Coley. "The detectives on the
case found a phone number in his shop, jotted on a pad by the
phone. The name written by the number was Peaches."

Coley rose from his chair, slapping his fist into his hand.
"Bingo is right! Did they follow up on the phone number?"

O'Reilly studied the report. "Nothing in here says so. If you
hang tight for just a few minutes, I'll check with someone on the
case. I saw him down the hall." He backed away from the table
and walked down the hall, leaving the report on his desk.

Moving quickly, Coley spun the report around and scanned
the page. There was the notation, Peaches, and a phone number.
He heard Sean O'Reilly shouting down the hall, his voice getting
closer. Coley spun the report around to face Sean's empty chair,
committing the number to memory.

"Not a lot of luck yet, Coley. The phone number traces to an
address on Twenty-first Street. Our man went over there but she
wasn't home. The landlord lives in a basement apartment and says
our friend Peaches strips in Buster's Hotzy Topless on Ninth Avenue."

"You mind giving me the address on Twenty-first?" Coley

knew he was pushing his friendship. The lead hadn't been followed up as yet.

O'Reilly stared at the police report on the table. "Sure, Coley, you can put it next to the phone number."

"Thanks, Sean. How did you know I had the phone number?" Coley, stunned, asked the question sheepishly.

"Relax, Coley. I wouldn't have left the report there if I didn't want you to read it. Don't think you put one over on me, pal." Sean grinned and pointed to the old scarred table. "See that hole some idiot drilled right through this perfectly fine table? The corner of the report was right on it when I left the room."

"Thanks, Sean." Coley stared at the report, a full six inches from the ugly hole. "I'll keep the info right up here." He tapped his temple.

"Coley, be careful. It's an ongoing investigation. The boys will be getting a warrant to go through her apartment. Lay off that angle until they do." O'Reilly rose from the desk and extended his hand to Coley. "So when can I tell Kathleen you are coming out for dinner? She'll make life miserable for me if she finds out you were in town and didn't."

"I'll do it Sean. I'll give you a buzz later in the week." Coley moved toward the door.

"Oh, Coley, just in case you don't know, Buster's Hotzy Topless is up around Twenty-fourth." Sean shrugged. "It's a dump, Coley. Don't fall in love."

"You make a man's life easy, Sean. Thanks again. I've got to be in Dobbs Ferry in a couple hours. I have to cope with rush-hour traffic, but I may take a quick peek at Buster's place."

Coley's long strides took him to the topless joint within minutes. Sean O'Reilly was right. It was a dump. He sat at the bar and ordered a beer, waving off the glass offered with it.

A tall bony brunette was bumping lazily along the bar. A half dozen customers stared trancelike at the mechanical thrusts of her pelvis. She worked her way down to him and smiled a hello through brown teeth. Coley gave her a quick wink then probed the corners of the shabby place now that his eyes were getting used to the darkness. It was not only a dump, it was an empty dump.

He motioned to the barmaid. "A buddy of mine told me about a dancer here named Peaches. Said she was a blast. Was he telling the truth?"

"Peaches works nine to five." She shrugged. "She ain't got nothin' I ain't got. Come on in later and take a peek. Hey, how tall are you?"

"Guess."

"I'll bet you're plenty big enough." She leaned over the bar, the ample cleavage carefully positioned to his advantage. "Peaches ain't got nothin' like this."

Coley stared, winked again, and downed his beer. "Got to go. Maybe I'll be in later." He rose from the bar stool.

"Hey doll, I get off at two. Come on back. You can look at Peaches all you want, but she ain't much fun." She winked back at him. "She's got this big ugly boyfriend."

Coley walked out of Buster's Hotzy Topless and headed toward the parking lot. He'd have to come back. Right now he was going to be late for dinner in Dobbs Ferry. But he had learned a lot. Willy should be pleased. The homicide of Finehouse had been a shocker. There was, however, absolutely nothing to connect it with the theft of the AMERI. Yet there was this gnawing feeling in his gut that the two events were related.

He was anxious to meet this Cliff Blaylock, the intelligent guy who thought nothing of leaving a hundred grand treasure in his driveway.

Coley stepped down on the gas as he swung onto the Henry Hudson Parkway. He thought of Marissa back in LA. What a babe! She made the dancers in Buster's look like a lower species. He'd call her tonight and tell her so.

21

Heavy Laval lit a cigarette and slumped behind the steering wheel. From his vantage point just off Route 9, he watched Blaylock and the woman having drinks on the open deck of the fancy yacht. They were with another man and woman who evidently came with the yacht.

He had to finish his business with Blaylock soon, he reasoned. He didn't like the way that Blaylock had sped up exiting the toll booth on the Tappan Zee Bridge. It was almost like he knew that he was being tailed. From then on he had kept his distance and damn near lost him.

Trying to ransom the coin was giving him problems. He had heard of guys that specialized in blackmail. But that wasn't his specialty. Whenever he really wanted anything, his specialty was beating the piss out of whoever it was, and taking it. Getting the hundred G's from Blaylock meant that he had to have the money on him and turn it over without using the revolver he had shot the kid with. Blaylock looked like a wimp, but as long as he carried the equalizer he was dangerous.

The four people had now stepped off the big yacht and were standing on the dock. One of them was pointing at something high up on the fancy boat and seemed to be explaining something. Blaylock had started walking down the dock far ahead of the others and seemed impatient to get going. Laval wished they would hurry up. The sun had set and it was rapidly getting dark.

Finally, the four of them reached the BMW and piled in. Soon Blaylock's car was winding its way up the steep incline from the shore road. From where he sat in the Cherokee, they would have to pass right by him if Blaylock headed north on Route 9, or move away from him if they headed south.

They turned south. He let them get a headstart, then pulled into the light traffic several cars behind them. They passed the exit to the bridge and drove south along the Hudson River. By the time they reached Dobbs Ferry Laval felt more secure. It was dark and all Blaylock could see would be his headlights in a line of many others.

Soon the BMW made a sharp right turn and began to snake down a winding road toward the water. It pulled into the large parking lot of the Chart House Restaurant. Laval also entered the lot and swung around to a position facing the exit and watched the foursome walk to the entrance. Suddenly they were met by a tall black man, neatly dressed in slacks and a sports jacket. The man was incredibly tall and lean. Blaylock's guests evidently knew him. They stood chatting and occasionally he could hear a burst of laughter from one of them.

They all had entered the restaurant when Blaylock suddenly emerged from the doorway and walked rapidly to his car alone, as if he had forgotten something. About half way, he stopped and stared at the Cherokee and began coming slowly toward him. Laval with lights doused, gunned the engine and pulled out of the lot and headed up the hill. Near the top, he looked back through his rearview mirror and saw Blaylock still standing in the road several hundred yards behind him. No question about it, he had the Cherokee pegged.

Laval tried to put himself in Blaylock's shoes. The guy must be scared shitless, he reasoned. After all, he had committed murder. Laval fingered the envelope beside him in the seat. Hell, what did he have to be afraid of. Blaylock had no choice other than to do as he asked.

Laval sped north toward the Tappan Zee Bridge, crossed over it, and headed south toward Stag Creek. He drove confidently into the quiet little town, down the short cul-de-sac and stopped in front of Blaylock's mailbox. He flipped the manila envelope into the mailbox, glancing up and down the empty street. There was a porch light here and there shrouded in the dark shrubbery. There wasn't a person in sight anywhere. The suburbs were a mystery to him. I wonder what they are all doing, he asked himself. He smiled to himself, decided that they were all either screwing, dead, or out at some fancy restaurant living it up like the Blaylocks.

Back in Dobbs Ferry the diners were in the midst of their main course. Cliff Blaylock had sat without comment during the pre-dinner conversation dominated by Coley Doctor telling the group about his day and Willy asking questions as they went along. Once, Blaylock had groaned aloud when Coley told them about the apparent homicide of Finehouse, and mentioned that he had seen nothing about it in the papers.

"As an avid collector, I suppose I have been to most every coin dealer in the city. I vaguely remember going into Finehouse's shop once. I recall a nice old gent. This is terrible." Having said that, Blaylock lapsed into silence for a moment. "Of course, there is nothing to suggest that the homicide had anything to do with the AMERI." He looked at Coley.

"Right," replied Coley, "but even though one door on our investigation is closed permanently, we do know that a woman named Peaches brought him an AMERI to appraise a few days before he died. It would be nice if the old guy would have survived so we could have talked to him." Coley thought it best not to tell the group that he would be eyeballing Peaches later that night, though he made a mental note to tell Willy when he got him alone.

"Coley, I think you've made a lot of progress for one day," Willy observed, obviously excited. "So what's our next step?"

"I think we ought to keep doing what we're doing. David

Blackwell said the guy that brought the AMERI into him didn't seem to know beans about numismatics. He's liable to show up again someplace. I think we ought to notify as many coin dealers as possible about the stolen AMERI, maybe even get on the Internet. There must be a lot of them trading information. We can give them Blackwell's description of him."

Willy looked questioningly at Ginny. He knew they were both counting the hours until they would leave for the Caribbean. "I think you're right, Coley. Let's give it a couple more days if you can find the time."

Blaylock sat silently, brooding, looking out across the Hudson River and the palisades on the other side. He wished they would stop their investigation before someone else got killed. He thought of the beige Cherokee tailing his every move since they had left Stag Creek. He thought of Willis McCord. "What did you do that for, Mr. Blaylock?" His last words haunted him a hundred times a day.

"I wish you would stop it!" Cliff Blaylock spoke tersely. "I don't care about the damn coin!" He paused, now conscious of everyone staring at his abrupt re-entry into the conversation. "Look at it this way. The insurance company will take care of the loss."

Sandy Blaylock gaped at Cliff along with the others. "Cliff, I'm amazed at you. Wouldn't it be wonderful if they would catch the thief? I don't know about you, but it scares the hell out of me that someone would come right in our driveway and do something like that. I can hardly sleep anymore."

Cliff looked at her with the same sober, brooding look that had dominated his visage lately.

"Look at yourself, Cliff. You are just as much of a nervous wreck as I am. Let your friends help you," pushed Sandy, pleading with him.

"Let Coley have the ball for a couple more days, Cliff.

I've seen him perform miracles." Willy smiled confidently at Coley who was still staring at Blaylock, trying to fathom his attitude.

"Oh, what the hell, give it another day or two," Blaylock said without any enthusiasm. "I guess the fact that Finehouse was killed really upset me. What if he were somehow involved with the thief. I'd hate for any of you guys to get hurt."

Coley listened and watched Blaylock as he talked. He never looked at anyone. He just kept staring across the Hudson. What Blaylock said sounded to him like a warning, like he knew something they didn't. "Okay, pal." Coley patted Blaylock on the back supportively. "We'll give it another day or so. Believe me, then I am headed for LA. I got the cutest little woman alive out there. I wouldn't leave Marissa alone any longer for a whole stack of your AMERIs."

Blaylock smiled weakly, and then again sat quietly as the others chatted over dessert. Coley attempted to buck up Blaylock's spirits by regaling him with outlandish stories of his and Willy's escapades in the past, but he guessed that the man's mind was somewhere else.

At the end of the evening, Blaylock drove everyone back to the marina. Willy and Ginny climbed aboard the *Tashtego*. Coley said good-bye, got in his rental Buick, and headed back to Manhattan to pick up the lead on Peaches.

Sandy snuggled as close to Cliff as possible as they started their trip back across the Tappan Zee Bridge. "Cliff, you are so fortunate. They are such wonderful friends. And I think Coley is an absolute hoot. I'm sorry you weren't in a better mood. I think your friends are worried about you."

"They shouldn't be . . . I'm sorry. I'm just not myself. Maybe I ought to have a checkup." He kept glancing in his rearview mirror. When he made the cloverleaf to leave the Thruway and go south on the Palisades Parkway, he slowed down to a crawl to see if anyone raced to catch up to him. He breathed a sigh of relief when he still found himself all alone on the Parkway. Could he have imagined it all?

After he pulled into his driveway, he strolled out to the mailbox as Sandy went ahead into the house. He reached inside and grasped his fingers around several pieces of mail.

The five-by-nine manila envelope with no stamp and no postmark sent a chill along his spine. He walked back toward the side door of his house and ripped the flap from under the metal clasp. A Xerox copy of the same news photo of Willis McCord slid out. He turned it over, holding it under the glare of the porch light. A message was scrawled in heavy marker pencil. "Starting at noon, Saturday, you will carry one hundred thousand dollars in cash under the front seat of your BMW at all times, until it disappears. Shame on you!"

Blaylock's hands shook as he stuffed the picture and the message back into the envelope. He entered the house, and tossed the mail onto the kitchen table, first stuffing the stampless manila envelope into a side pocket of his jacket.

He turned off the porch light and stared out into the darkness. He could hear Sandy moving around in the bedroom upstairs. Slipping his hand inside his jacket pocket he clasped his fingers around Sandy's small .22 automatic. He had killed already, he thought to himself. It would actually be easy to kill someone who really had it coming. He started shaking violently. The burly man in the ski mask was a professional lowlife, and he was armed. He remembered vividly the large caliber revolver he had pointed at him before his struggle with Willis McCord.

Blaylock looked at the puny little automatic in his hand. He began to sweat, realizing he was a poor match for a professional thug.

22

The *Jersey Trick* rolled slightly in her slip at a marina a half mile inside the Barnegat Light. Red Irons sat tensely in a deck chair, his back to the cabin bulkhead. A large wake of a passing motor yacht had caused the *Jersey Trick* to bob uncomfortably. Irons wondered how anyone ever got used to life on a boat. He hoped any plans for time afloat didn't include him.

Immediately after their arrival from Newark Airport, Bocco Lamas and Veronica had vanished below deck. A deckhand had led him to the deck chair, and fixed him up with a drink and a cold turkey sandwich. He stretched his legs and tried to slump more comfortably in the chair. The sandwich and the drink were long gone. He had been left alone to enjoy the scenery around the remote marina, and his queasy stomach had had enough of it.

Irons stood and walked a few paces, wondering where the deckhand kept himself. To his left a small line was clipped across the entrance to the steep gangway leading ashore. Glancing quickly about, he unclipped the line and walked slowly down the gangway onto the service dock, then a few paces to the parking lot. He sat on a small bench next to the lot and lit a cigarette. This is much better, he thought, his queasy stomach settling to normalcy.

A sound of Veronica laughing came from somewhere below deck on the *Jersey Trick*. He guessed that she and Bocco were continuing their backseat sexual marathon that had lasted from Newark Airport to Barnegat. Red Irons decided he could hardly blame Bocco for ignoring him. The chick was built for action. He looked at his watch. One or the other of them ought to get tired soon. Another squeal of delight came from behind the tightly curtained porthole, just below the bridge of the sleek yacht.

He groaned and lit another cigarette. He pictured Veronica swinging up the concourse toward him at the airport. In his whole life, he had never bedded a legitimate number ten. Why an ugly bastard like Bocco? Of course, that had to do with money, lots of money, probably more than he would ever see.

"Hey Red! Where the hell are you!" Bocco's voice boomed from the deck area he had vacated.

"Right here, Bocco, just taking a little stroll." Irons got up from the bench and strode toward the gangway.

Bocco Lamas bounded down the gangway. "Takin' a little stroll? You must be losing your marbles, Red. Stroll around the deck, for Chri-sakes. I bring your ass down here to experience a little of the good life, and you spend it walking around the parking lot. Lemme give you some advice, Mr. Irons, unless you aspire to the good life, you'll always be a nothin'. You'll never have a fancy babe like Veronica with a motor in her throat."

Lamas grinned lewdly at Red as he approached and finally got so close he could smell a strange mixture of garlic and aftershave that hung in the air around him.

"I get seasick just sitting in the slip, Bocco. I can't help it."

"That's too bad, Red, because some day you may have to take a long ride on the *Jersey Trick*." Bocco was scowling at him now. "Tell you what, Red, I think you better get your ass back up to Hoboken."

"Tonight?" Irons tried to look disappointed and not show how relieved he was to leave the *Jersey Trick*.

"Yeah, tonight. While you were strolling around the parking lot and Veronica was taking care of business, I was on the telephone." Bocco paused, still scowling at Irons. "Business in Jersey is going to hell, Red. I warned you that Heavy Laval was a troublemaker."

"He's a tough guy. He don't leave any loose ends, Bocco," Irons said defensively.

"Bullshit! I told you on the phone that we saw that red Corvette parked in front of Heavy's place a bunch of times. We checked the plates from the pictures in the paper." Bocco paused and lit a cigar. "The kid gets himself killed and now Heavy spends all his time cruising up and down the Palisades Parkway like a chicken with its head cut off. The kid was Heavy's man, Red. And business is going to hell."

"Heavy lied to me then. I'll have a little talk with him. Everything is going to be alright, Bocco." You bastard, he thought to himself. I wonder how many guys he's got snooping into my setup.

"It's too late for talk! Clean-cut guys in suits and collars have been sniffing around Peaches. I hear Peaches is starting to peddle her ass around Chelsea. I'm telling you, Heavy's lost control!" Unexpectedly Lamas thumped his forefinger into Iron's chest.

Irons glanced toward the yacht. One of Bocco's bodyguards was standing on the deck with his arms folded staring at him. "I'll take care of things, Bocco."

"Damn right you will!" Bocco poked him again with his forefinger. "If I were you I'd start with Peaches. We'll think about Heavy Laval a little later. But I want to know what he's up to with all that gallivanting around."

Red Irons nodded. "Gotcha boss. Don't worry. I'll do what I have to do."

Bocco stuck out one hand and slapped Red Irons on the back with the other. "Good boy, Red. I'm sorry I got a little rough with you. Sometimes business gets a little unpleasant." Lamas smiled patronizingly. "It's all history. I'm gonna forget all about it. I know when my pal, Red Irons, says something I can bank on it." Lamas slapped him on the back again and turned toward the gangway.

Irons' eyes followed him all the way up the gangway and into the cabin before he climbed into the Cadillac to drive back to Hoboken. He looked at his watch. It was still the shank of the evening. Maybe he would have time to check into a few things yet today.

23

Coley Doctor pulled the Buick into an open-air parking lot near Twenty-fourth Street, and walked west toward Ninth Avenue. Peaches wasn't due to start her topless gig for a few minutes yet. Planning what to say to her was tough. He hoped the NYPD hadn't grilled her yet. If so, she would want no part of questions from a stranger.

He had a little time to kill so he altered his route to take him back to the storefront that used to be Finehouse's shop. It was pitch black inside. He eyeballed Ninth Avenue in both directions. It hadn't changed a whole lot since his college days when he and a bunch of guys would pile in a car and drive down to the city for fun and games. But it was visibly rougher now. Dingy bars, restaurants, bodegas, video and porn shops lined the street. Peddlers and hookers outnumbered potential customers at this hour.

In a neighborhood like this, he decided that Finehouse could have gotten knocked off by anyone if he were careless as to who he let in the door. He looked at the smattering of baseball cards and posters scattered along the inside of the window and suspected that the old man's shop had been a dying proposition. Rare coins didn't fit well in this neighborhood.

Music blared from the door of Buster's Hotzy Topless. The windows were carefully painted and curtained to prevent those outside from seeing what went on inside. The thought occurred to Coley that if one could clearly see inside, they would never go in.

He entered and made his way to a stool at the end of the bar. A half-dozen customers sat at the bar, and a few more at tables in the dimly lit club. A tiny Oriental woman was systematically removing her clothing, undulating to an overly loud jukebox. Not bad, thought Coley, a decided improvement over the brown-toothed brunette he had seen earlier in the day.

His buxom barmaid, cleavage now spread to reveal just a trace of nipple on the right side, greeted him with a smile and a bottle of Bud. "Hi, big man. You come back for the action I see."

"Action is my middle name. Is that Peaches?" Coley nodded at the petite dancer.

"No, that's Pussy LaFrance."

"You could have fooled me. She looks Oriental to me." Coley grinned at the barmaid. "And who are you?"

"I'm Tracy. And that's the only honest name you'll get in here, handsome." She studied Coley's features. "You a cop?"

"Hell no. Why would you think that?"

Tracy shrugged. "I don't believe you. When you work this neighborhood for a while you get so you can spot a dick a block away."

"My name's Doug Johnson, and I ain't no cop."

"Have it your way, Doug. Hell, I don't care. I like my men big and tall. I wouldn't care if you were the Chief of Police."

"Now Tracy, that's more like it. Let's be friends." Coley shoved her the change from a ten dollar bill. "Peaches fly the coop?"

"Nope. She's in back getting ready to go on." She leaned across the bar and whispered. "I think our dear Peaches is working on a little damage control. Her slob of a boyfriend must have worked her over again."

Coley shook his head in disapproval. "Tracy, I got no use for guys like that."

"I told Peaches to pitch him out." Tracy shook her head in disgust. "She's a born loser, big man. She actually puts a roof over this guys head, feeds him, and God knows what else. She treats him like a bigshot, and he uses her for a punching bag. The bastard!" She caught Coley's eyes raptly staring at her widening cleavage, then smiled. "Now I bet you would treat a girl real nice."

"You got that right, Tracy." He winked at her in assent. The small dancer bounded off the stage and disappeared behind the curtains to the rear. The tempo of the music changed to a loud, heavy beat as the drapes parted and a long bare leg poked skyward.

Tracy slid another beer in front of Coley. "Here comes your Peaches, big man."

Peaches moved slowly, pausing to twirl and jiggle a bit in front of each customer at the bar. When she reached Coley, she swung her hips and torso into serious action. A blond ponytail flipped freely as she swept her head up and down the bar eyeing each patron. Finally she concentrated on Coley, meeting his stare and running her tongue lasciviously along her lips. She was good enough to provoke a few hand claps and shouts of encouragement from the small jaded crowd.

She danced in front of Coley for the longest time, locked in a staredown, which Coley refused to break. Not bad, Coley thought to himself. Not bad at all for a Ninth Avenue dump. Even though she was no spring chicken and had a pound or two that jiggled where it shouldn't, she was a good-looking bimbo. He slid a ten spot up her leg and under a garter.

Peaches gave him a smile and a wink then moved on down the bar. Finally she finished her first set and moved behind the drapes to an unenthusiastic sprinkling of clapping hands. Coley noticed that several customers never looked at her and continued in uninterrupted conversation. Coley decided she had a tough job. She garnered only a couple of other tips besides his.

"Did you fall in love, handsome?" Tracy was back.

Coley shrugged. "She's a cutie, but she ain't my style. I don't know how she does that all night long. There must be a better way to turn a buck."

Tracy glanced toward the curtains shielding the dressing room. "Why don't you ask her about all that. Here she comes."

Peaches walked the length of the bar until she reached the stool next to Coley and sat down. "Hi mister, thanks for the tip." She smiled at Coley, then looked him up and down. "Wow, you must be a tall guy. You make me feel like a midget."

"I can't help it. I never wanted to be this tall, but I just kept on growing. The world ain't built for guys my size." He looked at her. She did have beautiful blue eyes. She had applied heavy makeup near one cheekbone. There was a hint of puffiness that made her face non-symmetrical. "Can I buy you a drink?"

"Sure. I'll tell you right up front that it won't be nothin' but soda pop. But it will pay the rent on this stool." She continued to size him up.

"Hey listen, thanks for being honest. A guy appreciates that. It makes me feel special." He spoke facetiously with a sly wink.

"You a cop?" She blurted it out, still gaping at his tall frame.

"Hell no! How come everybody in here wants to know whether or not I'm a cop?"

"I can't imagine." She leaned closer to him and whispered. "Actually it's okay with me if you're a cop. Some of my best friends are cops. My name is Peaches." She extended her hand.

"I'm Doug Johnson," lied Coley. "Just killing time, seeing the sights of the city. I fly out tomorrow. I used to carouse down in this part of town when I was a kid. Just checking it all out. I can't remember anything as pretty as you, back then."

"Thanks. Where you staying?" Peaches lowered her voice, and asked the question without looking at him.

"The Sheraton, uptown."

Peaches ordered another phony drink. Coley nodded his okay to Tracy, who had been keeping an eye on him. "That's a nice place. It beats the dump I live in." She downed the small glass of Coke quickly and then ordered still another. Peaches rose from the stool and pressed next to Coley. "I've got another set coming on. I'll be back soon, okay?"

"Hell yes, Peaches. By the way I just love peaches."

She rolled her eyes at him, and then headed backstage.

Coley glanced at his watch. He hadn't been there an hour yet, and he had spent over fifty bucks. He was going to have to find an ATM machine nearby if he were to stay until five A.M. when Peaches got off. He decided he'd get down to business and get it over with.

Peaches paid little attention to him on her next set except for a couple of quick winks. She concentrated her bumps and squats on several new customers along the bar. Coley figured she thought she had him nailed for a big tab for the night, so she was hustling fresh money.

Funny, one guy came in, clean and neat with thick, curly red hair and a neatly clipped beard. She totally ignored him even though he had a pile of cash in front of him, and had his eyes glued to every bump and grind. When her act was completed, she quickly emerged from the dressing room in the loose rayon robe and joined Coley again on the stool next to him.

"Hey, I bet you don't have to go to the gym at night. You get a helluva workout up there."

"I try to keep my mind on my work. It keeps me from getting some creep overheated. If I start staring back at them, they follow me home."

"You stared back at me," Coley reminded her.

"That's because I'm gonna follow you home mister." She nudged him playfully in the ribs with her elbow.

"Whoa, slow down! When do you get off work?"

Peaches groaned. "Maybe four in the morning."

"Maybe I'll come back." Coley offered. "I can't sit around

here and drink all night. Nothing personal, but I don't like your neighborhood very much."

"You look big enough to take care of yourself. I know, you are getting cold feet."

"Believe me, Peaches, I can handle myself. But I'm on strange turf. I found out only this afternoon that an old friend of mine got mugged and killed a couple of blocks from here." Coley turned toward her so that he could watch her face for any reaction to what was coming.

Peaches shrugged, "Really?"

"Yeah, I used to have a baseball card collection. I'd come down here on Ninth to a little coin and card shop. There was a real friendly old gent there that would feel sorry for me sometimes and toss in a couple extra cards after we made a deal. I went in to see him today."

"I betcha I know just the place you mean. In fact I went in there a couple of weeks ago. He is a nice man." Peaches talked as if he still existed.

"Yeah, he was a prince of a guy, but he ain't no more. He was robbed and beaten to death about ten days ago. The guy in the bodega next door told me so."

Peaches turned toward him with a look that could only be described as one of horror. Her big blue eyes stared at him in disbelief. "Let's see ... Finehouse ... that's it! His name was Finehouse."

"You got that right. Too bad! He was one of the good guys." Coley studied her face. If she knew anything about the killing, she was a great actress. "You a card collector?"

"Card collector? ... Oh, no ... I found this old coin in a box of junk ... I wanted to find out if it was worth anything."

"Was it?"

"No ... no, I could never be that lucky." Peaches edged away from Coley, not wanting to talk anymore about Finehouse. She was thinking of Heavy Laval. The last time she saw the coin, she thought he had gone out and sold it to Finehouse. Maybe he did and maybe he didn't. She tried to think back and fix a date in time, but she couldn't. Heavy was a bastard, but she couldn't imagine that he would kill anyone. She quickly dismissed it from her mind.

"Sorry, Doug. It's time to dance. See you at four o'clock?"

"I'll try, baby. I'll try." He sipped at his beer and watched her make her way to the dressing room.

"Strike out, big guy?" It was Tracy, pushing another beer his way.

"She keeps weird hours. Hey, you're right, she does have a shiner and a puffy cheek. Her guy must be some jerk!" Coley stared down the cleavage she persisted in putting in front of him.

"Speak of the devil and he walks right in." Tracy nodded at the back of a new customer who walked all the way to the back and sat down next to the guy with the red beard. He was thick-set, with very broad shoulders and thick black hair that hung in unruly curls.

"You know his name?" Coley bluntly dared to ask Tracy.

"I don't know whether he's got a name. Everyone just calls him Heavy. Been in and out for years. It's always been just Heavy."

Coley shoved a twenty dollar tip at Tracy and glanced again at Heavy. He certainly fit the description Blackwell had given him uptown. "Thanks, doll. I'll be seeing you."

"At two o'clock, I hope."

Coley winked at her and walked toward the door.

Down at the end of the bar Heavy Laval glanced away from Red Irons who was telling him his troubles. He saw the tall nat-tily dressed black man leave the bar. Briefly, he thought of another tall black man he had seen that night up in Dobbs Ferry. It had been from quite a distance. Nah, it couldn't be, he said to him-self, and then dismissed the thought.

24

One hundred thousand dollars was a lot of money for him to put together in small bills in a couple of days. The blackmailer would have to take hundreds. That would still raise eyebrows in his bank. Most of it would have to come out of his brokerage account, or Sandy would see something peculiar was going on right away. She seldom took an interest in that account.

Blaylock's continual anxiety permitted not one minute of sleep. His eyes, now fully accustomed to the darkness focussed on Sandy, facing away from him in deep sleep. Ever so cautiously, he slipped from their bed, donned a robe, and slipped downstairs. He opened the drapes on the living room window about halfway, and then sat in a recliner facing the window. He could see out to the road. He could see the mailbox, which now sped his pulse every time he looked at it.

Tonight's communication from the thief said nothing about the AMERI. It was purely a matter of blackmail. He decided to stall. He would tell the thief that it would take a couple more days to get all the money together, which well might be true. He would also tell him to mail him the AMERI at once. After all, the coin, having the pedigree that it did, would be very difficult to market through the legitimate numismatic channels. He and the thief both knew that the hundred thousand was blackmail to insure that Willis McCord's killer would remain unknown.

He walked to his study and hand-printed the note. He placed it in an envelope and then into a small briefcase that was to have held the blackmail money. Blaylock went outside and walked to the BMW in the driveway. He shoved the briefcase containing the note under the front seat. He left the door of the BMW unlocked, vowing to continue to do so until it disappeared into the hands of the thief.

"Cliff! You scared the wits out of me." Sandy confronted him reentering the side door from the driveway. "Where on earth have you been?" She quickly flipped the light switch, flooding the foyer with light.

"Sandy, I had no idea I would frighten you. I just plain can't sleep. I took a little walk, that's all."

"In your robe and slippers? Cliff, look at you."

He looked down at himself, forcing a smile. He wore a robe, slippers, and no trousers. She had a point. These were strange walking clothes. "Well, it's after three in the morning. I went no farther than the driveway, Sandy."

Sandy put her arms around him and held him for a few moments. "Oh Cliff, promise me you'll go to the doctor tomorrow. I've read that insomnia is caused by physical difficulties sometimes. You've got to get checked out."

Cliff raised his voice, "I just had an annual physical a couple of months ago. There is nothing wrong!"

"Nothing wrong? You are standing here in the middle of the night shouting at me. Something's wrong, Cliff." She pulled away from him, shaking her head. "By the way, Cliff, a few minutes ago when I heard you rattling around downstairs, I reached for that little automatic in my nightstand. I know that sounds silly. I haven't done that in years."

"So? That's understandable, Sandy."

"But it's gone. The gun is not there. Cliff, I swear I have never moved it since I put it there."

"I have it Sandy. I took it downstairs a few weeks ago to clean it. In all the excitement of the past few weeks, I just plain forgot about it. I'll go get it right now." He could feel the same quavering in his voice and wondered if Sandy could detect it.

"Oh what a relief! It'll wait till morning, Cliff. Maybe it should wait forever. I seriously doubt that I could ever actually shoot any-one." She laughed a little and hugged him.

"Well, I'll get it back where it belongs tomorrow. It's com-forting in this day and age . . ." There was his voice, trailing off into a whisper again. "Under the right circumstances I think any-body can pull the trigger."

She kissed him. "Tell you what, you keep the silly old thing in your nightstand. I think I've forgotten how to use it. Now, if you don't mind, after scaring the wits out of me, I am going back up-stairs and sleep. Why don't you join me. At one time in our life, until quite recently, we had our own special little formula for in-somnia. Maybe we could resurrect that." She kissed him again, provoking a slight response.

"Mmm, suppose that would take care of my little problem, whatever it is?" he hastily added.

"It always did, Cliff. Have you forgotten?"

"Of course not. I'll join you in a few minutes. I promise." He watched Sandy run up the stairs, then returned to the recliner in the living room. He stared at the mailbox across the front lawn at the end of the driveway.

He was lying to Sandy all the time now, even about joining her upstairs. The only reason he was getting away with it was be-cause it was so out of character and unexpected to her. But he re-alized that some day she would catch him in some blatant lie. Then he would either have to level with her and reveal the whole sordid story, or he would have to leave her.

He couldn't make himself go upstairs. His insides churned as he gaped, open-eyed, at the mailbox. He thought about Willy and Coley working so diligently to help him. Sooner or later they would trip him up in a lie also. He wished that they would leave him alone.

Suddenly he was jarred from his trancelike state by the slam-ming of a car door. He arose and walked, through the darkened house until he could see the McCords' driveway.

In the moonlight, he saw Adrienne McCord climbing slowly from behind the wheel of her car. She rocked unsteadily as she slammed the door, then propped herself against the side of the car for a moment before starting for her front door. She was alone, obviously drunk.

She teetered and then fell to the lawn next to the sidewalk. He watched the beautiful woman laboriously struggle to her hands and knees. She crawled a short distance and again got to her feet and wove her way to the front door. She stood propped against it for some time until he saw Alex's robed figure silhouetted in the now open door, helping her in.

He couldn't help but believe that the pathetic scene he had witnessed was probably his fault.

25

It was four-fifteen in the morning when Peaches hailed a cab on Eighth Avenue for a trip uptown to Sheraton Center.

Detective Sean O'Reilly set the now cold coffee in the holder protruding from the dash of the beat up old Ford, pulled away from the curb and followed the cab. He had been waiting for over an hour, ever since Coley Doctor had called him to identify Peaches as Heavy's girl. From the way Coley had described him, Heavy could only be one person, Heavy Laval, West side pusher and occasional stoolie. He was a most unlikely person to try to peddle a rare coin at Blackwell's on Fifty-seventh.

According to Coley, the coin dealer in White Plains had told him that Peaches had shown an AMERI to Finehouse, who was now dead. O'Reilly had a warrant to bring Peaches in for questioning, but first he wanted to see if she would lead him to Heavy Laval.

Peaches entered Sheraton Center and immediately took an escalator to the lobby floor where she located a house phone. The hotel operator had no record of a Doug Johnson being registered. A conversation with the front desk produced the same results.

"That bastard," she muttered to herself. She had thought this guy was on the level. Usually she had a sixth sense about things. It was a quarter to five. Now all she wanted to do was collapse and go to sleep. She walked outside the hotel to hail a cab when she was met by Sean O'Reilly who had tailed her every step of the way.

O'Reilly flipped his NYPD identification at her. "Peaches Collins, you'll have to come along with me, I have a few questions for you. It shouldn't take long."

"I can't believe this bullshit! I'm here minding my own business after working all damn night. I'm going home and going to bed. Now please, buzz off." She started walking at a fast pace, but the detective persisted in following alongside her.

"I wasn't doing a damn thing. Some jerk stood me up. I'm telling you I haven't broken one of your damn laws." O'Reilly had maneuvered her next to his car.

"Of course you haven't. This is not an arrest Miss Collins. There's been a homicide. I have a couple of questions. . . . Now get in and I'll drop you off at your apartment on Twenty-first."

"A homicide?"

"Yes."

"Who?"

"Jonathan Finehouse. That mean anything to you?"

"Yes, he was a nice man. I sure as hell didn't kill him. I just found out about it tonight."

"Mind telling me how you found out?"

"Doug Johnson told me. The bastard stood me up. He was a

black guy about seven feet tall. The bastard! He came on to me after my act at Buster's."

O'Reilly smiled. His friend Coley Doctor hadn't wasted any time. "Where's Heavy Laval tonight, Miss Collins?"

"There's another bastard. You've got a whole list of bastards tonight. He was in Buster's a few hours ago. I hope I never see him again."

"Come on, hop in. I'll run you home." O'Reilly opened the door of the old Ford. To his surprise, she slumped wearily in the front seat.

"Look, copper, you're on the level, right?"

"Don't worry kid." Peaches was obviously a marshmallow. He could see that. He couldn't help but feel sorry for her. Not a bad looker. What did she see in Heavy Laval? "Hey, I hear you're the star of the show down there."

"Buster's is a dump, copper. There ain't no stars in a dump. I am what I am. I hustle drinks in a dump." Peaches buried her face in her hands as he drove south along Eighth Avenue. Suddenly she looked at him questioningly. "I bet you know Doug Johnson. The bastard looked just like a dick."

O'Reilly smiled and patted her hand. "Nope. No self-respecting detective would stand up a dish like you." With all of her troubles, O'Reilly could see that Coley's standing her up hurt the most.

The detective pulled over to the curb, finding a parking spot a few doors from her walk-up. "Tell me a little bit more about the rare coin you showed to Finehouse, Peaches. Where is it right now?"

"I don't know," Peaches replied softly. It was the truth. She had thought that Heavy had sold it for the three grand. "Mr. Finehouse said he didn't know what it was worth. I might have tossed it in the trash," she lied.

"You gave it to Heavy Laval, didn't you?" O'Reilly persisted.

She shrugged. "Maybe he swiped it." It was the end of a long night. She felt tired. All at once her weariness turned to fear. If Heavy did kill Finehouse, she could be next. Especially if he got wind of her talking to a cop.

"Heavy live at your place?"

"Off and on, when he wants a little piece. Is that what you're up to? If you are why don't you just come out and say it. You cops are all the same." She crossed her legs provocatively, hoping that would take the detective's mind off his questioning.

"Look, young lady, I figure you're in a peck of trouble. There is a matter of grand larceny, and murder, and we followed the trail to you. You're playing with dynamite. I want you to think real hard and tell me if there is anything else I should know." He wrote a phone number on a card and gave it to her. "If your memory improves, call me."

She glanced at the card. "Sure copper, tell me one thing. Does that son of a bitch Doug Johnson work with you?"

O'Reilly shook his head negatively. She was still pissed off at Coley's standing her up.

Peaches got out of the old Ford and walked down the block. O'Reilly waited until the lights went on upstairs before leaving his parking space. The dim light of dawn was showing in the eastern sky. It would soon be time for him to report for a new day down at the precinct. He pointed toward Brocklyn and a couple of hours sleep.

"Hey kiddo, put on your fancy duds, you're going out stompin'." When she turned the lights on, Heavy Laval was sitting on the sofa next to the red-haired guy she had seen him with at Buster's. "Meet Red Irons, baby. You're going to a big party out at Port Jefferson."

"Stuff it, Heavy. It's sack time and I mean sleep time." She walked by the two men and into her bedroom. Turning to shut the door, she found Heavy Laval right in her face.

"Sorry, baby, but all the sudden you're talking to fuzz all the time."

A resounding smack dealt her a stunning blow, dropping her
to the floor. Red Irons hustled into the room to help him get her to
her feet. Propping Peaches between them they maneuvered her
down to the street and into the Cadillac where she lay unconscious
behind the black tinted windows.

The two men piled into the Cadillac and pointed north on
Eighth Avenue, soon making a left and entering the Lincoln Tun-
nel. Dawn was breaking when they pulled up next to where the
Jersey Trick was rolling gently against a dock just north of Hoboken.

Peaches, now drugged and wobbly, was assisted aboard and
placed in a small cabin below deck.

Red Irons drove Heavy Laval a few short blocks to Hoboken
Terminal where he would catch the PATH Train back to New
York.

"What do you think, Red. Is Percy LeRoy gonna have company?" Heavy asked, knowing whatever happened now was none
of his business.

Irons shrugged, his deep blue eyes a stark contrast to his flaming red hair in the dawn light. "She'll get a nice change of scenery,
Heavy. Sometimes people get too involved and they need that."

Heavy Laval waved good-bye as Red Irons pulled away from
the terminal. He breathed a heavy sigh, hoping that would be the
last time he would see that bastard for awhile.

He entered the terminal and walked quickly downstairs to the
PATH Train that would take him under the Hudson River back
to Chelsea. As he sat quietly on the train for the fifteen minute
ride, he couldn't push Peaches out of his mind. He got the re-
curring image of Peaches, all dressed up in fancy duds with this
big chain around her feet, floating side by side with Percy LeRoy,
looking up at the Narrows Bridge.

26

Willy Hanson met Coley Doctor for breakfast at the Hilton, a short distance from the marina in Tarrytown. Coley had lots of news. Willy listened attentively as he told him about his meeting with Peaches and NYPD detective Sean O'Reilly. Then came the bombshell. The man named Heavy Laval whom he had seen in the strip joint was a dead ringer for the man described to him by Blackwell, the uptown coin expert.

Willy smacked a fist into his palm. "That's it, Coley! Case solved! It's time to go to the police and dump this in their lap. Let's hope Laval hasn't got rid of the AMERI yet." Willy pushed back a chair from the table and crossed his legs. "That s good work pal. Only a day and a half of real work. The last time we got together on a case, it lasted months and wound up halfway around the world."

Coley grinned and stretched his long legs. "Yeah, we're pretty hot stuff, partner." Coley winked. "And just a little bit lucky."

"I can't wait to get Cliff Blaylock on the phone and tell him," enthused Willy. "I hope the news will wipe that perpetually constipated look off his face. Sandy's going to fly the coop if he don't lighten up."

Coley's demeanor sobered. "I can't quite figure that guy out. You know, he doesn't match your prior description of him at all. A simple case of robbery, for which he is wholly insured has turned him into a real mongrel. If I were Sandy, I would dump him. I know he's your friend, but that's just the way I feel."

"Can't blame you. Well, this news should restore the old Cliff Blaylock personality." Willy pulled a small cellular phone from his jacket pocket and dialed Blaylock's number. He answered on the first ring.

"Cliff, this is Willy. You seem to be home all the time. Don't you ever go into the office anymore?"

"I can do most of my work here, Willy. This is the day of modems and computers. You retired much too soon. I'll bet you would have your office right on the *Tashtego* if you were still fighting the battle. What's happening?"

"Big news, Cliff! We're about to put the screws to your thief. Coley struck pay dirt down in Chelsea."

"Really?" Cliff's weak comment sounded distant and far away. Willy waited a second for more to come, but there was only silence.

"Cliff, are you there? Did you hear what I said? I think we've busted the case!"

"Well . . . now that's good news. Who stole my coins?" Blaylock's voice seemed void of any real excitement.

"Coley and I are having breakfast at the Hilton over here in Tarrytown. We are getting ready to go downtown and talk to Coley's friend on the NYPD. We'd like you to come along. That would save a lot of paperwork. The detective could get all the details right from the horse's mouth." Again, dead silence on the line for several moments.

"I . . . I'm kind of in the middle of something here, Willy. Can it wait a day or two?"

Willy was amazed at the request. It was all he could do to keep from exploding. "Cliff, maybe you don't understand me. We can nail this bastard if we act fast. Hell, you might even get the AMERI back. It hasn't turned up anywhere yet. Coley's got to get back to LA. It's urgent that we act fast."

"Okay, Willy . . . okay . . . I'll put my work aside here and meet you at the Hilton. I guess you're about twenty minutes from here. We'll talk about it."

"Tell you what, Cliff. Meet us at the marina, aboard the

Tashtego. Coley and I have finished breakfast here. We can talk more freely on the boat."

"Okay. . . . Have they got the guy in custody yet?"

"No, but it's just a matter of time. The detective down there needs your input."

"Okay, Willy, I'll see you as soon as I can at the marina." Blaylock hung up without another word, still sounding totally unexcited.

"The unappreciative bastard!" Willy muttered to Coley. "I'm sorry I got you into this, Coley. You'd think that Blaylock would be turning cartwheels over the news."

"He's your friend, old buddy. I've been trying to fathom his strange behavior all along." Coley rubbed his chin, in deep thought. "You know a lot of victims get cold feet at the thought of coming face to face with a perpetrator."

"Maybe that's it. He only said he'd come after I told him he wasn't in custody yet. Let's get back to the marina. I'd like to wrap this up today. Ginny's anxious about getting the *Tashtego* pointed south before the weather breaks. I think it's important that Cliff meets your detective."

"Absolutely," Coley agreed. "You know, Willy, if I don't get back to LA soon, Marissa will be on the hunt for a more reliable man. Of course, there ain't none. But I don't want her looking."

"Hey, I meant to ask. What kind of a looker is that Peaches babe? Did she take it all off?"

"The answer to your questions are pretty nice, and not quite all. The answer to the question you haven't asked yet is, no I didn't. In fact I stood her up."

"Next thing I know, you'll be showing up at church, Coley. I'll give Marissa a good report someday." Willy smiled broadly as they walked out to Coley's rental Buick. Their success in helping Cliff Blaylock had them walking on air. Too bad, Willy thought, that Blaylock didn't share more of their elation.

Back at the *Tashtego,* Ginny was methodically polishing the brightwork that made the *Tashtego* stand out wherever she went. Not only was the rugged ketch a pleasure to handle in heavy seas, but Ginny's constant devotion to detail kept it in meticulous order, shipshape in every detail.

"Hi guys! Blaylock called. Said he was running a little late. How was breakfast?"

"Grand! Coley put it on his hotel bill. That made it even grander." They watched as Ginny applied varnish with a fine-haired brush at the base of a cleat.

"Hey, there's paint and brushes in the cabin if you gents would like to help."

Coley beamed a smile at the remark. "Ginny, there is one thing you don't want to do, and that is to put a paintbrush in my hand and turn me loose on this boat. The *Tashtego* would be a mess very soon. I painted my house out in Anaheim once, and the neighbors chipped in to pay a real painter to do it over."

Willy dialed Blaylock's home again only to be greeted by an answering machine. He terminated the call in disgust. "Coley, it's been about an hour since we talked to him. Maybe we ought to go wrap things up with O'Reilly ourselves. I know for a fact he's only fifteen minutes from here, across the Tappan Zee and a few miles south, all parkway."

"Relax, Willy, here he comes now." Blaylock's BMW was winding down the steep road to the marina. He parked next to Coley's rental car and walked leisurely toward the dock. Every now and then he would stop and glance back over his shoulder, looking back up the steep road. "He sure ain't bustin' his tail, is he?"

Finally he drew near enough to be heard. "Sorry I'm late, had to stop for gas. We still going downtown?" He asked the question like he was hoping it had been called off.

"Hell yes, Cliff. We'll get the whole case wrapped and maybe you'll get your coin back in a few days. How about that!" Willy looked up at him, waiting for a response.

"That's nice, I really appreciate what you guys have done. I just hadn't planned to go into the city today." Once again he glanced back up the hill beyond the marina.

Willy looked openly disgusted with him. "Let's get the damn trip over with. Come on, we'll take Coley's rental car."

They piled into the rental Buick sitting in the parking lot next to Blaylock's BMW. Coley turned and faced Blaylock in the back seat. "Hey, Pal, is your car all locked up?"

"It's fine," he said, avoiding a direct answer, and glad that Coley hadn't tested the door. "Let's go." Blaylock tried to act anxious to get to Manhattan. "Have no fear, I've learned my lesson there."

Blaylock tensed as Coley raced up the hill and turned south toward the city. "What kind of questions do you think the detective will ask me?"

"O'Reilly will want to hear the details of the robbery from you and the chain of events that led us to Heavy Laval. It might be necessary to get him extradited to New Jersey in which case New York would want a copy of your complaint to the local police and documentation of the loss. Of course if they find he is connected to the Finehouse homicide, they will want to keep him there. You'll like O'Reilly. Don't sweat about his questioning."

"What if this Laval fellow says he found the coin someplace and was just trying to get an appraisal?" Blaylock asked.

Coley glanced back over his shoulder at Blaylock. "Look, Cliff, this guy's got a record a mile long. He's a thug, a pusher, and all sorts of minor junk. He isn't too bright. He's a born loser. O'Reilly will have ways to nail him."

Willy sat quietly listening to Coley talk about the theft and began to reconstruct the robbery in his own mind. He had a problem. "Coley, why do think a street-smart city thug would venture out to Stag Creek and pick out Cliff's BMW for a hit?"

"That bothers me too, Willy," Coley agreed. "But it's kind of a trend. The crud in the city is seeping out to the suburbs. It's easy pickins out there for a smart operator. Yet they usually pick some spot closer in. Stag Creek is kind of in the boonies. There isn't even a train station there. I would guess that Laval was at the Wellington Inn looking for an easy mark at the coin show. He probably followed our boy Cliff home. Possible, Cliff?"

"I guess it's possible, but I didn't see anyone." Blaylock found himself getting very nervous. He was glad they were in the front seat and not looking right at him. He wondered if they would be present when O'Reilly questioned him.

He couldn't tell them what really bothered him. He couldn't tell them the reason he was late getting to the boat was because he had led the beige Cherokee far up the Palisades Parkway in an attempt to lose it. Finally, after having been followed through several cloverleafs, the vehicle had disappeared. Of course, the Cherokee had been to the marina near Tarrytown before. Laval might well look there again while they were in New York. Blaylock hoped he would. It would be a perfect time for Laval to pick up the empty briefcase with the note.

Back at the marina, Ginny was working on the strips of teak that framed the forward hatch. She was standing inside the *Tashtego* on a small ladder rubbing at the finish with fine steel wool, her head and shoulders protruding from the forward hatch. On this beautiful fall day the *Tashtego* was tied to the end of the long guest dock. Many of the vessels in the marina had been pulled for winter storage. The only boats nearby the *Tashtego* were several smaller powerboats that were being offered for sale.

As far as she could tell there was no other activity in the marina. Weekdays in the late fall were usually like this. A few weekenders tried to stretch the boating season with a day trip now and then, but not today. It was a perfect day to work uninterrupted on preparations for their long sail to the Caribbean.

From her vantage point now, looking out over the Tappan Zee as she worked, she didn't notice the beige Cherokee that wound down the steep hill behind her and parked next to Blaylock's BMW.

Heavy Laval sat for a few moments in the Cherokee and surveyed the marina. There was no sign of life anywhere. He figured Blaylock must be aboard the fancy yacht at the end of the dock where he had visited once before.

Laval lowered himself to the parking lot between his vehicle and the BMW. Glancing cautiously around, he opened the door of the BMW. He reached beneath the front seat and felt the small briefcase, wrested it from its tight storage place, and then turned and tossed it through the window of the Cherokee onto the front seat.

Within a few moments the Cherokee was slowing, winding its way back up the shore road. Heavy looked back toward the marina several times into the side mirrors. No one stirred. What passed for a grim smile crossed his craggy, pockmarked face. It was the easiest hundred G's he ever made. In fact, he told himself, it was the only time he had ever scored that big. Screw Red Irons! he thought. He had his own big deal going now.

Before turning on to the Cross Westchester Expressway, Laval pulled the Cherokee into a roadside diner. He rolled up the dark tinted windows, glanced around, and then unzipped the small briefcase. He pulled out several tightly rolled newspapers and a small envelope. Already cursing with rage, he ripped the unsealed flap from the envelope and read Blaylock's carefully lettered note.

"Mail me the AMERI at once. Once I have it, I will put the money in the same place you found this note. It will take me a couple more days to get the money together. It is almost impossible for you to sell the coin. It is too well known. It has a pedigree."

"That fuckin' pipsqueak!" Laval roared and slammed the briefcase to the floor of the Cherokee. He then read the note again. "Pedigree?" mumbled Laval. What in the hell was this jerk talking about. Dogs had pedigrees. This guy was nuts, he reasoned. "Right now is the time to teach that bastard a lesson."

Laval backed the Cherokee out of the diner parking lot, and pointed it back toward the marina. He fumed aloud, "It's time this damned asshole knew who was calling the shots."

The Cherokee wound slowly down the hill. The marina looked the same as he just left it. Blaylock's car was parked in the same place. There were only two other cars in the entire lot. Laval parked the Cherokee close by the long floating dock that led out to where the *Tashtego* was tied up at the far end.

The *Tashtego* showed no signs of having anyone aboard. He glanced back at the BMW and decided that Blaylock must be inside the boat. After all, he had seen him visit there before. What's there to be afraid of, he asked himself. He'd walk right up to the fancy yacht and confront Blaylock. He wouldn't dare identify him to anyone else that might be aboard. He'd seen him kill Willis McCord.

Laval reached under his seat and fished out the nine millimeter Glock and stuffed it into his waistband under the heavy sweater. He climbed out of the Cherokee and began to walk slowly along the floating dock. Laval stopped briefly now and then to appear as if he was examining the several powerboats that were offered for sale.

As he neared the *Tashtego*, Ginny suddenly emerged from the cabin door, carrying several brushes and a small can of varnish. She glanced quickly at Laval. He was now feigning inspection of the small Bayliner near the *Tashtego*. Ginny sat on a side cushion in the cockpit and became absorbed in refurbishing a bit of brightwork.

Laval sauntered close to the *Tashtego*. "Lady, I'm sorry to bother you, but I'm looking for Cliff Blaylock.... He told me to meet him here."

Ginny, startled, snapped her head up from her work and

gaped at the rugged, broad-shouldered man. "Cliff? Cliff told you to come here? Are you the detective?"

"Yes, ma'am, I am. I'll talk to him if you don't mind."

Ginny instinctively found the man frightening. He neither looked nor talked like a detective. "Well, sir, you're out of luck. He's not here. I'll tell him you dropped by . . . Mr . . . who can I say called?"

Laval kept walking slowly toward her as she talked. "That's bullshit, lady. His car is right out there. I got to see him." No sooner did the words leave his mouth, when he vaulted with surprising agility over the life rail into the cockpit.

Ginny panicked, knocking the varnish can to the deck as she tried to reach the cabin door, and the .38 revolver that was in a side keep behind it.

Laval was at her like a shot, shoving her into the cabin and closing the door behind them.

"Oh my God!" she screamed. "Help!" And then a loud scream as blood-curdling as she could manage. She groaned, realizing that inside the *Tashtego* her screams probably would attract no one in the small marina. She thought of the forward hatch, and in a twisting effort wrenched free of Laval and tried to run, but he was on top of her with his massive frame.

Whap! The slap of the Glock's barrel across Ginny's face dropped her to the deck of the forward stateroom, where she lay without movement.

"You got no sense, bitch!" muttered Laval. He quickly ransacked through the boat. Blaylock obviously wasn't there. He glanced back at the fallen woman. Now there's a fancy piece of tail, he thought to himself. Maybe he ought to help himself. He looked at her close up and decided she might be dead and quickly rejected the thought of ravaging her.

Laval calmly inspected the living quarters of the *Tashtego*. He rifled through a large woman's handbag, which he pulled from a side keep, and grunted approvingly at finding several hundred dollars and a cache of credit cards. Then he quickly made his way through the cabin door into the cockpit and walked down the small gangplank.

Within a couple of minutes he had made his way back to the Cherokee. He climbed behind the tinted windows and surveyed the quiet marina. Nothing stirred! He laughed aloud, marvelling at the ease with which he had pulled off the simple robbery. This would teach that damn Blaylock to do what he was told, and in the process he had turned a neat little profit.

He drove out of the marina and back through Tarrytown. Hardly anybody walked the streets, and so many windows of the parked cars were rolled down. It was like a big candy store out here in the suburbs. He decided he would find a nice little apartment and set up shop out here. Red Irons could just plain go to hell.

27

H eavy robbed somebody. That's usually not Heavy's game. He must have found a soft touch. He got some gold and some rare coins." Peaches sat on a sofa next to Veronica and across the small salon from Bocco Lamas. They were aboard the motor yacht *Jersey Trick* lashed up to a guest pier near Hoboken. "He got rid of the stuff at a few coin shops. A couple days after that, the cops started coming around, and a couple of detectives too. That's all I know." Peaches held the side of her head where Heavy Laval had given her a whack.

Bocco rubbed at a dark growth of beard. He eyed Peaches thoroughly as she talked. Actually she could be cleaned up to be a pretty snazzy chick, he thought to himself. The bruise on her cheek would go away. "I want you to stay away from Heavy Laval. Never talk to him again. Got that, kid?"

"You don't have to worry about that. I never want to see that bastard again." She looked around the salon. The towers of Manhattan loomed across the Hudson from where they were now. "How did I get here?"

"We had to get you away from the cops. I don't want you nosing around those guys either. I'm sorry the boys were a little rough on you. You can thank your pal, Heavy. Red wouldn't hurt a fly. We'll take care of Heavy. You'll never have to worry about him again. Where do you suppose he is?" Bocco stared at Peaches. The babe had too much on the ball to waste. Under Veronica's wing, she would turn a nice profit as a party girl.

"He has a room over Murry's Bar on Ninth. Of course, lately he's been hanging around my place a lot." Peaches shook her head, and smiled at Bocco. She really had to stay away from Heavy now, she thought, after spilling her guts to Bocco.

"We checked out the place on Ninth. He ain't there. The boys are cleaning out your place right now. The son of a bitch flew the coop."

"Cleaning out my place!" Peaches realized she was totally at their mercy. "I got some nice stuff there. Mostly clothes and dance costumes."

"Don't worry, kid, you'll have them soon. Meanwhile, I got a place for you right here, working for Veronica." Veronica had been silent until now. The dazzling blonde smiled at her assuringly.

"I hear you're a dynamite dancer," Veronica said. "So you'll just keep on dancing, only at private parties. We've got a little shindig up in Port Jefferson in a couple days. You'll be a smash. Maybe we'll put on a little show together." Veronica winked at her and crossed her endless legs. "You'll make a few bucks and live like a princess."

Peaches looked a little dubious. Bocco and Veronica staring at her at the same time made her nervous.

Bocco broke the silence. "Kid, I might as well put it to you straight. You gotta be willing to turn a trick now and then for a big spender. Real class. No Ninth Avenue stuff. In two days, Veronica will have you looking like a movie star. Deal?"

Peaches nodded her head in approval. "Why not?"

Bocco thought to himself that there must have been a long list of answers to that question, but she would get not a one from him. "Good! You're on the payroll, kid."

Veronica reached over and squeezed the hand of her new charge. "We'll have a ball, Peaches. Let's get started right now. We've got to do something with that face."

Veronica rose and stretched her tall, well-endowed body. Peaches noticed that Bocco couldn't keep his eyes off her. Veronica seemed to be someone special to him.

Bocco quickly rose and headed for the door. "You two can stay right here if you like. I've got to get up on the bridge. We're out of here in a few minutes."

"Where we going?" asked Peaches. "I've got none of my things yet."

Bocco smiled at her. "It don't matter where we're going, kid. Water is water. We're going to be on the water for a couple days. Don't worry about a thing. Veronica will see to it that you have some duds." Bocco left for the bridge, leaving them alone.

"Bocco likes to be mysterious sometimes, Peaches. We're headed for Long Island Sound and the party in Port Jefferson. Come on, let's go to my cabin and get started on those bruises."

Veronica's cabin was a posh layout, a queen-size bed loaded with fancy pillows, a small sofa and lots of mirrors. An etched glass door opened into a shower just like you might expect in a nice apartment. "Wow! This beats my cubbyhole."

"Well, doll, you just drop by whenever you want to." Veronica studied the bruises on her cheekbone up close. "You're gonna survive, kid. It's not as bad as it looks. Give it a couple days. Do you do drugs, Peaches?"

"Nope, that's the only bad habit I don't have, I guess. Oh I've smoked a joint a few times. But I really don't like it."

Veronica sprawled on the sofa. "Tell me, do you do women? You know, like tricks?"

Peaches gaped at her, feeling herself flushing red. "No . . . nope," she stammered. "I guess that's two bad habits I don't have." She forced a nervous smile.

Veronica laughed softly. "Well don't get uptight, doll. I have to know these things. Bocco gets some weird ideas sometimes."

All at once there was a throb of a powerful engine as the *Jersey Trick* pulled away from the dock. Slowly the sleek cruiser turned from its berth and pointed out across the Hudson, south of the twin towers of the World Trade Center.

Veronica bounded from the sofa and opened an accordian door to a closet. "Let's see what I can find you to wear. There are plenty of bathing suits, and cover ups, and lots of underwear I've never worn. That just about makes a complete wardrobe for this trip."

"Veronica, you have to be a foot taller than I am. I couldn't wear anything else of yours anyway." Peaches grinned at her, and decided she liked her. At least she seemed direct and to the point. "Is Bocco really rich? I mean rich rich. I've only seen boats like this from Battery Park. How does he really make the big bucks?"

Veronica sobered and stared at her. "Tell you what. I'll forget that you asked. Just remember never to ask again. Okay, doll?"

"Gotcha!" Peaches replied, happy to see the warm smile return to Veronica's face.

The engines of the *Jersey Trick* rumbled louder as the cruiser picked up speed. Soon Peaches could see the Statue of Liberty out her window. From there the boat swung sharply to the port and passed the tip of Manhattan. A few minutes later they pointed north into the East River, and slipped under the big bridges one by one.

It was a new experience and adventure for Peaches. Strangely, she felt safe, even though realistically, she was a prisoner.

"Tell me, Peaches, where would you look if you had to find Heavy Laval real quick?" Veronica's question was unexpected. Peaches supposed that it was really Bocco who wanted to know.

Peaches shrugged. "Heavy kept his business pretty much to himself. He hung out at Murry's off and on. He came to my place when he wanted to get laid. Once in awhile, he mentioned having to run up to north Jersey. But he never took me with him. I don't ever want to see the son of a bitch again."

"Smart girl! Bocco's really pissed off. He was supposed to check in late last night and this morning, and didn't. If you get any ideas, let me know."

"Sure thing, Veronica. I wish I could help." Right now she was glad that Heavy hadn't confided much in her when it came to business.

28

It was about three in the afternoon when Willy, Coley, and Cliff Blaylock left the precinct house down in Chelsea. The meeting with Detective O'Reilly produced little new information. Heavy Laval hadn't been picked up yet, though O'Reilly said he was a familiar character to a lot of policemen, and said it should be only a matter of hours.

O'Reilly had listened to Blaylock as he told him his version of the robbery of the BMW in his driveway. "I was a damn fool I guess. I'll never leave anything of value in my car again." He informed O'Reilly that a detective from the Stag Creek police department had investigated the scene and had written up a report. O'Reilly said that he would follow up by contacting them.

O'Reilly did have one bit of new information. The detective reported that two other coin dealers besides Blackwell's in the city had bought several gold bullion coins from a man that fit the description of Heavy Laval. These two did not say that he offered them the AMERI. One place reported that he came in with a woman whose description fit Peaches Collins. "Heavy Laval ain't too bright," O'Reilly had said. "He's leaving a lot of footprints."

Now they were driving north on the Saw Mill River Parkway, heading back to Tarrytown. Blaylock turned into a clam once they left O'Reilly. If he was excited about the progress in the case, neither Willy nor Coley could tell it.

Willy broke the silence as he drove. "Cliff my boy, if I were you, I'd be feeling pretty good right now. I would guess it's been quite a trauma for Sandy, having been robbed right in her own driveway. They say that people always feel violated when something hits that close to home. To get this thing wrapped up this quick has got to make you feel good."

"Yes, Willy, it will be good to get it over with. I want to thank you fellows again."

Coley turned around in his seat to look squarely at Blaylock. It wasn't what he said, it was how he said it. There wasn't a hint of a smile on his face or elation in his voice.

When they got to the marina, there were only three other cars in the lot, one of them a Tarrytown police car parked near the ramp to the floating dock. They could see a policeman talking to someone standing next to one of the boats that were for sale.

Coley surveyed the quiet marina. "Tell you what, Willy, I betcha a buck that cop is trying to buy one of those boats. Fuzz are big on that stuff you know."

"You're on for a buck, Coley." Willy pulled up next to the

BMW. Blaylock was the first to open the door. "Thanks for everything, guys. Keep in touch." By the time Willy and Coley climbed out of the rental Buick, Blaylock was getting into the BMW. He started the engine and waved half-heartedly as he started to leave the parking lot.

Driving with his left hand, Blaylock poked his right hand under the seat, and immediately broke into a sweat. The briefcase was gone! Heavy Laval had his message. Driving slowly up the incline, he looked back at the parking lot. Heavy's van was certainly not there. There were just three other vehicles, including the police car.

Coley and Willy paused to watch the BMW wind up the hill. "Strange guy, Willy. I thought today would buck him up and make him feel good. Hell, I think I'll send him a good fat bill for our services. That might get a rise out of him."

Willy nodded his agreement and started walking toward the dock holding the *Tashtego*. Ginny was nowhere to be seen. The policeman who was chatting with someone sitting on one of the powerboats glanced their way. He abruptly stopped his conversation and started his way down the dock toward them.

"Sorry sir, access to this dock is closed right now." The policeman stood spreading his stance in front of them and holding his arms outstretched.

"I belong on that ketch out there, officer." Willy nodded toward the *Tashtego* and started to walk around the policeman.

The policeman stepped directly in front of him and eyed him suspiciously. "That your boat?"

"Well, not exactly, it belongs to my partner. She must be aboard. What the hell is going on here!" Willy reddened, getting irate.

Coley stood a step behind Willy trying to figure out what was going on. "Officer, this man lives on that boat. He has a perfect right to go aboard." Coley looked ahead to the *Tashtego*.

"Now wait one damn minute you two!" The officer backed off

a couple steps and put his hand on his sidearm. "There's been some big trouble out there, and I'm telling you there is going to be a lot more right here unless you both settle down."

"Trouble! What kind of trouble?"

The officer looked at the distraught Willy. "Just who the hell are you?"

"I'm Willy Hanson, and I live on that boat with my partner, Ginny Dubois."

"Follow me and we'll see about that." He turned toward Coley. "You stay right here and keep your distance." Willy followed the policeman to the *Tashtego* and up the gangplank, The policeman tapped lightly on the door to the main cabin. "Miss Dubois, may I speak to you please?"

"Ginny! It's me. For God's sake, what is going on?" Willy plunged right past the policeman into the cabin. "Jesus!" He couldn't believe his eyes.

The cabin was a shambles. Ginny sat on the edge of her bunk, her head swathed in a white bandage that showed a huge spot of blood. She looked at him, eyes welling with tears trying to speak.

"Willy . . . Willy, thank God you're here," she spoke softly as if speaking were painful to her. "It was awful, Willy. Some guy came in here with a gun and ripped this place all apart. . . . We fought, Willy, he was an animal!"

Willy held her in his arms trying to make sense of it all. "Ginny, we've got to get you to a hospital. Look at you."

The policeman broke into their conversation. "We had an ambulance here, sir. Tried to get her to a hospital and she absolutely refused. I think she should be looked at."

Coley had climbed aboard and was standing behind the policeman gaping at the obviously battered Ginny. "Willy, we better get her to an emergency room somewhere. She's got to be checked out."

The policeman nodded his head in agreement. "I'm sorry I was so rough with you boys when you first got here, but this thing looked very serious. The detectives just left. One of them will be back in a few minutes."

"When did it happen?" asked Coley.

The policeman shrugged. "We're not certain. The lady was evidently out for a while. She called 911 about two hours ago."

"Ginny, what do you mean, you fought? You could have got killed." Willy held her close. She was trembling. Ginny was a tough cookie. He looked around the ransacked cabin. All the drawers were dumped and wires were ripped loose from the radio. "This guy must have been a monster."

"Willy, he was strong as an ox. I think he smacked me with a gun." Ginny touched the crude bandage on her head. "He was huge, like a damn gorilla. I'll never forget that face, never!"

"Did he rape you?"

"No. He probably thought he killed me. He knows your friend, Blaylock."

"Blaylock! What makes you think that?"

Ginny was breathing more easily now, and the details of her violent confrontation with her assailant were coming back vividly. "When he first approached he asked for Blaylock. He said he knew he was here, and then just muscled his way into the cabin. When he found that Blaylock wasn't here, he began to start ripping at things."

"Blaylock? It just seems inconceivable that he could have anything to do with this." Willy glanced up at Coley who was taking in the details of the destruction. "What about it, Coley, any of this make any sense to you?"

Coley shook his head and then addressed the policeman. "Has there been any trouble like this recently around here?"

"They run a nice family business here. Once in a while, you get some youngsters cutting up in the summertime, but I've never seen anything like this since I've been on the force." The officer seemed as stunned as they were about the event.

Coley walked around the cabin trying to picture what had happened. "Ginny, do you have any idea if this guy took anything?"

"He emptied my purse. That's all I can be sure of right now. I'm missing over six hundred dollars and our credit cards. I told all that to the detectives when they were here." Ginny's eyes roamed the ransacked cabin. "It was all so neat and organized. We were all set for the Caribbean, Willy." She smiled weakly and then winced with pain as she attempted to adjust the bandage.

Willy stood up, and helped Ginny to her feet. "Coley, I'm going to take our wounded battler here to the nearest emergency room. Why don't you head over to Stag Creek and see if Blaylock can shed any light on who this bum might be. Ginny, you've been through hell. Are you absolutely sure that this guy mentioned Blaylock?"

"No doubt about it. That happened when things were still peaceful around here."

Coley was anxious to get started. He would like to question Blaylock before he had too much time to think about things. "You say this guy was tall and beefy. What about his face?"

"Scarred, maybe pockmarked. He had a greasy mop of black curly hair. He was ugly, Coley, fat and ugly." Ginny shuddered.

Coley's eyes met Willy's, two men with the same thought. She had just described Heavy Laval.

29

It was the wrong time of evening for Coley to head for Stag Creek. The Tappan Zee Bridge was jammed with bumper to bumper rush hour traffic. Commuters were pouring from Manhattan into Westchester and across the Hudson's longest bridge into Rockland County. The stop-and-go traffic gave him some think time.

He tried to raise Detective O'Reilly on his cellular phone, but kept getting his answering machine. Finally he opted to leave a message. "Check with the Tarrytown police on the armed robbery at the marina. The victim was Willy's partner, Ginny, who was beaten and robbed aboard their yacht. He's the guy you met this afternoon with Blaylock. The ID fits Heavy Laval perfectly. Laval's crazy. He could have killed her. You boys have got to pick him up. Later tonight I'll be at the Hilton in Tarrytown."

Actually, his good friend O'Reilly probably had a full plate, he thought to himself. The only reason O'Reilly wanted Laval was to question him on the Finehouse homicide. The precinct down in Chelsea must have an awesome workload. He was afraid that a larceny over in Jersey would suffer from lack of priority.

Coley's thoughts returned to Blaylock and his quiet, almost hostile attitude. He knew Willy was doing the right thing by trying to help. But it seemed to him that Blaylock felt amazingly unappreciative. And now, this thing at the marina. If it were anybody but Ginny, he would be certain that she got the name wrong. Of course, there was the chance that some other thug might look just like Heavy Laval. He decided that was not likely.

Finally, he reached the west side of the Hudson and turned off going south on the Palisades Parkway into New Jersey. Willy had drawn a crude map, showing the way to Blaylock's house in Stag Creek. It was dusk by the time he pulled into the heavily wooded cul-de-sac where Blaylock lived.

The driveway was empty. Coley knocked on the door, rang the bell, but there was no response. He wound up walking around the house. The BMW was nowhere to be seen. He looked at his watch. It was six-thirty. He decided to drive around a bit and come back later on.

He found his way to Stag Creek Road, which Willy had called the main drag. He drove south until he came to a restaurant, the Prospect Inn. His stomach was growling. He hadn't eaten since the breakfast with Willy.

There was a rectangular bar inside with a half-dozen patrons chatting and having cocktails. He couldn't help but notice that at the far end of the bar sat an absolutely dazzling woman, dazzling enough to quickly switch his thoughts away from Blaylock. After all a man shouldn't work every split second of the day, he thought, sitting down on the bar stool beside her.

"I'll have a Tanqueray, rocks, olive," he asked the tall bartender. He sneaked a glance at the woman next to him who pretended not to notice him, bent on staring into her straight-up martini.

"My name's Coley," he said to the bartender returning with his drink, and offered his hand. "And yours?"

"Ted," the bartender replied tersely, staring at the six-foot-seven black detective. "Hey you look like one of the Knicks."

"You mean I look rich, which I'm not," smiled Coley

"No, you really do look like one of the Knicks."

"You mean because I'm black?" Coley decided to needle Mr. Ted a bit, but he gave just a hint of a smile. "Actually I'm looking for a friend of mine, Cliff Blaylock. Thought he and Sandy might be having dinner here."

Teddy shook his head. "Haven't seen him lately. He comes in here once in a while though."

"Have you tried their home?" A soft, throaty voice came from the vision next to him.

He turned to meet the dark blue eyes set in a flawless face, framed with long jet hair meticulously brushed. "Yes, they're not at home."

"Good! Let's hope they are out having a good time. They are my neighbors, wonderful neighbors."

"Well, I'll bet you are a wonderful neighbor too. By the way, my name is Coley Doctor."

"I'm Adrienne McCord." She extended an elegantly manicured hand. "I'll tell Cliff I ran into you."

"Please do that," replied Coley, pondering the familiarity of her name. Of course! It was Blaylock's neighbor who had lost a son in a shooting at a local hotel. Willy had told her all about the McCords. The shooting had been the same day of Cliff's coin theft. He decided to do a little detecting. After all he was a detective.

"Adrienne, I have a question. You must be related to the boy who met with tragedy a few weeks ago." He saw the woman wince. "I've heard the story from Cliff and Sandy. I'm sorry. Maybe I shouldn't have mentioned it."

"Oh, that's alright." She looked at him soberly. "I'm the boy's mother. I find that it helps to talk about it now and then. For the first few days I couldn't bear to. The Blaylocks were very special people to young Willis."

Coley decided to switch the conversation to the Blaylocks. "Well, I find Cliff an interesting man. I guess he has made quite a name for himself in publishing."

"My son found him fascinating. When he was a small boy, Cliff inspired him to collect coins. Willis spent many happy hours with Cliff Blaylock in the early years. It was a hobby that he kept all through his life." She stopped abruptly, stumbling over the word, life, reminded again that it was at an end.

Now Coley really felt pity for her. He decided to change the subject completely. "How's the food in this place? I just remembered I haven't eaten since breakfast."

She actually smiled at him. "It's good. In fact it is probably too good for a slim, trim fellow like you. I bet Teddy is right. You're an athlete, a basketball player."

"Well thanks for the compliment, but he is wrong. I'm an investigator, doing some work for Cliff. I did have dreams at one time of being the next Dr. J., but fell just this much short." He held up his thumb and forefinger about two inches apart. "Tell me, are you waiting for someone? Perhaps you'd join me for dinner."

"No and no. I am afraid I'm still very poor company. I just stopped in for a cocktail. Alex is away on business. I must get home. I'm expecting his call. Tell you what, I will take a rain check, okay."

Her unexpected remark stunned him. After all, she didn't know a thing about him. It didn't make sense. The woman must be extremely confused in her grief. Quite soon after the remark, she nodded a good evening and left.

"Teddy, what's good to eat?"

"Everything. The specials are on the board behind you." He nodded to the mirrored wall behind him.

"Is the corned beef and cabbage any good?"

"You got me there. I don't eat the stuff, but I get no complaints. I heard you talking about Cliff Blaylock. He eats it sometimes."

"I'll have some. Say, by the way, that Adrienne McCord seems like a very nice woman."

Teddy looked thoughtful for a moment. "She is. But she put up with a hell of a lot with that kid. I feel sorry for her." The bartender walked away shaking his head.

Suddenly the thought hit Coley like a ton of bricks. The McCord kid was a coin collector. There was a coin show at the Wellington Inn the day he was shot. Cliff Blaylock's coins were stolen the same evening, when Heavy Laval showed up in his driveway. He decided that he would tell Willy he wanted to spend a little more time on the case.

30

Adrienne McCord drove slowly down Lamplighter Place, swung around the wide cul-de-sac and into her driveway. The porch light was lit at the Blaylocks. Maybe she would call Sandy, she thought. Perhaps she would come over and have a drink. The tall black man at the Prospect Inn who called himself Coley had been interesting. Too bad she hadn't taken up his offer for dinner. But the fact that she had halfway considered it shocked her.

God she felt lonely! There was a couple of days of activity right after the funeral and then the house was empty. Alex, not really sharing her grief, had escaped on a business trip to Seattle this morning, finally leaving her totally alone. She turned out the lights of the Mercedes and sat behind the wheel staring at the house, steeling herself to go inside.

As she sat, a vehicle entered the cul-de-sac with only its parking lights lit. It stopped briefly in front of the Blaylocks. An arm extended from the window and stuffed something into the mailbox, and then moved on. Strange time for a delivery, she thought.

Adrienne sighed, got out of the car, and went into the house. She began turning on lights everywhere as she went to the bar in the family room. She splashed half a glass of Beefeaters into a rocks glass. She glanced at the clock. It was only seven-thirty. If she went to bed now, she would be up at two in the morning. A call to the Blaylocks produced only a message from the answering machine. Taking a large swig from the glass, she looked up the stairwell and remembered she had been putting off something for a long time, and decided now was the time.

Adrienne climbed the stairs, stared at the closed door at the top, took one more swig of Beefeaters, and opened the door to Willis's room. The huge, neat pile of clothing was still on the bed where her visiting sister had put them. A carton of plastic bags sat on the bed. Their church would send someone to pick Willis's clothes up tomorrow.

She opened the door to the large walk-in closet, turned on the light, and went inside. It was cleaned out except for a pile of luggage in the rear. She decided she might as well get rid of them also. Alex and she had all the luggage they needed. She began moving the empty bags into the bedroom. Underneath them were two thick black Samsonite briefcases. She stopped to pick them up. They were not empty like the other luggage. They were heavy.

She took them into the bedroom, sat them on a chair and opened the latch on one and peeked inside. She gasped and started to breathe heavily when she realized what she saw. There were hundreds of small ziplock plactic bags filled with white powder, just like the ones Alex used to bring home from New York. There was enough cocaine there to last a person a lifetime. The other briefcase produced the same contents. Carefully, she closed the latches on them, put them in the farthest corner of the closet, and again piled the luggage in front of them.

She sat on a chair and started to weep. She thought she had finished the weeping bit days ago. But now she couldn't stop. She gulped the rest of the gin.

The phone rang, jarring her from her melancholy state. It was Sandy. "Oh Sandy, thank God! I tried to get you a little while ago. Sandy, have you got time to talk? Let's have a drink."

"You naughty woman! Sounds like you've had a couple."

"I can't fool you, Sandy, I can fool Alex, but not you. Speaking of Alex, he is in Seattle. And I am at my wit's end over here."

"Sit tight, I'll be right over. Maybe you'd better put on a pot of coffee."

"You got it."

"Give me five minutes. I want to leave a note for Cliff. He's not home yet."

Adrienne went downstairs to the den, poured another glass of gin, and then fired up the small coffeemaker behind the bar. All that cocaine, she thought, what am I ever going to do with it. The rumors about Willis reached her more than once, but she had chose not to believe them. When they had found all that cocaine in his red Corvette, she tried to convince herself that it had been planted. She wouldn't tell Sandy about her discovery. She couldn't tell anyone. Someday, she thought, she would put it in trash bags and dump it in one of the refuse cans along the parkway.

There was the doorbell. That would be Sandy.

Sandy took one look at Adrienne and could see that she was smashed. "Adrienne dear, you are a bad girl! Cliff and I have a rule that we never drink alone. It's a good rule. Maybe it's for you someday, when you get back to normal." Sandy hugged her.

"Sandy, I don't know what I would do if you weren't my neighbor. I think I would have gone mad by now. It seems that I just get things in focus and everything blows up again. Do you think I'll ever be able to forget about the past few weeks?" Adrienne dabbed at the corners of her eyes with a tissue.

"Probably not, but time will take the focus away from all this. You have so many years ahead of you. You'll find other interests that will take over." Sandy felt inadequate. What could she say to console this woman?

"I don't know . . . something always turns up as a reminder that Alex and I are . . . well, damn it, failures."

"Oh come on! This will pass, Adrienne. It's going to be tough for a while, but it will pass." She watched as Adrienne poured coffee with an unsteady hand.

"Did your detective find you?" Adrienne asked.

"Detective?"

"Yes. I met him at the Prospect Inn about an hour ago. He said he tried your house, looking for Cliff, and that he would be back later. He was an incredibly tall, good-looking black man."

"Oh, I know who you mean. That's Coley Doctor. He's helping Cliff to try to find the coin thief. He's a friend of a friend, and supposed to be quite good. I had forgotten all about our little problem. I hope that Cliff gets home soon so they can talk."

"Sandy, I have to show you something. It's driving me crazy." Adrienne paused. She had to show what she had found to someone she could trust. She just couldn't keep everything inside like she had planned. "Do you mind?"

"Of course, Adrienne. You have me on pins and needles now. What is it?"

"Follow me." Adrienne set her coffee down, and walked to the staircase. "Promise not to tell a soul?"

"You've got it." Sandy followed her upstairs. She opened the door to Willis's room and led her in. They walked right past the clothes piled on the bed, and then into the large closet.

Adrienne moved several pieces of luggage until she could reach the two briefcases, and brought them out to the bedroom. Wasting no time, she popped the latches on one and and opened it wide. "Look, my dear, at what my darling son had stashed in his room."

Sandy gaped at the hundreds of tightly packed transparent bags that filled the briefcase. "Is that what I think it is?"

Adrienne confirmed that it was with a silent nod of her head. "You see, our problem goes on and on. When they found more of the stuff in his Corvette, I kept convincing myself that Willis had been framed. Now I know that the worst is true. He was involved, big time." Her voice cracked as tears came. "My son, my brilliant class president."

She sat on the bed weeping openly. Sandy sat beside her and wrapped an arm around her shoulders. "Does Alex know about this?"

"No, I just found it today."

"You'll have to call him and tell him. He should fly home."

"Oh, Sandy!" She looked at her pleadingly. "Do I have to tell him? It's just something else he can blame on me. I thought I might dump it in garbage bags and stuff them into a refuse can along the parkway. Why does Alex have to know?"

"Adrienne! You can't keep piling up all this guilt on your own shoulders. Alex should know." Sandy eyed the neat rows of bags in the briefcase. "You've got to tell the police. This is a substantial bit of evidence. Don't you want them to catch whoever shot Willis? According to the papers, they already found plenty of this in the Corvette. It isn't like you just discovered something new."

"I guess you may be right, Sandy. I need time to think about it. Do you think it can wait a day or two?"

"Sure, why not? I have an idea there will be a lot of questions and reports to fill out. They may want to search further around the house. At least wait until morning. You don't want to face all of that tonight."

"I'm glad that I know someone that can think clearly, Sandy. Thanks." She forced a weak smile. "I'll call the police the first thing in the morning."

Coley Doctor pulled into the Blaylock's driveway heartened by the fact that lights were lit in several rooms of the house. There was a car in the driveway, not the BMW, but surely someone was home. He rang the doorbell several times and then rapped the heavy brass knocker. There was no response. He got back in his car and decided to wait a while.

Coley looked at the long driveway leading to the rear of their house. He figured that it was at least two hundred feet from the street to the point Willy had described where the thief had broken a window and robbed the BMW. He shook his head. Brave thief, he reasoned. It was so damn quiet in this little town. There hadn't been a car on the street since he had got there.

Lights shone on the trees at the end of the cul-de-sac as another car pulled into Lamplighter Place. It paused for a couple of seconds and then pulled slowly into the driveway alongside Coley's rental Buick. Coley could see it was the BMW, and got out of his car to greet Blaylock. "Cliff, sorry to bother you this late, but Willy and I have a couple of questions."

Blaylock walked toward him, extending his hand. "No problem, I hope I can help. Did you ring the bell? I see Sandy's home."

"No answer, Cliff."

Blaylock fished a key from his pocket and opened the door. Once inside, the foyer light was already on. Coley looked at the powder blue carpet where Blaylock had walked, and then at Blaylock's feet. His shoes were soaked, as were his pant legs, showing wetness several inches above his ankles. "Hey Cliff, you're getting mud on the carpet."

Blaylock stared down at his feet. "Oh boy! Sandy isn't going to like that." He couldn't help but notice that Coley was still gaping at his shoes. "Over in Park Ridge they were hosing down the street. I stepped off the curb right into a mess. I guess I should sue them for a new pair of shoes."

"Yeah, I'll be your witness, Cliff." He watched as Cliff read a note left on a foyer table.

"Sandy's next door. She spends a lot of time with Adrienne McCord. She ought to be back soon." Cliff sat down, took off his muddy shoes, and put on some slippers he took from a coat closet in the foyer. "So what's up?"

"I'm glad you asked that, Cliff, and I'm glad you are sitting down. We've had some real excitement at the marina." Coley studied the man. Blaylock was looking down at his wet trouser legs. One was soaked almost all the way to the knee.

Before Coley could go on, the door chimes sounded. Blaylock got to his feet, opened the door, and Willy Hanson walked in. "Willy, come on in. Coley was just starting to tell me about some excitement at the marina."

"How's Ginny?" asked Coley. "I'm sure you didn't leave her alone."

"She's going to be fine, Coley. They're going to keep her in overnight in Nyack Hospital for observation. She has a serious concussion." Willy still hadn't acknowledged the presence of Blaylock.

"What happened, Willy?" Blaylock whispered his question, sensing Willy's hostility.

"Damn it! You tell me! And it better be good." Willy glared at him, trying to suppress his rage.

Blaylock backed off a couple of steps. "Now wait a minute here! I have no idea what you're talking about."

"While we were in Manhattan, your friend, one Heavy Laval,

ransacked the *Tashtego*, and pistol-whipped Ginny. She's in Nyack hospital. Why? What in the hell is going on!"

"Laval?"

Willy thrust his hand at Blaylock, grasping him firmly by the front of his sweatshirt and threw him roughly to a sitting position on a foyer bench. Holding him firmly by one shoulder, he shook a finger menacingly into his face.

"Willy!" Coley tried to intercede but Willy waved him aside.

"Now, Cliff, I want you to think very carefully. I'm going to give you one chance to tell the truth about why you were supposed to meet Heavy Laval in Tarrytown." He dropped his hand from Blaylock's shoulder and backed away a couple of steps. Then he shook his fist at him. "And if I think you're lying, I am going to knock all your teeth out."

Blaylock looked sullenly at the floor. Maybe now was the time, he thought to himself. Maybe now was the time to get the whole story off his chest. Maybe Willy would understand how, in defending himself, he had killed Willis McCord. Then he thought of all the police he had talked to and everyone else that he had lied to. Who would believe him?

"Okay . . . I'm sorry, Willy. You deserve to know. This Laval guy offered to sell me back the AMERI." The minute Blaylock said it, he knew it sounded stupid.

"That's all?" Will shook his head in disbelief. "That's wonderful. All you had to do was tell us or the police and go ahead with the contact. We could have filled the whole woods with police and nailed this guy." Willy started to pace the foyer nervously, thinking through the scenario. "Instead, you made some sort of an arrangement with this Laval to meet you at the marina while we all went into New York. Was the money in the BMW, Cliff?"

"No . . . I left a note. I refused him. I put him off. I insisted on getting the AMERI first."

"You refused him? You didn't tell us about your plans. Then

you went into New York to talk to O'Reilly with the two of us, leaving Ginny totally out in the cold, back in the marina. She was a sitting duck for Laval who saw your car and probably thought you were on the boat. Right?"

"Yeah, Willy, I guess that's about it."

Willy stopped pacing right in front of him. "The whole thing doesn't make sense. Why didn't you tell us? What were you afraid of? You're leaving out something, Cliff. I want to know what it is."

Blaylock closed his eyes and grimaced, then he stared down at his wet feet. Now was the time to make a clean breast of everything. But he couldn't make himself do it. "I guess I was just stupid, Willy . . . I was just stupid," he stammered, not making eye contact.

Gathering all his strength into one furious burst of motion, Willy slammed his fist against Blaylock's jaw, dropping him savagely to the floor.

"Willy! For God's sake, you could kill him!" Coley tried to step between Willy and Blaylock at the last instant, but was too late. Now he stood in front of Willy watching Blaylock on the floor, moaning and spitting blood. "Good, very good, you didn't kill the son of a bitch." Coley looked at Willy who was grinning with satisfaction at seeing Blaylock writhing on the floor.

"That felt real good, Coley. The nerve of that lying jerk, putting Ginny in harm's way like that. Why don't you take a crack at him too, Coley. Be my guest."

"I'll take a rain check on that, old man. You've done your job well. Why don't we get out of here."

"And leave this mess for Sandy?"

"Don't worry, when he gets on his feet he'll have some sort of story to tell. He's good at that, Willy."

"I'm going back to the hospital and spend a little more time with Ginny. You might hang around for awhile and explain to that son of a bitch that we're staying on his case. I'm going to stay until I nail Laval for his assault on Ginny. I hope I find him before the police do. I owe him a little damage. I swear, Coley, if I could get him in the right spot, I'd finish him."

"I'm sticking around too, Willy. This whole damn case is getting interesting. I feel the same way you do about Laval, but you can't go around busting people up like that. Settle down, pal." Blaylock groaned again and managed to push himself up on one elbow.

For the first time Willy stared at his muddy feet and wet trouser legs. "Where the hell's he been, I wonder?"

"Let's see. He told me that they were hosing down the streets over in Park Ridge."

"Really. That's only about a half mile from here. I'll check it out before I head for the hospital." Willy walked toward the door, Coley following him. "I just don't believe him," he whispered to prevent Blaylock from hearing. "Sandy might be pretty upset when she gets here. He'll blame the whole thing on me. I suspect the friendship is over anyway."

"Willy, I'm going to bring Sean O'Reilly up-to-date tomorrow morning. I think he ought to know about Cliff's effort to ransom the AMERI. Agreed?"

"Yep, we've got to play it square." Willy climbed in his car and headed back to the hospital.

His lights had just disappeared when Sandy Blaylock met him in her driveway coming home from her visit with Adrienne McCord.

"Hi, Coley, welcome back to Stag Creek. Adrienne told me that you met her at the Prospect Inn."

Coley decided to get his bad news over with fast. "Sandy, Cliff and Willy had a fight. Cliff's okay I think, but you might check him over."

"A fight!" Sandy looked dumbstruck. "I can't even imagine that."

"He'll be fine. I'd rather you get the story from him. I've got to be on my way. Ginny's in Nyack Hospital. Willy's on his way there. I may drop by."

"Hospital? What happened!"

"She got assaulted on the *Tashtego* by some goon, the same guy that stole Cliff's coins. I'd rather you get the rest of the story from Cliff. Good night, Sandy." Coley got in his car and drove away as Sandy entered the front door.

Coley glanced at the clock on the dashboard. As soon as he got to his hotel in Tarrytown, he decided he would call Adrienne McCord. He wanted to cash in the rain check for dinner tomorrow night.

31

The next evening, Red Irons sat in a dark corner of the Bee's Knees disco looking out on the crowd. The disco, attached to the Wellington Inn was jammed, even though the night was still young. There were a lot of suits and ties mixed with the more outlandish disco chic worn by many. The babes looked fancy, slick and clean, even though their dancing was down and dirty. The suburban crowd looked like money, lots of money. No wonder Heavy Laval had done so well in this neck of the woods.

Irons lit a cigarette for Lila. He had brought her along thinking that he would be more unnoticed with a date, tucked away in the corner. Lila, his favorite among Veronica's girls, was dressed down for this evening. Her tight black sheath, with black hose, blended in with the darkness. Her ample cleavage was held in check by a leotard she wore beneath the dress. Shoulder-length permed brunette hair was quite similar to many of those now twisting and gyrating to the disco beat.

"Red, I got news for you. This is not a Heavy Laval kind of place. What makes you think we'd find him here? Big and ugly as he is, I don't think he'd get past the bouncer." She licked her lips after every puff from the cigarette. Irons liked that. He decided that Veronica must give all her gals lessons in hot.

"Lila, baby, maybe you're right. But look at that guy over there." A tall, solidly built man with a fuzzy growth of beard stood at the bar, moving with the music. He wore a black leather jacket emblazoned with the legend, DILLIGAF.

"Biker," Lila murmured. "Do I look like I give a fuck?"

"What!" Red Irons gaped at her.

"Dilligaf, that's what it means."

"That's the trouble nowadays. You young chicks know a lot of things, including a lot of things you shouldn't know."

"Are you complaining, Mr. Red? I noticed there is only one bed in our room in this hot pillow joint." Lila rubbed knees with him under the table.

"You're probably right. I don't think Heavy would show up here either." Irons studied the crowd. "Heavy did a lot of business in velvet dumps though. I bet he had this joint covered by the kid who was knocked off. Now, business is way off, and a lot of stuff is missing. But I'll betcha Heavy's around somewhere trying to find a new talent. At first he even lied about the kid being his contact, tried to play dumb."

"It ain't hard for Heavy to play dumb." Lila nestled up and kissed Red Irons' ear, and then pulled back to stare at him. "Hey, you're handsome tonight. You never spiff up like this when you come into Hotzy's."

"Thanks, doll. That kind of talk will put you right on the midnight menu. But first we've got to do a little work. I want you to scout out the ladies' room a couple times, and mix around a little bit at the bar. See if anyone's doing anything but booze. No questions, just open your eyes."

"Sure boss, anything you say."

"After a while we'll take a look at a couple more places. I'll bet Heavy's roaming around these hills someplace."

"Mmm ... now there's some class. I think I could even do that." Lila nodded toward a tall woman, jet hair down to her waist brushed to a sheen that caught the spinning lights. She had a perfect face and wore the black jumpsuit like it was painted to a model's figure. Heads turned when she walked. "And I'll bet you that's money, too."

Red Irons stared at the striking woman, now standing at the bar, derierre moving subtly with the music. "Probably just another dumb young chick. Looks like she is by herself."

"I'll bet she's your age, Red. What do you want to bet?" Lila now locked her leg around his under the table.

"Who cares, babe. The world's full of beautiful stuff. We want Heavy Laval. There's a big difference." Red Irons leaned back in the booth, looking mesmerized by the undulating bodies and the monotonous heavy beat of the music. "Check out the ladies' room, baby. Stay awhile, see if there is any action. There's a steady parade in and out of there."

"Sure, boss. You just keep looking at the babes and get yourself all steamed up. You're gonna need all you got tonight to keep up with me." She probed her tongue into his ear for a moment and then left on her mission.

Red Irons stretched out in the booth and sipped his drink. Making this scene with Lila certainly beat the hell out of fighting off seasickness up in Port Jefferson. He slid his hand casually inside his jacket and felt the heft of the Glock snugly in its place. He wanted to get it over with Heavy as quick as possible. He liked the area. Lots of woods and lots of water around. Poor Heavy, a loner in the world. Nobody would miss him or even care.

He stared at the babes now bumping and grinding to a faster beat. Lila's a match for any of them he thought. Maybe not the tall black-haired dish who sat at the bar soaking up a martini. He had noticed that she turned several guys away.

Irons finished his drink, his eyes searching for Lila in the semidarkness. I guess she's still in the powder room, he thought. What in the hell was she doing in there? His eyes automatically went back to the fancy woman at the bar.

Now she had company. A tall, very tall, black man was standing at her elbow. They were chatting. He was drawn to the appearance of the tall man. He wore fancy duds. Broad shoulders were obvious under a sport jacket that was cut a tad too big, draping loosely under his arms. Red stared at him. He would bet he carried a piece.

The tall man, standing next to the dish, turned toward her, his face catching a bit of the spinning light. Red Irons stiffened to attention. No, it couldn't be, he assured himself. Except that it was! It was the same tall dude he had seen down on Ninth Avenue talking to Peaches a few hours ago! Now what were the odds against something like that? He was thirty miles away from Hotzy's. There must be a thousand watering holes between here and there. And here was the same athletic-looking tall dude.

Irons slumped down in the booth, and sipped at his empty glass. There was little likelihood that the guy would be able to spot him in the dim light. Irons wondered idly if the man had followed them there. It seemed impossible. He rejected the thought. He decided the guy had to be a cop.

There was Lila at his ear again. "Hi boss, still getting an eyeful?"

"Sorta. Where the hell you been? You've been gone long enough to turn a couple of tricks." Irons frowned at her as she again wrapped her leg around his.

"Geez! Is that all you think about? I've been getting an earful from the chicks in the john. I locked myself in my private little stall and heard more grungy dirt than you can imagine."

"Like what?" Irons asked, still watching the tall guy and the fancy babe.

"They're really pissed off. They're having trouble getting their noses full. Seems the stuff used to be all over this place. Now a good time is hard to find."

"Yeah, we know all about that, baby. What else?"

"Seems that all the action is over at a place called Sweetie's on Route 17. Don't ask me where that is."

"Good work, Lila. See that tall guy at the bar . . . I mean the really tall guy."

"How could I miss a hunk like that? He's talking to Miss Fancy Ass. What about him?"

"Ever see him before?" Now the tall man was smiling. Apparently they were having a pleasant conversation.

"Nope. I would remember something like that. I'll bet he's a basketball player." Lila studied his face as he turned, almost facing them.

"I think he's a cop. I'll bet you a sneak under the covers that he's got a piece under his left shoulder." Irons shook his head. He couldn't buy that the tall dude's presence was a coincidence. "Tell you what I want you to do. Wiggle over there and try to work your way next to them. See if you can pick up a word or two. It's gonna be tough with this damned music. Break in and ask a few dumb questions. Smile and turn on the charm. Maybe you'll get real lucky. They both might want your body." Irons leered at her.

"Red, don't be a creep. You want information, I'll get information. Just leave it to me to figure out how." Lila stopped talking as Irons pushed himself out of the booth.

"I'm going up to the room. When you find out all you can, join me. Then we'll take a quick look at Sweetie's over on 17." Irons left the room without looking back.

Alone in the booth, Lila fixed her attention on the two at the bar. She didn't like cops. If the guy was a cop, what the hell was she supposed to do. If it was just some guy chasing a skirt, she could handle it. She got up and made her way between the dancers and squeezed next to the tall black man, now bending close to the ear of the woman. No way in hell that she could hear much of anything over the din of the disco music.

"Sir! Excuse me, please!" She pushed her way to the bar, shoving her breast against the tall man's arm.

"Well, excuse me. I just bet you're trying to get the bartender's attention." Coley looked down at her and broke into a smile. "Be my guest." Coley stepped behind Adrienne's bar stool. As he turned she pressed close to him, her arm firmly against his jacket. Coley tensed, as he eyed her sharply, still affecting an affable smile. He had had women do that before. It was a move to determine whether or not he carried a gun.

"Did you find out what you wanted to, young lady?" Coley returned her stare without blinking.

"Yeah, big man. It turns me on. My name's Lila." She turned on a warm smile.

"Well, now, Lila is a pretty name, isn't it, dear?" Coley turned toward Adrienne and winked. In the process he could clearly see that the red-bearded man was no longer in the booth. Incredible! thought Coley. A patron from the sleazy joint in Chelsea in this place at this time. He remembered that red beard that sat next to Heavy Laval. There couldn't be two like that.

"Lila is a pretty name." Adrienne looked her right in the eye and went along with Coley's little game.

"Now, Lila, my friend and I are leaving, so you will be the lucky one to inherit our bar stool, and hopefully the bartender also." Coley nodded toward Adrienne and the two of them headed for the door before Lila could say anything else.

Adrienne spoke as they hurried to Coley's rental Buick outside. "What in the world was that all about? Not that it matters. It's a poor place to have conversation. I hadn't been there in a long time. My, how it has changed."

As they left the parking lot of the hotel, Coley checked his mirrors carefully to see if they were being followed. He decided they weren't. He swung onto the Palisades Parkway. "Okay, Adrienne. I've had enough excitement. I guess I'm not used to brazen young ladies like that. Next time let's make it a nice quiet place, where we can hear each other without shouting."

"Coley, I'm sorry I suggested the Wellington. But it was close by and it used to be quiet. Get off at the next exit. I know a nice quiet spot. Actually Lila was kind of cute. Poor thing, it takes all kinds I guess."

"Tell me, Adrienne, did you ever see her tall red-bearded companion before?"

"Companion? I thought she was alone. Where was he?"

"Watching us, sitting over in the dark. He and Lila locked tonsils once in a while."

Adrienne laughed. She seemed very much at ease. "My! You are a detective, aren't you? I missed all of that. Why do you suppose she bothered to talk to us?"

"Adrienne, I promise I will tell you that some day, when I know myself."

"Is it so important?"

"It could be. I think I was being followed. You don't know how that upsets a private investigator. It upsets me so much that I'm taking you home. Believe me, that's hard to do. Can we do this again?"

"I look forward to it. You make me feel . . . comfortable." Adrienne leaned across the console and brushed a kiss along his cheek. "I just love a man who knows when and how to take charge. I trust you, Coley." Then she fell back in silence.

Coley didn't know quite what to make of it. He had heard of grieving widows being hot to trot now and then, but grieving mothers? And how about old Alex, way off in Seattle. Did he give a damn?

"Coley, I've made a decision and I'd like your opinion about it." Adrienne was looking away from him, pausing to take a long drag on a cigarette. "I found two briefcases filled with cocaine in

Willis's closet. They must weigh fifteen or twenty pounds. I'm turning them over to the police in the morning."

"Adrienne, don't tell another living soul. Contact the police and get it out of your house as quickly as possible. Show them where you found it, and let them pick it up."

Adrienne held her head in her hands, trying to hold back tears. Coley leaned over and held her gently for a few moments.

He glanced at the clock on the dash. It wasn't eleven o'clock yet. Buster's Hotzy Topless would be open for hours. And Tracy would be there till two. He had to find out who the red beard was. He was sure that Tracy would know. She might even know more about Heavy Laval.

32

Peaches arrived in Bocco's stateroom dressed in flaming red short shorts and a mini halter that had difficulty containing her well-endowed female form. Veronica, garbed in a similar black satin version, sat at a small bar sipping a Grand Marnier from a snifter while leafing through a stack of papers. If she noticed Peaches making her entrance, she gave no indication of it.

"Peaches, I want you to meet Judge Roy. He's a good friend of ours from upstate." Bocco paused to emit one of his rare chuckles. "He's gonna be our guest for the evening here in Port Jefferson. Judge, Peaches here is in charge of making you happy. You name it, you got it. You'll find her very accommodating."

The man introduced as Judge Roy was easily three hundred pounds of grinning obesity. "Peaches is it? That's my favorite kind of snack." The monstrous man guffawed loudly at his own idea of a joke. "My, my, you're somethin'. I never saw anything the likes of you down in Carolina."

"Well, thank you, Judge." She noticed that he was cradling an empty glass in his palm. "How about me fixing you a fresh drink. What are you having?"

"That would be right nice. Chivas, right out of the bottle, no ice or nothin'."

As Peaches walked over to the bar, Veronica kept right on reading the papers, still not acknowledging her presence.

"Here, Judge, how's that?" Peaches bent over to hand him his drink. The man's eyes locked on her barely contained bosom.

"That's just fine, young lady. Say, maybe you just better call me Roy. We'd best forget the Judge part right now."

"You're the boss, Roy." Peaches giggled nervously. "I think everybody ought to be called just what they want."

Bocco stood up abruptly. "I'm going up to the radio shack for a while. You guys get on with it. We'll talk a little later."

The instant Bocco left the stateroom, Veronica got up, walked over and threw the bolt on the door. She turned and winked at the judge. "A little privacy, Mr. Roy, just a little. Okay?"

"That's fine."

"Peaches, I need you for a minute in the other room." Veronica paused long enough to turn on some soft rock, and then followed Peaches into a small adjoining galley. "Peaches, Bocco is really upset. They've been looking everywhere for Heavy. We can't find him. You know him better than anyone. Bocco thinks you two guys were too close not to know a lot about each other. You better strain the brain kiddo, while you're working on this guy. Bocco's getting very impatient."

"While I'm working on this guy?" Peaches looked at her questioningly.

"Yes, that's what I said. This guy's very important. Bocco wants him happy."

Peaches shrugged. "The way he's pouring down the Scotch, he's soon gonna be out of it."

"Not likely! He's been thinking about this all afternoon."

Peaches grimaced. "Well, I'll try. As soon as you get out of here I'll damn well try."

"Not possible, not possible at all, dear. The judge has a specialty." Veronica reached for a dimmer switch and brought the cabin lights down to a mere glow. "You see, his specialty is oral sex, with a watcher."

"With a watcher?"

"You got it kiddo. I'm the watcher."

Up on the bridge of the *Jersey Trick*, Bocco had finally established contact with Red Irons' cellular phone. "Hey, what the hell is going on? For your sake, I hope you've found the son of a bitch."

"Not yet. But, Bocco, there's something crazy going on up here in Bergen County. There's this big tall black guy. He must be near seven feet. I saw him down in Hotzy's the last time I saw Heavy. Less than an hour ago, I saw him here at the Wellington Inn. That's where some of Heavy's inventory finished up in the red Corvette. The SB is around here someplace. I'd bet on it."

"That ain't good enough, Red. You haven't got a lot of time left. We've got to find Heavy before the cops do. It's your funeral, pal. It ain't mine. Let me talk to Lila."

"Lila isn't here. She's down in the disco. I sicced her on the tall guy. Maybe we'll find out something soon."

"I want you and Lila right where you are until you find Heavy Laval. I expect you to have him by the time I pull into Nyack with the *Jersey Trick*. That's less than forty-eight hours. Hey, he can be living or dead. But either way I want him. Reasonable, huh?"

"Sure, Bocco. Don't worry about nothin'." When Red Irons

hung up the phone, a shaking hand rattled the phone in its cradle. He had just had a terrible thought. What if the cops had already picked up the bastard? There was no doubt in his mind that Heavy would play canary if it meant saving his skin.

33

Buster's place was boiling with action. Coley groaned. Cutting short his abbreviated date with Adrienne to check out Buster's was indeed going from the sublime to the ridiculous. But duty called. He had to know who the red-haired guy was. Adrienne had been a real sport about it.

The late night crowd from an undertakers' convention up on Thirty-second had gone south for whatever nightlife they could find. Coley wedged himself between two black suits at the bar and read the prominent convention badge of the mortician sitting next to him. Coley decided to ask him a question that he had thought about many times. "Hello friend, my name is Doug Johnson. I've always wondered why a man would go into your type of business."

The slight pale man pulled his eyes away from Pussy LaFrance, who was undulating her way along the bar, and studied the tall, athletic-looking black man next to him. The sharply dressed man looked very much out of place in Buster's topless joint. "When I was heading for college, my father drove me all around this little town in Iowa where I still live. He showed me all his bank accounts, and he showed me all the property he owned. He pointed out all the people that were probably going to die before I would finish my education. It was a no-brainer. I opted for being rich, and being able to come to places like New

York and seeing something like this." He nodded toward Pussy Lafrance, the tiny Oriental dancer now in front of them.

Coley actually respected the man for being candid, but if it were himself in from Iowa with a pocket full of money looking for a good time, Buster's Hotzy joint would be at the bottom of the list. "Thanks, pal. I hope it was worth the trip, but I guess Uncle Sam eventually pays. Tell you what. I'll bet if you slide a twenty under her garter, you might see something you just won't see every day back in Dubuque." Pussy Lafrance had overheard and gave Coley a smile and a wink of recognition just as Tracy the barmaid approached.

"I caught ya, handsome, making eyes at Miss LaFrance. Shame on you. There's not enough woman there for you at all." Tracy slid a Coors across the bar. "It's on me. I like it when old friends come back."

"Thanks, Tracy. I didn't know we were old friends."

"You just hang around till two o'clock and see how friendly I can be."

"What about Peaches? I ain't no two-timer." Coley saw her smile vanish for just an instant.

"I'll bet you've got our little Peaches tucked away somewhere, haven't you?"

"Nope. Life's been rotten."

"Peaches flew the coop. She hasn't showed up for work for a couple of days. It's not like her. She was pretty reliable for her kind. They do come and go in that profession. They get all messed up with money and men." Tracy stepped back so Pussy LaFrance could aim a few bumps his way.

Coley ignored the diminutive dancer, sorry to hear he had wasted the trip into town. "What about that gorilla of a boyfriend?"

"Heavy? Heavy must be in trouble. He's got more guys looking for him than I can count. He just plain don't come in. Maybe he and Peaches flew the coop together, though the last time I saw

Peaches she swore she wouldn't have anything more to do with him. Heavy used her for a punching bag once too often."

Coley groaned to himself, thinking of the beating Ginny had taken up on the *Tashtego.* "Guys like that deserve the worst, and eventually get it. Heavy live around here?"

Tracy lifted her eyes and stared at Coley. "You ask too many questions, Mr. Doug Johnson. You're a damn cop for sure, aren't you?" Then she leaned over the bar and whispered, "Don't get me wrong. The best lay I ever had I got from a cop. But if you want to ask questions, you can't do it here. No telling when and if we have company in this joint." Tracy moved down the bar to serve other customers.

Coley sat for awhile, hoping that maybe Peaches or Heavy Laval would wander in. But no such luck. He should have stayed at the Wellington. He had the distinct feeling that he had disappointed Adrienne, and that if it were up to her, he fantasized that they would be getting it on about now.

He pulled a fifty dollar bill from his wallet and folded it neatly into a small rectangle and then signaled to Tracy. "You ever get a day off, doll?"

"Only Sundays, and I have a rule. Never on Sundays."

Coley positioned the bill in his palm where she could clearly see the number fifty. "One more question?"

"You are a persuasive man, Doug. For you I might even break my Sunday rule." She quickly glanced around her to see if anyone were paying attention.

"The last time I was in here, Heavy came in and sat next to a guy with a red beard. He looked like he visited a barber frequently, and he packed a heater. I could tell. Who was that man?"

"You must mean Red Irons. I think he might own a piece of this joint with Buster, but I'm not sure. The rumor is he has big connections. I ain't about to say anything else, because I don't know anything else, and I don't want to know."

"Connections with dope?" Coley whispered.

Tracy stared at him in silence. It was obvious that he had pushed her as far as she was going to go. "Thanks Tracy." he enclosed the fifty in her palm. "I'll see you again real soon, and we'll celebrate."

"Celebrate what?"

"The best lovin' you ever had in your life. I'm not about to be outdone by some cop," Coley lied.

Coley left Hotzy's and decided to take a quick look at the precinct station to see if he were lucky enough to catch Sean O'Reilly. No such luck, he would have to ask Sean about Red Irons at some other time.

He returned to the parking lot, picked up his car and drove west until he reached the Henry Hudson Parkway going north toward his hotel in Tarrytown.

It was about one A.M. when he dialed Willy's cellular phone as he drove, deciding that he had to find out how Ginny was doing. Willy wouldn't mind. He answered on the first ring. "Hi pal, how's Ginny?"

"Feeling damn good, but they're keeping her one more day. She is flaming angry about this Heavy Laval creep. He caught her in a position where she couldn't reach her automatic. I think she would have killed him in an instant. I think the whole incident has turned Ginny into a vigilante. God help the next guy who tangles with her."

Coley brought Willy up on the events of his day. "This Red Irons guy seems to be some sort of a big mucky-muck. If he is, I'm sure that O'Reilly can fill us in. Hey, I hope you are keeping your eyes peeled there in the marina."

"One of the local cops has stationed himself in the lot. My .38 is in the side-keep six inches from my hand. I hope Laval comes back."

"He seems to have disappeared. I think our best chance is to nail him when he tries to contact Blaylock again. Have you heard from Blaylock since you did the dental work? Jesus, Willy, that wasn't nice at all."

Willy could hear Coley chuckling. "I haven't heard from him. I called Sandy this morning to apologize. Blaylock wasn't there and she didn't know where he was. She was pretty cool toward me, but did say that Cliff hadn't been himself for quite a while. He don't know how lucky he is that Ginny is going to be okay. I haven't lost my temper like that in a long time. To tell you the truth, it felt good. I still can't figure Blaylock out. We're missing a part of the puzzle for sure."

"I've decided one thing, Willy. I'm going to stick around here until I'm an old man if I have to. Everything else is on the back burner till we nail Heavy Laval."

"Glad to hear you say that, Coley. You know how I feel. But it's obvious you have additional motivation."

"And what could that be?"

"Well, let's see. It is an interesting case. There's Adrienne, there's Peaches, there's Tracy, and now there's a Lila. According to you, they're all lookers. I think it's time to bring Marissa up to date."

"Pal, God is putting me to the test. And I am as pure as the driven snow." Coley decided to put a question to Willy that had bothered him for a while. "Willy, if you don't mind, I think it's time for us to have a chat with the Stag Creek police, and see if they have turned up anything on the robbery. Also, I wonder if there has been any progress on the homicide of Blaylock's neighbor at the Wellington Inn. The whole story seems to have vanished from the press."

"Be my guest. I've been thinking about that, but keep in mind that the McCord kid was killed in another jurisdiction. Actually I'm sure the local police are interested, but the other town in New Jersey would be directly involved. I doubt if they would have

much interest in the robbery in Blaylock's driveway. Give it some
thought and we'll talk later today."

After Coley hung up, he couldn't rid himself of the thought
that the two crimes were connected. But it remained a hunch and
nothing more.

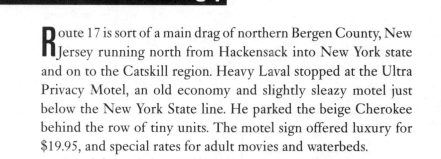

34

Route 17 is sort of a main drag of northern Bergen County, New
Jersey running north from Hackensack into New York state
and on to the Catskill region. Heavy Laval stopped at the Ultra
Privacy Motel, an old economy and slightly sleazy motel just
below the New York State line. He parked the beige Cherokee
behind the row of tiny units. The motel sign offered luxury for
$19.95, and special rates for adult movies and waterbeds.

Laval figured that Cliff Blaylock knew his vehicle by sight.
But the Cherokee was registered to Peaches Collins. He doubted
if anybody knew that but him. He had used her established credit
to buy the vehicle only a few months ago.

Blaylock was due to show up early in the morning and leave
his parked car a quarter of a mile down the road as he had been
instructed in the latest drop-off in Blaylock's mailbox. No doubt
the silly bastard would be watching from somewhere around
when he picked up the hundred G's. But that didn't bother him.
If Blaylock were going to the police, he would have done it long
ago.

Laval opened the road atlas, and traced his finger along the
intended route to Florida. He would be on his way seconds after
Blaylock made the drop. Too bad Peaches had screwed up. He
could have banged her all the way to Florida, he reflected, won-

dering what they had done with Peaches. He vowed that someday he would get even with Red Irons.

Right now he had no options. When Irons delivered the
twenty kilos, he had wanted cash on the barrelhead. The McCord
kid had screwed him out of it. All he had was the money from the
gold, and the expected payoff from Blaylock. If the newspapers
were right about the stuff they found in the Corvette, there was
a lot more stashed somewhere. But the kid was dead and there was
no way Red Irons would buy any further excuses. So it was time
for a long overdue paid vacation. The alternative was to join Percy
LeRoy, deep under the Narrows Bridge.

Laval fell sound asleep during the second running of *Ten
Coeds and Their Slave*. Their slave was continually running out of
gas. Too bad they didn't use a real man like himself for the role,
he thought, thinking of the night he and Peaches had kept it up
all night long.

At six A.M. came the loud jangle of his wake-up call. He took
the nine millimeter Glock from under his pillow and stuffed it
into his jacket hanging on a chair next to him. Within five minutes he was inside the Cherokee, inching around the side of the
motel until he could see the broad shoulder of six lane Route 17,
which ran in front of a used car dealer at that point.

It was there! Blaylock's BMW was parked right where it was
supposed to be. From where Laval sat, it looked empty. He
scoured the surrounding terrain. Except for an occasional semi
rolling down Route 17 there was little activity anywhere at this
hour. He pulled the Cherokee out of the driveway and proceeded
cautiously toward the apparently empty BMW.

He stuffed the Glock into his waistband, fastening the bottom
portion of his zippered jacket to conceal it. Then he continued
driving until he was directly behind the BMW. Waiting until
there was no traffic behind him, he left the Cherokee, walked a
few paces and opened the door of Blaylock's car. He reached
under the seat and produced a heavy manila envelope that was

fairly hefty with its contents. Again glancing nervously about as he walked, he climbed back into the Cherokee.

Laval pulled around the BMW and sped toward the crest of the hill on the roadway ahead of him, glancing frequently into his rearview mirror. The BMW stayed right where it was and there was still no traffic behind him once he cleared the crest of the hill. He made a right turn as soon as he could and sped along a winding side road feeling totally confident that he had not been followed.

Heavy pulled into the small parking area in front of a convenience store, feeling it was time to celebrate with a coffee and a bag of donuts before he proceeded on his way. First he picked up the fat envelope and ripped the sealed end. There was a small roll of newspaper enclosing a smaller unsealed envelope. Panic started to build. It just wasn't thick enough to contain a hundred G's.

He began to finger through stacks of crisp new hundred dollar bills. His count stopped abruptly at one hundred. He stared off into the distance, finally deciding that he held ten thousand in his hand. It was a far cry from a hundred thousand.

Laval peeked in the envelope and unfolded a small typewritten note. "If you leave me the coin, I will deliver the rest of the money at the same spot, same time, in forty-eight hours."

"The nerve of that bastard!" Laval bellowed in rage inside the Cherokee. His hand went to his pants pocket, and produced the AMERI. The once pristine, but soft copper coin showed several scratches from being jangled around with other pocket change. He grimaced at the artifact with rage. "I'll fix that son of a bitch," he vowed aloud as he gripped the hilt of the gleaming Glock in his waistband. He stared down in the seat at the stack of hundreds. The oversized portrait of Ben Franklin evoked an evil smile. He would milk the bastard for every dime he had on earth. Then he would kill him.

Laval went inside and bought coffee and a sack of chocolate-covered donuts. As he perfected his plans for the future he sat in the Cherokee and sipped coffee and munched at the donuts until he had eaten the whole bag.

Actually he had a big advantage over Blaylock. The only time he had ever seen him face to face, Blaylock was staring at a ski mask. Blaylock had never seen his face. Hell, this would be like taking candy from a baby. Blaylock must be scared shitless to even part with the ten grand so easily.

Laval reached into a pants pocket and produced a small pocketknife, then fished the AMERI out of the wad of change he carried in the other. He reasoned that it was too risky to peddle the coin to a coin dealer. Those bastards spoke a different language. He opened the smallest, but very sharp blade on the knife. Holding the AMERI flat against the armrest, he began digging at the soft copper. He continued until he had scratched the name WILLIS into the metal. It was crude, but unmistakably, WILLIS.

Laval admired his handiwork. Now the pipsqueak would know he meant business. He stuffed the ten thousand inside his jacket. Not a bad payday after all, he reasoned. And there was no cut to be paid to Red Irons. He decided that he would live high on the hog until the final payoff from Blaylock.

Heavy Laval exited the driveway of the convenience store and turned back to retrace the route he had just taken. By the time he passed the used car dealer, Blaylock's BMW was gone. He kept going north on Route 17 for awhile, then turned eastward over a network of winding rural roads.

Finally, there it was! The Wellington Inn stood tall among the trees. He checked into a room, locked the door, and looked at his watch. He had a whole day to kill. He stolled over and looked out the window. He could see the beige Cherokee parked near the grove of trees at the end of the parking lot. Looking the other direction he could see the very spot where Cliff Blaylock had shot

Willis McCord. Good thing it was about dark on that day. Otherwise anyone looking out almost any room would have seen the kid get it.

The kid had no idea that Blaylock carried a gun. Laval remembered asking him pointedly whether or not the man would be armed.

He walked away from the window and looked at the movie menu sitting on the TV set. What luck! *The Ten Coeds and Their Slave, Part II.* Heavy Laval stripped, climbed into the sumptous king-size bed, and prepared to spend the day in luxury. He figured he was about fifteen minutes away from Blaylock's house.

35

The *Jersey Trick* pulled away from Port Jefferson about ten in the morning, and revved up to full speed, plowing down Long Island Sound toward Hellgate. Bocco Lamas sat at the helm steering the fast cruiser as Veronica stood behind him giving him a vigorous back rub. She continued until they passed through the churning waters of Hellgate and pointed south into the East River.

"Bocco, I thought we were headed north to the Tappan Zee. That's what you told me last night." Veronica resumed her massage.

"Big change in plans, baby. Heavy Laval has vanished. We've got to find the SB before the police do. They want to question him about a homicide in Chelsea. We're headed for Hoboken. We'll pick up a couple of the Miami boys and head for the Tappan Zee. We'll find a mooring near Nyack. We're going to turn that area upside down, find Heavy, and give him a long vacation. He's cost me and the boys a lot of dough."

"You gotta do what you gotta do, Bocco." Veronica sat down at a chart table on the bridge, crossing her long sleek legs toward Bocco. The bare legs and short shorts made quite a display.

"How'd Peaches get along with Judge Roy last night?" Bocco leered at Veronica, knowing the judge's preference. "I understand you were a witness."

"You'll be happy to know that Peaches is a champ. The judge is still sleeping like a log."

"Get him up and moving. We're going to dump him out in Hoboken. Our business up there is none of his business," Bocco growled, really not happy at the change in plans.

"What about Peaches? You leaving her in Hoboken?"

"Are you crazy? That little tootsie knows too much. She stays aboard. Even in Nyack she stays aboard. Down the line we might have to use her as bait for Laval."

"She might know a lot, Bocco, but she really isn't too bright. I don't think she has any idea what we're all about. She's good at her work though. The judge thought he was in heaven. I can picture her as one of our regulars out in the Hamptons this summer. With a little training, of course." Now it was Veronica's turn to smile at Bocco.

Bocco slowed the pace of the *Jersey Trick*. The East River was crowded with pleasure boats bound for a weekend on the sound. Several mid-size freighters probably bound for Bridgeport or New Haven were working their way up the busy channel. "No use pushing it baby. We don't want the Coast Guard on our ass." Bocco frowned at the small cutter making its way up the channel, the big red slash across the bow identifying it as a Coast Guard vessel.

"Bocco, you look worried. Usually after your massage in the morning, nothing bothers you." Veronica had heard one end of an early A.M. phone conversation. Evidently it had been bad news.

"We got problems, kid. That damned Laval was way over his head up there in the suburbs. If we don't get him out of circulation soon, we'll have to back out of a very lucrative area."

Veronica started her back rub again. "Want to talk about it?"

"Damn it, I couldn't sleep. I get this call from Chelsea. Some tall black character, they say he must be six foot seven or eight, and packs a heater, has been asking questions. First he pretended he had the hots for Peaches. Then he started nosing around for information on Heavy Laval."

"So, sounds like a cop, Bocco. It's probably just a cop trying to do his thing. Did you get a name?"

"Doug Johnson. Ever hear of him?"

"Nope. That should be easy to check."

"I did. The NYPD ain't got no such person of his name or description. That comes straight from the roster file." Bocco paused and lit a small cigar. "Last night this fellow comes into Buster's and asks around for Red Irons. All kinds of questions, like, who is he, and what business is he in."

Veronica shrugged. "Maybe he's checking credit. Or maybe he's a fed, or maybe somebody owes him some money."

"Veronica, I don't like the way he keeps climbing up the ladder. First it was Peaches, then Heavy, then Irons. Next time it might be me." Bocco stared at Veronica, blowing a perfect circle of smoke her way. "I've told the boys to get a tail on him the next time he shows. I think the boys maybe should teach him a lesson."

It was a beautiful fall day. By the time the *Jersey Trick* reached the tip of Manhattan, Judge Roy and Peaches had joined Bocco and Veronica on the aft deck. The judge steadied himself at the rail with his massive arm around Peaches. Battery Park, the Twin Towers, and the Statue of Liberty all passed their view before they pulled up to a ramshackle old pier near Hoboken. Bocco walked up to join them at the rail.

"Judge, I've got a limo waiting for you. They'll take you straight to Newark Airport." Bocco nodded to Peaches with a jerk of his head, that told her to get lost.

"Very good, Bocco, I enjoyed my visit." He leaned forward to whisper. "I'll do what I can when the parole hearings come up." The judge eyed Peaches wriggling away from them in a thong bikini. "When the hearings are over I'd like an encore with that one."

"You got it, Judge," Bocco said tersely, scowling at the bridge as the *Jersey Trick* bumped along the pier. Ahead of them he could see two men pushing a small hand truck along the pier.

Bocco walked Judge Roy to his limo and then returned to greet the two men who were preparing to move the contents of the hand truck aboard the *Jersey Trick*. Veronica walked over the gangway to join him.

"Veronica, these are the boys from Miami. This is Elvis and this is Crackers," Bocco said, still wearing his scowl.

She smiled a welcome, especially at Elvis, who actually looked quite a bit like the Elvis. Crackers was just like his name, wizened and dour, a skinny, humorless little man.

Bocco seemed more preoccupied with the huge beer cooler stowed aboard the hand truck. It took the strength of the two men to hoist the cooler onto the deck of the *Jersey Trick*. Elvis and Crackers then carried the cooler, following Bocco who led them to a hatch leading below deck. The three then disappeared from view and closed the hatch behind them.

Bocco knelt on the deck of the engine room and applied a small screwdriver to the floor panel. From all appearances it was riveted down, just like all the others. But the rivet heads were phony and the panel lifted easily on metal pegs set in the corners, revealing a compartment constructed in the bilge measuring about three feet by four feet.

"Okay, open it up," Bocco nodded toward the beer cooler. "I've got to know what the hell we've got aboard."

Crackers swung the cover back on its hinge. From his kneeling position Bocco viewed an arsenal that included four Uzis, two high-powered rifles, and several nine millimeter Glock handguns.

"What's in the boxes?" Bocco asked, pointing to the ten-inch-wide compartment running the length of the cooler, thickly padded with sheets of insulation.

Elvis grinned. "Charges, remote detonators, and enough hot stuff for a small war. There's two dozen hand grenades under the panel holding rifles."

"Good work!" Bocco enthused. "Where'd you get this stuff?"

"Brought it up from Florida last night. Crackers drove all the way. Crackers forgot how to sleep. Sometimes that comes in handy." Elvis chuckled. Crackers's face remained as lifeless as a cadaver.

"Okay, I don't want anyone aboard to know where this stuff is, even Veronica. You guys got that straight?" Bocco stared at the two men.

"You're the boss, Bocco." Elvis looked at Crackers who just nodded his head in agreement.

When the three emerged on the main deck, Veronica and Peaches were stretched out in deck lounges, soaking up the late afternoon sun. Veronica crossed her long legs and smiled at Elvis. "We met in Miami, remember?"

"I like to forget the past, lady. I made a stupid mistake. Now I make sure whoever I hit on isn't the boss's squeeze. Live and learn." Elvis grinned, switching his attention to Peaches.

Bocco mustered one of his rare half smiles. "It's a damn good thing you learn fast, kid. You're here in Jersey because you're an expert at one thing. And it's got nothing to do with that thing in your pants."

Elvis wandered away and lit a cigarette near the life rail. Bocco looked at Crackers. If Crackers had the ability to move a facial muscle, he hadn't yet shown it. But what the hell did that matter? He was the best anywhere at blowing things up.

The *Jersey Trick* rumbled to life. Bocco stood and watched his crewman free the lines from the pier. He glanced up at the bridge and waved a signal to his skipper. The handsome motor yacht inched away from the dock and pointed out to the mid-Hudson where it turned north toward the Tappan Zee, some thirty miles away.

36

Cliff Blaylock groaned and gingerly probed at his swollen jaw. Since the night that Willy Hanson had slugged him, he had moved downstairs in the den. He fully understood Willy's loss of temper, and couldn't condemn him at all. That was a puzzle to Sandy who had actually wanted to call the police about the assault. Sandy's words still rang in her memory. "What kind of a friend is that? He assaulted you in your own home! Trying to buy your coin back from the thief was stupid. But it was your business. I'm sorry, Cliff. I don't want that man in our home again."

He had watched the clock on the desk turn through all the hours of the night. Sustained sleep was virtually impossible. Now it was becoming daylight. He walked into the bathroom, drew a glass of water from the tap, and took a couple of painkillers. Staring at himself in the mirror, he was pleased to see that the swelling had gone down somewhat, but the pain around the loosened teeth persisted.

"Cliff, where were you yesterday?" Sandy startled him. He turned to face her in the doorway to the den.

"What are you doing up at this hour?" Sandy stood red-eyed in her robe. She looked as if she hadn't slept either.

"I asked you a simple question, Cliff. Where were you yesterday? Don't answer me with another dumb question."

"I went into the office and got involved reading through a lot of stuff. I got home late and didn't want to bother you."

"That's not the truth, Cliff. I called your office repeatedly. No one saw you all day."

"Alright! Alright! I just drove around all day, trying to figure out a way to get out of this mess." There he was again, he reflected, putting another lie on top of all the others. "This... thug, the man who robbed us must be a maniac to do what he did to Ginny. I didn't have the wildest idea that it would happen ... I guess I'm afraid for us."

"Cliff, I think I'm going to go away for awhile. I'll go visit my sister. I realize that we have problems, but we have always faced our problems together. Now you go out and drive around all day alone. I don't believe you, Cliff."

"Then go visit your sister. Maybe that's the best thing." He couldn't face her and turned to stare out the window.

"Cliff, look at me! What is happening between us? We got robbed. So what!" Sandy walked over and stood next to him. "What if we had the McCords' tragedy to deal with? Adrienne has been seeing a shrink! I'll tell you that's the only reason I have stayed around this long, to spend time with her."

"I think that's wonderful, Sandy. But eventually she will accept what has happened. It's good that you have spent time with her." While saying that, Cliff was really thinking that it would be great if she would go away for awhile. "But now maybe it would be a good idea to go to your sister's for a few days."

"Cliff, do you think our problem really amounts to anything at all?" Sandy paused. Adrienne had told her not to tell a soul. But she knew that Cliff shared everything with her. "Do you know what Adrienne found hidden in her house yesterday?"

"What?" Cliff replied lifelessly, not at all expecting the answer he would provoke.

"Upstairs, in Willis's room, underneath a stack of luggage, she found two large briefcases that must hold twenty pounds of cocaine."

"Oh, no," Cliff murmured. "How can you be sure? Did you actually see it?"

"Yes, I saw it! Oh, Cliff, I am so afraid for her." Sandy put her arms around him as her eyes filled with tears.

In his own mind, Cliff began to see things clearly. The detective in New York had said that Heavy Laval was a pusher. Heavy had been Willis's partner in the robbery at the Wellington. A lot of cocaine had been found in Willis's red Corvette. What in the hell was he going to do? He thought of the ten thousand he had given Laval yesterday. Maybe he would be happy and go away. But more likely he would be furious, and return quickly.

"So what in the world is she going to do with what she found, Sandy?"

"She's going to turn it over to the police, maybe today. Obviously, she just can't let it lie there. It's got to be worth thousands, God knows how much!" Sandy dried her eyes on the sleeve of her robe. "So see, honey, our problems are nothing compared to what they have next door."

Cliff became nauseous. The more he thought about his escalating problems, the more confused he became. Realistically he couldn't expect Heavy Laval to just go away. "Yes, Sandy, Adrienne, and Alex have gone through hell, and I guess it's not over. I want you to think about going to your sister's for awhile. I'll see if I can get back to my work and get all this out of my mind."

Sandy left his arms and walked toward the stairs. "Cliff, if it would help you sleep, come on upstairs. Please, I'd feel better."

"Okay Sandy, I'll be up in a little while."

Cliff looked outside again. The sky was cloudless and getting bright. It would be a perfect time to go back to the river where he had dumped his gun. It was so dark the other night that he couldn't make out a thing. The water in the upper Hackensack had virtually dried up during the autumn drought. It was scarcely a foot deep. He remembered exactly where he had dropped the gun within its pouch. He wanted to look again in the bright daylight. Finding it should be easy.

He picked up his car keys and walked outside. He glanced at the mailbox. He hadn't heard anything stir during the night. It was probable that there would be nothing in it. He decided to take a peek anyway. He walked to the end of his driveway and looked inside the rural box.

His heart started pounding at the sight of a small envelope with his name printed in crude block letters. He reached in, pulled out the envelope and opened it. Inside was a note. When he pulled it out, something dropped to the ground. It was the AMERI!

He bent down and picked up the coin, looking back toward the house. If Sandy was in their bedroom, she could see him. He quickly dropped the AMERI into his shirt pocket, then read the note. "Fool! Bring the rest of the money, same place, 6 A.M. Sunday. 90 G's."

Hands trembling, he stuffed the note into his pocket, and walked around the house to his BMW. He turned on the engine and sat for a moment, fishing the coin out of his shirt pocket. "Oh, my God!" he exclaimed aloud.

Ugly scratches dominated the previously mint-state coin. He turned it over to the obverse side, and gaped unbelievingly at Willis's name carved in the antique copper. It was ugly, so ugly, and now also virtually worthless.

He sat in the BMW for a long time before dropping the mutilated AMERI back into his pocket. Finally, he drove slowly out of his driveway down to where the road to Old Tappan crossed the Hackensack River.

Cliff drove a few yards beyond the short bridge and parked

his car on the broad shoulder where fishermen often parked. Walking back to the middle of bridge, he peered down into the water running in a shallow stream perhaps eight feet below the bridge. The smooth stones on the bottom were clearly visible. There it was! One oval stone looked different from the others. It was the special zippered leather pouch that held his gun. Unless one knew exactly what it was, it looked like another of the many round smooth stones that dotted the bottom.

An occasional car passed by, early commuters on their way to train stations, or small-business people heading for their shops. One car, a maroon Buick, crossed the bridge behind him, slowed down and parked just beyond his own car. The door opened, and out stepped Coley Doctor! Blaylock stiffened as he approached.

"Hey, Cliff, what the hell are you doing out here this time of day?"

Blaylock moved toward him, wanting to get as far away from the position where he had seen the gun case as possible. "Oh, it was a beautiful morning. I couldn't sleep. I decided I'd go get the morning papers. Just stepped out of the car to get some fresh air." Blaylock instinctively rubbed his sore jaw.

"How you feeling? My partner packs quite a punch." Coley stared at Blaylock. He was nervous. Why? Coley peered down into the small stream and then along the banks. "It's a beautiful spot."

"Yes," replied Blaylock. "I used to come down here as a kid and fish. In the spring, we used to catch trout here. What brings you back to town this morning?"

"The policeman who has your case, Detective Hinkle, is on duty this morning. I asked him if I could drop by and discuss a few things. Want to come along?"

Blaylock appeared to think about it for a moment. "No, Coley you go ahead. Sandy's alone. I better get back to the house. Bring me up to date if you find out anything." He started walking toward his car.

"Hey pal, you ain't keeping any more secrets are you? Willy

and I are anxious to get this case over with." Coley glared at him. Why was he so nervous?

Blaylock paused and shook his head, suddenly very conscious of the mutilated AMERI he carried. "No. I am really sorry about the whole thing. If I hear anything, I'll let you know."

"You do that," Coley advised. He watched Blaylock climb into his car and drive away. Coley peeked over the railing of the bridge once again, sweeping his eyes along the banks of the shallow little stream. Blaylock was a strange duck. He thought about other friends of Willy he had met over the years. Invariably he had liked them all. Blaylock was different, but then of course, he wasn't Willy's friend anymore.

37

It was nine A.M. when Willy picked Ginny up at the hospital in Nyack, almost straight across the Hudson from the *Tashtego*.

"Ginny, I hope you feel as good as you look. I've missed you." He leaned over the console to embrace her as they sat in the hospital parking lot. They were still locked in a kiss when a couple of nurses walking by their car gaped at their prolonged smooch.

"Willy! For heaven's sake. We are right out here in front of God and everybody!" Ginny smiled at the two nurses and squirmed over against her door. "I have a great idea. You can take me to breakfast. They were very nice to me there but I am famished for a big greasy breakfast. Sausage and eggs, with piles of buttered toast." Then we'll go back and start to work on the mess in the *Tashtego*.

"Good idea! I know just the spot. By the way, don't worry

about the *Tashtego.* I've got everything gleaming again. That big gorilla must have kicked over a can of varnish in the cockpit. Now that was a challenge! But I think it's okay now. You can take a look at the wiring on the ship-to-shore. It works, but picks up a lot of noise. Nothing appears to be permanently damaged."

Ginny sighed. "Willy, it's like two days were stripped right out of my life, just lying there with this roaring headache every time the painkiller would wear off. But now, I'm ready for action. When do we leave for the Virgin Islands?"

"Very soon, I hope. Coley and I want to help the police nail that bastard first. It shouldn't take long. He leaves footprints all over the place. He must be as dumb as he is vicious." He glanced at her as they drove back across the Tappan Zee Bridge. "Of course, if you want to leave right now, Coley can wrap up the investigation. He's out this morning meeting with the police jurisdictions involved. How do you feel about it?"

"I want to meet that guy face to face. I don't want any slip-ups at the arraignment. I guess the Virgins can wait a few more days. I always liked autumn sailing anyway."

"That's the spirit! Coley will appreciate our hanging around. He's done a bangup job so far." Willy fell silent for a few moments. "It's Cliff Blaylock that confuses me. I think Cliff has gone off his rocker. He's like a different person from the old Cliff I used to know. I guess I don't have a friend anymore. I guess I really lost it. But I'd say one smack in the jaw deserves another. At least I didn't put him in the hospital like that goon did to you."

Ginny stretched across the seat and kissed him. "Thanks lover. I think you were magnificent. If I were there and got the double-talk you did, I would have slugged him myself." She became silent as they passed by the toll booth. "You really should watch that temper though."

After breakfast at a diner near the exit in Tarrytown, they drove down the winding road to the marina. The *Tashtego* stood

magnificently handsome at the end of the long dock. The several
boats that had been tied up near her had been moved. A lone policeman sat in a cruiser near the entrance to the dock.

"The police feel terrible about this thing, Ginny. They evidently don't ever have that kind of trouble here."

"I'll have to apologize to them. I got pretty feisty when they
tried to get me in an ambulance. Actually they were right. I *did*
need help." They parked near the police car. "Hey Willy, take a
look at that."

A long sleek motor yacht passed near the jetty on the other
side of the marina. It continued slowly along the shore, the powerful engines rumbling in a near idle. The fancy yacht circled and
then pointed toward Nyack across the Tappan Zee. As it pulled
away, it was easy to read the large name written in script across
her transom. *The Jersey Trick, Weehawken, N.J.*

"Yeah, that's pretty nice. I wouldn't trade a dozen like her for
the *Tashtego* though."

"You mean I've finally made a real sailor out of you?" They
embraced again as the policeman smiled and gave them a thumb's
up for approval.

Once aboard the *Tashtego*, Ginny walked through the cockpit
into the main cabin, her eyes assessing the result of Willy's clean-
up job. "Great doll! You do good work. For the past two days I've
been worrying about this. When I left it looked horrible." She
walked over to the side keep until her hand touched her small .22
automatic, and then lifted it out to examine it. "Willy, I remember being just inches away from this when the bastard hit me. I
swear, he was an instant from being shot."

"Well, since you're okay now, maybe it's best this way. Actually shooting someone, no matter how much he deserves it, hangs
around to haunt you for quite a while. I know." His mind raced
back to a long-past adventure when he had to pull the trigger to
save their necks near the airport in Los Angeles. He could still
remember the look of shock and horror on the man's face. "From

now on, till we head for the Virgins, wherever you go, I go, and we carry our weapons."

"I wouldn't have it any other way."

"I think our problem will be gone in a day or two. The NYPD and three suburban police departments are working on the case. And this guy is stupid. The local police got some great footprints in the varnish up front. The bastard evidently wears a size fourteen."

"That's a lot of action for a driveway break-in, Willy."

"Well, there are drugs involved and maybe a murder down in Chelsea where his girlfriend tried to peddle the coin. Coley says the FBI is even in on it now. The robbery in Cliff's driveway is the least of it." Willy proceeded to bring her fully up to date on everything she had missed since going into the hospital.

The cellular phone signaled a caller. It was Coley. He had just finished a briefing with the Stag Creek detectives. "Willy, an insurance investigator has been talking to the police here. They just flat out don't believe Blaylock's version of the robbery in his driveway."

"You know something Coley, neither do I. Hey, Ginny's here. She looks great. When you coming over here?"

"Soon, Willy. I am going to stop off and talk to Blaylock again whether he likes it or not. On the way to the police station this morning, I saw him wandering around by a creek that runs through town. He acted funny. Of course, he always acts funny."

"What did he say he was doing?"

"Said he was just out to get some newspapers. Hell, it was six in the morning."

"Maybe he was. That was the most logical thing I've heard him say so far."

"He acted strange, Willy. I think he thought I had been following him. Actually I was on my way to the police station. This one long road through town passes right by the creek. I couldn't miss him."

Coley hung up. Willy walked forward where Ginny was
hunched over the deck that had taken the spill of varnish.

"Ugh, Willy, it's still sticky. It has to be sanded off and done
over. This one footprint is perfect. It looks like some kind of
sneaker."

"New Balance, size fourteen. The police have some dandy
pictures and measurements. Leave it there. It will remind us to
carry our artillery."

Straight across the Hudson, perhaps two miles away, the *Jersey
Trick* had picked up a mooring. Bocco stood on the bridge with a
pair of binoculars, sweeping back and forth along the coastline,
a hundred yards to his port. His skipper was assuring him that this
was what they had arranged for. "Yeah, this is the right mooring.
There is plenty of room for the boat to swing around here. This
is all tidal water. Right now the tide is going out, so we have our
portside to the shore. Later she'll swing around and the starboard
will face the shore."

"I know that, anybody knows that. You think you can teach
me about boats?" Bocco snarled at the captain. "If you want to ed-
ucate some dummies, talk to the broads."

"I'm sorry Bocco. I didn't mean anything by it. I just wanted
to assure you that later on, your cabin will face the shore as you
wanted it." The captain turned away. He had never seen Bocco
quite so surly as he had been on this trip. Sometimes he wished
he had never hooked up with the *Jersey Trick*. He wistfully eyed
the big sailboat towering above the jetty over in Tarrytown. Now
there was a vessel he would relish commanding!

He pulled his eyes away from the idyllic ketch and turned toward the business of lowering the small runabout. Bocco had
told him that he and the two hands from Miami would be going
ashore in the late afternoon. He would first go in and make certain that all the proper arrangements were made with the small

marina for ground transportation. He instinctively didn't care for the boys from Miami. He had seen killers before. The little guy called Crackers was a dead ringer for Percy LeRoy, now looking up at the Narrows Bridge, swinging around and around with the tide.

38

Red Irons scanned the parking lot from his fourth floor window at the Wellington Inn. Lila was sound asleep. The bucolic change from Hoboken and Manhattan unnerved him. It was 5:45 A.M. on Sunday morning and nothing stirred in the broad parking lot below or in the wooded hills around it. The lavish yellows, reds, and rust-colored fall foliage painted a picture foreign to him.

About a dozen cars were widely scattered on the broad expanse of blacktop. When the Bee's Knees disco closed early Sunday morning, and the corporate tenants of the hotel sent their seminar participants back home, the Wellington Inn was virtually empty. The few tenants remaining in the hotel slept in, evidently happy in their planned isolation.

A lone figure emerged from under the canopy in front of the Wellington's entrance beneath Irons's room and started walking briskly across the blacktop. The husky man wore a loose fitting parkalike jacket with the head cowl pulled down and bunched at the back of his neck. Red Irons's eyes followed every step of the only pedestrian in the lot. In the beginning, it was because he created the only movement in the lot. Yet the bulky man's stride had a familiarity to it. Lila mumbled something from the bed, momentarily distracting him.

"Red, please close the drapes. What are you doing up? We just went to bed."

"It's creepy around here Lila. It's like we're in a big cemetery and everybody is dead." Irons glanced again at the figure in the parking lot, now probably a hundred yards away. Ahead of the man was a tan-colored heavy duty vehicle parked next to the woods.

He squinted, trying to see more clearly. It was a Cherokee, he decided. He rubbed at his eyes furiously. When the man unlocked the door to the Cherokee, he turned toward the hotel for an instant, then climbed in. If it wasn't Heavy Laval, it was someone who looked just like him!

Red Irons stood up, nose to the window, as the vehicle began to weave its way through the maze of ornamental plantings that separated the lot into different sections. Soon it found the long driveway and sped away from the hotel and onto the winding rural road. It quickly disappeared.

The last view Red Irons had of the Cherokee, was of the spare tire, mounted considerably off-center in the rear. Irons sprang into action, pulling on his clothes amidst a stream of invectives. "Heavy Laval, that two-bit bastard! Lila, he just left the hotel in the Cherokee. It had to be him!" He pulled on his shoes and stuffed his Glock into his jacket.

"Red, relax, it can't be him. What in the hell would Heavy be doing in a place like this?" Lila sat on the edge of the bed as Irons opened the door to the room.

"Baby, you stay put till I get back. Lock the door. Don't let anybody in the room." He shook his finger menacingly at her as he left the room. "Get yourself dressed. We may have to blow this dump fast."

"Red, for God's sake, I just got to sleep. If it was him, he's gone." Irons, ignoring her protest, slammed the door and bounded down the hall toward the elevators.

Once outside, Irons began jogging toward the black Lincoln

parked well away from the hotel, placed in its remote spot because of the crowded lot when the Bee's Knees was jammed the night before. About midway to it he stopped and stared down the road to the point where the Cherokee had disappeared. If it had been Laval, he had to have a ten minute jump on him. Another vehicle passed lazily down the road.

Lila was right. The impossibility of a successful pursuit was obvious. He walked on slowly toward the Lincoln. Now that the crowd was gone from the night before, he decided to move the Lincoln close by the hotel, directly under the windows of his room. Fumbling in his jacket pocket he produced his car keys. He paused for a moment, looking back at the hotel. Lila stood at the window on the fourth floor.

He waved almost imperceptibly and then unlocked the door and climbed behind the wheel. Lila, he had long ago decided, was sort of a dumb bitch, but she was loyal. He looked up at the room again. Lila still stood there. Even though she didn't know it, he thought, in ten minutes they would be screwing again; but first he just had to repark the car. Grinning at the prospect of returning to the room, he rubbed at his unshaven red stubble with his left hand and turned the key in the ignition.

A whoosh! And then a deafening roar filled the Wellington Inn parking lot. Black smoke billowed aloft and the vehicle became engulfed in sheets of flame as shards of glass and bits of metal sprayed the landscape in every direction. Red Irons, frozen in his stance at the wheel quickly became a shriveled, charred cinder.

Behind a stand of trees, down the main road, a few hundred yards away, Crackers crouched behind the wheel of a rental car alongside the road. His frozen, cadaverlike visage, broke into a broad grin and a gurgling, maniacal sound that was his version of ecstatic laughter filled the air.

Lila screamed in her room as the concussion from the blast rattled the window in front of her. She stared at the car, now only occasionally visible between the billowing clouds of smoke, and scanned the area around the car in the hope of seeing Red Irons. Then, in the shifting smoke, she glimpsed the shattered windshield of the burning automobile, distinctly seeing a dark mass huddled behind the wheel. She screamed again, and with her pulse pounding began to dress in furious haste.

Stepping again to the window, she now saw perhaps a half-dozen people standing in the parking area, all a considerable distance from the flaming vehicle. In the distance she could hear the sound of fire equipment moving toward the hotel. A succession of police cars began arriving. The quiet, idyllic fall day had been turned into the worst of nightmares.

Now dressed, Lila stood again at the window looking at the scene below. She didn't know what to do next, go downstairs and join the growing crowd outside, or stay where she was. She sat on the edge of the bed and continued to observe the fire, soon transformed to a pillar of steam as the firemen trained hoses on the remains of the car.

A thought crossed her mind that started her retching and trembling violently. Whoever was responsible for the explosion would have likely reasoned she would also have been in the car with Red Irons. That would have been the plan!

Fear gripped her. She started again studying the faces one by one in the parking lot trying to identify someone she knew. Her own judgment told her that this had to be Bocco's work, and once they found she was still alive, she would be next.

But why? She was a nothing in Bocco's vast organization. Veronica had picked her out to accompany Irons. She had always figured Veronica as a friend. The blatant murder performed before her eyes on the parking lot below reminded her of her relationship with Bocco. She knew a lot more than she wanted to know about Bocco. Veronica had told her a lot of things when they were together. After all, Veronica selected her to be with Irons.

She looked around the room, thinking only one thing. She had to disappear, and quickly. She immediately gathered everything she had brought with her together and tossed them into the large leather tote bag that had served as her luggage. Irons had told her it would be only an overnight stay.

Next she went through the few belongings that Red Irons had left in the room. Unzipping his shave kit, she smiled weakly. Fingering quickly through a wad of money, she counted over fifteen hundred dollars, and then stuffed it into a zippered compartment within her leather bag.

The shoulder holster to his Glock hung on the closet door. She figured he probably had stuffed the weapon into his waistband.

Again she sat on the edge of the bed and stared out the window. The crowd in the parking lot was now quite large. Sightseers, attracted by the explosion and smoke had pulled off the main road to watch the unusual Sunday morning show. Policemen were sealing off a large area around the remains of the smouldering vehicle with bright orange cones and wide yellow tape.

Lila stared again at the faces in the crowd one by one, hunting for someone familiar to her. She recognized no one. She felt alone and more afraid than she had ever been in her life.

Now she focussed on one thought. She decided to get to an airport. Red's wad of money would get her anyplace in the country. California came to mind. She would hide away in some obscure corner of LA, and start a new life. But first she had to get to an airport.

Now she moved closer to the window where she could look straight down and see the people standing in front of the Wellington Inn. Standing with arms folded was the hunk, the tall, sharply dressed black man she had met the night before at the Bee's Knees with Miss Fancy Ass. He was just standing and watching, apparently detached from the activities of the many local police and firemen.

Could he be Bocco's man? She thought not. He had sure

looked her over. If he hadn't been with Miss Fancy Ass, she thought she might have had a positive reaction to her come on. Maybe he would be worth a shot. Hell, all she was looking for was a trip to the airport. Bocco would be checking everywhere once he learned she didn't die with Irons. She looked out the window again at the incinerated car and wondered if it were possible to identify any remains.

Lila found a plastic laundry bag in the closet and stuffed in the few items Iron had left in the room, the bulkiest of which was the shoulder holster. She took one last glance around the room and headed for the elevator. Once in the lobby she headed straight for the corridor that led to the Bee's Knees Disco, not yet opened for the day.

Glancing about to make sure she was alone, she entered the women's powder room, walked directly to the waste receptical, and took the laundry bag from her large purse. She slipped it easily into the refuse can.

Heading out the front entrance of the Wellington Inn, she spotted the tall black man still standing where he was when she had observed him from her room. She stood near him, but slightly behind him, wanting him to approach her first if possible. It would be better if he thought that she was not seeking him out.

Coley stood quietly, watching the firemen in action. The flames were now out, and the shriveled remains of the Lincoln now only smouldered and hissed once in a while as the firemen continued to hose it down. Whoever had been in the car would certainly not be recognizable.

He took a step forward preparing to returning to his car, which he had parked some distance away. The pillar of smoke had attracted him as he had been driving on his way once again to visit Cliff Blaylock.

Coley spotted Lila as he turned to leave. "Lila, my, you are a pretty lady this morning."

Lila feigned a warm smile. "Thank you. What's with the fire? I hope there isn't anyone in the car."

Coley looked beyond her, wondering where Red Irons was. "I've overheard that there is at least one person inside. There, I believe they are trying to remove the remains now."

He watched Lila turn away. She might be a tough cookie but the scene was too much for her. Coley glanced at his watch. "I think I'll go inside and have a cup of coffee. Care to join me?" As he asked, he continued to search the crowd for her companion of the night before.

Lila hesitated before replying. "That would be nice. I'd love to. Where's your beautiful friend this morning?"

This wasn't the way Coley wanted it. He was the detective. He should be asking the questions. He smiled at the brassy Lila. "Well, she went the usual way of the ships I bash with in the night." He led the way to the coffee shop inside the hotel.

"So where's your friend?" Seated and sipping at a scalding hot cup of coffee, Coley felt it was time to start playing detective.

"My friend?" Lila feigned a puzzled look.

"Oh come on now. I saw the little smoochy game over in the corner." Coley watched her squirm for an answer.

"Oh, him!" She finally answered. "I had to blow that bastard off. He thought he was God's gift to women."

"Where you headed this morning?" smiled Coley, not believing her.

"The airport. Got to get to Newark Airport. I was about to make arrangements when I saw the trouble in the parking lot. But I still have plenty of time." She kept her dark brown eyes fixed on Coley and began to move her crossed leg nervously under the table, repeatedly brushing against Coley's trousers.

"Are you checked out of the hotel?" Coley asked, now wondering how much time he should waste on Lila. He wanted to catch Blaylock at home before he started out the day. In a strange way, Lila was a pretty little thing. But he figured her for a kind of an airhead, probably a one night stand that Red Irons had picked up somewhere.

"Yeah, all checked out and ready to go," she replied. Irons had signed for a room when they checked in. It was one bill the hotel would never collect.

"I suppose the bell captain can arrange for a limo whenever you are ready." Coley left his legs planted firmly where they were as she intensified her contact.

"I suppose so," Lila mused softly. No way did she want to deal with any of the hotel personnel.

Coley decided to liven up the conversation a little bit and get it over with. "Say, that red-haired guy you were with last night. I would like to talk to him. I think he and I can cut a deal."

"Deal?" Lila visibly tensed. The swinging of her leg against Coley's stopped.

"Yeah, I'd like to move a few kilos of stuff. I was told that was his business." Coley had a sudden thought. What if she were a cop? He had certainly put his foot in it. The notion was soon dispelled.

She leaned over the table and spoke in a low voice. "You big bastard," she smiled. "I knew you were cool. I could just feel it." Her toe found his open cuff and went searching.

"I think you are a cool chick, too. Take me to your leader, the red-haired dude."

"Can't." She again leaned across the table. "That's impossible. But I can introduce you to a contact."

"That him burned to a crisp in the car out front? Is that Red Irons?"

"You ask a lot of questions, Mr . . ."

"Johnson, Doug Johnson," Coley frowned. He hated his alias. He'd have to pick another name sometime.

"Look, Doug, you help me and I'll help you. But no more questions about Red Irons." She glanced out the window of the coffee shop. A crowd of people now surrounded the burned car.

"Just get me out of this place and to someplace we can talk. I don't feel safe here."

"Suits me." Coley was gaining respect for her. Maybe she wasn't an airhead. "Let's get out of here. Follow me."

Outside, Lila followed him to the rental Buick, walking along the edge of the crowd still watching workers attempting to extract the body of Red Irons from the car. After Lila got in the car, Coley swept his eyes around the entire parking lot one more time. If they were being observed it wasn't apparent.

Coley drove several miles on rural roads, constantly watching his rearview mirror. Deciding that they weren't being followed, he turned onto the Garden State Parkway and headed south into New Jersey until he reached the Montvale parkway service area. He pulled into a parking place near a fast food complex, shut off the engine, and turned to face Lila. She was sexily posed on the seat next to him, her supple legs tucked up under her, exposing a wide expanse of nyloned thigh.

"You like what you see, Mr. Johnson?"

"Yes, as a matter of fact, stuff like that has made a shambles out of my life more than once." Coley grinned.

"Let me tell you, Doug, there ain't no stuff anywhere like this." Lila gave him a big warm smile and a provocative lick of her lips. She glanced around the very public parking area. "We going to talk here?"

"Yep, I think we should. Then we can get on with other things, like you heading for Newark Airport."

"Doug, I told you I was in no hurry. I like the other things. Pleasure before work, that's how life should be."

"Damn, Lila, I had that all twisted up. I could love your philosophy. I got twenty kilos, high grade, I want a buyer for the full lot." He watched her big brown eyes grow bigger.

"Look, Doug. That car, burning in the Wellington parking lot, I was supposed to be in it. I'm dead meat unless I make it to lala land. I'm amazed that we got out of the hotel. I'm going to tell

you one thing and that's all, mainly because it's all I know." Lila
hesitated, staring at the tourists pouring into the rest stop at lunch
time. "There's a yacht, the *Jersey Trick*, on a mooring off Nyack
in the Hudson. You'll have to take it from there. . . . Now, let's get
me to Newark."

"That's it? What about Heavy Laval?"

"I said no more questions."

"Look at it this way. You say you're dead meat if you're ever
caught. Wouldn't you like to see the *Jersey Trick* boys out of com-
mission forever?"

"You are a cop, aren't you?" Lila reached over and stroked his
smooth shaved face. "I feel bad about giving you any information.
I've just signed your death warrant." She paused and took a deep
drag on a cigarette. "I don't know where Heavy Laval is. He's
around here someplace." Lila swept her hands in a circle. "Red
was getting ready to chase him when the Lincoln blew up. Good
luck, copper."

"See that long building right over there behind the fast food
complex? That's an airline ticket counter. They run limos every
few minutes to Newark."

Lila stared at him in disbelief. "You mean you don't want any
goodies?"

"Maybe someday, Lila, someday." Coley handed her a card
with an 800 number on it. "If you ever have anything to say, call
this number. No voice will ever answer. Leave a message at the
beep. Now get over there, get your ticket, and get on the next limo.
I'll wait right here until you pull away. Get your sexy ass to California and crawl in a hole somewhere." Coley reached across and
shoved the door open.

Lila walked slowly toward the ticket office, glancing back at
Coley just before she entered the building. He waited a full twenty
minutes until she emerged and climbed into a limo, quickly blowing a kiss his way as the door closed behind her.

39

There was very little traffic on Route 17. Cliff Blaylock parked on the broad shoulder in front of Happy Hal's used car emporium. He got out of the BMW and made certain that the door was unlocked. A package containing sixty thousand dollars lay on the floor of the front seat. It was a full half hour before Heavy Laval was to show up.

He shoved his hand into his jacket pocket and gripped the hilt of Sandy's small .22 automatic, looked up and down the empty highway and began walking. A quarter of a mile later, he walked into the parking lot of Dolores's Pancake House where he had parked the small rented Ford Pinto several hours ago.

He went inside, sat at the counter where he could see the grill of the BMW a quarter of a mile down the road, and ordered a cup of coffee. The sixty thousand was all he could scrape together. Laval would have to wait a long time for any more. It was a sizable sum of money. Perhaps it would be enough to get him off his back.

At a quarter past six, he spotted Laval's Cherokee coming over the rise in the road, slowing down until he pulled alongside the BMW and stopped. Laval sat in the Cherokee for a full minute, evidently waiting until there was absolutely no traffic on the road behind him. Then he got out, approached the BMW quickly, opened the door and picked up the package in the front seat. He bent over, evidently searching under the seat before shutting the door and climbing back into the Cherokee.

By then, Blaylock had left the diner and sat in the Pinto observing the Cherokee in his rearview mirror. Laval pulled away from the BMW, accelerating rapidly as he approached the pancake house. Blaylock let him get a quarter of a mile ahead before he entered the traffic lane behind him and several other cars.

At the first opportunity, Laval exited Route 17, crossed an overpass and proceeded in the general direction of Stag Creek. Two cars behind him did the same thing, so Blaylock was able to keep his distance. On and on he drove until he reached the broad circular driveway of the Wellington Inn and turned in. Blaylock followed and parked several hundred feet from the spot where Laval parked the van. It was easy to keep unobserved. Between him and the van were several police cars and a small crowd of people watching the remains of a burned-out automobile being dragged aboard the tilted flatbed of a huge truck.

He watched Laval stride rapidly to the entrance of the Wellington Inn, carrying his package clutched under an arm. It was unbelievable! Here was Heavy Laval evidently living only a few miles from his house.

Noting carefully where the Cherokee was parked, Blaylock drove back to Route 17. He parked the Pinto behind his BMW and then got in the BMW and drove away. Stopping at Dolores's Pancake House once again, he called the rental car people to report that the Pinto was disabled and told them where they could find it.

He drove slowly back to Stag Creek deeply disturbed by the proximity of Heavy Laval. He decided that he would see that Sandy left to visit her sister as soon as possible, and that he would himself disappear for awhile. He reasoned that Heavy Laval couldn't harass him if he couldn't find him. In time he would just go away.

The morning had gone according to plan until he pulled into his own driveway. A car was parked toward the back of the house about where he usually kept the BMW. He saw Coley Doctor talking to Sandy, standing just outside the side door.

The chronic nausea that had plagued him through the past couple of weeks returned. What did he want this time? His hand automatically slipped inside his jacket to feel the bulk of the the ruined AMERI. Maybe he should just flat out tell Coley to get off the case. He would handle things himself. After all Willy was helping him just as a gesture of friendship. The friendship was fractured, so it made good sense for them to go their merry way.

"Hi dear!" Sandy waved. "Look who's here. Coley's got some good news."

Cliff offered a limp handshake to Coley. It bothered him a little that Sandy seemed very impressed with Willy's sidekick. Her anger with Willy over striking him in the foyer did not extend to Coley Doctor. "Hi, Coley," he said weakly. "I guess we could all use a little good news."

Coley accepted his handshake rather tentatively, amazed that he did not first inquire about Ginny's progress. "Cliff, there is all kinds of good news. First of all Ginny's back on the *Tashtego* and feeling much better."

"That's wonderful, I was just going to ask about her."

Coley gave him his blank look. He reminded him of several men he once knew in a brief fling at sales management. Whenever someone would come up with an obviously fine idea in a think session, there were always several others who stated that they were just about to say the same thing. "Well I was just about ready not to mention Ginny, but I figured you'd be interested."

Blaylock stared at Coley, looking puzzled. "Of course I'm interested. What's the other good news?"

"The Stag Creek police, and a couple of other jurisdictions up in Rockland County and in New Jersey are working together to nail Heavy Laval. Seems he is into narcotic distribution big time. Because of the murder of Finehouse and Laval's movement across state lines, the FBI has joined the hunt. It looks like they'll have him soon."

"I'm glad to hear it. I know Willy is anxious to get to the Virgin Islands. I refuse to impose on you guys any longer. It's wonderful that you took the time and effort, but I insist you get on with your lives. With all those people interested, I'm sure it won't be long."

"Cliff, I'm sorry but I think you're forgetting something."

"And what's that?" Blaylock couldn't hide his irritation with Coley.

"Ginny took a stiff shot in the jaw from this punk. He could have killed her. If I know Willy Hanson, he ain't about to leave until he gets a piece of that son of a bitch."

Blaylock nodded and then shook his head negatively. "Well, don't think I don't appreciate your efforts, but I don't want anyone else to get hurt." Blaylock turned abruptly and walked into the house, then returned to the doorway. "Sandy, I'm going to change clothes and go into the office for a few hours. It's been awhile."

Sandy just nodded and then walked with Coley to his car. "You can see how upset Cliff is. I'm sorry. He and Willy were so close at one time. But maybe it's best you two get on with your lives."

"Mrs. Blaylock, that's just not possible until this thing is wrapped up. It won't be long." Coley climbed into his rental Buick and then rolled down his window. "If you ever need me for anything, Sandy, you know how to reach me."

Sandy smiled. "I have your card, Coley." She went back into the house as he pulled out of the driveway.

A few minutes later Cliff Blaylock came down the stairs dressed in a business suit.

"Cliff, are you actually going into the office? That's the first time I've seen you in uniform for a long time." Sandy smiled at the reminder of happier days for both of them.

"Sandy, it's time to go forward. We've both been too depressed for a long time." He hugged her, pecked her on the cheek, and left.

She watched him pull out of the driveway in the BMW wondering where he was really going. His attempted swift reversal to normalcy was as frightening as it was unexpected.

She went upstairs, feeling ill at ease, wondering if life would ever be like it was just a few weeks ago. She hoped that Coley would be right, and the thief would be caught soon. It bothered her that Cliff didn't share Coley's optimism. What really bothered her was the thought that a simple thing like a theft in the driveway, covered by insurance could turn their life upside down. She walked into their bedroom and picked up the flannel shirt that Cliff had deposited on a chair next to the closet. She smiled faintly. Maybe things were getting back to normal.

She held the shirt at arm's length to determine whether to hang it up or drop it into the dirty clothes, and decided on the latter. Instinctively she ran her fingers into the shirt's pocket, felt the bulk of a coin and pulled it out. She started to put it in a tray on Cliff's dresser as she always did and then glanced at it.

It felt and looked unusual. Holding it in her palm, she studied the unusual chain links design, then read the legend around the coin. The United States of AMERI. It was the AMERI! She had never actually seen it before, but had heard Cliff describe it many times.

Her hands trembled with nervous excitement as she turned the coin over to examine it. There was the crude replica of Liberty with long flowing hair. But there were ugly scratches on the coin that Cliff had told her was pristine. She tilted the coin so that the bright scratches caught the light. Crudely but unmistakably the deep scratches formed letters that spelled WILLIS.

She knew very little about numismatics, but she knew enough to know that someone had virtually destroyed the value of the AMERI. And why did the scratches clearly spell Willis? All she could think of was Willis McCord. What could one possibly have to do with the other? And why hadn't Cliff told her about the return of the AMERI?

40

A brisk wind swept down the Hudson canyon on a prematurely cold fall day. The *Jersey Trick* rolled more than usual at its mooring. Bocco's face was a perpetual scowl as he talked to his two killers. The morning papers were piled in front of him. "We have to assume Lila got away. They found only one body in the Lincoln and they say it was probably a male, identified by a pair of large size men's shoes."

Crackers shrugged and stared at Bocco, in a look that said, I did what I was told to do.

Veronica sat on a lounge toward the back of the salon fussing with her fingernails. "Don't worry about Lila. She doesn't know enough to be a problem. She'll probably show up before the day is over." Veronica spoke calmly, continuing to buff her nails.

"I'm not so sure," Bocco growled. "She and Irons spent a lot of time in the sack. Irons liked to play the big shot. You think he wouldn't run off at the mouth to impress a babe like Lila?" He shook his finger at the two killers. "That's why I want you guys to spread your charm around. Don't get stuck on one bimbo. They all got the same equipment."

Veronica got up from the lounge and walked in front of Bocco, letting a terrycloth robe she wore fall open to reveal her nude form. Stretching languidly, she spoke. "Bocco, baby, you really don't mean that, do you."

Elvis risked a broad smile. Crackers just stared. Bocco put his arms around her and yanked her close until his chin rested on her navel. "Everybody knows you're special, Veronica. You and I got our own rules. Now sit back down over there and don't butt in."

Elvis kept grinning at her as she returned to the lounge. Crackers stared at Bocco without expression.

"Elvis, since you like to drool so much, I want you to scout out the McCord woman. That ratfink son of hers had to have a big stash somewhere, and it's our property. You've got to follow her somewhere and catch her alone. The whole area around her house is crawling with cops, and will be until they find Heavy Laval. Heavy's too stupid. He won't get very far. But I want to find him first. Got that, Crackers?"

Crackers blinked his eyes and nodded.

"You guys know your business, now go do it. Any questions?"

"What do I do with the McCord dish when I find her?"

"Anything you want, Elvis. Get invited to her home so you can get a look around. Get her high. Get in her pants. Make her happy. Bring her aboard the *Jersey Trick* if you want to impress her. Enjoy your work. But you've got to do your job. If you can't charm her, you have to get nasty. I'll leave the details to you and Crackers. Did you catch her picture in the papers?"

Elvis nodded. "Rest easy, boss. I'll find out if she knows anything about the stash."

The three men left the salon of the *Jersey Trick* and made their way to the aft deck where a small dinghy swung on a stern line.

"Make any calls on the cellulars brief," Bocco cautioned as the two men climbed into the dinghy. Crackers took a quick pull on the starting cord and they putted away.

"You can buy me one of those, Bocco." Veronica's voice came from behind him as he stood on the aft deck watching the dinghy make the short trip to the small marina.

He turned around to find her staring at the big ketch in full sail pointing north in the Tappan Zee. The vessel had tall masts

and unusually wide spreaders that made her stand out from all
the others he had seen.

"Baby, I hate sailboats. Those guys are nuts. They move like
snails and get in the way. The *Jersey Trick* could split that son of
a bitch right in two before he knew what happened."

"They're pretty, Bocco," Veronica persisted.

"So's Lila, baby. But a fat lot of good it's going to do her when
we find her."

On shore, Elvis and Crackers tied the dinghy to the dock and
proceeded to the small Pinto. Within minutes they were speed-
ing down Route 59 in the general direction of the Wellington
Inn.

As they pulled into the parking area of the hotel, Crackers extended his arm and tapped Elvis on the shoulder. Elvis turned to
find Crackers actually smiling. "Easy job. Already it is an easy job."
He pointed off into the distance.

At the end of the lot, near a stand of tall trees sat a beige
Cherokee. Crackers swung the Pinto around until he could read
the license numbers. "Yep, that belongs to Heavy."

Elvis swept his eyes around the huge parking area. There
was still a police car parked near the taped off area where the Lincoln had burned. "Crackers, this place is probably crawling with
fuzz. We'll go in, find an out of the way spot in the lounge and
bide our time for awhile. Heavy's got to be in there somewhere."

Crackers merely nodded his head.

"Pal, you've got to remember. No trouble! Be nice, Crackers."

The two men sat in the lounge area in a spot where they
could observe both the front entrance and the hall that led to the
elevator bank. The Wellington, a suburban convention mill, evidently was without a major business meeting. Very few people
passed through the lobby.

"Maybe we better check and see if Heavy's got a room,"
Crackers said, breaking his usual silence.

"Wrong, Crackers, wrong! Heavy's nuts, but not crazy enough to use his own name. If Bocco's right, the fuzz have probably cued in the desk to report on him." Elvis sipped at his beer as time began to pass. "We've got to get out of here soon. We're the only people around. If the cops have this place staked out, sooner or later they'll find an excuse to check us out."

They sat for a moment in the rental car in the parking lot. Elvis took stock of the situation. "Tell me, Crackers, would you have any trouble getting into the Cherokee if it were locked?"

"No. Best do it after dark." Crackers showed just a hint of a smile. He had uttered more words today than Elvis had heard him speak in a month. Now he was anxious to get to work.

In his room on the fifth floor of the Wellington Heavy Laval counted the money. Sixty thousand dollars! He piled the hundreds up on the desk in neat stacks of ten thousand each. The beauty of it was that it was all his. There would be no cut for Red Irons and his friends. Counting twenty G's for the gold and another ten G's in cash he had pried out of Blaylock, he had ninety thousand all to himself. It was time for the Florida trip, he decided. He would lay off Blaylock for awhile, until he was needed. He looked around the fancy room. If he only had Peaches here to bang once in a while, life would be perfect.

He called room service and ordered lunch, a New York strip with all the trimmings. He rubbed his eyes at the price, thirty-seven dollars, all written out in script on the fancy menu. What the hell did he care? It was on Willy Hanson, whoever he was. The gold credit card had worked like magic when he had checked in.

He walked to the window and looked out over the acres of parking area. His Cherokee sat barely in view to his far left. It was all gassed up for the Florida trip. He'd leave after dark.

Room service knocked on his door. He signed the check care-

fully, remembering to spell Hanson with an "o," and then slipped
the boy a twenty dollar bill for a tip.

"Thank you, Mr. Hanson. Will there be anything else?"

He thought for a moment about asking for a babe, but decided
not to. Instinct told him not to attract too much attention. He
shook his head. "That'll be all right now."

He fastened the chain on the door, and walked over to the television set and picked up the movie guide. What do you know, he
observed. There was a long list of X-rated stuff. He turned on a
movie and sat down to his steak. If only Peaches could see him
now, he thought. The stupid bimbo could have been right beside
him if she had played her cards right.

The way he figured things, Blaylock still owed him thirty
thousand. After all, he had the funny looking cent now. He wondered how he liked the reference to Willis McCord. That would
sure teach the bastard a lesson. In the future when he asked for
more money, Blaylock wouldn't dare shortchange him.

The couple in the porno movie were beginning to get it on.
"Damn, I wish Peaches was here," he murmured aloud, then
vowed to teach her a lesson someday.

41

That morning, Willy and Ginny made the decision to move the
Tashtego out of the marina and find a mooring offshore.

"I'm sorry, Willy. I just can't sleep knowing that animal is out
there someplace. Even with you here and the policeman in the
parking lot, I can't sleep."

"I don't blame you, lover. That was quite a trauma. It may be a while before you feel safe on the boat. The weather's great. We'll feel safer on a mooring."

The dockmaster at the small marina turned out to be a big help when Willy explained their problem to him. He would make a few phone calls and see what he could do. In a half hour he rapped on the hull of the *Tashtego*.

"I have a friend, the Janzens, very nice people. They have a private mooring across the river. They've pulled their boat for the winter. You can even use a small dock at the back of their property for a dinghy base. The mooring is about two hundred feet out. No one will bother you out there."

"Sounds nice. It will probably be for only a day or two. Okay Ginny?"

"Sure! I want to get rid of the dark circles around my eyes before they become permanent." Ginny forced a smile.

"You folks just stay there as long as you like. These folks have no use for the mooring until spring." The dockmaster stepped aboard the *Tashtego* and pointed to an area about a half mile north of the Tappan Zee Bridge on the west side of the Hudson River. "If you go over there, off shore from that tall white house, you'll find a mooring float that has a letter 'J' painted on it. That's the Janzen's float. It's about halfway between that big motor yacht over there and the bridge."

Ginny looked at the swanky yacht across the river. "We saw them moving north on this side of the river this morning. I remember the name, the *Jersey Trick*."

Willy studied the shoreline. There were no other vessels in the vicinity, and the yacht would be at least a half mile from them. "I want to thank you. This should be ideal."

They said their good-byes to the dockmaster as the engine of the *Tashtego* rumbled to life. Within minutes they were in the main channel where they hoisted the main, then the jib, and pointed north. Ginny beamed for the first time in days. "Let's give her a little workout."

Willy nodded his approval and moved to strap in the sheets to take advantage of the fresh breeze. The *Tashtego* heeled smartly in the breeze and gathered speed on the northern course. They proceeded until the Bear Mountain bridge loomed just ahead, then came about to follow a course south along the palisades of the western shore.

Their return took them within a hundred yards of the *Jersey Trick*. The tall blonde in a bikini hoisted a cocktail glass in appreciative salute and they responded with the friendly wave.

They had no trouble finding the Janzens' float. Ginny brought the *Tashtego* slowly about and inched toward the mooring until Willy grabbed it expertly with the boathook. Within seconds, they had the *Tashtego* safe and secure on the new mooring.

Willy reached Coley Doctor on his cellular phone and gave him their new location, and the Janzens' street address along the shore. There was a dinghy inverted on the Janzens' small dock. Willy tried to picture the tall Coley making use of the tiny dinghy and oars. "Ginny, I can't wait to see Coley make use of that dinghy. We could charge admission to see that."

Ginny smiled. "Coley is really a landlubber. I think he actually detests the *Tashtego*. It's a wonder you guys ever became good friends."

"He isn't much of a seaman, but he's a hell of a detective, Ginny. If you had to have one man in a tight spot, you'd pick him."

"Where is he this afternoon?"

"Snooping around, trying to find Laval. Sandy called him, says she's got to see him quick. So by now I guess he's headed over there. We'll go ashore and meet him for dinner at the Prospect Inn, in Stag Creek. The dockmaster should have our car here soon. He was waiting for someone to follow him, so we wouldn't have to drive him back."

42

Cliff Blaylock slapped his hand against the railing of the small bridge in exasperation. Once again, he bent low over the railing and stared down into the clear water. The flow of water in the narrow creek was even less than it had been a few days ago. Every stone and pebble was clearly visible to the naked eye, covered by only a few inches of water.

The large kidney shape of the pouch holding his handgun was not visible anywhere, though he had clearly seen it on the day when he had been interrupted by Coley. It had looked like many of the smooth flat stones now still visible. Again he walked down by the water, just to make sure the gun pouch was not there. "Damn it!" He cursed his stupidity. The weapon was registered to him. He had to find it.

"Hi, pal, fixin' to go wading again?"

Startled, he jerked his head upward to face Coley Doctor, now standing on the bridge. "Coley! You scared me. I had no idea anyone was around. I'm just walking around. This is one of my favorite spots. I used to wade around in here when I was a kid."

"Oh yes! I remember. You told me that once before. It must be great to have a favorite spot so near your home. Someplace where you can hike around, commune with nature, and forget your troubles. You folks out here in the suburbs really have it nice." Coley leaned against the rail, looking totally relaxed.

"We like it out here, Coley. I'll bet you grew up in the city. This must seem like strange behavior to you." Cliff Blaylock stepped away from the edge of the water and turned around to ascend the narrow path back up to the bridge.

"I was born and raised in Watts, out in LA. There's nothing like this in Watts. No place to commune with nature and gather your thoughts. Just concrete, asphalt, and a few basketball hoops."

"And you chose the hoops. Willy told me about your basketball days. That must have been great." Now Blaylock was back up on the main road. He saw Coley's car just around the bend.

"Where you headed this afternoon, Cliff? You're all dressed up like a commuter."

"As a matter of fact, I'm going into the office. Sandy and I both think I'd better get back in the old routine. I guess the robbery has everyone all upset. Of course, I did a very stupid thing in trying to deal with the thief. But I've decided to put everything behind me."

Coley gave him his coldest stare. Right now he was nervously wiping at his shoe propped up on a crosspiece of the small bridge, trying to clean a bit of mud from between the sole and the top of his shoe. "Cliff, at least you didn't ruin your damn shoes, like you did the other night."

"The other night? Oh, that happened over in Park . . ."

"Bullshit!" Coley stopped him in mid-sentence. "You were down here wading around, right in this creek, looking for the gun!"

"The gun!" Blaylock gaped at Coley, trying to read his mind. "That's preposterous. What gun?"

"The one I found in the creek this morning, Cliff. The .38 revolver. It looks brand new. Of course it will have to be thoroughly cleaned now. I used to have one just like it." Coley paused and decided there was no time like the present to test his theory. "Why'd you kill the kid, Cliff?"

"What in the hell are you talking about? I don't have to stand here and take this from the likes of you. What kid?"

"The kid next door." Cliff Blaylock now turned and walked rapidly toward his car, Coley following. "For some reason, you killed the kid and then threw the .38 in the river. You had some sort of a squabble. I figure the McCord kid was maybe in cahoots with Heavy Laval. You had this confrontation when they tried to rob you, and you killed him. Right Cliff?"

"You're insane!" He opened the door of the BMW. "You're nuts, just like Willy Hanson. He's about to get an assault charge sworn out against him. Now get out of my way."

Coley's body blocked the door. "You want to go to the police station and bring charges against Willy. Be my guest! I'll go with you, one-stop shopping. I have to turn in the gun anyway."

"I'll have charges brought against you too. I've lived in this town a long time."

Coley grabbed him by his tie and collar and shoved him against the headrest. "Look, punk, I've had enough of you. You don't dare go to the police with me. I may not be totally right, but I'm damn close. At least two other people have been killed and Ginny beaten up because you are trying to cover your tracks. Now, do you really want me to go to the station with you?"

Blaylock squirmed under Coley's tight hold. Coley released him and his head sagged to his chest. Breathing heavily now, he spoke. "Do what you have to do, Coley. Turn in the gun if you think you should. I don't want any more unpleasantness. Willy was a good friend. Please, just leave me alone. I need some time to think."

Coley backed away and shut the door to the BMW. Blaylock's remarks were a virtual confession to some sort of complicity in Willis McCord's death. They were good enough for him but perhaps not yet a strong case for the police.

Blaylock turned the car around and proceeded south on Stag Creek Road. Coley followed him as far as the police station. When the BMW did not turn in, Coley pulled over to the side of the road for a few minutes, and then turned around and headed north, wondering what the phone call from Sandy was all about. He decided to question her about the .38 that lay in the leather pouch beneath his seat.

Within minutes, he swung his car around the cul-de-sac and

pulled into the Blaylocks' driveway. Sandy waved from the front door as he got out of the rental Buick. "Hello, Mrs. Blaylock, enjoying this fall day? All these colors are really dazzling to a Californian."

"Yes, they must be, but I'm afraid I haven't even thought about enjoying them this year. I am extremely worried about Cliff. Please come inside, I want to show you something." He followed her into the house and into the den. "I found this in the pocket of the shirt Cliff wore yesterday. Cliff disappeared this morning. I found it after he left. Frankly, I'm worried sick over him." She handed him a small unsealed envelope.

Coley peeked inside and then let the AMERI slide into his palm. "Well, I'll be damned. Cliff got back his AMERI. That's wonderful." He raised his head to find her staring at it as if it were an abomination, a black widow spider, perhaps. Her eyes were red and damp from crying.

"Now, turn it over, Coley."

Coley flopped over the large cent in his hand. "Oh no!" he gasped. Several heavy scratches desecrated the coin. Then he read the crudely etched name, WILLIS. "I don't know much about coins, Sandy, but I do know that someone has virtually destroyed the value of this one."

"I may be wrong, but I think Cliff, himself, might have done this. I've never seen him in such a despondent mental state. I notice that he just can't stand to talk about Willis McCord."

"Sandy, I think you're wrong. Numismatists search all their life for a perfect rarity like this. I don't think they have it in themselves to destroy it."

"Ordinarily I would agree with you, Coley. But Cliff hasn't been himself since Willis McCord was killed next door. It affected him beyond belief. He's been totally unpredictable ever since then. And now, I find this coin with Willis's name scratched on it."

Coley stared at the AMERI in deep thought for several moments. "For the time being, Sandy, I would put this back in the shirt pocket where you found it, or hide it in a book or something. That would probably be better. To be quite frank, I don't believe that Cliff is very stable right now. I don't think it is time for you to confront him with this. But if you do, perhaps it would be best if I were around."

"Oh my, Cliff would never hurt me. He is really a very gentle person. But I'll do as you say. I hate the idea of anymore unpleasantness. Actually I am going out of town to visit my sister for a few days." Sandy dabbed at her eyes.

Coley nodded. "Maybe that's a good idea. By the way, Sandy, does Cliff own a handgun?"

"Yes, he has a small .38. I got a .22 at the same time, and we both took shooting instructions. Cliff kept badgering me until I agreed a few years ago. He's a big law and order fan and insists that the world has turned into an unsafe place. Although until very recently, I never heard of anything happening in Stag Creek."

"Do you know where he keeps the handgun?"

"Yes, usually on his closet shelf. But it's not there. He told me he took it downstairs to clean it. But it's not there either. Frankly, the fact that it is missing has me quite worried."

"Mrs. Blaylock, I think he bears watching. He seems a little confused right now. He'll be okay when we get all this figured out."

She wrung her hands together and sighed heavily. "Thanks, Coley. I feel better now that I've talked to you."

Coley left the house feeling that he had learned quite a bit. There was no doubt in his mind that the gun he had retrieved from the river belonged to Blaylock. The fact that Blaylock had chickened out on his threat to go to the police made him feel that his theory was close to the mark.

He glanced at his watch. It would soon be time to meet Willy and Ginny at the Prospect Inn, only a couple of miles away. He decided to turn the .38 over to the police before meeting Willy.

Also, he wanted to check with the police to see if a slug had been found in Willis's body, or at the crime scene.

Coley had a few minutes before the date with Willy and Ginny at the Prospect Inn, just enough time to familiarize himself with the town a little. Stag Creek seemed to be built all along one main road that ran on for six or seven miles, abutting the narrow, winding Hackensack River on one side. Every time he turned westward, he found himself in another community within several blocks.

He paused to read a historical marker. Vaguely he had read of the Baylor Massacre somewhere in an old history book. In 1778 a group of Continental dragoons were surprised and wiped out at that site in a Revolutionary War action. The bodies of the slain were dumped in a tannery vat nearby, not discovered until recent times. It was difficult for him to visualize such carnage now in the pristine setting nearby a golf course. As nearly as he could tell from chatting with a couple of shopkeepers, that was probably the last real excitement these sleepy bedroom towns in northern New Jersey had experienced.

He found himself driving to the north on Stag Creek Road toward New York state. From there it was just a few miles to the Wellington Inn, the site of Willis McCord's last day and the theft of Cliff's AMERI. He could visualize the whole thing, pretty much the way he had described it to Cliff Blaylock. How did the big cocaine stash fit in? He couldn't find Heavy Laval too soon. The answers were obviously with him.

By the time Coley showed up at the Prospect Inn, Willy and Ginny had not yet arrived. Teddy, the bartender was practicing golf swings, ala Johnny Carson, behind the bar. He kept it up until he satisfied himself with a perfect follow-through.

"Yes sir, what'll it be?"

"A little scotch and water, then you can get back to your golf." Teddy scowled as if he didn't think that was very funny.

"Did you ever locate Cliff Blaylock?" Teddy asked, placing the drink in front of him, obviously remembering his last visit.

"Yes, thank you, I did. He and Sandy seem like nice people," he added, trying to draw the bartender out on the subject.

"They're good people. I haven't seen them for quite a while. Cliff told me about a robbery he had the last time he was in. Whoever pulled it off sure took a chance." Teddy went away shaking his head just as Willy and Ginny walked in.

The three of them took a table in the cocktail lounge rather than wait for an opening in the dining room. Teddy interrupted his golfing pantomime and seated them in a darkened corner where they would have some privacy, yet had a full view of the lounge area. Coley was impatient to get started with all his fresh news.

"I just came from a visit with Sandy Blaylock. She had a bit of news that would qualify as slightly earthshaking. Cliff Blaylock got his AMERI back."

"That bastard! That means he's been dealing with Heavy Laval again, without telling us." Willy reddened with anger.

"Relax, that's only part of the news. Someone took a sharp knife and carved Willis McCord's first name into the obverse side. Sandy thinks Cliff probably did it. She as much as said she thinks Cliff needs a shrink in the worst way."

Willy and Ginny gaped at Coley, dumbstruck with the peculiar information.

"Did you actually see the AMERI, Coley?" Willy had trouble believing that anyone would deliberately ravage the coin.

"I held it in my hands. I told her to put it back in the shirt pocket where she found it, or hide it somewhere. Now I have one other bit of news that tops everything. Remember the night Blaylock traipsed mud all over his foyer?"

"I sure do," Willy nodded. "He told us he stepped off a curb in Park Ridge where they were washing the streets. I went right over there and crisscrossed the business section after I left you. Everything was high and dry. The guy at the firehouse didn't know what I was talking about. Our boy Cliff lies again!"

"Well I caught him again with his feet wet. Down south of here a ways, there is a little bridge as you turn to the left. He was wading around in the creek under the bridge. I caught him hanging around the same spot one other time. Today I got there before he did. I went wading first."

Coley paused, sipping at his drink, leaving Willy and Ginny hanging. He always got great pleasure at making people wait for the other shoe to drop.

"So you went wading. I know you want me to ask you why," smiled Willy. "We don't give a damn, Coley. Keep it to yourself."

"No, I insist on telling you. I found his .38 revolver."

"What! What in the hell are you talking about?"

"Exactly what I said. I have just turned it over to the Stag Creek Police." Coley proceeded to tell them the whole story of his meeting with Blaylock, including Blaylock's initial threat to swear out assault charges against Willy. "He denied any knowledge of the gun, but then backed down pretty fast on my offer to go to the police station with him. I struck a nerve, Willy. I think he shot the kid next door!"

Ginny gasped. Willy gaped at him, stunned. "Coley, you're making a long leap, considering the information you have. You're even guessing that it is his gun."

"It's a pretty good guess. Sandy just told me it was missing." Coley said confidently. "Sandy's leaving town, incidently. She's going to visit her sister. There's lots of trouble in their little paradise."

"I'm glad you turned the .38 in to the police, Coley. We're gettin' mixed up in something far beyond a simple driveway break-in. Blaylock will have to swim or sink on his own story as far as I am concerned. You know how Ginny and I feel about that bastard now."

"You still want to nail Heavy Laval?" asked Coley.

"I not only want to, Coley, I'm going to." Willy sipped at the Chivas.

"I've got a lead. Remember little Lila?"

Willy grinned and winked at Ginny. "Another one of his good-looking babes. Okay, Coley, what about Lila?"

"She's off to sunny California. Thinks she's on the mob's hit list. She says the key to Heavy Laval is a fancy yacht moored down in the Tappan Zee. She called it the *Jersey Trick*."

Ginny and Willy looked at each other in frozen silence. Then Willy turned and stared out the window and watched a car park in the restaurant parking lot, trying to put all the information together. "Ginny, of all Coley's news, that bit of information may be the worst of the lot."

Now it was Coley's turn to be surprised. "You mean you know about the *Jersey Trick*?"

"Yeah, Coley, it's moored off our bow, about a five iron shot from the *Tashtego*."

A drienne McCord didn't mind wearing black. It was her favorite color. Her sleek figure wore it well. She had been losing weight. She found it was easy when you didn't eat. The ankle-length form-caressing cocktail skirt, slit to the thigh, fit perfectly. She sipped from the Scotch in a glass on her dressing table, then stood tall and walked back and forth in front of the mirrors. She looked at her neatly packaged derriere undulate provocatively as she glanced over her shoulder into the mirror. She laughed softly, sipping again at the Scotch, as she made a decision not to wear a bra, and selected a low-cut knit blouse that tied at the waist.

Looking close up in the mirror, she saw the stubborn lines that refused to go away, inconsequential in soft light, but hell in the sunlight. Alex took rude delight in pointing them out in the soft light.

It was still early. Sandy Blaylock had dropped by earlier to say good-bye. She was going to visit her sister. Seemed that Cliff had fallen off his pedestal in some way. But she was unclear about what came between them. Silly woman, she thought, if she had Alex to live with, putting up with his constant sniping at her dignity, she'd know what a real bastard was.

She planned to have dinner at Louis Quatorze down by the waterfront in Piermont. She and Alex were known there and she felt confident going alone. Maurice was always a kick. His delightful piano was soothing and his compliments outrageous. Tonight Alex wouldn't be there to inhibit him. But first she had to take care of something.

Adrienne walked downstairs and went into the library. It was always a depressing room for her. Most of the shelves were filled with books never read by either Alex or herself. Early on she had subscribed to several book clubs, and each month's selections were probably still in the niche where they were originally placed, except for the ones Willis had chosen to read. Alex had bought a set of encyclopedias taking up two full shelves. To her knowledge, none of them had been moved since they were purchased. Alex always said that a library made a home complete. She had no idea what he meant by it.

Adrienne stretched, reaching high to a shelf that held a row of her old college textbooks and selected *An Introduction to Calculus*. She had made a private hideaway out of the book figuring that it was the least likely of all to be pulled from the shelf. She opened the book, which had been hollowed out, and withdrew an oblong cookie tin, then carried the tin upstairs and opened it. She sniffed the empty contents. It had been empty a long time, but still she imagined the odor of marijuana and smiled. Memories of old college days and faces long forgotten returned to her mind.

Now in Willis's room, she dug down through the pile of luggage and extracted one of the two matching briefcases. She sat it on top of the pile of luggage and opened it. Then she filled the cookie tin with as many bags of cocaine as she could cram inside. Who would know the difference, she asked herself. Now she would follow Sandy and Coley's advice, and turn the remainder over to the police. Up to now she couldn't bring herself to further implicate Willis. But the damn newspapers wouldn't leave the story alone. The whole world would soon know all about Willis.

She went downstairs and quickly returned *An Introduction to Calculus* to its niche. Alex would never have to know about her little secret, she decided. She poured another couple inches of Scotch in the low glass and went back upstairs to finish dressing, and realized that she felt stone sober. Her tolerance for Scotch was building to an incredible level, and usually ended only after over half a bottle had been consumed.

It was seven o'clock when Adrienne walked outside and climbed behind the wheel of their Mercedes. Yesterday, the constant vigil of a police car had been discontinued, although she did see officer Hinkle drive by several times. Frankly, she felt relieved. She had grown weary of their attention, though she felt that their interest was genuine. But if they had got any closer to the apprehending of Willis's killer, she was unaware of it.

She backed out of her driveway and pointed toward Stag Creek Road just as another car entered her cul-de-sac. The car passed and seemed to pause at the Blaylocks' as she turned north on Stag Creek Road. She drove slowly in the waning daylight, crossing into New York State and within minutes was heading north on the winding road along the Hudson through Piermont, and finally parked facing the River at Louis Quatorze Restaurant.

Adrienne sat for a minute. She felt warm. Testing one of the little white packages was probably a mistake, though she had sniffed just a bare little white dot from her finger. As she entered the cozy piano bistro, Olga, the always stately and proper hostess hugged her warmly.

"I am so sorry dear. It's so good to have you back."

"Olga, no more sorrow. It's over. It's good to be out among friends." She waved at Maurice at the piano who gently saluted her. "Olga, I'll just sit at the piano bar awhile, okay?"

"Certainly dear. Maurice will be thrilled. Will Alex be joining you?"

"He's in Seattle. Business. He's making money hand over fist."

"Wonderful! So you can spend it," Olga tittered as Adrienne sat facing Maurice at the piano. "You'll be having Scotch I presume."

Maurice was all smiles. "In honor of your return, I have just compiled a medley of all your favorite tunes. If anything displeases you, just snap your finger."

"Thanks Maurice. It's good to be back. And the best part is that Alex is not here to interfere with our taste in music."

"Yes! There will be no Michigan fight song tonight."

He launched into his medley as she gazed out on the Hudson. There was no wind and the flat water mirrored the eastern shore. Adrienne felt good, for the first time since the funeral. Should she feel this way? Now just for an instant she felt guilty about it. The feeling went away. She had tortured herself ever since the funeral. Her life was going on, whether she liked it or not. Maurice was reading her mood, and now was determined to change it. She smiled her approval and toasted him as he livened up his little medley.

Elvis Clock parked his car directly behind the black Mercedes. Traffic had been light all the way from Stag Creek and he was able to follow her at a distance. He lit a cigarette and sat in his car, giving her time to get settled inside. He got out of his car and walked over to a dock along the edge of the Louis Quatorze Restaurant. Diners ate at candlelit tables along the waterfront. Piano music drifted his way now and then. And then he glimpsed her, sitting at the piano bar near the front. There was space all around her.

What a stroke of luck, he told himself. At least now she was all alone. She was a classy looking babe. He'd have to pull his best manners out of mothballs and give her the queen bee treatment.

He ground out his cigarette on the asphalt. Glancing far up the river he could see the tall sail on the other side of the bridge that had taken a mooring that day. Just beyond, long and low on the water were the lights of the *Jersey Trick*. He glanced at his watch. Bocco would be having his steak on the aft deck with Veronica about now. Lucky bastard! And here he was with work to do.

Inside, Elvis took a stool at the piano bar, leaving a space between them. He watched Maurice play for awhile noting that Adrienne McCord was quite attentive, sharing smiles with the piano player at times.

"Do you have a favorite?" Maurice asked him after finishing his little medley for Adrienne.

"You're doing just fine. The young lady seems pleased. I'm not about to change that."

Adrienne smiled his way. "Oh come on, you must have a favorite or two. I love just about anything Maurice plays."

"Okay, Maurice, how about a real oldie, 'Anything Goes.' "

Maurice riffled the keys softly for a moment, closed his eyes and quickly picked up on the lively tune.

"He's very good. I've never been able to stump him with a tune." As she spoke, Adrienne looked squarely at the tall, handsome young man. Thick black hair, dark eyes, and gleaming teeth shown in his youthful easy smile. She doubted if he was much over thirty.

"Well, let me test him. I'll give it some thought. By the way my name is Elvis and actually I'm partial to old Elvis's music."

"Really! So am I," enthused Adrienne. "And you actually look a little like Elvis, at least the Elvis I've seen in old movies. I'm Adrienne, and I guess that you've gathered this is Maurice."

"Adrienne, that's such a beautiful name. I don't think I've ever known an Adrienne." He engaged her deep blue eyes, which had a wide awake intensity about them, almost too intense. "You must be waiting for someone. Every time I meet one of the beautiful people, they are always waiting for someone else."

"Well you are wrong. I am alone with Maurice and his music. I haven't been out in awhile and frankly, I got stir crazy. And you, are you from around here?"

"I call Miami home. Right now I'm serving as second mate on a yacht that moored in Nyack a couple days ago. You can see it way off in the distance beyond the bridge. It's the low line of lights you see on the water."

Their vantage point was poor, but Adrienne was able to make out the location. "What a life! Elvis, I admire you. A mate aboard a luxury yacht. I would imagine that you like that very much."

"Oh I know you wouldn't believe me, but it's hard work. It's sort of a business headquarters for the owner. There are good times, but there are also times when everyone is hard at work. Tonight is party time aboard. I decided to take the night off and explore the wonders of Nyack. And I'm glad I did." Elvis beamed an approving smile toward Adrienne.

"That's exciting. Now what kind of business does your employer run from his boat?" Olga passed by and Elvis renewed their drinks.

"Importing, exporting. The boss is a wheeler-dealer. I know very little about his business, except when it calls for my specialty, as second mate of the *Jersey Trick*." He smiled engagingly, at the same time wondering what this gentle woman would think about his real specialty.

"Well if I were a young man, and I can't imagine that," she laughed, "I would very much like your job." Adrienne sipped at her refilled Scotch, feeling just a little light-headed. She wished she hadn't indulged so heavily at home. She thought of the sight of the dab of white powder in her palm. Perhaps she should go to the ladies' room. Another sniff or two would clear her head.

They talked. Elvis had a knack for being a listener, saying just the right things to egg her on. She told him about Alex being in Seattle. She even told him about Willis. She told him about her good friend that was going away, and admitted her loneliness. Soon Elvis touched, then held her hand as they talked.

Maurice began to play loud and lively tunes. Once she saw him frown, and question her with his eyes.

"Adrienne, I think perhaps we need some fresh air. I'd like to show you our yacht. If you don't want to do that, perhaps we should go someplace else, or just take a walk along the water."

"Elvis, you are a rogue. I can tell it." She smiled faintly. "But I like rogues. There's another very nice quiet place just down the street. Let's go there instead of to your boat. But first I must make use of the powder room here."

"Of course, whatever you say. My night is yours to spend as you like." Corny, he thought as she walked away. But she bought it. She really had a buzz on, and his experienced eye told him it wasn't the Scotch.

Coley Doctor sat outside of Louis Quartorze behind the dark tinted windows of his rental Buick. Sometimes he wondered if he was just nosey or if he was a good detective. Earlier he had parked in the Blaylocks' driveway after having dinner with Willy and Ginny at the Prospect Inn. No one was home. Sandy had evidently left as she said she was going to do. Both cars were gone.

He decided to wait awhile and see if Cliff came home. He wanted to confront him one more time before the FBI got in the mix.

Then Adrienne McCord, dress fetchingly slinky, had gotten in her Mercedes next door. He watched until she disappeared from Lamplighter Place and turned north on Stag Creek Road. He almost screwed up when he passed a car, and then that car immediately passed him. Some guy, alone in a car, was hanging right on Adrienne's tail. Now that was interesting!

He had chanced one quick peek through the window and saw Adrienne sitting with the slick-looking, tall dark man who had scouted out the scene through the windows before going in. He figured that if the meeting were preplanned, she would have waited for him to escort her inside Louis Quatorze.

An hour and a half passed. He chanced another peek inside and saw the two all touchy-touchy at the bar. Within a few minutes they both came out the door, walked about a block down the sidewalk and entered another bistro. Adrienne was having difficulty standing in her high heels and was willingly supported by her handsome friend. He thought of poor Alex in Seattle. He thought of her boldness the night he was out with her. This woman was loose as a goose and asking for trouble.

He looked north along the Hudson River and saw the majestic masts of the *Tashtego* just beyond the bridge. He picked up the cellular phone, deciding to check in with Willy and Ginny, and tell them not to expect him tonight.

"All's quiet here, Coley. Everything looks quiet on the *Jersey Trick* too. Do you suppose your Lila gave you a bum steer?"

"Maybe so, but I don't think so. Someone's got Adrienne McCord in tow at a bar about a mile south of you. I've decided to play detective."

"I think you're jealous, Coley. You thought you had Adrienne under your wing."

"Willy, this guy was following her, all the way from Stag Creek."

"Careful, Coley. Don't do anything stupid. We don't know what we're mixed up with here. Check back in an hour if it's convenient. I'm not going to sleep anyway."

"How's Ginny?"

"Out like a light. She's right at home on a mooring."

44

H eavy Laval stirred in his room. He had dozed off during the repetitive viewing of flesh rubbing against flesh on the TV screen. He flipped it off and walked over to the window. The dimly lit parking area at the Wellington Inn was perhaps half full. The disco was probably beginning another busy night. He glanced at his Cherokee, still isolated at the far end of the lot next to the woods.

He splashed some water on his face, and rubbed at his stubble of a beard with a towel, deciding not to shave. There would be plenty of time for that on the way to Florida. He stuffed the Glock into his belt, put on his jacket, and checked to make sure the weapon did not show.

Heavy was very pleased with himself, grinning as he shoved the package containing the sixty thousand dollars into a laundry bag with some dirty clothes. No more bosses for him! Down the line he would take another chunk out of Cliff Blaylock. The way he saw it, everything Blaylock had would someday be his.

He decided against checking out. The cardholder would have to argue that out with the hotel some day. There was a real spring in his step as he walked out of the hotel. There was nothing like a bag full of money to make a guy feel good, he thought. No more sharing. It was great to be the top dog.

He strode across the parking lot, stopping only once, to watch several classy suburban chicks get out of their car and ankle toward the Bee's Knees Disco. Just for an instant, he thought about how great it would be to have one of them stashed away in the Cherokee to bang around on during his trip. Then he thought about Florida and reasoned that there would be plenty of chicks there, maybe even one with a nice place to stay.

He unlocked the Cherokee, opened the door and tossed the bag into the back, and climbed inside. The instant the door closed, a rude nudge of cold steel pressed into his neck.

"Heavy, keep both hands on the steering wheel. You take even one off and I blow your brains all over the place." Crackers leaned forward, pressing a nine millimeter against the base of his skull, and wrapping his other arm around his neck to prod him with the sharp point of a rigging knife. "Drive out of here, slowly please, and follow instructions. Understand? We all know how stupid you are. You try anything stupid now, you die."

Laval froze, thought briefly about going for his gun, but realized that he must wait for a better time. "What do you want? I have nothing of value. What do you want?" he grunted again.

"We'll have to see what Bocco says. I'm sure he will tell you what he wants. He says you are a piece of crap. Now what would he want from a piece of crap?" Crackers rasped out the words, laughing when he finished.

Crackers jabbed him with the ice-pick sharp rigging knife. "Feel this? You make one move and it will come out the other side of your neck." He reached over and pulled the Glock from Laval's belt. "Nice gun. I can always use a new one. Now go, get us out of here."

Laval drove out of the hotel parking lot onto the main road, following frequent instructions from Crackers, who kept his weapons prodding into his neck.

"Friend, we can be friends you know," Laval grunted, barely audible.

"Just keep driving, and tell me how we can be friends."

"I have a lot of money. I can make you rich. As much as twenty five thousand dollars. Now please put your weapons away." Laval marvelled at the appeal of his simple proposition.

Crackers prodded him again with the knife. "Okay, friend, since you bring it up, tell me where you will get the money. And tell me right now, or I will cut off your ear. This knife is very sharp. Don't worry, you'll hardly feel it." Crackers persisted with his rasping maniacal laugh. "Now!"

"The money is nearby. It won't take long," squealed Laval.

"Sorry, that's not good enough. You can tell your story to Bocco." Crackers lifted the point of the rigging knife to Laval's ear and scraped it along the edge.

"No! Stop! I will pay you now. Is it a deal?"

"Of course it's a deal. Pull over on the shoulder and keep your hands on the wheel." Crackers prodded his ear with the knife one last time, as Heavy Laval pulled over on the shoulder of the road.

"In the bag, on the floor next to you. There is a package inside. Take your twenty-five thousand."

Crackers still holding the gun to Laval's head reached down and picked up the plastic laundry bag. Fumbling around inside he produced the large envelope. "Okay, I have it. Thank you very much. I can see that you are not always stupid."

"Now open the envelope and help yourself to twenty-five thousand," Laval instructed nervously as he again felt the knife at his ear.

"You are stupid, aren't you? I prefer to keep the whole bag. How much do I have?"

"I thought we had a deal," persisted Laval.

"How much, fool?" Another jab came at the ear.

"Sixty thousand." Laval could feel warm blood running from a small wound.

"Thank you very much. If you think you've been cheated, you may bring it up with Bocco. You have my permission." Again the maniacal raspy laugh came from the back seat. "Now, my friend, turn left up ahead, along the big river."

Within a few minutes they were headed north on a winding road along the Hudson River. The roadway passed beneath the approach to the Tappan Zee Bridge. About a mile ahead Laval could see the *Jersey Trick* moored offshore. A short distance behind it he saw the familiar outline of the sailing yacht he had plundered in Tarrytown. Strange, he thought to himself.

They passed the *Tashtego* and kept driving until the *Jersey Trick* was visible a few hundred feet away. Crackers smacked Laval alongside the head with the knife blade and instructed him to turn down a long driveway that led to a small dock.

"Now, blink your headlights four times and then shut them off," came instructions from the rear seat.

Laval, still with a gun to his head watched two men board a small runabout tethered to the stern of the *Jersey Trick*. There was the cough of an outboard motor and then the steady throb of the small engine as it pointed toward the dock in front of them.

"Crackers, that you?" A voice came from the runabout.

"Yes, I have Mr. Laval, who likes to make deals." He prodded Heavy with the gun as they walked to the runabout in the darkness. Crackers carried the hotel laundry bag.

Within a couple of minutes they were aboard the *Jersey Trick*. Bocco sat on a deck chair on the fore-deck waiting as the men approached him.

Crackers tossed the laundry bag on the deck in front of Bocco. "Compliments of Heavy Laval. He thought I was a cheap bastard. He thought he could buy me for sixty thousand dollars."

"Heavy, sorry to hear about your companion."

Laval didn't expect such civility. "Companion?"

"Yes, Red Irons, he was burned beyond recognition in a car fire at the Wellington Inn." Bocco smiled in the dim light.

"I didn't know. What happened?" He remembered clearly the

charred remains of the vehicle in the Wellington Inn parking lot, but didn't have a thought that it might have been Red Irons.

"We're sorry about Irons, Heavy. We thought he was a thief. We thought he was holding some product. We didn't know you were going to bring us the money for some of it."

"Glad to help, Bocco. I was on my way to Hoboken to bring you the money, until I was stopped by your man here." He nodded at Crackers.

Crackers roared with his insane rasping laugh.

Bocco lifted a hand to hush Crackers. "Crackers, I'm going to put you in charge of this dimwit until he tells us everything he knows. Take him down to the security cabin. Tie him up and if you have to, beat the truth out of him."

"Bocco, please, I've told you everything I know... I... I brung you the money, didn't I?"

"As a matter of fact you didn't; Crackers did. Enough of this talk. Take him below deck."

Laval, helpless, was led below deck, handcuffed to a stanchion and left in a barren locked room. Crackers pointed a finger at him. "I'll be seeing you soon. You heard what the boss said. Everything you know. Relax. That can't be much." Laughing again, Crackers closed the door behind him.

Willy Hanson sat in the hatch of the *Tashtego*, field glasses trained on the *Jersey Trick*. Fascinated, he had watched the lights blink on shore, and then the runabout sent to pick up the two men. In the dim light, he could not pick up much of the conversation. There was a lot of swearing and some obvious animosity among the members of the group.

Twice he thought he heard the names, Bocco, and Heavy Laval. Voices tended to travel clearly over the water that separated the two vessels. Yet, he couldn't be sure. He wished that Coley

Doctor would check back with him. An hour had passed. He decided he would feel a lot better with Coley aboard. If it were okay with Coley, he would like to bring the FBI aboard the *Tashtego*. There were listening devices that would pick up practically everything said aboard the *Jersey Trick*.

Then a thought crossed his mind that raised the hair on his neck. If indeed Heavy Laval was aboard the *Jersey Trick*, he would spot the *Tashtego* in an instant.

Willy went below deck and contemplated waking Ginny, but then decided he'd wait. He went aft to a stern hatch, went below and opened a security locker and withdrew a high-powered rifle. Once again he positioned himself in the hatch where he could keep a low profile as he continued to watch the *Jersey Trick*. Damn it! He wished Coley would call.

A small lantern was lit, illuminating the stern deck of the *Jersey Trick*. He framed the deck in his binoculars. A half dozen people including two strikingly attractive women were hoisting glasses, laughing and giggling about something. He heard the number sixty thousand dollars emphasized several times. And then once, for sure, he heard Heavy Laval's name mentioned loud and clear, and then everyone laughed, as if there was some big joke about him.

45

Coley crouched low in the rental Buick. Adrienne and her companion came out of the Shad Bin, a run-down little joint that looked out of place in an otherwise picturesque area. She staggered and he caught her in his arms, and then held her against him and locked lips with her. She started squirming and grasping, obviously enthralled by the mouth-to-mouth resuscitation.

Coley eyed her companion, half-walking, half-carrying her back to Louis Quatorze where their cars were parked. He fumbled in her purse until he found the keys to the Mercedes and then helped her enter the passenger side door. At least he's going to do the driving, he thought, otherwise he'd have to come up with some excuse to butt in.

He followed the Mercedes south through Piermont. It finally made a right turn and they soon wound up on a road that Coley knew pointed in the general direction of Stag Creek.

He kept his distance. Losing them was not a problem. There was virtually no other traffic at this hour. She was all over him as they drove. Their heads merged as one and then became one as her head disappeared. The Mercedes started to weave erratically as they approached the New Jersey State line. He slammed on the brakes when they stopped about a quarter mile in front of him.

"The bastard!" Coley muttered to himself. They must have met before tonight, but why then would he have had to follow her in the first place? The Mercedes moved away slowly from the shoulder and drove straight to Lamplighter Place. Coley passed the short street and returned a couple of minutes later, not wanting to be obviously on his tail. The porch light was on and there was a light upstairs. Acting quickly, he doused his lights and turned into the Blaylocks' driveway next door, making sure the house hid him from view. There were no cars. Sandy had left and Cliff was still missing as far as he knew. He got out of his car and positioned himself in the darkness where he could see Adrienne's front door and the parked Mercedes.

He waited and waited, for over an hour. Now he was sure that Adrienne must have known him before tonight. She didn't strike him as the kind of woman who would pick up a one night stand and take him to her own home. He had surely misjudged her. Yet she had come on to him as well. He remembered her hyperintensity. There was something odd about her.

Adrienne's porchlight went dark. He saw the man walk to the Mercedes in the shadows. He carried a small suitcase or a box that he tossed into the back seat. He stood for a moment and looked back at the house, seeming to stare at the lighted room upstairs. He made a move to walk back, then hesitated and quickly got into the Mercedes and drove away. Coley followed him after he turned north off Lamplighter Place. He eased his car onto Stag Creek Road with his lights out and already the Mercedes had disappeared around the curve about a quarter mile away. He started to follow and then stopped. The guy was no doubt headed back to Louis Quatorze to pick up his own car.

He made a U-turn, raced back to Lamplighter Place and pulled into the McCords' driveway. He couldn't live with himself without checking on Adrienne McCord. It was just instinct, but something was wrong.

The light was still on upstairs. He rang the bell, then rapped on the door. No answer. He tried the knob and the door swung open. "Adrienne! It's Coley!" Still not a sound.

Then he smelled it, the smell of raw gas. Then a strong whiff that was almost overpowering. He flung the door open, paused to throw a foyer chair through a large picture window in the living room. Taking a deep breath, he ran straight back to where he expected to find the kitchen and he did. The hiss of gas came from the range. Frantically he turned the knobs and then yelled, "Adrienne! Adrienne!" No answer. He raced up the flight of stairs to where he had seen the light. Adrienne's nude form was draped across the bed.

"Adrienne!" He shouted as he reached her. Wasting no time he grasped her around the waist and hoisted her slender form to one shoulder, went down the stairs and into the front yard. He laid her down in the grass far away from the house and collapsed a few seconds beside her. He saw her arm move. She was alive!

He shook her and tried to breathe more life into her, finally propping her up against a large oak tree. She moaned then retched as she struggled to maintain her balance. "Stand there," he ordered, "I don't want you to lie down. This is Coley! You've been gassed. Try to stay awake!"

He fished inside his jacket pocket, withdrew the small cellular phone and dialed 911. "Gas victim, possible fire, McCord house on Lamplighter Place. Need an ambulance and fire equipment."

"Stay calm mister. We hear you. Please repeat and identify yourself."

Seconds after he was off the phone, a police cruiser, lights flashing, entered the driveway, quickly followed by another.

"She needs help." He pointed to Adrienne tottering against the Mercedes. "The house was full of gas, I don't know whether I got it all turned off or not."

Coley had taken off his jacket to drape around the nude Adrienne. His weapon in the shoulder holster was in full view.

The policeman drew his own gun and leveled it at Coley. "Keep your hands up! Up!" Another policeman grabbed his weapon and patted him down. "Just stay right there and don't move. We'll get to you in a minute."

"He's okay." Patrolman Hinkle, who had just arrived on the scene spoke "That's Coley Doctor. He's the one that brought the gun into the station. He's working on the Blaylock case. I know all about him."

Coley interrupted them. "You guys better get in touch with the police over in Piermont. There could be a blue Pinto in the parking lot of Louis Quatorze that belongs to the guy who turned on the gas burners here. Also there should be Adrienne McCord's Mercedes. Last three digits, 209. He drove Adrienne's car out of here less than fifteen minutes ago. He's probably gone by now. Some of the restaurant employees might be able to tell you something about the guy."

"We'll see about that," said the policeman with a gun. "Just stay right there. You've still got a lot of explaining to do."

Coley started to breathe a little easier. The cops had their job to do. "I'm the one who made the 911 call. This can all be explained, but it will take a while."

And it did. It was a full two hours after the ambulance took Adrienne to the hospital before he was free to leave the police station.

"Coley Doctor! Playing cops and robbers again!" The familiar voice startled him just as he was accepting his weapon back from the police. He turned around to face an old poker-faced, sardonic friend, Mark Whitcomb of the FBI.

"Mark! You don't know how welcome a sight you are. The last time I saw you, we nailed that son of a gun over in Hong Kong."

"When I heard you and Willy were up here nosing around the Blaylock case and the McCord case, I insisted on taking a look. I guess you knew we were involved now."

"Hell yes, the NYPD and these guys all know the FBI is involved. But not in my case. All I'm trying to do is nail the thief of Blaylock's rare penny."

"The two cases have turned into one case, Coley." Whitcomb frowned. "And the further we dig in, the messier it gets."

"Let me guess. You think Blaylock might have been involved in the McCord case."

"Right. Ballistics is running more tests. The weapon you found is registered to Cliff Blaylock. A spent bullet lodged in a tree near the shooting could be a possible match." Whitcomb studied Coley's face. It was obvious he had a lot of respect for the man, though he did tend to run wild once in awhile. "Coley, tell me all you know about this incident tonight, at the McCords' house."

Coley and Whitcomb adjourned to the front seat of Whitcomb's car where they spent the next half hour or so talking. Coley tried to fill him in with his total involvement in the case.

"Where's Willy Hanson these days?" Whitcomb asked knowing that in the past, wherever Coley was, Willy was not far away.

"He and Ginny are on a mooring off Nyack in the Hudson, on the *Tashtego*. I'm sure he wants to talk to you."

"Coley, I suggest we all meet at the Wellington Inn at seven tomorrow morning. I'm staying there. We'll have some breakfast and compare notes. Willy, Ginny, the Rockland Police, the local police, you and I. We're close to breaking this thing. We've got to be sure that we're not stepping on each others' toes."

"Sounds good to me," Coley agreed. They paused while Whitcomb received a call.

"That's strange," Whitcomb said. "They found the Pinto in the parking lot at Louis Quatorze. It was a rental car, some small company around Newark. The papers on the visor say it was rented by some guy named Percy Leroy."

"Ring a bell?"

"Yes it does, Coley. He was a small time hood in Chelsea who disappeared a couple years ago. The rumor is he's wearing concrete shoes, looking up at the Verrazano Narrows Bridge."

"How about Adrienne McCord's Mercedes?"

"It's not at Louis Quatorze. The guy must still have it or maybe he ditched it someplace. We've notified all close jurisdictions."

Coley nodded his approval. He had to hand it to Whitcomb. He was thorough. "Mark, if you don't mind, I'm going to cruise on over to the hospital and check on Adrienne."

"I'll go with you, but it's probably a wasted trip. The boys just spoke to the hospital. She's in rough shape. She's full of natural gas, booze, and cocaine."

"Cocaine! How do they know that already?" Coley's mind was going a mile a minute. That may be why she looked so odd to him at times.

"She told the boys in the ambulance. I hope she lives, Coley. Where's your car?"

"Behind Blaylock's house."

"You come with me, Coley. Maybe Blaylock will be home when we get back over there."

"Mark, it's just a hunch. But I'd bet Blaylock's flown the coop. He knows I fished his gun out of the Hackensack River. If he really had anything to do with McCord's death, he's quaking in his boots someplace."

"You've met him several times. Is he dangerous?"

"Nope, he's a wimp. But right now he's a desperate wimp." Coley shrugged. "What bothers me is that he keeps playing footsy with Heavy Laval. There must have been a big payoff for the AMERI."

"Under the circumstances, Coley, I think I'll get a warrant and search Blaylock's house. I think the AMERI should be held as evidence until we get some explanation for the scratches."

"You know, Mark, I just recalled something that I had forgotten in all the excitement. When Adrienne's date came out of the house, he was carrying a small suitcase. In view of what happened, I'll bet it was the cocaine stash."

"Possibly. If he was the kind of a guy who would try to asphyxiate someone, he could be mixed up in anything."

"I guess at the time, when I saw the suitcase, I thought maybe he had shacked up at her place last night and they had some kind of a spat."

"You think a lot about things like that, don't you, Coley. I'd worry about myself if my mind was in the gutter as much as yours."

Coley frowned at the agent. Sometimes Whitcomb's perfection got on his nerves. He tried to imagine him in bed with a woman. He couldn't.

When they arrived at the hospital, they found Adrienne McCord had been placed in intensive care, and were advised that no visitors were allowed. The physician on duty told them that a conversation with anyone other than close family members was out of the question.

"Thanks, doctor, I'll check back in the morning. She didn't happen to mention the name of the person she spent the evening with tonight, did she?" Coley persisted.

"No, she didn't. She was in no condition for conversation of any kind, I assure you."

"Relax Coley," Whitcomb interjected. "I have a report from the boys who questioned a piano player at Louis Quatorze. The guy she was with called himself Elvis."

Coley shrugged. "That doesn't help us much." He looked at his watch. It was past midnight. "You mind if I go on up to the Wellington Inn with you? I'll get a room. I hate to pester Willy and Ginny on the *Tashtego* tonight. That way I'll be fresh for your big meeting in the morning."

"Good idea, Coley. I warn you, the joint charges an arm and a leg."

"Good! I'll send the bill to Blaylock."

The drive to the Wellington took about fifteen minutes. Coley registered at the desk, and then had a casual afterthought. "By the way, I would like to make a reservation for a friend of mine for tomorrow." He decided that if Willy and Ginny didn't want it, it would be easy enough to cancel. It would be his treat. Somehow he couldn't imagine being comfortable on the *Tashtego*.

"The name, sir?" queried the pert miss behind the counter.

"Hanson, Willy Hanson." He watched the clerk work with the computer.

"Sir, we have a William Conrad Hanson here now. He checked in a couple of days ago. Would that be the same party?"

"Yes it would." Coley stared at the clerk in shock. He had talked to Willy several times recently aboard the *Tashtego*. He turned toward Mark Whitcomb, who was waiting for him before he went up to his room. "William Conrad Hanson is Willy's full name, although I've never known him to use it."

Then it hit him. The credit cards! The credit cards stolen from Ginny by Heavy Laval! Could it be the guy was stupid enough to use one? He quickly explained the situation to Whitcomb.

Whitcomb swung into action, showing the desk clerk his FBI credentials. "Call the man's room. When he answers just tell him it was a mistake, and you're sorry."

The phone rang on and on. "He doesn't answer, sir." Meanwhile the manager emerged and she was explaining the situation to him.

"It's imperative that we get into that room right away." Whitcomb addressed the manager.

The manager hesitated. "Does this pertain to the investigation of the car bombing in our parking lot?"

"Yes, yes, yes! Hurry man, let's get up there!" Whitcomb watched as the manager produced a pass key. "Come on, Coley, you come along. Keep your weapon ready when we get upstairs." They followed the reluctant manager to the elevator.

Upstairs, the manager tapped repeatedly on the door. There was no answer. Whitcomb nodded toward the pass key in his hand. The manager stepped nervously away from the door, handing the key to Whitcomb, who now stood with gun drawn as did Coley.

Whitcomb and Coley burst into the room the instant the door opened. A quick check revealed no one at home. A small pile of dirty clothes lay on the rumpled bed. Several empty liquor bottles and room service trays were on the floor by the bed. The closet was empty.

Whitcomb, looking disappointed, holstered his gun and turned toward the manager. "Seal off this room. Let no one in until my boys have secured the contents they need for evidence."

Coley looked at a room service chit on one of the trays. It was dated that day. "He can't be far, Mark. He's too stupid to last very long."

46

Cliff Blaylock sat at the small wooden desk in his motel room just off the Garden State Parkway. Writing the letter to Sandy was the hardest thing he ever did. He counted five pages written on a legal-size yellow pad, and was not finished. He had spelled out all his misadventures starting with the day that he shot Willis in the parking lot of the Wellington Inn. He tried desperately to include every last detail.

Rising from his chair, he walked to the second story window and looked outside. Home was probably five miles away. From where he stood, he looked out across a wooded area. In the distance he could glimpse the pristine parkway winding southward through the autumn colors. He and Sandy had always especially loved the autumn. Their life together had been so good for both of them. But his spur of the moment action had brought it to a halt. Every action he had taken since that event had mired him in a situation that was impossible to justify to anyone. But at least he would make this last effort with Sandy.

He looked at himself in the long mirror that hung on the bathroom door. His thinning blond hair was shaggy and the three days' growth of unshaven stubble on his face made him look like a stranger to himself. Of course, he seldom ate anymore. Always slender, now he looked emaciated.

Walking back to the small desk, he glanced at the bed. He had placed a heavy bath towel across the two pillows stacked one on top of the other. Sandy's gleaming .22 automatic lay in the center of the white towel, clip inserted, ready for action.

But there was still work to do at the desk. He would prepare a detailed accounting. In a way, this was the hardest part of his task. They had scrimped and saved for all their years for a security they had hoped to share together someday. But now he would put a halt to those dreams while there was still enough left for Sandy to find a life that would be rewarding to her.

First there was the seventy-eight thousand he had spent for the AMERI. That was a shrewd investment, now rendered worthless as a result of the scratches. The insurance company had made it clear that they were rejecting his claim. There was the sixty thousand he had given Heavy Laval just a few days ago, plus the first payment of ten thousand dollars. Then there was the twenty thousand in bullion that Laval had stolen. It all added up to 168,000 dollars.

Sandy didn't know that he had lost his job. He hadn't done a lick of work since the slaying. Justifiably, his company had rejected all of his excuses and flimsy alibis. He could see now that the truth in the beginning would have been better. Or would it? Truth would have demanded his confession, and his life would have deteriorated in another painful way.

Now finished with the accounting of his days since the slaying, he reread the letter carefully, and heard himself sigh with satisfaction. He put it in an envelope, sealed it, and printed Sandy Blaylock's name on the front in large block letters.

Leaving the envelope in the middle of the writing desk, Blaylock walked over to the bed and picked up the small automatic. He laid down and propped his head on the towels atop the two thick pillows. He could see the autumn leaves outside the window, watching one occasionally fall and waft its way toward the ground.

Before releasing the safety lever, he pointed the gun first at his forehead, then at his temple. He put it to his lips and pointed it slightly upward, finally deciding that would be the surest way for success. He then remembered reading somewhere in a mystery novel, that the thumb was the best trigger finger for such a procedure, thus reversing the small automatic for an accurate aim. He carefully released the safety lever and brought the weapon to his choice of positions.

He hesitated. He could feel the sweat on his palm as the gun slipped against it. His heart was beating so hard, he could actually hear it. Sweat from his forehead found its way to his eyes. Then tears gushed for no reason at all.

After perhaps thirty seconds, he carefully reversed the gun and re-set the safety. He laid it on the night table next to him and lay without perceptible movement for a long time. "My God!" he finally screamed. "I haven't the guts! Please, please help me do it. Somebody. Anybody with guts!" He rolled over trembling, and buried his head in the pillows.

After a half hour or so, Cliff Blaylock got out of bed. He doused his face with cold water, and rubbed his head vigorously with a towel. He stuffed the envelope into his inside jacket pocket and the automatic into a side pocket and then went downstairs to pay for the room.

The desk clerk eyed the unshaven man suspiciously. "Something wrong with the room, sir?"

"No, not at all. I just wanted to catch a little nap. I'll pay cash for that." He forced a smile toward the clerk who kept staring at him as he tore up a credit card impression he had taken earlier.

"Here's your receipt, sir. Come again when you can stay a while." The clerk flashed a weak smile.

Outside, Blaylock climbed into his BMW, drove a few blocks, and then turned north on the Garden State Parkway. Soon he was on the New York Thruway heading toward the Catskills. He rolled the windows down. The cool air felt exhilarating.

And then he had an idea! Blaylock rubbed at the ample stubble on his face. He wished he had shaved. He got off the thruway at the Harriman exit and made a U-turn. From there he sped along with the heavy evening traffic toward the Tappan Zee Bridge.

47

Willy had dozed on and off once the noise aboard the *Jersey Trick* began to calm down. The group seemed to be doing a lot of celebrating about something. There were two women aboard who, from his distance, were gorgeous. They seemed to be the center of attention in the early part of the evening. Twice he heard Heavy Laval's name spoken, but no one above deck filled the description that Ginny had given of him.

Coley had called him twice, the last time reporting the use of his credit card by Heavy Laval at the Wellington Inn. At least the room service people gave a description of the guest that matched Ginny's description of Laval.

It was about midnight when his cellular phone beeped. He snapped wide awake, rising up in the sleeping bag he had spread on a bench in the cockpit, noticing as he did so that all but a couple of lights had been turned out on the *Jersey Trick*.

"Willy, did I wake you up?" It was a muffled voice that he struggled to recognize. "I ... I ... just had to call. I'm in my car in Tarrytown. You've obviously moved the *Tashtego*."

"Cliff Blaylock! This sounds like Cliff Blaylock."

"Right! I've got to see you Willy. The sooner, the better." There was a long silence.

"Okay, okay, so you have to see me. Can it wait until morning?" The thought of leaving Ginny, given the proximity of the *Jersey Trick*, was unthinkable to him.

"Please, Willy. Right now."

"Can you row a dinghy?"

"Yeah, actually, I'm pretty good at it."

"If you are in Tarrytown, cross the bridge. You'll see the *Tashtego* moored about a half mile north of the bridge. Take the shore road until you reach a sign lettered, THE JANZENS. Take the driveway down to the dock at the edge of the water. There is a dinghy there. Come on out, I'll wait in the cockpit. Try to be quiet. Ginny's catching up on her sleep."

"I'm glad to hear that Willy. I hope Ginny forgives me someday."

"That's a tough one, Cliff. You're going to have to handle that." Blaylock hung up.

Now what was that all about, he wondered. What wouldn't wait till morning? He rubbed his eyes, then stored the rifle in the keep beside him. The *Jersey Trick* was now totally dark. A rising new moon lit the Tappan Zee. He felt it safe to doze until Blaylock arrived.

It didn't take long. In fact, it seemed to happen instantly. Blaylock dimmed the lights once he entered the Janzens' driveway. Willy watched him walk out on the small dock, and then bend to loosen the lines that held the dinghy. As he started across, Willy saw that he was an excellent rower, pulling strong on the port oar to compensate for the outgoing tide.

Willy dropped a ladder over the side. Finally the dinghy thumped against the hull of the *Tashtego*. Willy took his bowline and secured the dinghy to an aft cleat. Blaylock scrambled up the ladder, climbed aboard, and then sighed heavily as he sat down on a cockpit bench. "Wow, that was a workout. I'm not used to physical stuff. I was on the water a lot as a kid in Wisconsin. Rowing, I guess, is something you never forget how to do."

"Sandy left town, I hear." Willy studied Blaylock's unshaven visage in the moonlight. He found it very difficult to be cordial. "So what's up, Cliff. I hear the AMERI is ruined. If you had just left everything to us, you might have got it back."

"You're right about all that, Willy. But the condition of the

AMERI really doesn't matter anymore. Hell, I'd never sell it anyway. It's all the other stuff that matters."

"What other stuff?"

"Like the fact that I killed Willis McCord with my .38. In my mind it will always be self-defense. But I killed him. I meant to kill him. If I had it to do over again, I'd do it."

Willy gazed steadily at Blaylock as he blurted out his confession. He had now lost his voice for a moment, choking up to the point that he couldn't go on.

Ginny popped her head from the hatch. "What the hell is going on out here? It's sleepy time."

"I'm sorry, Ginny, I should have told Cliff to wait until morning." Willy scowled at Blaylock, who now just sat staring in the distance toward the lights of Manhattan, far down river, below the Tappan Zee Bridge.

"I wrote a letter to Sandy. I guess she'll be leaving me. Rather than telling the story, I want you to read it. I might forget something." He handed Willy the envelope that he produced from his jacket pocket. "Ginny, I want you to read it too."

Willy got up and entered the cabin hatch, turned on a small lantern and started to open the envelope. "Cliff, maybe you should give this to your lawyer first."

"No, you deserve to know everything right now."

Willy read the laboriously written six pages, pausing once in awhile to read certain portions again. "I'll be damned. It looks like Coley Doctor had it figured pretty well." Willy handed the letter to Ginny.

"Yeah, I know he did. Coley confronted me with his version when he beat me to the gun in the river. It seemed like every time I did anything, things got worse."

"Cliff, you've dug yourself quite a hole. Coley might be able to put you next to the right lawyer. It's likely you could spend time in jail. There's bound to be a manslaughter charge, weapons charges, insurance fraud, and that's just the beginning of a long list." Willy shook his head. "What do you think, Ginny?"

Ginny was still absorbed in the letter to Sandy. Once finished, she looked squarely at Blaylock. "This is a suicide letter, isn't it?"

They watched Blaylock drop his head in agony. A spate of tears came, clearly visible in the moonlight. "It . . . it was. But I couldn't do it. I'm okay now."

Ginny shrugged her disbelief. "Cliff, you better get some help with that problem too. Look at yourself. You're far from okay. Are you going to give this to Sandy?"

Cliff nodded. "As soon as I can."

"Then tell her you love her somewhere in there, Cliff. Maybe at the end. No! Better you put it right at the beginning."

"I forgot. I guess I didn't think it was appropriate in a suicide note. I just wanted to tell her how it all happened. She'll probably leave me anyway."

"Cliff, tell me, was having Sandy so disappointed in you the main reason you considered killing yourself?"

Blaylock thought for a moment. "Yes, that was really the only reason."

"Then write the damn thing over and tell her you love her." Ginny handed him the letter and went out the hatch to the aft deck.

Blaylock nodded at Willy. "She's right, Willy. Ginny's a smart lady."

Willy grinned. "Don't tell her that, she'll send you a bill for counselling. Let's go outside and get some fresh air."

The lights of the small towns around the Tappan Zee were now mostly dimmed, letting the moonlight bathe the shoreline. You could almost read by the moon's brightness. Willy cast a quick glance at the *Jersey Trick*, now dimly lit and quiet. He thought for a moment about explaining the significance of the vessel to Cliff, but decided he had enough to think about. Evidently he was unaware of the hornet's nest he had stirred up with the drug cartel.

"It's beautiful out here. I see why you guys like this." Cliff was taking in the scenery when he paused, staring at the shoreline abeam of the *Jersey Trick*. "Mind if I borrow your glasses, Willy?" He pointed to the binoculars in a side keep.

"Help yourself." Willy felt apprehensive as Cliff began scanning the nearby shoreline.

"I don't believe it!" gasped Blaylock. "That's Heavy Laval's four-wheel drive. I'd know it anywhere!"

"There are a lot of Cherokees around, Cliff. It may not be his."

"I can read the plates. I've been playing tag with that Cherokee for days."

"Willy, that means the guy that slugged me might be right there on the *Jersey Trick*." Ginny glared at the fancy yacht.

"Relax, babe. We'll leave it to Whitcomb to find out. It looks like Coley was right about the tip he got from his friend, Lila." Willy looked at his watch. "In about three hours Whitcomb will be having his war council. Meanwhile he's got a tail on everyone that leaves the *Jersey Trick*."

Blaylock looked puzzle. "It looks like I missed a lot. Who is Whitcomb?"

"Whitcomb is FBI. You opened a Pandora's box you wouldn't believe. By the way, Cliff, who carved Willis's name in the AMERI? I didn't see that in your letter."

"Heavy Laval. I guess the stupid fool did it to make a point that he was serious when he tried to shake me down. Like a lot of non-collectors he probably had no conception of what he was doing. Of course, the AMERI is comparatively worthless now."

Willy nodded, studying Cliff's every word. The man seemed incredibly calm now for having been through such an emotional meat grinder. "Cliff, I would like to keep your letter to Sandy for awhile." He tapped the envelope against his palm, as he continued to look at Blaylock. "I'll get a copy made before our meeting with Whitcomb. We'll drop by your house and give this back to you sometime today."

"Of course, Willy. Mind if I ask why?"

"There are facts in here Whitcomb should know. He's an old friend. I know him well enough to hold him to confidentiality until you're ready to go public."

Blaylock rubbed his chin in deep thought, knowing that there could be no logical way to turn back from his confession now. He shook his head decisively in the affirmative. "Anything you want, Willy. I want to help the investigation if I can."

"Good boy!" Willy looked pleased with his lost friend for the first time in a long time. "Hang around. We'll rustle up some bacon and eggs. Then we'll all take the dinghy in together. The FBI is due for a boarding party in an hour or so."

48

Elvis Clock was abruptly awakened by a tapping on his cabin door. It was five-thirty A.M. He opened the door a crack, and there stood Veronica, her five-foot ten draped in a sheer robe hanging agape over nothing but her sun-bronzed body.

"Bocco wants you front and center by six. We're having breakfast in the salon." She tossed her long blond hair and gaped openly at his nakedness. The smell of jasmine wafted through the doorway.

"Where's Bocco right now?"

"In the shower. Then he's got a stack of morning papers to read. Crackers went out and got them."

"Come on in." Elvis grasped her hand and trailed kisses up to the hollow of her neck. He led her in and then closed the door behind them.

"Look, we've got maybe fifteen minutes, and I don't like to be left hanging. You know what I mean?" She thrust herself boldly against Elvis.

"What happens in fifteen minutes?" Elvis asked as he began trailing kisses down her form.

"Bocco comes looking and you get shot."

"Hell, someday I'm gonna get shot anyway. This is worth the risk. Now be a bad girl and cooperate." Elvis maneuvered her to his unmade bunk and began to assault her furiously with his tongue and his manhood.

She was compliant, but totally unresponsive. He caught her smiling provocatively as she laid motionless to his attentions. "You bitch," he mumbled. "Playing one of your stupid games."

"You've got about five minutes left, baby. Bocco reads very fast. Now let's see if you're any good."

Within seconds her mood changed to a wildly uninhibited response. Soon came a low moan that built into a mindless scream. Elvis cupped his hand over her mouth as she bit into his finger, drawing blood.

When he pulled back she struggled from the bed and slipped on her robe. "Thanks. As the commercial says, I needed that! It's time to go see Bocco."

He glanced at his watch. It was a couple minutes to six. "What about me?"

"You? Gee, I hadn't given it a thought. Ask me again sometime." Veronica quickly slipped out the cabin door, and made her way to the salon on time.

Elvis wandered in five minutes late. If Bocco cared, he didn't say anything. He was still poring over an article in one of the papers. Veronica was lolling calmly in a deck lounge looking thoroughly engrossed in a paperback novel. Cracker wandered in and joined them. He filled a coffee cup and stood sipping from it at a porthole that overlooked the *Tashtego*.

Bocco broke the silence, taking his eyes from the newspaper. "The DA says they are going to make an arrest in a day or two. In fact, the way he put it, it sounds like a promise. He says there has been a lot of new evidence. Anybody here got any ideas, or are you all stupid?"

He paused for a few seconds to let his question sink in while he filled a coffee cup. "Well, I guess one thing is obvious, you're all stupid!"

Crackers turned from the window and sat on the edge of a deck chair. He sipped at his coffee and stared emotionlessly at Bocco. He had taken care of his jobs. He had taken care of Irons and brought Laval in. The boss couldn't be unhappy with him.

"Crackers, how's our prisoner?" Bocco spoke softly to his number one hit man.

"He is unhappy, boss. I keep him handcuffed to the stanchion except for food and bathroom." Crackers surrendered one of his rare smiles. "I tell him I will see to it that he is unhappy for the rest of his short life. He gets very mad when I say that." Crackers smiled again.

Bocco turned his attention to Elvis. "Mr. Clock. It seems we have a shortage. I'm surprised at you."

"Shortage?" Elvis tensed. He had no idea what Bocco meant.

"The cocaine. There's a couple of kilos missing. You told me you got them all. But there's a bigger problem than that, Mr. Clock." Bocco turned the last pages of the *Bergen Record* and gave him a cold stare. "I don't read a thing anywhere here about the mysterious demise of a certain Stag Creek socialite."

Elvis looked at Veronica, still outwardly absorbed in her book. He felt uncomfortable that she had a full audience to all Bocco's conversation. Who the hell was the boss anyway?

"Bocco, maybe it's too soon for the papers. Maybe they haven't found her yet. Who knows?" Elvis shrugged and tried to casually sip at his coffee.

"There also ain't no story about any house blowing up. Maybe you turned on the water and not the gas."

Crackers emitted one of his raspy maniacal laughs. "That is so funny, boss."

Elvis shot his co-killer a withering look. "Bocco, I did my job. Read tomorrow's papers for Chri-sakes."

"There ain't gonna be no tomorrow's paper. We're leaving tonight. For your sake, I hope you're right, Mr. Clock." Bocco kicked his heels up on a deck chair and crossed his arms. "Now let's get back to our other problem, the missing two kilos."

"I got everything she had. It was there beneath a pile of suitcases in the kid's room. There ain't no more, unless Heavy short-changed the kid on product. Ask Heavy." Elvis felt a surge of confidence. The handcuffed Heavy was obviously out of Bocco's favor.

"That's a good idea, Mr. Clock." Bocco turned to Crackers. "Bring our prisoner up here. We're gonna have a chat with him."

"Do I leave his cuffs on, Boss?"

"Hell yes. The guy is like an ape. He could do a lot of damage."

"No chance, boss." Crackers drew his nine millimeter. "He'd be fulla lead real quick." Again came the raspy chuckle as he rose to go below deck to where Laval was being held.

"Yeah, except we don't want a lot of noise right here in the middle of all the gentle folks in suburbia, do we? Right, Veronica?"

"You got that right, Bocco." Veronica stood up, letting the gauzy dressing gown flare open as she turned. "If you guys don't mind, I'm going to go dress for the day. I don't want to offend all the gentle folks in suburbia." She strolled to her stateroom, leaving all of them ogling her departure.

The fact that Veronica could come and go without the usual command from Bocco once again nagged at Elvis Clock's mind, this time seriously. Who was really in charge?

Bocco pressed some buttons on the intercom. "Peaches, come on up to the salon. I want you to meet an old friend."

There was little more than a grunt from the other end. Peaches had been sleeping soundly, resting up for a planned encounter with Judge Roy later in the day. Finally, after prompting, came a mumble, "Okay, Bocco. Be up in a couple of minutes."

Bocco scowled at Elvis. "Nobody knows Heavy Laval like Peaches. She'll know whether he's telling the truth or not."

Crackers quickly returned with Heavy Laval. His bushy unkempt hair and heavy stubble of black beard made him indeed look like a gorilla. He lumbered clumsily ahead of Crackers, hands cuffed in back of him.

"You stink, Heavy," Bocco growled. "Please don't sit down anywhere. Crackers, when we're finished here take him back on the aft deck and hose him down."

"Right boss. I told him he stinks too." Crackers beamed at the thought of hosing him down later on.

Laval became distracted as they ridiculed him. His bloodshot eyes caught the sight of the *Tashtego* out the bow window. The big sailboat was mooring nearby. As he watched, several men were climbing aboard from a small runabout. They were being met at the top of the boarding ladder by the tall, fancy babe he had beaten. He had hoped she might be dead.

"What'ya staring at Heavy? Haven't you ever seen a sailboat before?" Bocco glanced briefly at the *Tashtego*, but had no reason to be troubled by what he saw.

"Bocco, I'm hungry," replied Laval, snapping his eyes away from the sailboat.

"Hungry?" Bocco questioned with mock sincerity. "Crackers, what has our man here had for breakfast?"

"Nothing sir. I felt it was a waste of food and he would make more of a mess." Crackers was dead serious in his answer. What could be more logical than that, he thought.

"Nonsense, see that he gets some sweet rolls and coffee. Being a doomed man is punishment enough right now. Wouldn't you say so, Peaches?"

Peaches entered the salon and stood gaping at the seedy spectacle of the disheveled Laval in handcuffs. "Bocco, you promised I would never have to look at this bastard again."

"Relax Peaches, let's just say that he was caught with his fingers in our cash register. He'll be leaving us quite soon. That's a promise."

"Peaches, I'm sorry about what I did. I never meant ya no harm, Peaches." Heavy was desperately trying to find sympathy from her. After all, she had always forgiven him before.

Bocco held up his hand. "Enough bullshit. Heavy here claims he sold the kid ten kilos. Two are missing. Heavy shot the kid, so we can't ask him. We found the stuff in the kid's house, minus two kilos. Laval claims he didn't shoot our pusher, Willis McCord. Now tell me Peaches, do we believe Heavy Laval or not?"

"Heavy's a liar. He's always been a liar. You can't believe anything he says," Peaches snapped. "If any of that happened, I know nothing about it. May I go now?"

"Yeah, Peaches. Get some rest and then get dolled up. Your judge has just arrived in Newark." Bocco leered at Heavy Laval. "Peaches sure knows how to please the judiciary, Mr. Laval. Did you teach her all that?"

Laval hung his head on his chest not wanting to meet Bocco's stare. He instinctively tugged at his handcuffs, and then once again stared out the window of the salon and looked at the *Tashtego* in the distance. He squinted his bleary eyes. There were now three people in a rubber dinghy paddling toward shore, the fancy dark-haired babe, a man who he didn't recognize, and Cliff Blaylock! "Bocco, Peaches is mad at me. You know how women are. I guess I ain't too smart, and sometimes I forget things. But this I know. That man in the dinghy wearing a grey sweatshirt is Cliff Blaylock. He shot Willis McCord. If anything is missing, that son of a bitch has it."

Bocco jumped to the window and looked at the rubber dinghy. Several men on the bow of the *Tashtego* were watching them row ashore. Bocco shook his head. "Heavy, you gotta make up something better than that. What's the guy doing on that sailboat?"

"The kid, Willis McCord, pointed it out to me once. He said the guy next door to them, Blaylock, was a good buddy of the guy who owned the big sailboat. Blaylock bankrolled his drug deals." Heavy Laval paused. He began to sound logical, even to himself. He saw interest return to Bocco's face.

"How do you know that guy in the boat is McCord's neighbor?" The question came from Veronica unnoticed by the others, now standing again in the door to the salon.

"I saw him up close. The McCord kid said he was carrying a bundle, and the kid had planned a heist. We wore ski masks. I saw Blaylock. He didn't see me. When the shooting started, I lit out." There was enough truth to the story to make it sound convincing. Laval knew that he was fighting for his life.

Veronica strode into the room, still not dressed for the day, and stood squarely in front of Heavy Laval in a diaphanous dressing gown, hanging open over her statuesque bronzed body. "Mr. Laval, have you ever heard of Percy Lercy? He worked your Chelsea district long before you did."

"Yeah, I heard of him." Laval murmured, remembering the popular legend that he had been dumped under the Narrows Bridge.

"If you're lying, you'll join Percy. Tonight! If you're telling the truth, Bocco's got quite a job getting us out of this mess. But he will, and then you'll get another chance."

"Veronica! For Chris-sakes, the guys a damn liar." Bocco, furious, blurted his objection to the fact that Veronica was giving credence to Heavy Laval's story. "How the hell can we trust the bastard. He would have been out of sight with our sixty grand if I hadn't sent Crackers to haul him in."

"Settle down, Bocco, we'll know soon, won't we. Send one of the boys out to follow those guys in the rubber dinghy when they get ashore. Have him report to you every half hour." Veronica strolled from the room. It surely sounded like Veronica was really the boss.

Heavy Laval was hustled back below deck and put into the empty cargo room once again a prisoner. But he noticed that Crackers had stopped his insane cackling on the way back to his improvised cell. He was his usual silent self. He felt that things were looking up for him. At least he had a long-shot chance.

The woman, Veronica, had them squabbling among themselves. His story concocted of truths, half-truths, and lies would buy him time.

Anything was better than the alternative, looking up at the Narrows Bridge for an eternity, swinging around and around with the tide.

49

Willy phoned ahead, rousing Coley from his room as they drove from Nyack to his hotel. He wanted to bring Coley up to date on the Blaylock suicide letter before the meeting with Whitcomb, and get a copy of it made at the hotel. In front of him, Blaylock, in his BMW waved as he turned off toward Stag Creek and they continued toward the hotel. Willy was satisfied for the moment Cliff had purged his conscience and was no longer an immediate threat to end his own life.

Coley was waiting outside the hotel when they arrived. "Hey, good to see you guys! Let's go get a cup of coffee someplace. This joint's crawling with cops and FBI. We'll see enough of them at seven." Before leaving, Coley had the front desk make a Xerox of Blaylock's letter.

"Good work, Coley. We might as well run this over to Blaylock's house right now, in case we get tied up later on." Deep inside, Willy wanted to confirm that Blaylock had indeed gone to his home. Within minutes they arrived and saw his BMW next to the house.

Coley ran to the front door and surprised Blaylock with their quick delivery service. Willy watched as he handed Blaylock the letter and exchanged a few cordial words with him before returning to the car.

Next door, a patrol car sat in the driveway, and yellow "crime scene" tape fenced off the entire McCord property.

Willy glanced at the house. "You really did a job on the picture window, Coley." The chair was still lying in the front yard with the shattered glass.

"Man, I was scared to death. All I could smell was gas. I wanted some fresh air quick. I thought the house was going to blow up." Coley paused, remembering his impulse to turn a light switch. Only his haste to get to Adrienne had probably averted a disaster. "The police are getting search warrants right now for both houses."

Ginny had been quiet since leaving the *Tashtego* in the hands of two FBI men, and a Nyack police lieutenant. "Willy, those men aboard the *Tashtego*, they wouldn't try to put her under sail would they?"

"Not a chance. There isn't a sailor in the bunch. They're just using her for a listening post. The river is covered by at least two police launches spaced to the south, and a Coast Guard cutter standing by beyond the Narrows Bridge."

The *Tashtego* was home to Ginny. It was obvious she wanted

no more trouble with Heavy Laval. "What if the *Jersey Trick* gives them trouble? That boat is big enough to ram her and survive."

"Ginny, you saw the big duffle bag they brought aboard with the fishing poles strapped to it. There's more artillery in there than you can imagine. If they are crazy enough to start trouble, they'll have a big hole in their fancy boat." Coley sounded confident. Also he had a lot of respect for Whitcomb's decisions. "Don't worry about Heavy Laval. He's small fry. There are a lot bigger fish to fry aboard the *Jersey Trick*."

The trio arrived at the Wellington Inn about fifteen minutes after Whitcomb had begun his briefing. He stopped talking until all of them were seated, and then stared at his wristwatch. "Private investigators march to their own drum," he observed sarcastically. "They show up any old approximate time. We can't fire their asses, so we'll put up with it for now. I'm sorry, Ginny, for using such language, but certainly I don't include you as a PI. Miss Ginny Dubois is with us today because she is owner and skipper of the *Tashtego*, the sailboat we are using as a listening post down on the waterfront."

Ginny couldn't keep from butting in. "Mark, are those men capable of putting the *Tashtego* under sail? I had very little time to brief them. They seemed to be intimidated by the few things I did show them, like operating a marine toilet for instance."

Her remark drew a hearty laugh from the assembly of policemen.

Even the laconic Whitcomb flashed a smile. "Rest easy, Ginny, they have no intention of putting her under sail. They would probably have trouble finding the anchor line. But believe me, they do have their expertise in sophisticated weapons and listening devices. The rest of you gentlemen should know that Miss Dubois is the one who suffered a severe assault at the hands of Heavy Laval, whom we believe to be aboard the *Jersey Trick* right now."

Whitcomb went on and on with his briefing. For the last few

hours they had kept tabs on everyone boarding the *Jersey Trick*, and put a tail on everyone leaving the yacht. "They seem to be having some sort of a conclave aboard. A guest that boarded her a few minutes ago has been identified as a prominent judge from South Carolina."

Whitcomb concluded his briefing with a large map of the Hudson River on an easel. The map covered a section of the river running from West Point to the north, to the Verrazano Bridge to the south. Pointer in hand, he identified the position of everyone connected with the operation. "We plan to move in as soon as we are sure that everyone we're after has returned to the *Jersey Trick*. Remember at all times the prime objective of our joint effort is the capture of Bocco Lamas, whom we know to be a major player in the Caribbean drug trade. Keep alert. He's slipped through our fingers before. We anticipate moving in on them by surprise, just after dark."

Willy and Coley studied the highly detailed map. Willy leaned toward Coley and whispered. "Whitcomb should work for the Pentagon. He makes me feel like a kid playing cops and robbers. The man's a genius."

Coley shrugged. "A genius with a big budget. I sure hope the taxpayers get their money's worth."

"Miss Dubois." It was Whitcomb addressing Ginny. "It's time to get the *Tashtego* out of harm's way. I ask that you you move her south late this afternoon. We'll keep a couple of men aboard. We've arranged dockage for the night near Weehawken. Can you have her ready to go?"

Ginny looked at Willy for an answer.

"Hell yes, I'm ready if Ginny is. We'll be twenty miles closer to the Caribbean. When you going to make the pinch on Blaylock?"

"The Stag Creek police will attend to that this very afternoon. Any questions?"

Whitcomb's war council ended. Everyone rushed out to begin

working on the final details of their participation in what promised to be a memorable day.

Ginny had a last word of caution for Mark Whitcomb. "Mark, all your guys should keep some rain gear handy."

Whitcomb rolled his eyes at the sunlight outside the window. "Ginny, you are far too young to have misbehaving arthritic joints. What makes you think it's going to rain on our parade?"

"Mark, I suggest you listen to the marine weather radio. It was pretty iffy last night."

"I'll do that." The imperious Whitcomb blessed her with a condescending smile.

50

Captain Lorenzo circled the deck of the *Jersey Trick* two times, pacing at a slow, measured step. His response to an advertisement in a Miami paper had resulted in his being hired at a ludicrously high wage as skipper of the luxury yacht. He had been aboard her almost a year now, and knew little more about her owners than he knew the day he was hired.

The size of the *Jersey Trick* compared with the several vessels he once had in his command in the Chilean Navy. This sleek one hundred twenty footer had the engine of a beast. She'd do forty knots easily and had a penchant for knifing through rough water with little difficulty. He had heard that it was built for an Argentine billionaire with no restrictions as to cost.

He had a crew of seven. The first mate served as engineer. He had a cook with two assistants, two additional hands served as seamen assigned to maintenance most of the time. When guests were aboard, the two seamen worked as servers or bartenders in the salon. He had a communications officer that was really under the control of the chief corporate officer aboard. Bocco Lamas filled that slot at the moment.

Right now he stood at the rear of the bridge digesting a weather chart he had just been given. It was going to be a nasty little storm. Thirty to forty knot winds were possible just outside the Narrows. It was the remains of a tropical storm that had broken up over Hatteras.

"Perhaps we should wait until morning." He addressed the communications officer who sat looking at a duplicate of the weather map.

"That is not possible," came the reply from the radio shack.

Lorenzo shook his head in disappointment. "It will be uncomfortable until we can tuck into the Chesapeake."

"Comfort is not in Bocco's vocabulary once he has made a decision. You know that, Captain."

"What does the woman say?" The captain hesitated to call Veronica by name.

"I'm sure she knows Bocco's plans. Are you worried, Captain?" He peered intently at Lorenzo.

"Heavens no. We've been in much worse weather. We'll be pummeled a little for a short time, but the calm of the Chesapeake will come quite soon. I just worry about the comfort of the guests."

"That's not your worry, Captain. Veronica knows all about the possible weather. If she knows, Bocco knows."

Captain Lorenzo retreated from the radio shack and paced the deck one more time. He had a strange command, indeed. The staterooms up front were a virtually sealed private set of apartments, as was the main salon, and the several smaller cabins immediately below the salon. As captain, he was welcome in the isolated compound only under urgent circumstances. The cook and his catering staff were more welcome there than he as captain.

The fact was, he hated his strange command. He had made

up his mind that even his outlandish pay didn't justify being half a captain. He had overheard his engineer refer to him as "Half-Captain" Lorenzo once. He could even smile at that, because it was true. It was what went on up front that bothered him. He had seen enough to know that something very evil was going on up there.

Just as he reentered the bridge, he saw Bocco Lamas making his way toward him.

"Lorenzo, we leave at seven sharp. We will make a slow-down stop at the dock in Hoboken to drop off Judge Roy. As soon as he gets ashore, it's full throttle. Understood?"

"Yes sir. I expect that will be just in time for a little rain and a little breeze." Lorenzo watched him closely, trying to figure out if he had already been briefed about the inclement weather.

Bocco's face twisted into one of his rare smiles. "Nothing we can't cope with. Right Captain?"

"Absolutely." He watched Bocco make his way back toward his private compound. Under ordinary circumstances he would have recommended they either leave right now, or wait until the blow was over. But he, of course, was only Half-Captain.

He took off his cap and brushed his hand through his steel grey hair. He could already smell the moisture in the breeze. Personally, he didn't give a damn. A little rough weather now and then furnished the scant excitement he experienced. "Ah! Now that's a sight." Lorenzo murmured as the looked down the Tappan Zee. The big sailing ketch with the wide spreaders broke out in full sail and glided out and under the Tappan Zee Bridge. It brought back memories of his prepping days for the Chilean Navy.

Bocco strolled into the salon. Peaches was there boozing it up with Judge Roy. She winked at Bocco. The gal was learning. She was deftly seeing to it that the judge was getting three or four drinks to her one. His hands were clutching each boob like she was a giant radio. She was singing different little songs each time he changed the dial. He looked at his watch. Judge Roy would be out of it by the time he caught the limo in Hoboken. Bocco poured himself some scotch and sat down at the bar. Everything was falling neatly into place. The five hundred kilos he had picked up in Port Jefferson would soon be on their way to Baltimore.

His private intercom buzzed. He glanced at the master board. It was Veronica. "Bocco here," he answered.

"Bocco, baby. I've got the squirming hots just lying here thinking about you. Please come see me."

"Sure, why not? I'll be right down."

Bocco poured himself a couple more fingers of scotch and made his way toward Veronica's stateroom. They had some time to kill. It was certainly thoughtful of the bitch.

The door to her stateroom was slightly ajar. Her bronze body lay stretched out on the bed, legs spreadeagle, hands behind her head.

Grinning broadly as he seldom did, Bocco swung the door open and stepped inside.

The eight pound hammer dropped him like a steer at the stockyards. Veronica rolled over, her back to the scene while Elvis Clock dragged the body of Bocco Lamas to a big steamer trunk, already open against the wall. Folding the slender Lamas neatly at the hips, he stuffed him inside, shut the lid and closed the latches. He quickly threaded a heavy padlock into place and closed it until it clicked.

Elvis then sat on the trunk as Veronica rolled over to face him. "See baby, I told you all the time that it would go slick as a whistle. No problem."

"Elvis, you're the one that's slick. That was awesome."

"All for you baby. It's high time you had a guy around who can do you a few little favors now and then."

Veronica rose on her elbow and brushed her fingers through her heavy blond mane. She looked at her wristwatch. It was all that she wore. "This time, instead of fifteen minutes, we've got a couple of hours. Lock the damn door and come to baby. I've got a little something you can do right now."

51

Cliff Blaylock watched as the shopkeeper fitted the AMERI into the small gold frame. The large cent looked as pristine as ever with the reverse side up. The ugly, scarred obverse side would be pressed against the soft cotton forever as far as he was concerned. He had it wrapped in a small gift box, smiling with satisfaction at his last minute idea. He hoped the agents would permit him to board the *Tashtego* one more time.

Cliff groaned with disbelief as he drove along the river road toward Nyack. Far from shore, he saw the *Tashtego* in full sail passing under the main span of the Tappan Zee Bridge. The stately ketch was pointed south. He pulled over and watched for a couple of minutes feeling helpless as the *Tashtego* moved steadily down river in a fresh breeze over a full mile from where he sat.

He reached for his cellular phone and tapped out Willy's number. He answered on the first ring. "Willy, this is Cliff."

"Cliff, I figured you should be in jail by now. What's up?"

"Not much, I wrote another paragraph on my confession as Ginny suggested. I guess I blew the socks off my lawyer when he read a copy. He's going to accompany me to the Stag Creek police in a little while."

"Good boy, Cliff."

"I wanted to see you and Ginny before you left. In fact, I'm on shore, watching the *Tashtego* right now. She looks beautiful."

Cliff listened as Willy explained that Whitcomb had decided he wanted the *Tashtego* out of harm's way when they went after the *Jersey Trick.* "Whitcomb arranged for us to dock near Hoboken tonight. I guess we'll be off to the Caribbean in a day or two. Take care, Cliff. You'll be hearing from us soon. Coley will drop by and confer with your lawyer, okay?"

"Thanks, Willy. I'm sorry for all the trouble. You guys are something special." Blaylock felt sad as he continued to watch the ketch. He looked at the time. From what he knew about sailboats, it was probably making about eight knots or so down river. I could be in Hoboken long before they get there, he thought to himself. The *Tashtego* would be easy to find along the waterfront. What the hell, his inevitable date with the police could wait a wee bit longer. He'd surprise them in Hoboken. If he hurried, he might beat the evening rush hour traffic.

By the time the *Tashtego* reached the George Washington Bridge, the clouds in the thickening overcast were cutting down visibility considerably. A light mist began to further blur the shoreline from the *Tashtego.* The fresh breeze had virtually stopped blowing, and the jib sail began to luff and fall slack. Finally Ginny decided to haul down the sails, and switch on the auxilliary engine so they could run closer to the shoreline until they reached Hoboken. As darkness grew nearer visibility was reduced to perhaps a thousand yards. The concrete canyons of Manhattan disappeared on the port side.

In a half hour they scooted past the Port Imperial Ferry landing, busy this hour of the day bringing commuters from mid-town Manhattan to New Jersey. At that point a police launch pulled alongside. Willy confirmed by radio that they were to follow them.

Just south of the Hoboken Ferry Terminal they were guided to an unused commercial dock where they quickly secured the *Tashtego.*

"Gotta hand it to Whitcomb," Coley observed. "It was nice to have them meet us. It would have taken awhile to find this dock in the lousy weather."

The police boat waved their good-bye and rumbled back north in the heavy mist.

Back at the mooring in Nyack, Veronica was having a chat with Captain Lorenzo on the bridge of the *Jersey Trick.* "Bocco is really under the weather. He's decided to lie low for awhile. We'd like to get out of here in a half hour. The judge has passed out. He'll be going all the way to Baltimore with you."

"There'll be no docking in Hoboken then?"

"Captain, I want you to just brush up against the dock and then keep going. Peaches and I are headed for the airport and Miami, so we're getting off. I've set an alarm. Bocco will be back on the bridge with you after you clear the Narrows."

Lorenzo nodded. He hated the idea of docking in Hoboken anyway. "The weather bother you, ma'am? The winds are due to kick up in a half hour or so. It should be over pretty quick, but we might toss around a bit."

"Don't bother me a bit, Captain. This tub can take it can't she?"

Again Lorenzo nodded, then pointed through the rain to a commercial boat landing. A half dozen men in rain slickers were walking toward the dock. Two of them were carrying a long chest that looked to be heavy from the way they were toting it. Toward the end of the dock another man was standing aboard a thirty foot open launch. "They don't look like fishermen; I wonder what that is all about."

Veronica studied the group on the shore, all garbed in similar foul weather gear. "I can smell a cop a mile away, especially when you get seven of them together. Let's get this thing rolling, Lorenzo."

"Now?"

The man in the radio shack opened his door. "An officer of the Nyack police would like to talk to the skipper. Something about a missing persons report."

"Tell him you can't read him!" Veronica glared at Lorenzo. "Move, damn it, now! Let's get out of here."

The engines of the *Jersey Trick* rumbled to life as rain began to pelt against the windows. Now, on the shore, they could see several additional men moving toward the launch in the driving rain.

The two seamen on the bow of the *Jersey Trick* freed the hawser from the cleat leading to the mooring buoy and they were now moving slowly ahead, picking up speed steadily as Lorenzo opened the throttle.

Soon the shoreline dimmed in the rain. By the time the *Jersey Trick* passed under the Tappan Zee Bridge, Lorenzo had her up to thirty knots, pointing due south in the main channel of the Hudson River.

Veronica glanced toward the stern. Low on the water she could see the running lights of the launch. "More throttle, damn it!"

Lorenzo shook his head and pushed the vessel to three-quarter speed. The running lights off the launch faded into the mist. Visibility ahead was poor. Lorenzo tensed, realizing if anything were in their way, it would be difficult to avoid a collision.

"Ease off a little, Lorenzo. We've lost them. I'm going below for awhile. You okay?"

"Certainly." Now that he knew what she wanted him to do, he would do it. In fact, he would concentrate much better if she were not looking over his shoulder.

Below deck, Crackers sat playing solitaire in his cabin when Veronica approached the open door. She came in and locked it behind her. Crackers continued with his game of solitaire as she sat on his bunk facing him.

"How's Heavy Laval doing?" Veronica asked.

"He's in his cabin. I gave him two bottles of rum. He drank it all. He's no problem." Crackers squeaked just a little of his raspy laugh.

"Crackers, baby, can you swim?"

"Like a fish."

Veronica crossed her long legs and smiled, as Cracker's eyes stayed glued to the cards. She realized that if all men were like Crackers, she'd have a tougher time in the world. But his first and only love seemed to be weapons and explosives. "After Peaches and I jump ashore in Hoboken, I want you to wait until the boat has covered another hundred yards, and then swim for shore. Any problem with that?"

Crackers met her eyes, showing no emotion at all. "None. If I get caught, I will just say I'm drunk and fell off the dock into the water. What about Elvis? He cannot be allowed to discover what I am about to do."

"Don't worry about Elvis. I'll take care of him." She smiled to herself. Right now he was out like a light in her stateroom. "If you need me, I'll be in Peaches's cabin. Crackers, only you and I know about the explosive charge. Bocco's already fertilizer. That clear?"

Crackers merely nodded, and then whispered, "Yes, boss." He kept his eyes on his card game until she had left his cabin and closed the door behind her. He carefully picked up the cards and started to put them back in their small box. Then he thought better of it and tossed them into the wastebasket. He wouldn't need them anymore.

Outside his cabin now, Crackers stared at the shoreline, very close to them, and barely visible in the driving rain. He hoped that the Captain knew the waters. They were moving quite fast to be so close to the shore.

Because she asked, he decided to check on Heavy Laval one more time. He opened his tiny cabin. Laval was sprawled on the floor, the empty rum bottles lying on their sides, rolling with the movements of the boat. "Good-bye, bastard!" he muttered.

Soon he knelt on the floor of the small cargo room. Using a rigging knife he lifted the false section of flooring and leaned it against an adjoining wall. He opened the chest and secured some sticks of dynamite, a cap, and a timer. Working rapidly, he wired the explosives to the timer. He looked at his watch, then carefully set the assembled device back inside the box with the remaining explosives. He replaced the floor panel and stood back to make certain that it fit snugly and looked like all the others.

Crackers returned to his room, put his nine millimeter into a waterproof belt pouch along with some cash. As he prepared to leave he could hear the engines of the *Jersey Trick* revving down. The big yacht was steadily losing its forward speed.

Crackers went topside. The wind had abated, but the downpour of rain was torrential. The lit buildings and docks along the shore were barely visible. They passed a waterside restaurant perhaps two hundred feet away. He could see diners pause to stare at the *Jersey Trick*. He saw Peaches and Veronica huddled together at the rail far ahead of him. Then the running lights of another vessel appeared, and he heard some unintelligible shouting through a bull horn.

Then he saw something he didn't expect. Heavy Laval was staggering down the port side of the *Jersey Trick*, slipping and falling frequently, holding desperately to the handrail. "Bastard!" He whispered in the driving rain, and hoped that Veronica would not see Laval. He slipped and fell again, grasping a stanchion to keep from sliding overboard as the *Jersey Trick* lurched when its engines were put in reverse.

Then there was a scraping and bumping as Lorenzo slowed them to a near stop. Crackers watched as Veronica and Peaches jumped off onto an empty pier. Almost immediately Lorenzo threw the *Jersey Trick* into full forward throttle and swung her out toward the Narrows. Crackers hurtled himself into the water.

52

A board the *Tashtego*, Ginny, Willy, and Whitcomb were startled by the sudden roaring throb of the big yacht being given full throttle. They hurried outside the cabin and saw a large boat pulling away from a dock a couple of hundred yards to their stern. "God, I hope he sees us," yelled Willy.

The vessel bearing down on the *Tashtego* now swung to the port and left them wallowing in a mighty wake as it thundered past them.

Ginny recognized it instantly. "That's the *Jersey Trick!*"

Willy leaped to the marine radio, and using the channel Whitcomb had designated, got through at once. Whitcomb, sounding harried and excited, "What have you got for us Willy?"

"The *Jersey Trick* right off Hoboken damn near ran us down at the dock." There was a frantic conversation at the other end.

"We know, Willy, we're right behind the *Jersey Trick*. Nothing to worry about. He's running right into the U.S. Coastguard. They're about ready to put one over his bow. You folks okay?"

"We're all okay, aside from a few more grey hairs."

Aboard the cutter, a couple hundred yards from the *Jersey Trick*, crewmen at the gun mount awaited orders from their captain to fire a warning shot.

The radio man was trying desperately to communicate with the *Jersey Trick*, but got absolutely no response. The captain stared helplessly at the renegade yacht. "Prepare to give chase," he ordered.

Before he could order the warning shot across the bow, there was a tremendous explosion no more than a hundred yards from the cutter. For an instant the night sky was lit with blinding light as all lights aboard the *Jersey Trick* went dark. Still having some forward motion, the vessel seemed to be gulping water as the massive hole under her bow filled the hull in a matter of seconds.

Slowly she slid beneath the waves just south of the Verrazano Narrows Bridge. Shouts came from the water and the cutter moved in to pick up survivors.

Whitcomb arrived in the police launch and his men began to assist in the rescue of survivors.

Willy, Coley, and Ginny saw the flash and heard the thundering explosion.

"Damn!" screamed Coley, "I bet they ran into the cutter."

Willy worked furiously at trying to raise someone on the radio. Finally Whitcomb's voice came through loud and clear. "The *Jersey Trick* just blew up, Willy. The skipper of the cutter didn't even have time to fire the warning shot. She just blew sky high and sank. It looks like we have four or five survivors. The cutter's okay and our boys are okay. We'll keep you posted."

The trio aboard the *Tashtego* breathed a sigh of relief with the news that the explosion had not involved the cutter or the police launch. "My God! I wonder what that was all about?" muttered Coley.

They stood in the cockpit of the *Tashtego* as the radio continued to monitor the activity of the rescue party around the sunken yacht. They could see the powerful searchlight of the cutter sweeping back and forth across the water. About ten minutes later, Whitcomb directed a message toward the *Tashtego*.

"Willy, we have four survivors. We've got the skipper who calls himself Captain Lorenzo, two deck hands who don't speak English, and a chubby Oriental who says he was the cook. If anyone else was aboard they went down in deep water. We're going to cruise around awhile just to make sure. It's all over Willy."

"No Bocco Lamas? No Heavy Laval? No women?" Coley persisted.

282   RALPH ARNOTE

"I'd be jumping with joy if I could say yes, Coley. The answer is no. We'll check with the Coast Guard and see if it is possible to send down divers in the morning. It's deep water here. Lots of current." Whitcomb's voice was filled with disappointment.

"Hey! There's someone out there." Ginny pointed down the long empty wharf. Someone was walking toward them, perhaps a hundred yards away. He stumbled along erratically for several steps and then fell, scrambling clumsily to keep from falling into the water.

"Must be some drunk from town. He must have taken the wrong way home," Coley said. "He's going to kill himself if he isn't careful."

Willy vaulted over the rail of the *Tashtego* and jogged quickly toward the man on the edge of the dock, stopping just short of him. "What's the matter, partner, you okay?"

"Hell yes, somethin' wrong?" The man's speech came between heavy breaths. The man extended a hand, which Willy grasped to help pull him to his feet.

Willy saw the man's face clearly for the first time as he stood in front of him. The broad shoulders, the heavy mop of black hair and unkempt beard glistened with wetness as Ginny beamed a spotlight their way from the *Tashtego*. He had never actually seen Heavy Laval before, but he knew it was he from Ginny's frequent descriptions.

"Heavy Laval?"

"Yeah, piss ant, what's it to ya?"

Willy crouched low and started an uppercut from below his knees that crashed into Laval's chin. The huge man wavered, but did not fall. He stumbled forward and bearhugged Willy to the edge of the old dock, then wrestled him down slamming an elbow across his face as they hit the wooden planks. Laval raised up and straddled Willy, measuring him for a final blow.

Coley yelled and leaped over the rail of the *Tashtego*.

Before he could reach Willy, two shots rang cut in quick succession. They sounded more like a cap pistol than anything else. Laval slumped to the very edge of the pier and then tumbled over into the Hudson River.

Coley spun on his heels and faced Cliff Blaylock, a dozen feet away, Sandy's tiny .22 automatic in his hand. Before Coley reached him, Blaylock hurled the gun into the river with all the strength he could muster.

"You crazy fool!" Coley held him tight for a minute, then dropped his arms and ran to kneel at Willy's side. He moved, struggled to his elbow and stared at Coley.

"What happened?"

Blaylock walked over and sat down on the pier next to them. Ginny ran from the *Tashtego* and joined them, and then fell sobbing on Willy as he managed a grin.

Coley got up and peered over the edge of the dock into the darkness and the swift moving tide water below. "He killed the son of a bitch, Willy. Cliff shot Heavy Laval."

The four of them walked back to the *Tashtego* in silence. Coley looked down the isolated long pier. Nothing or no one was visible in the rain. They climbed aboard the *Tashtego* and sat in silence listening to the radio from Whitcomb's launch. "Hey Willy, where the hell are you? Everything okay?" It was Whitcomb.

Willy grabbed the mike. "Everything's okay here. Any other survivors?"

"No. We're going to keep the cutter here, and see what we can find in the daylight. Might as well try and get some sleep, Willy."

Willy turned the receiver down low and switched off his microphone.

Coley stared at Blaylock, and then Willy. "So what do we do now? I saw the look on Cliff's face. I tell you it was an execution!"

Willy shrugged. "I think Cliff has already done everything there is to do."

Blaylock was fidgeting nervously, glancing repeatedly at the edge of the dock where Laval had disappeared. "I've killed two people now," he whispered softly. "I just didn't know what else to do."

Willy shrugged. "I guess one killing kind of avenges the other. But Cliff my boy, that isn't the way the law is supposed to work. By the way, thanks. I guess he was getting ready to do me in." Willy got up, stretched and rubbed his neck and jaw where he had taken the blow from Laval.

"But what do we do now?" Coley persisted.

"Damn it! I said we've already done it!" Willy rasped. "The guy saved my life, Coley. If you want to report this, I'll have to back you up. But I say let's wait a while. Cliff will be doing some time, anyway."

"I'm willing to try, Willy. Let's hope the case goes down to the bottom with the *Jersey Trick*." Coley looked off in the distance. "We've got company. Looks like a police car."

Blaylock looked at his wristwatch. "I'll bet that's the Stag Creek police. I called my lawyer and told him I'd turn myself in down here." Cliff then grinned broadly. "Oh, I almost forgot why I came. Here, Willy." He handed him a small package.

Willy ripped the wrapping away. "Why, it's the AMERI!"

"I wanted you to have it, Willy. Of course it's a one-sided coin now. It isn't worth much anymore."

"Thanks, Cliff. It's a real treasure for a rinky-dink collecter like me."

The police cruiser drove out onto the dock, stopping near the *Tashtego*. Blaylock's lawyer got out along with two policemen. Blaylock stood up and climbed down the short ladder to the dock. The police patted him down, cuffed him, and read him his rights.

The officers stared at the *Tashtego* and smiled appreciatively. Blaylock, now overcome with emotion, just waved.

The cruiser made a U-turn and drove slowly away. The lettering on the side proclaimed that it belonged to the township of Stag Creek.

"Nothing ever happens there," Coley said, affecting great sarcasm.

Meanwhile high overhead a big jet thundered out of Newark in a steep climb preparing to turn south toward Miami. Veronica gazed at the lights of Verrazano Narrows Bridge. Pushing her face next to the glass she could see several small boats circling the waters just south of the bridge. Then the clouds wiped away her view. Peaches slept soundly at her side.

Far below, in the depths of the Hudson, a heavy bag, which held the skeleton of Percy LeRoy, anchored firmly by a chain and cinder block, still swung around and around with the tide. Now it was joined by an old steamer trunk that lodged nearby in the muck after tumbling out of the gaping hole in the hull of the *Jersey Trick*. Bocco Lamas had joined Percy LeRoy for an eternity.